He could not _____ sing at
every breath. Fear, grief, anger would _____ chances
of escaping and warning his mother, as his father had
asked.

He was only nine years old, and perhaps he had a right to
cry. But he thought he knew how to stop it . . .

Arris found a curtained alcove where he was reasonably
safe and closed his eyes, still as a stalker in sight of his prey.
He focused his concentration inward. The turbulent
thoughts and emotions that battered him whirled in a cone-
shaped spiral, sweeping from side to side in his mind,
leaving no room for reason. He summoned strength from
his fingertips through his storm-tossed mind and watched
as a spherical shape began to form. It was an extension of
how his mother had taught him to block unwanted
intrusions from his thoughts. Arris opened his eyes,
gasping like a landed fish, and stood for a moment. Then
he returned to the image and compressed its size, shrinking
the sphere until it lodged in a dim corner of his head, out
of the way.

It was done.

CATHERINE COOKE

The Winged Assassin

Futura

An Orbit Book

Copyright © 1987 by Catherine Cooke

First published in Great Britain in 1988
by Futura Publications, a Division of
Macdonald & Co (Publishers) Ltd
London & Sydney

ISBN 0 7088 8266 8

Printed and bound in Great Britain by
Collins, Glasgow

Futura Publications
A Division of
Macdonald & Co (Publishers) Ltd
Greater London House
Hampstead Road
London NW1 7QX

A member of Maxwell Pergamon Publishing Corporation plc

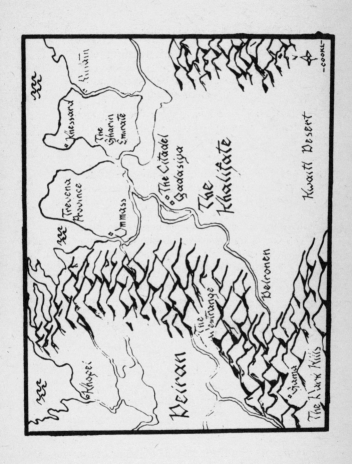

PROLOGUE

THE CRIMSON GODDESS dreamed of the perfect lover.

It was the most pleasant dream she had had for a long time. She was called Rehoman the Destroyer, and her dreams were usually dark with blood and burning and the desire for vengeance against the upstart godlings who had stolen her worship and tricked her into sleeping for almost a thousand years.

She would have a consort worthy of her when she woke, she thought. He would not be one of the frightened, half-witted beauties she had had to settle for in the years of her power. He would burn from within with the crimson fire. Together they would regain what she had lost.

There came a rent in the fabric of her dream. Her enemies were setting forces in motion to oppose her. Rehoman shifted slightly in her sleep and moved to counter their play. Her Messenger would have to fly far under a rising sun on wings used to moonlight, but the Goddess still had enough power to compel obedience from her servants.

Her dream was growing more and more pleasing. She could almost taste the sweet smoke of sacrifice rising from every temple of the land, as it had so many years ago.

BOOK
ONE

CHAPTER
1

THE LOSSIRAN HAD come again. Arris sat very still and closed his eyes. He could hear it seeking around the outside of the north tower, calling for him, screeching its wordless bird cries in a voice that was not a bird's. The Mother of Vultures. The Messenger of Rehoman. In the middle of the day, at the Citadel, a week's journey from the Dark Hills where it belonged. If his mother had been there she would have greeted it warmly, but Arris wished it would go away. He did not want to listen to it. He did not want to learn any more of the Crimson Goddess's dreams.

Would Sasha ever decide where to move? Arris opened his eyes and looked across the oak table. Maybe if he ignored the Lossiran it would go away. It was Sasha's ninth birthday, and Arris was beating him again. His friend's bright blue eyes were narrow in his pale face, and he twisted a strand of his curled golden hair between his fingers as he tried to decide how to counter Arris's strategy. Sasha reached for his Vizier piece, then retreated. The lines of battle on the gameboard were one-sided. There was no way Sasha could win. Arris tried not to smile. Sasha might be the Crown Prince, and his father might be the Khalif, but Arris's father was the greatest general in the Khalifate.

A breath of cold air put out the fire. Arris almost jumped out of his cushioned chair. Sasha seemed not to notice. Arris looked past the sleeping form of the Prince's old nurse Letha to the leaded-glass window of the high tower room. It was closed. But the hearth was cold. Not even the coals in the grate glowed. The Lossiran had found him.

Maybe it would just talk to him, as it sometimes did in his

dreams. Maybe it would not force him to say anything. Maybe it would give him no prophecies. It had only come once before in the year he had been at the Citadel, and that time had been bad. His father had gotten into a lot of trouble. The Lossiran had made Arris say things, but no one in the North believed in the Lossiran. He was not even sure his father had believed him.

He could see it now, taking form inside the room next to the window. Its scaly head bent, its black wings outspread to either wall, it stared at him with its dull red eyes. Arris could smell its breath, like the breath of a long-buried corpse, the charnel stench of rotting meat. He whimpered softly and clenched his hands into fists beneath the table to try to keep from shaking. He wanted to scream for help; but he knew Sasha could not see it, did not even know that a huge Goddess-sent vulture, the color of deep night underground, was standing in the upper room of the nursery, was walking toward Arris with its wings spread to embrace him.

Arris closed his eyes again and murmured a childish spell to ward off evil. He could not think of anything more effective. He could not remember his mother's training. He felt the cold creeping nearer, and heard the hollow click of the vulture's massive claws on the flagstone floor. The Lossiran breathed in and out, rasping, shallow breaths, as if breathing was difficult for it. Then Arris felt a chill wind as its wings closed around him.

The boy clamped his teeth against a scream when the rattling feathers touched him. He opened his eyes on blackness. He was drowning at the bottom of a midnight well, frozen, stiff, his thoughts slowing with his heartbeat as the ancient will of the Messenger of Rehoman thrust like an icy knife into his mind. His desperate defenses were brushed aside like brittle white feathers. He tried to struggle, but he could not move. His tears were frozen and he could not cry. It hurt. He could not remember hurting this much before. The Messenger left its message coiled insistently in Arris's mind, and opened its wings to release his body.

He could not say anything else if he wanted to. His tongue moved like a rusty marionette. "The Khalif is dead."

Like a bright shadow before his clouded eyes, Sasha moved suddenly to advance a pawn into the line of check between Arris's Priest and his Khalif. "Not yet! Not while he's got a squire to protect him. Look. It'll take you at least three moves to get him now." He laughed.

"The Khalif is dead," Arris repeated tonelessly. The Lossiran croaked in triumph and sprang away, flapping its vast wings once before it vanished through the window. The fire in the hearth crackled and burned again.

Arris crumpled in his chair. He pressed his hands against the velvet cushions, gaining small comfort from the napped softness after the frostbite cold of the vulture's scales. He gasped for breath as his heart thudded to regain the beats it had lost. Why had his mother refused to teach him how to resist the Lossiran effectively? Surely she knew. She had been a priestess of the Crimson Goddess before his father had taken her.

Sasha stared at him. "What's wrong? You'll still win. You always win. It must be because you're nine months older than me."

His stomach hurt. He could not tell his friend what the vulture wanted him to. But he had no choice.

"Arris-ka?" The golden-haired boy leaned across the game board, scattering jeweled pieces to the floor. "Are you sick? What is it? Should I wake Letha?"

"No," he said quickly. "No, I'm not sick, I . . ." He looked down at his hands, shaking in his lap. "Do you remember three months ago when the Lossiran told me about the ambush at Brethil Pass?"

"And my uncles thought your father was a Yaighan spy, when it turned out to be true." Sasha nodded. "I had to beg them for days to let you visit me again. I remember."

"It happened again. The Lossiran came." Arris swallowed hard. "I didn't want it to. But I had to listen, and I have to tell you what it said. The Khalif is dead. He died while we played."

"What?"

"Your father. Rasul Ilkharani. I'm sorry."

Sasha shook his head. The light from the window flashed on his curls. "That isn't funny, Arris."

"It isn't a joke. It's true."

"Stop it," the Prince said. "I don't like games like this. The Lossiran? A giant, invisible bird, from an outlawed religion? And it was just here, and it told you my father was dead? That's stupid."

Arris stood up and walked over to the window to look out into the Garden Court. "I'm sorry," he said helplessly. Dizziness swept over him, and he sat down abruptly on the marble window seat. The vulture had taken much of his strength.

"Come back, Ris-ka," the Prince said. "Don't get upset. I don't believe you, but how can you expect me to? I saw my father not three hours—"

The Palace bells began to toll wildly, without rhythm, breaking the midday stillness with deep-toned mourning. Arris shivered. Why did the Goddess have to send her messages to him? He did not even worship her.

"Evening prayer so soon?" muttered the old nurse, surprised from her nap.

"Mother of the gods." Sasha ran to the window, his hands and face pale as alabaster above the starched ruffles of his birthday finery. "Sygathi Ylla . . . it can't be . . ."

"Such language!" the nurse admonished, putting aside the needlework she had fallen asleep with.

Below in the landscaped garden a bare-legged slave stumbled as he ran. He climbed the pedestal steps to the pole where the banner of the Ilkharani flew. The bright standard fell, and a black pennant rose in its place. Keening wails began to sound from the Women's Court on the other side of the wall, where Rasul had his wives and concubines.

"My father is dead." Sasha turned from the window, his sapphire eyes wide.

"Myrdethreshi defend," Letha breathed, brushing the sign of the Five Gods across her wrinkled forehead.

Arris whispered, "He was poisoned."

The Prince stared at him. "How can you know that?"

"I told you. The Lossiran."

"There is no Lossiran, Arris. It's only a children's nightmare story. And I'm not stupid enough to believe it."

"I wouldn't lie to you," Arris said, rising from his seat. "We swore to be brothers, Sasha. We vowed to keep faith." He pulled a small gold ring from his left hand and held it out. "I swear to you, the Lossiran told me your father was dead. If you don't believe me, you can take back your pledge gift."

The Prince reached out slowly and took the ring. He spoke softly. "If you really think the Lossiran came to you, the priests could accuse you of heresy. Goddess worship. But I think you overheard your father plotting to kill mine, just like you heard him plotting the Brethil Pass ambush. My uncles were right. The Lord Areyta is a Yaighan spy."

"And a regicide," the old nurse Letha said harshly. "The Lossiran indeed."

"No," Arris said, his voice growing shrill. "That's not true."

"You knew he was dead before anyone could have known. I should have listened to my uncles before."

"He betrayed your friendship and your kingdom," Letha said, "if he knew of a plot against your father's life and did not warn you. Call the guard, Your Highness. He'll know who conspired with Areyta, and that information will be easily got from a child."

"It isn't true, Sasha," Arris said urgently.

"You are your father's heir, Saresha Ilkharani," the nurse admonished. "Do what you must do."

"Go." The Prince hurled Arris's ring into the fire. "Leave my kingdom."

"What?" Arris backed toward the door. He did not believe this was happening.

"I won't call the guard. I won't tell them what happened here." Sasha turned his back, his voice barely audible. "If I ever see you again, I'll kill you."

"Your uncles will want to question him!" Letha protested, clawing at the cloth-of-gold tunic Arris had worn for the birthday celebration. The boy writhed away from her and hurtled out past the heavy carved door.

A vise gripped his chest. He ran down the winding tower stairs, not feeling the polished railing or the worn stone beneath his slippered feet. He did not cry. It was too sudden, too overwhelming. The Khalif was dead, and they thought his father had done it, and Sasha would kill him if he did not leave the Khalifate. Even if Sasha kept quiet about the Lossiran vision, Letha would tell. And his father knew nothing about it. He had to be warned.

A long arm reached out to stop him: Maenad, the older of Sasha's uncles, climbing the stairs to tell his nephew of the Khalif's death. Arris ducked under the Emir's grasp and ignored his command to stop.

He hated the Lossiran. He hated the Crimson Goddess. He wished he could run all the way to the Dark Hills, all the way to his family's estate, Delronen, where his mother would take him in her arms and tell him it had only been a dream.

Arris had never seen the Audience Chamber so crowded. Everyone was shouting, nobles and courtiers and slaves, and soldiers were trying to make orders heard above the chaos. He stopped in dismay at the door, gasping for breath after his headlong descent. Where was his father? He could not see past stomachs and sword belts. There was nothing to do but ask and hope no one was looking for him yet.

"Have you seen the Lord Areyta?" he called, pulling at the sleeve of the nearest nobleman, a portly dandy who reeked of wine.

"What? What is it, boy?"

The noble's companion, a slim, handsome youth with a languid air and heavy-lidded eyes, peered down at him. "It's Areyta's changeling, the little dark one. Beautiful, isn't he? If he were only a slave . . ."

"Aye, you're one of Kerami's own, Taifid," muttered the older man. "I thought you were after that new kitchen girl."

"I'll have her before the night's out," the youth said. "Would I be a true servant of the Lover if I failed to appreciate beauty? Where's your bright twin, boy? You should see the Prince and him together, Lucan, it would break your heart."

Arris felt his face flushing. "Excuse me, sir, my father? Have you seen him?"

"Areyta?" Taifid shook his head. "Not likely, lad. Haven't you heard? Nievan's accused him of the poisoning. There's a warrant out. They'll lack proof, but when does that stop the Vizier?"

So soon. Arris nodded his thanks and began to struggle through the press toward the distant portal of the south tower. There was a chance he could still warn his father. The Khalif had not been dead long. The warrant would have to go through the channels of command until it reached someone with enough rank to arrest a province lord. Perhaps the two of them could escape before a general search began. Arris knew the maze of the Citadel and the Palace better than most. Well enough to hide from soldiers, if necessary. Well enough to get his father out safely.

He stumbled on the broad stairs of the south tower. The

Lossiran had drunk deeply of him. At home when it had come his mother put him to bed for a day afterward.

His family suite spread out from a door on the fourth-floor landing. The door was open. His father sat calmly at his desk looking out over the stairway. He was lacing his best robe over an exquisite surcoat of diamond-patterned blue and gold. His red hair and beard were freshly combed and perfumed, his boots polished, his silk turban set with a huge sapphire. With the heavy muscles of his arms and shoulders disguised, he looked like a prosperous merchant.

"Where's your sword?" Arris cried. "We have to run! They'll be coming for you."

"Run? That would be admitting my guilt. Let them try to prove I killed the Khalif."

"They'll find proof. They want it to be you. That's what Taifid said downstairs." Arris pushed a strand of long black hair from his eyes, wondering if he should tell his father the rest.

"Taifid? That mincing catamite?" His father chuckled. "I've been at court fifteen years, son. I know it well. There may be some hysteria. I've no doubt Vizier Nievan would love to see me dead. But no one else will listen to him."

"They'll kill you." For a heart-stopping moment, the boy saw a hand tattered with rotting flesh reaching toward him, and a grinning skull beneath the turban and its sapphire, and he thought: a dead man. I am talking to a dead man. Then he took Areyta's firm, strong hand and allowed himself to be pulled into a fierce embrace. The perfumed beard tickled his skin.

"No, little one. Not with the Khalif dead, and everyone from the Deirani Empire to the Yaighan to the Kwaitl nomads aching for revenge. They won't let Nievan make a scapegoat of the best battle commander they have."

A sob caught him. "They'll have proof," he said miserably. "Sasha said he wouldn't tell, but they'll find out, and they'll say I heard you planning to kill the Khalif. And they'll kill you."

"What do you mean, son? What happened with the Prince?"

"The Lossiran came." Arris felt his father stiffen. "It told me the Khalif was dead, before I should have known . . . we have to run! I know a way they won't think of." Then he heard the booted feet in the hall, and the jingle of soldiers' harness.

"Behind the tapestries. Quickly." Areyta gave him a hard shove. Arris slipped into the recess of the wall, trying to keep from sneezing at the ancient dust of the hangings. His father patted him lightly from the other side. "Perhaps Saresha will keep his word to you, and all will be well. But for now be silent. Wait for me, and if I don't return, try to get word to your mother. She must be warned, do you understand?"

He would not return. Arris bit his tongue hard to stop the tears and pressed against the rough stones to keep his shadow from showing on the tapestry.

The soldiers proclaimed their warrant loudly as they entered the room. Arris could see them dimly through the weave. His father greeted them as if he was inspecting the troops on a summer's festival day.

"Smile, my lord Areyta," said a sibilant voice. "You will have little chance to do so again." The Vizier Nievan was a younger brother of the Khalif by their father's fourth wife. He had always hated Areyta.

"Your time would be better spent courting favor downstairs, Vizier," said Arris's father softly. "If you want the Consulate to elect you one of the Prince's regents."

"It is well spent here. They'll look kindly on the man who brings my brother's murderer to justice."

"Be reasonable, Nievan. You have no proof. You yourself saw the Khalif later than I this morning."

"You claim innocence?"

"In the name of Sygathi, I swear it."

The Vizier laughed. "Then you are forsworn—if calling on one of the Brothers Ylla has any meaning for you at all. It is well known you tolerate the worship of the Crimson Goddess among the Yaighan, your wife's people. My brother thought you would be a strong lord when he gave you their lands. But the conquered have corrupted you. Or perhaps the Lady Tauena herself."

"I forbade that worship, as the Khalif's law demands."

Ignoring him, Nievan continued. "Not long ago, the Dark People had a habit of sacrificing their kings on occasion. I trust you see the connection. Rest assured your judges will."

• • •

Arris did not come out from behind the tapestry for another hour. They had bound his father and marched him off like a common criminal, and Arris had feared they would return to search his rooms, but no one had yet appeared.

He could not stay here. He changed his cloth-of-gold tunic for a dark brown one, and tucked a dagger into a fold of his belt. Then he crept down the stairs to the third floor and took a narrow passage beyond the usual turning. There, the close walls bore flaking traces of old mosaics, and an empty wineskin and a few scraps of bone lay in a dark corner where some exploring slave had brought a stolen feast. Arris's feet remembered the way, though his mind was dizzy with weakness and fear. Another turning, and he descended a long, cramped flight of spiraling stone steps. They had been built when the south tower was the outermost defense of the ancient Citadel, and were nearly forgotten.

The boy stumbled and bruised his shoulder on the harsh stone. Tears jerked from him and would not stop. He was ashamed, though there was no one to see him cry. The sobs clutched at his throat. He fought for breath, for control, as he descended blindly into the dark. Perhaps he should rest before he attempted to thread the maze of the Palace that lay between the Citadel and the last wall.

The floor was gritty and cold and smelled of damp earth. Arris woke, sore from being curled in a tight ball, his stomach empty and cramped, his throat swollen and hoarse with tears. He looked around in vague surprise at the dark pillared corridor, the cracked and deformed walls where the weight of settling earth had broken through. He wondered what sort of dream this was. Then he remembered. He was in the bowels of the Citadel, and if they found him they would kill him.

He got to his feet, so light-headed he could hardly stand. His muscles groaned, unwilling to stretch. How long had he slept? There was no way to guess the hour. Arris hurried through the deep corridors, trying to remember the paths he and Sasha had used in their explorations of the Palace. His slippers padded softly on the uneven stones. He was slight, and he was dark of skin and hair, as were his mother's people. If anyone noticed him, he would have seemed only another shadow, or a ghost of the buried Citadel.

His father would die a traitor, Arris knew. The Lord Areyta, who had offered his Khalif unswerving loyalty and an unquestioning sword. He would die, a convenient scapegoat, to satisfy the people's need for vengeance. Arris wondered who had poisoned the Khalif. Surely not the Yaighan. It would bring the weight of the Khalifate down on them again.

But it was their fault. It was his mother's fault, for giving him her blood, for making him sensitive enough to hear the Lossiran. He knew that once the judges heard what had happened in Sasha's room his father would be lost. It was as if he had lit the pyre himself. Tears pressed behind his eyes. He slammed his fist against a wall. It hurt. He looked at the bloody scrape angrily.

Arris leapt back into a crevice of the stairwell as a globe of light passed nearby. It was a sentry; he had reached the inhabited parts of the Citadel without realizing. The danger slashed into the chaos of his thoughts. He could not go on like this, with his throat convulsing at every breath. Fear, grief, anger would destroy his chances of escaping and warning his mother, as his father had asked.

He was only nine years old, and perhaps he had a right to cry. But he thought he knew how to stop it. A vague memory: a Yaighan slave caught stealing pigs had been whipped in the courtyard at Delronen until his skin hung in bloody shreds; the man had not screamed, and had walked away with an enigmatic smile on his face. Arris, five or six, impressed, had asked his mother how the slave had done it. She had told him, but made him promise never to try the technique.

Arris found a curtained alcove where he was reasonably safe and closed his eyes, still as a stalker in sight of his prey. He focused his concentration inward. The turbulent thoughts and emotions that battered him whirled in a cone-shaped spiral, sweeping from side to side in his mind, leaving no room for reason. He summoned strength from his fingertips through to his storm-tossed mind and watched as a spherical shape began to form. It was an extension of how his mother had taught him to block unwanted intrusions from his thoughts. Arris opened his eyes, gasping like a landed fish, and stood for a moment. Then he returned to the image and compressed its size, shrinking the sphere until it lodged in a dim corner of his head, out of the way.

It was done. Its ease was deceptive, he knew. It would be hard to maintain. The suppressed emotions would grow, and would have to be released eventually. They would overwhelm him. He had heard of people going mad from it. But if he was safe with his mother or another Yaighan by that time, he should be all right.

Pleased with the success of his spell, Arris turned away from the stairs and started up a broad, low ramp that would lead him to the east tower. His mind was clear and sharp now, his senses subtly heightened. He would escape. He was sure of it.

CHAPTER

2

SOME OF THE BEDROOM windows on the third floor of the east tower opened onto the roofs of covered walkways, guarded passages connecting the Citadel to other buildings of the Palace. Arris and the Prince had used those roofs several times, amusing themselves by eluding the guards. Tonight it would not be a game. Arris hoped some of the bedrooms' occupants would be late retiring.

He saw no sentries in the third-floor corridors. Ornate doors lined the walls, marked with family crests. He chose that of Taifid, the Lord Collector's son, the young bravo who had spoken to him in the Audience Chamber. Surely he would not be home so early. So great a romancer would still be attending the Court of Dreams beyond the Garden Wall.

The door was unlocked. As Arris slipped inside, the firm step of a soldier sounded in the hall. He could not alter his choice. He crept through the anteroom of Taifid's suite, and stopped like a hawk-frightened mouse at the open bedroom door. The youth was inside. By her accent, the girl with him was the kitchen slave his companion Lucan had mentioned.

Arris melted into the shadow behind the door, his heart beating so loudly he was sure the laughing pair would hear.

A chill breeze blew through the open window by Taifid's bed. Arris breathed deeply, remembering his spell and the courage it had given him. The thumping in his chest calmed. He was small, and could be as silent as a cat if he chose. The rug between the door and the bed seemed vast, but it was black char-cat fur, which matched his long hair and his hosen. With a short prayer to Verchaki Ylla, the god whose province was night and darkness, Arris dropped to his stomach and began to snake across the thick carpet.

"Darling, you make free with my time," the girl in the bed said archly, discarding the light covering from her naked limbs. Arris froze. "Again, you say, and it almost the first hour of morning, and me to be whipped if I reach the Quarters late!" She moved to rise.

The boy buried his hands and face in the rug. He was sure to be discovered. He wondered if Taifid might let him go. The young men in the bravo's set were held in open contempt by Nievan the Vizier.

"I'll give you something to bribe the guards with," Taifid said hoarsely. "You can't leave now."

There was a struggle on the bed, and the girl laughed. "Do I have a choice, my lord? I daresay you've never been whipped. Still . . ."

Arris raised his head cautiously, peering through a veil of black hair. Taifid pulled the girl down with one hand while moving the other between her legs. She chuckled, a deep, delighted sound. Breathing again, the boy crawled along the length of the bed's shadow. He glanced at the lovers, wishing he could watch more. They were oblivious as he pulled himself up the wall and out the window, landing heavily on hands and knees on the rough-shingled roof of the walkway. A foul-smelling puddle soaked one knee. He stood quickly.

The night was black and starless, befitting the death of a Khalif. Sentry lamps glowed yellow from the paths of the Garden Court below. They would be looking for Arris by now. He thought of his father, and what would be done to him by the Black Masks in the dungeons. The picture was distant and unreal to his spellbound mind; unpleasant, but not painful.

He swung down a bare grape trellis when the walkway

ended. He had passed the Garden Wall, the Court of Dreams with its laughing couples, and the Women's Court. The dead Khalif's wives and concubines had not been wandering in their gardens at this hour. Arris wondered which of them would die to send their lord safely on his journey to the Five. Was it true that those chosen loved their lord enough to want to follow him? Arris could not imagine his mother doing such a thing.

It was an endless night. He was almost caught several times. His heightened senses sharpened his path but blurred what lay behind, so that by the hour before sunrise he had reached the last wall without any memory of getting there. Unseen, he scuttled up the ramparts of the Soldiers' Walk like a rat boarding a ship. He crawled under the window of a guardhouse and slipped into a narrow archer's port, four feet high and the width of a man's waist. He hoped he had remembered the right place. Most sections of the many miles of moat were planted with six-foot spikes below the water's surface.

Arris breathed deeply three times and dived cleanly, without a splash, into the dark, foul-smelling waters twenty feet below. There were no spikes. He swam underneath as far as his small lungs could manage, then surfaced, gasping and sputtering, out of the range of the wall-hung torches. The water tasted vile. No doubt the refuse of the Palace was dumped into it.

By the time he crawled up the rocky embankment toward the forest, exhaustion hung from his limbs like leaden weights. He wrung the rank water of the moat from his slippers, and staggered into the tangled, leafless forest.

The morning sun was fierce to eyes accustomed to the filtered light of the Citadel. The road had been empty since the last Palace courier had raced past in a choking cloud of dust. The rider had not given Arris the barest notice. Not surprising, the boy thought. His bright slippers, his earrings and pendants, and his fine-woven hosen were buried under bracken in the forest, where he had slept until midday. His dark tunic was tattered around his bare knees, ripped and bloodied from pushing through tangles of dead trees. His long black hair hung rudely just below his ears, where he had hacked it off with his dagger. He was filthy, still smelled of the moat, and looked less than a house-carle.

A load of dry wood weighed on his back, tied with his long belt. He had thrust his dagger inside a knot of material at the waist of his tunic. The wood completed his disguise, and gave him a reason to go to the markets at Qadasiya. If he was lucky, he might actually sell the stickery stuff and eat for the first time since yesterday morning. He hoped no one would guess the source of the wood. It was forbidden to gather in the Palace forest, which was supposed to remain impassable to enemy armies.

Arris stumbled over a rut and fell to his knees, but rose again and kept his steady, slow pace. His mind, focused by his spell on his goal of reaching Delronen, would not allow him to stop or turn aside from the path without feeling a sharp tugging from the South. If only he had never left there. His mother had argued against his going; but his brothers had gone the year before, Falcmet and Husayn, thriving on the Northern intrigues and petty wars in a way Arris did not, and Areyta had not wanted to slight his youngest son. And Arris suspected his father had wanted to get him away from the ghosts of the Dark Hills.

Now Areyta would be a ghost, bound to the Wheel by his unjust death. He would not rest until his killers died in their turn, their blood shed by his kindred. This Arris knew to be true. Even the priests of the Brothers taught it. The thought was a thick, black place growing inside him, swelling the emotions trapped behind walls in his mind, straining the bonds of his clumsy spell.

"Hold up there!"

Arris jumped at the shout from behind him, but realized the voice was too high to be a soldier's. Shifting the load of wood, he turned, reluctant to stop when he was almost to the wall of Qadasiya. A dirty, pale-haired boy of eleven years or so was grinning at him from beneath a smaller load of sticks.

"You must've been out early."

Arris shrugged and resumed his slow pace. He saw no reason to be friendly. The boy was coarse-faced and of the lowest caste.

"It's luck we met," the older boy remarked. "It's hard to find space in the bazaar by yourself when most of the woodmen have wagons and families to help. You'll have had that problem before, little as you are." He looked sidelong at Arris. "Or are you a slave scrounging for his master's fire? I haven't seen you before."

"A slave?" Arris would not take that from a beggar. He drew his dagger, forgetting that the mountain of sticks on his back might hamper his movement.

"No harm meant. Kerami Ylla!" The blond boy backed away, palms forward. "Put that away, little fighting cock. Someone might steal it."

Arris sheathed the weapon, feeling foolish. Of course he looked like a pauper. That was what he wanted. The beggar boy meant no insult.

The northern gate of Qadasiya rose ahead, catching the slanting rays of the late afternoon sunshine. It was rounded with age and wind, not more than ten feet at its highest. It had been built in an age before catapults and siege machines, and was barely defensible now.

"You've just come to the city, then?" the boy said, seeing the way Arris looked at the wall. "You won't find a place in the bazaar without me. Think it over."

It was true he knew nothing of selling or bazaars. And he had no money, and a great hole where his stomach should have been. "All right," he said. "My name is Duan."

"Jamal," said the other, and began to ramble on about prices and undercutting and the best places from which to sell.

Even the soldiers at the gate were soft-looking and bored, like well-fed house cats who wouldn't chase a live mouse if they saw one. Arris did not fear them. His disguise was more than adequate for such observers. Still, this was the most obvious place for him to go. They would be searching for him here.

He detoured around a cursing old leper begging in the middle of the road and nearly tripped over a scrawny yellow dog. Inside the wall, the streets snaked narrow and congested, stuffed with tradesmen's shops. Jamal led him rapidly through the crowds. Buildings leaned crazily on one another, top-heavy as giant mushrooms, with shops on the lower floors and clothesline-bedecked residences on the upper. The sky showed through occasional cracks. Wide gutters ran down the narrow streets, stinking of refuse. Ragged beggar families were staking out areas for the night, building tiny smoking fires and guarding their small territories as fiercely as wolf-hounds. They frightened Arris. He had not known people lived that way.

Through the half-screened windows of the shops, he could see the shadowy forms of tradesmen and apprentices waiting on late afternoon customers. There were cobblers and tailors, clothmakers and jewelers, apothecaries and smithies. There were also food vendors. Arris lingered hungrily before their windows, gazing at the displayed meat pies and curries until Jamel had to pull him away.

Arris's head ached from the pressure of what was bound inside, and from the massed emotions of thousands of Qadasiyans that weighed on him from the outside. He could not distinguish thoughts, but the feelings were bewildering, deafening, violent in their intensity. Lust and greed and anger, and a few gentler emotions that did not scream so loudly. He wished his mother had dared to teach him more of how to control his sensitivity to such things. She had not wanted to anger her Northern husband.

Five priests of the Sun walked by, swathed in voluminous golden robes and turbans, their steps slow and measured, their clean-shaven faces grave. Arris was impressed by their bearing, and wondered whether the Brothers Ylla could be as real as the Goddess. Perhaps it was arrogant to assume that a god who had never spoken to him did not exist.

They passed the ruins of bathhouses and government buildings from the time long ago when Qadasiya had been the seat of the bureaucracy. Now the coastal city of Khessard housed most of the government machinery, and court messengers rode constantly back and forth with the requests of the bureaucrats and the orders of the nobility at the Citadel. The abandoned buildings in Qadasiya were now partitioned by flimsy wood-and-cloth barriers into dwellings for people of the underclasses. Jamal seemed familiar with the area. Arris wondered if his companion might not live in one of the decayed structures.

At last they arrived in an open-air bazaar. The colors and smells only overloaded Arris's wearied senses further. Booths were hung with eye-straining, dirty awnings of purple and yellow or red and green. The smells were nauseating to a boy who was used to the ancient dust and perfumes of the Citadel and the clean green scents of field and hill at Delronen. He stayed close to Jamal, feeling faint.

There were other fuel vendors with wagons piled with great mounds of wood. They scowled at the boys, but Jamal led Arris toward the other side of the bazaar, where the stalls of the butchers, fruit sellers, and other food merchants stood. One had packed up his booth early, so they threw down their loads in his space and spread them out.

"I can't guarantee luck at this hour," Jamal said. "But someone's bound to have forgotten to buy the night's fuel. We'll play on their sympathy. Look as young and innocent and hungry as you can."

They settled into cross-legged positions on the trampled ground. Arris found it easy enough to look hungry. The proximity of the food stalls was torture. He knew he looked much younger than his age, small and slim-boned as he was. In an effort to look innocent, he tried to wipe some of the grime from his face. If he had been less exhausted he might have enjoyed the game immensely.

A few soldiers passed, but none gave Arris a second look. He wondered if the spell he had performed had done more than lock up his unwanted fears. Everything seemed to be too easy. He had escaped the Citadel and the Palace, gotten to Qadasiya, found a helpful new friend when he needed him; and now, when the soldiers should be stopping and questioning every black-haired boy they found, they were ignoring him.

"Sir!" Jamal called out. A disheveled slave was passing, who had apparently been drinking away the time he was supposed to have been running errands. "Good sir, I have the wood you need. Dry and ready for your fire, choice and aromatic for cooking, priced for your purse as well. Only look a moment!" The boy leapt up and caught the slave's wrist, pulling him bodily toward the wood. Quickly, Jamal convinced the slave he needed it all. He left five copper hayim.

"A ridiculously high price," Jamal said with glee when the man was out of sight. "Come! This should buy us each plenty of food."

One haya apiece bought them meat pies and sourfruit, which they devoured unmindful of burning tongues and puckered lips. Arris's were gone in moments.

The ululating call for evening prayer assailed their ears. Arris winced, but Jamal touched his forehead with outspread hand in a reverent sign of the Five. "The Temple's nearby. We can thank the gods for our luck." He started away from the bazaar. Arris walked with him, curious. He had never been inside a Temple of the Sun. At the Citadel, his father had prayed wherever the call found him, saying he felt no need for priests between him and his gods. Arris had usually knelt with him, and sometimes tried to pray, but he had never worshiped.

The Temple was an ancient building, the largest in Qadasiya. It had been built by the first Khalif. Before then Rehoman had been worshiped on the site. Now the setting sun bounced brilliantly off the gold-layered minarets and shone in the complex patterns that scored the towering walls: patterns of plants intertwined, of scenes from the Mythos, of bright geometric shapes that led the eye inward past the walled courtyard to the pillared hall. The ceiling rose to many-domed heights above the crowds that pressed within. There were sweaty leatherworkers and armed soldiers, perfumed dandies and sober tradesmen, schoolboys and beggars. There were no women. The priests of the Brothers argued endlessly whether women had souls. They agreed their gods had little interest in women's doings except childbearing.

Jamal wormed through to the front of the Temple court. Arris followed doggedly, eliciting curses from men too large to do the same. He wanted a good view of the ceremony. But his head pounded with the effort of keeping out the crushing emotions and indecipherable thoughts of so many people. He wondered if the priests here had any training to help people sensitive to such things. He doubted it.

The gold-robed men who were gathered in the forecourt ranged in age from no older than Jamal to very old. Five of them stood forward. Arris knelt with the worshipers, unsure of the routine, but was able to genuflect and rise only a heartbeat after the rest. The prayers began to drone in low, monotonous rhythms, spoken aloud by the priests and, he supposed, silently by the others.

They chanted in an archaic version of the tongue of the Khalifate, which was only Arris's second language. He found it hard to follow. It seemed an invocation for the gods to enter the Temple. The Five Brothers were named and described at length: Verchaki of the Night, Sygathi the Truthsayer, Kerami the Lover, Myrdethreshi the Warrior, and Ogliatu the Eldest Brother, who lit the lamp of the sun in the morning and dimmed it at night.

Arris would have liked to believe in the Brothers Ylla. Their religion seemed controlled, bound up in ritual and the framework of sin and virtue. It felt safe, with no allowances made for the caprices of the gods it served; with no room at the edges for such creatures as the Lossiran.

But the whitewashed walls were faceless and devoid of design, the ceiling arched and scalloped, the stink of many bodies after a day's work pungent, and all was empty and without meaning. No presences could be felt but the collective guilt and half-belief of the people and the artificial fervor of the priests. Arris began to wish he had left the city as soon as he had eaten.

The sun was almost gone. He could feel dusk gathering beyond the thick stones of the Temple. Soon the moon would rise, waxing, and the Goddess would come into her own. Why did this religion not have a god of the moon? Verchaki held power only in darkness, not on the ivory-lit nights of the Goddess. Perhaps they had not really forgotten Rehoman, though they kept her out of their official rites. These ceremonies were powerless. Even if there were Five Brothers, surely they would not respond to such trivial mouthings.

The distant beating of wings caught the edge of his awareness. That could not be. This was the Temple of the Sun. It was only the beating of the hearts of the kneeling men in the hall, settling into rhythm with the morose chanting of the priests. It was only the soft, steady thud of a remote drum. It was only the footsteps of passersby.

It was the Lossiran. Rehoman had once been worshiped in this place, and perhaps she was not entirely gone from the hearts of the people. Arris closed his eyes and tried to pray. The Mother of Vultures was in Qadasiya looking for him. Not satisfied with the damage it had already done, it would make him speak in prophecy again, lay its spell of truth on him, betray him to the soldiers. He wanted to leap up and run, but that would only draw more attention to him.

His skin prickled with fear, and blood pounded in his ears. The Lossiran was flying around the minarets of the Temple.

Its darkness was a blanket of night settling over the building, though the sun was barely gone. And Arris was not the only one to sense its coming. He opened his eyes in surprise.

A young, blue-eyed priest clenched white-knuckled fists. The other priests were repeating a story from the Mythos, "Myrdethreshi and the Whore," a well-known morality fable. The young priest chanted different words with equal authority. His clear voice undercut the others.

"Seek protection to defend thee from evil, for the gods have that power. Find in them a shield against the chill things of night that seek thy blood and with it thy soul. For they are the Light of the Sun to drive away the most awful shadow. The sword of Myrdethreshi will be thy salvation, the love of Kerami, the truth of Sygathi, the power of Verchaki, the wisdom of Ogliatu . . ." The words were gasped now, between shudders of revulsion and horror.

The sound was meaningless to Arris. He cried out as the Lossiran broke through the ceiling, leaving no hole. It bore down on him, fanning its noxious wings, and he realized it did not mean to give him prophecy this time. Instead, it attacked the shields that kept his feelings imprisoned. Why would the Messenger do such a thing? His spherical cell was breached as if by a ram-tower. It crumbled. He could not let those emotions escape. They would overwhelm him, incapacitate him, perhaps drive him mad.

"Myrdethreshi, defend!" a cry came from ahead. The darkness of the vulture spread through the Temple like a malignant fog. The priests stood together with upraised arms, chanting in shrill voices. Panic battered Arris from every uncomprehending mind in the hall. They could not see the Lossiran, but they could feel it.

The stronghold of his thoughts was being overthrown, and his body convulsed with the fear of his escape from the Citadel, with the horror of Sasha's final words, with his father's unavailing innocence. He began to sob. The Messenger flew closer, and at his side Jamal whimpered in fear. But then there was a shriek of pain and dismay. The sound shrilled and echoed in Arris's ears. Something was there he could not describe, something bright with the sharpness of cold steel, that cut between him and the darkness and left him able to breathe again.

The Lossiran fled through the ceiling, followed by the

other power, and the hall was empty of spirits. But it echoed with murmurs of outrage from a thousand threats. Jamal screamed accusations at Arris, and the priests were approaching.

Arris ran, gripped by a horror of the gold-washed Temple that lent his feet wind speed. Evading grasping hands, he shot from the pillared hall like a bolt from a crossbow. The stones of the courtyard ripped at the soles of his bare feet, leaving bloody tracks.

The bright sword that had severed him from the Vulture's grasp had not mended the damage done. His mind whirled with the confusion of violent emotions that seeped through the cracks in his shattered walls, widening the fissures until they ran in floodwater torrents. Sobs shook his small body. Half-aware of the pounding of running feet behind him, he raced past the sparkling fountains in the Temple courtyard and around the inside of the walls like a penned animal. Then he found a side exit, a small priests' door. He lifted the latch, and was out.

Arris fled through the dusky city, randomly stumbling from shadow to fading light, in and out of the stinking alleys of the slums that crowded the beautiful Temple. Dogs and rats and children playing in the garbage scampered out of his way. He ran weeping, sick with fear and outrage, as the horror of the day before became even greater than it had been. He ran with the terror that he was going mad, as pictures flashed on the filthy walls of decrepit buildings like portraits in a gallery.

A bright ring scattering coals in a grate. A black banner rising. Statue hardness on the face of a golden-haired boy. Wind in his ears as he fled down tower stairs. Garish colors and crowds and a leering, handsome youth who saw through his clothing. A glittering sapphire above a beckoning death's-head. The musty smell of an ancient tapestry.

Unable to see where he was going for the tears, he ran at cavalry speed into a splintered wall where the alley turned sharply. The pain shocked him. His hands at his face came away bloody. His muscles cramped and twinged; his lungs screamed for rest. But the pictures would not stop. He might leave them behind if only he kept running.

Battered and bruised, whimpering, seeing the corridors of the Citadel in the streets of Qadasiya, he ran. Then a door opened in a dark lane and thin, rope-strong hands reached out and gripped his arms. He struggled, seeing through an overlay of memories. A horribly wrinkled face veiled with a kerchief. The bright black eyes pierced him from under jutting brows, and he screamed before he fainted into the muck and garbage of the alley.

CHAPTER

3

THERE FOLLOWED A DIM, twilight time of nightmares that were more real than dreams. Scenes played over and over in garish colors, as if by actors rehearsing for some tragic performance. There were memories: of visits by the Lossiran; of the day of the Khalif's death; of a night long ago when he lay on a forest's matted floor, an infant, watching dancers who moved like vultures and snakes, hearing songs he could not understand. His mother was one of the singers, he thought.

And some of the scenes were not memories at all, for he had never seen them. His mother, young and unformed as a fawn, lying in a dark stone ruin with a black-haired stranger not his father, then returning to her pale husband and blond babies. A scarred man, naked but for a belt of human hair, holding a squalling, dark infant over a fire and slowly lowering it until its wisps of hair began to smoke. His father, white-lipped, with clenched jaw and staring eyes, silent as his lacerated body was slowly ripped apart on a spiked wheel, until the light faded from his blue eyes. Faces floated in and out of this last scene: the pleasant smile of Nievan the Vizier as he directed the Black Masks; the disgust of the other regent, Maenad; and last, most familiar, the young Saresha Ilkharani, pale as new cheese, watching from an overlarge chair with a gilt circlet on his gleaming yellow curls.

Arris began to wake. He had been screaming for a long time, and trying to scream through a dry and soundless throat for longer afterward. His head was shot through with pains like needles in a cushion, and his stomach was tight and shriveled as a seasoned drum. His eyes were empty of tears, and his thoughts seemed empty as well. The horrible things he had walled up inside him no longer had the power to affect him. They were free from their bonds, but seemed distant.

"You've been drained," said a voice from his dreams in the Yaighan tongue. "Purged. Those things weren't any use to you."

"I walled them up," he whispered, shocked at the weakness of his voice. "But the Lossiran broke the walls."

"The Vulture knew you couldn't hold such thoughts long, your age and strength as they are, or they'd break through on their own. And then where would you be?" The voice was female, low and rusty with age. "Not here and safe as you are, young master. Your mother overstepped herself teaching you that trick, no matter the talent in learning you showed. A child shouldn't be taught to block emotions."

His dream was over. He felt a cup against his lips, and drank something that soothed and cooled his angry throat. It was taken away after only a few sips. "Where am I?" he asked with sudden urgency.

"You'll see in a moment. Oh, make no mistake, it was well done of you. And when you're a man grown, I've no doubt you'll control your feelings as well as any adept. Maybe even earlier, if we can get you out of this Goddess-accursed city and into the hills where you belong."

Drops of fragrant ointment fell on Arris's burning eyelids, and a soft cloth wiped them away. He opened his eyes. They ached, but he could see that he was in a tiny room hung with bunches of herbs and swatches of bright-patterned weave. An opaque curtain of black streamers cut his half of the room from the part that, judging from the noise, opened into the street. He could hear the clatter of wagons passing, and the morning hum of conversation. The room smelled of incense and spice. He lay on a soft pallet stuffed with feathers. The air was cool on his naked body.

An ancient, dark-skinned woman watched him from shadowed eyes. Her waist-length black hair was streaked with random gray. Her head was bound with a red kerchief, from which small coins hung. They jingled when she moved. Her dress was a gaudy print that fell, shapeless, against her shrunken body.

"Where are the clothes I wore last night?" Arris demanded.

"Last night you were bare, and the night before as well," said the crone. "It's been three days and three nights since I caught you and pulled you in with the priests close behind. As for your rags, I sent them to the trash heap. Don't protest, son of Tauena. I've had Terai find you others."

She moved with a smooth grace that seemed alien to her form. On a shelf beside two strange-hued bottles was a pile of muted red clothing: a tunic and hosen, short leather boots and a leather belt, a pleated cloak. Arris sat up with difficulty. His skin was clean of the filth of his escape. The old woman must have bathed him. He dressed in some embarrassment. The clothes fit loosely, and felt rough against his skin.

"You'll fill them out soon enough." She smiled toothlessly. "A few days' feeding will fatten those bones you wear. They said you were a pretty child, and I daresay you'll be so again."

The old woman turned and went into the outer room, and came back bearing a tray of meat pies and a pitcher. Arris was ravenous at the sight. He grabbed two pies and took a bite from one.

"Slowly!" she admonished, taking the second and replacing it on the tray. Her piercing eyes laughed at him. "A pretty child indeed. And you'll be a heartbreaking youth, and a man to turn heads. Don't gobble your pie, Arris j'Areyta. There are plenty, but slowly."

"How do you know my name?"

"The Goddess keeps watch on her own. It was no accident you ran from the priests in my direction." She smiled. "Now eat your pie, and be quiet. I have a customer coming, and you mustn't be seen."

"Wait," he called. "What's your name?"

"Mine?" She seemed pleased. "I'm called Ruena. In the city, they make it Ruena the Unbeliever." A chime rang from the outer room. She drew her kerchief over her face as an improvised veil, catching it on the other side with a pin. She touched her hand to a carved vulture's head that stood in a niche of one wall, and swept dramatically through the curtain.

The vulture's head was fashioned of ebony wood on a base of black stone. Arris shivered. It was the Lossiran, lifelike down to the dull red stones in its eye sockets. The small hairs quivered on the boy's neck, and a wave of dizziness made the object shimmer as if about to move. But why should he fear it? He had been terrified of the Lossiran before the visions and dreams of the last few days. Now that feeling was remote, unreal. In the Temple, the Messenger had not meant to hurt or frighten him, but to keep him from killing himself with the strength of his walled-off emotions.

His mother had told him once that the Messenger was not evil, only alien and cold. It did the bidding of the Goddess. Perhaps he should no longer be afraid of it.

His body seemed wavery and insubstantial, as if a breeze might blow through him. Arris lay back down on the pallet and turned his eyes to the wall, but he could still feel the dim red gaze watching behind him.

"I hate him," Arris said as his companion pulled him from the square.

Terai winced. "You can't blame the Prince," he said in his low Yaighan accent. "He only repeats what his uncles have told him."

"You don't understand," Arris muttered. He had seen it. Sasha in the public square of Qadasiya, flanked by his two uncles; Sasha proclaiming the lands of Delronen forfeit to the crown, the wife and children of the executed traitor Areyta exiled and homeless; Sasha calling for a hunt for Arris j'Areyta, convicted at a proxy trial of sorcery, heresy, and complicity in the murder of the Khalif. He had seen it, and heard the fervent strength of the Prince's young voice, and recognized the conviction on the angelic face. And he was beginning to hate.

Terai led a convoluted path back to Ruena's shop. The Yaighan hillman was trying to arrange to get Arris out of the city. Arris had met him that morning. He was small, thickly muscled, dark-skinned even for a Yaighan, older than Arris's father but far younger than Ruena. A taciturn man, he was friendly enough, but the boy was wary of him.

Ruena was packing a bag of blankets and food for his journey. Terai took money from under the old woman's cot and left without a word. Arris sat on the crowded counter for a while, waiting to see if she would speak, and finally asked a question he had been curious about for the last four days.

"If they know you worship the Goddess, why do they let you stay here? It's forbidden."

She laughed and gestured around the room, encompassing her herbs and spices, the vulture's head, the horned moon that hung over the lintel. "They suffer me to stay because they need me."

"Why?"

"To tell their futures, give them love potions, curses, amulets. The priests of the Sun won't do it. When they drove the Goddess out of Qadasiya, they forgot the needs of her people. I can fill those needs." She sighed. "It's important work, child, keeping her alive in the midst of her enemies."

"But you wish you were home, away from this place of alien powers and priests," he said, wide-eyed, reading her thoughts as clearly as inked words on parchment.

She was startled. "They'll teach you why I'm here, that and much else. I think they'll find you even more than your mother indicated. More, perhaps, than they can easily control."

Arris had never before sensed the very words in another's mind. He leaned forward eagerly. "Will they teach me power?"

The old woman ignored him, finished her packing, and went to wait on a customer in the other room. Arris remained where he was. When she finally returned, she looked at him and sighed.

"Yes," she answered, as if ten minutes had not elapsed. "They want to make you a force for them to use. They want to give you the highest rank the Goddess holds for a man. But you won't be the puppet they're hoping for."

"I'll be anything they want," Arris said. "As long as they teach me to destroy the ones who murdered my father."

Ruena turned away and did not speak again that morning.

"Here you go, lad." Terai swung Arris up into the second of the two gaudily painted wagons and tossed his bag after him. The hillman had removed the Northern turban he had worn earlier. He had limp, graying hair that hung thin and straight to his ears, and eyes that squinted hard as flint. Arris thought that he might once have been handsome, but wind and sun had leathered his face into a stern, unnerving expression that was rarely broken.

The journey was going to be unpleasant. Terai had appeared with a family of entertainers who had hired his services to guide them to the Dark Hills. They were to perform at something called the Winter Festival. A heavy, bearded man named Senna was their leader, and the father of the others, two girls and a youth. All were blond and sharp-featured, and spoke with the quick accents of the North. Terai had bought a horse with Ruena's money, and would be riding ahead, leaving Arris stuck inside a canvas-topped wagon with two giggling girls.

He sat sullenly on the hardwood floor between a large drum and a stack of striped poles, not trusting the flimsy walls enough to lean on them. The wagon began to jerk along the rough, cobbled streets of Qadasiya. How could he travel this way? He had come to court riding a fiery young horse alongside his father.

The two girls stared at him. They were unveiled, with rouged cheeks and painted fingernails. His mother had never worn a veil, but Arris had never seen a Northern woman without one. The priests would be scandalized. He tried to ignore them.

"Awfully little to be so much trouble," said the younger girl disdainfully. She looked perhaps twelve years old.

"Cute, though," said the older one, reaching out to ruffle Arris's hair and laughing when he pulled away. Her sister flicked the hard end of the harness she was mending at her, raising a welt of red on one pale arm. The older girl laughed again.

"I'm Vaessa, little boy, and this is Danae. Our brother who is driving is Van." She was fifteen, Arris thought, and trying to look older. He did not reply. "Come on, what's your name? We have to call you something. What shall it be? Boy? You there?"

"We're not supposed to ask," Danae hissed. "Terai said so."

"Oh, Kerami take Terai. We don't have to do everything he says. What's your name?"

"Duan," he muttered to quiet her.

"See, Danae? He can talk after all. But with that gruff voice he probably can't sing."

"Sing?" Arris said warily.

"Of course. We're to pass you off as a young cousin, a member of the troupe. Why else are you wearing our color?"

"You aren't wearing red."

"We don't wear our costumes for mending harness, stupid." The younger girl giggled.

"Ruena insisted he could sing." Vaessa frowned. "We'll see."

"That crazy old woman. All we need is an untalented little boy to smuggle all the way south. He'll be crying at every thunderstorm. And it's bad luck to have a child in a traveling company."

"So I keep telling Papa," said her sister.

"Oh, you . . ."

"I am not frightened of thunder," Arris said, beginning to be angry. "And I won't cry. Just leave me alone." He wrapped his arms around his knees, making himself as small as possible, and stared at the bouncing floor.

The girls were quiet for a moment. Then the younger one, Danae, crawled across the wagon toward him. She unbuckled three straps that bound a wooden case, and withdrew a small zither. "I hope you can sing," she said shyly. "Van cracks his notes unmercifully now. We think he'll be a baritone. But the descant part is missing." She flicked her fingers across the instrument. It sounded like a brassy harp. She began a light, breathy tune, obviously too high for her voice.

> *"Come lie with me in the forest green,*
> *My quick-fingered, light-fingered love,*
> *And there will all the joys be seen*
> *Kerami sent us from above.*
>
> *I'll taste your lips, the leaves will sway*
> *O'er things only lovers can know.*
> *Your breath, your body filling me . . ."*

"Stop it, Danae," said Vaessa sharply. "You don't teach songs like that to children."

"Papa taught it to me. He'll have to know it if he's going to sing with us in the show." She resumed her strumming. "Try this, Duan. It's the descant."

He matched the tones with ease. They were high, but he thought he reached them better than the girl.

"That's it!" Danae grinned. "Listen, Vaessa. I think he could be better than Van. He's certainly prettier."

Her sister frowned judiciously. "His voice is clear, anyway, and unstrained. We'd have to teach him everything. But he won't hurt the act, I suppose. With some audiences he might even help.''

Arris felt a strange wash of pleasure. Perhaps he would enjoy the trip after all, if he was not a hindrance to these people who were his disguise.

"He knows the songs, Papa,'' wheedled the younger daughter.

"And he'll forget them as soon as he's in front of a crowd,'' scoffed her brother Van, a thickset, heavy-featured youth with big hands.

The company had stopped that night beside a stream, not far from a camp of Deirani merchants who had agreed to a performance. It would not hurt, the girls said, to get a little extra money on their way to the Winter Festival.

"All the songs, Danae? In two days?'' Her father, Senna, smiled skeptically. He was a big, gruff man who had been indifferently friendly to Arris when he noticed the boy at all.

"Most of them. You'll like it, Papa. It really helps to have the third part again.'' Danae's tilted green eyes were lit with anticipation.

Arris liked her. She had taught him as quickly as he could learn; his mother had trained his memory almost since he could speak, and he rarely needed anything repeated twice. Danae had even convinced him to look forward to singing for strangers.

"He can sing Danae's part too,'' Vaessa said. "Better than she can.''

"I never claimed to have a good voice,'' Danae said. "But at least I always remember all the verses, and I never miss my entrances.'' She stuck her tongue out at the older girl. Vaessa scowled.

"Daughters,'' Senna warned. "We perform in an hour. Even if the Deirani won't understand a word we sing, we should look presentable. Get your costumes on.'' He paused. "Duan too.''

Arris grinned widely and ran to follow the girls to the wagons. He passed Terai picketing the horses and shouted, "I get to sing!''

The stocky Yaighan looked down at him unsmiling. "I suppose it can't hurt,'' he said in resignation, turning back to the horses.

Arris shook his head and walked on. He should not have expected Terai to be excited. Terai had not been excited about anything yet. Arris suspected the hillman had never wanted to shepherd him on this journey, but that he owed Ruena a favor.

He hoped Danae was not angry with him because he could sing better than she could. He did not think she would be. She had told him she wanted to write music for other people to sing one day. She had hummed a few tunes she had written, and he thought they were very good. She had even said she might write a song for him sometime.

They performed by torchlight for the Deirani caravan. Arris sang with the girls, playing a finger drum in simple rhythms behind their instruments. The songs mostly dealt with love. Many were explicit, and some descended into comic ribaldry. Vaessa and Danae flirted with their audience under the watchful eye of their father, tossing their long blond hair and swaying to the music. Arris merely stood and smiled while he sang.

The Deirani were honey-skinned and slant-eyed, traveling merchants from a supposedly vast empire beyond the mountains of the Westrange. Relations between their country and the Khalifate were uneasy at best, and there were frequent border wars. The merchants of this caravan were hurrying home in fear that either the new Regents or their own Emperor would choose the unsettled time after Rasul Ilkharani's death to launch a major attack.

The merchants wore long, sleeved robes over pleated trousers and knee-high, cuffed boots of beaten leather. Round caps confined their shoulder-length brown hair. Most were clean-shaven, though a few had mustaches. Arris liked their clothes. They looked more comfortable, and more durable, than the brocaded tunics, hosen, and slippers of the Citadel court.

When the singers had finished, the merchants applauded politely. Senna began a comic monologue on the virtues of an herbal medicine, accompanied by soft, technically brilliant harping. Van's big hands moved as surely on his instrument as they had earlier on the reins of his four-horse wagon.

"It was like playing to a bunch of corpses," Danae muttered as they laid their instruments back into their cases. The

wagons were quiet, and the soft harping sounded gently from
the Deirani camp.

"They're foreign," Vaessa said with a shrug.

"They liked us," Arris said. "Very much. I was watching
them." He wrapped himself in his pleated cloak in the corner
of the wagon where he slept. It would be cold tonight.

"They liked you," Vaessa said. "At least some of them
did. I hear the Deirani are that way. There are even rumors
that their Emperor keeps two separate harems. One of girls
and one of boys."

"You can't be serious," Danae said, shocked. "The priests
say that's a sin."

"Who knows what Deirani priests say?" Vaessa said.

"And who listens to priests anyway?" Arris added, interested. "I knew people at the Citadel who were like that. The
Lord Collector's son, Taifid—" He stopped abruptly. The
girls had turned to stare at him. He remembered they did not
know who he was.

"At the Citadel?" Vaessa repeated softly. "You're escaping from the court, then."

"Leave him alone," Danae said. "If we were supposed to
know who he was, Papa would have told us." She looked
worriedly at Arris. "But . . . be more careful, Duan."

He nodded miserably and turned toward the wall to try to
sleep.

"Eager to be home, Duan?" Danae teased. "Less than two
days to the Dark Hills, Papa says. That's where we're going.
Is it far to your home?"

"Not far," he said, and smiled. They had been more than
a week on the road. The fertile green land was achingly
familiar. Low rolling hills, the doorway of the Yaighan mountains, made a narrow purple band on the horizon.

Terai had whispered to him that morning that they would
reach his family's home just after dark. Arris's insides were
tightened like an overwound spring. He had not seen his
mother or brothers for over a year. If they were at Delronen,
he would see them tonight—if the soldiers had not gotten
there first. Nievan might not have waited for the official
proclamation in the square to send his men south. They might
all be dead. He did not think so, but they might be.

Danae was growing annoyed at his silence. To placate her,

he began to sing one of the songs she had taught him. This one was not in the show. It was an old melody, quick and lively, with words that made little sense but frolicked along like puppies. The horses picked up their pace as Danae joined in. From the back they could hear Vaessa crooning a slow counter-melody as she sewed a new costume for Van, who had outgrown his old one.

Arris would be sorry to leave them. They had been kind to him, had praised his singing, had not forced him to tell who he was. The way they bickered and fought and laughed reminded him of his brothers. He would not admit to himself that they reminded him of his friendship with Saresha Ilkharani; he was determined to hate the Prince, and could not do so effectively if he remembered loving him.

Delronen was no longer beautiful. The gates were thrown down, and the banner of the Ilkharani hung limply from a new wooden pole in the still air. Patrols of soldiers lounged in front of the distant manor, tiny silhouettes through burned groves of trees.

Arris tightened his grip on Terai's broad waist, but he did not avert his eyes. The wagons had been left behind several miles to the north, and only Senna knew where the two of them had gone.

"I have to know," he whispered.

"They aren't here," Terai said gruffly.

"But did they escape?"

"If they had died, son of Tauena, wouldn't you know?"

"Not if it happened while I was dreaming in Qadasiya with Ruena's herbs inside me." Arris surveyed his father's lands. There were no peasants in the huts along the roads, no animals in the fields. All was empty. Lifeless. There had been death here, but whether of the peasants or his family he could not tell. "I have to know."

A deep frown etched lines into Terai's weathered face. "We'll come back after moondark," he finally conceded. "I don't think we'll learn anything, though. For that we'll have to ask in Gama."

Gama. Arris remembered the name only vaguely. A word overheard from servants' lips, perhaps from his mother once. He knew so little of the high hills. His father had forbidden Tauena to tell her children much of her life before Delronen.

Arris did not even know much about the religion of Rehoman, beyond the truth of the Goddess's existence and the power of her Messenger. He thought he had seen some of the places she was worshiped, the stone circles built by his mother's ancestors, the groves of trees whose designs were too regular to be natural. He had heard the rumors and terror stories of priests and old nursemaids in the Citadel, but those he discounted.

Terai's dark face was set and still as the frozen waters of a pool, and Arris did not ask any of his half-formed queries. He barely kept his seat as the Yaighan moved imperceptibly in his furry saddle and the horse wheeled abruptly. They cantered over the desolate meadows, under the long shadow of the Dark Hills.

CHAPTER

4

THE WOODEN PILLAR crumbled under Arris's prodding foot, its carven grace reduced to charcoal. The boy's face was expressionless in its misery. Terai stood uneasily nearby, his sword loose in his belt, his narrow eyes leaping from one shadow to another. The moon had not yet set, but was deeply hidden in clouds. They were near the manor house, hidden by a group of fire-hardened birches.

"This was the summerhouse," Arris said. "We came here at night sometimes to watch the stars." Kicking through the debris that remained, he suddenly bent and freed an object. A small marble statue, layered with soot. Arris wiped it clean, revealing the figure of a man with a stylized spear in one hand and a measure of grain in the other. "One of their own gods." He showed it to Terai. "Sygathi. My father often prayed to him. It's strange. The soldiers destroyed the one place in Delronen that was sacred to their own gods.''

"Amusing," Terai whispered. "Come, lad. We haven't found what happened to your people, and we can't stay any longer."

"No. I'm going nearer. I want to listen to their talk." The boy started swiftly for the house. After a moment the Yaighan followed, muttering imprecations. When Arris was clear of the birch grove, the clouds over the moon suddenly parted. He was outlined as if by a flash of lightning.

"Who's there?" a guardsman called. Moonlight glittered on a ringmail coat.

Arris ran back toward the devastated summerhouse. Splinters of charred wood cracked and rustled under his boots, and dead branches broke as he stumbled through the trees. The soldier followed, drawing his longsword. Terai cursed in Yaighan, a strangely powerful sound, as if a standing stone had spoken. Arris turned in his flight to see Terai's short sword sweep under the Northerner's guard, slicing into the soldier's stomach. The Deirani steel cut through the chains of the light coat as if through cloth, and the smell of the gushing blood named it a true stroke.

The soldier gasped soundlessly as he crumpled onto the burned grass. The blood that pooled from his midsection looked black in the moonlight. Terai stooped, took the longsword from the nerveless hands, and passed it without a word to Arris. The boy watched, fascinated. He had never seen a dying man so close. The gorge rose in his throat, but he gripped the sword tightly and moved to where the blond soldier could see his face.

"Where are my mother and brothers?"

The soldier could not have been older than twenty. He stared at Arris and shook his head, his blue eyes pleading.

"Are they dead?" Arris spoke calmly, but a darker emotion than anger filled him. Terai watched silently.

"No," the Northerner choked out. "Gone."

"Before you came?"

The youth nodded, the effort costing him pain.

"But there is death here. The servants, then, and the peasants?"

The dying soldier nodded again. His face was white, and he was beginning to bleed at the mouth.

"Come, Arris," Terai growled. "He'll be missed."

The boy did not turn. He spoke in Yaighan so the soldier would not understand. "He isn't dead yet. He could tell them who we were. How long will it take him to die?"

Terai shrugged. "An hour, if he's lucky. More, perhaps."

"I'll leave him his sword," Arris whispered. He buried the blade into the soldier's neck, feeling the slight resistance give way. Blood spurted onto his red clothes. He did not step back until he was sure the youth was dead.

The hillman said nothing. He wiped his Deirani blade with a rust-colored cloth from his belt pouch and started back toward the riverbank where the horse waited. Arris stumbled after him, full of a sick triumph that was new to him.

The road was rutted with old tracks and washed out with disuse. The wagons jounced dangerously along, the only sound the protesting creak of the wheels and the snorting of the overworked horses. When Terai and Arris had returned that morning from the forests, they had said the main road was no longer safe. Senna and his children noticed the blood on the boy's clothing, but asked no questions. They harnessed their animals with the speed Terai urged, and followed him out of the draw where they had been hidden.

Arris sat miserably on the driver's board of the first wagon with Van. The youth had not so much as looked at him all morning, and it was now midday. The small caravan traveled now with no laughter or singing. Arris felt it was his fault. Somehow they had guessed what he had done, and no longer wanted to have anything to do with him.

Van swore by Myrdethreshi as one of the four horses stumbled over a small rockslide in the road. The animal nearly fell, and the traces tangled as the others fought to go on. Terai trotted his tired horse back to them, and soon had soothed the beast and convinced it to continue.

"Thanks," Van said rather grudgingly.

The hillman nodded. "Are you feeling better, lad?" he asked Arris in Yaighan.

"I'm all right." The boy was grateful for spoken words. "Will we be stopping to eat soon?"

"We dare not. They'll be searching for the killer, and they may think of this road. I know you're tired, young lord, but we'll be in Gama in two days. I imagine you'll find your mother there, and other things as well.'' He bowed over his saddle and spurred his mount forward.

Gama. Arris rolled the word in his mind. It felt mysterious, enticing. And Terai had called him ''young lord.'' He had never done that before. He knew Arris was the son of Lord Areyta, but none of the Yaighan had ever accepted that Areyta had any authority over them. It was very strange.

''What did he say?'' Van asked with a frown.

Arris answered, eager for conversation. ''We won't be stopping for a while.''

''Why? We're sneaking around like a band of highwaymen. The horses don't like this road, and I don't either.''

''Maybe it's a faster way to Gama,'' Arris suggested.

Van glared at him. ''Don't be stupid. It's all because we're hiding you. Papa should never have agreed to it, not even for Terai. He's breaking the law, and we are too.''

''How do you know that?''

''I know who you are. Vaessa and I figured it out. You're the one the Regents are hunting. The son of the man who killed the Khalif. They say you're a witch.''

Arris huddled into his cloak, looking at the dark stains. ''I'm not,'' he said softly.

''Last night, Papa wouldn't say where we were, but I think we were near Arcyta's old estate. You went there, didn't you? And someone recognized you, and Terai had to kill him.''

''Terai began it,'' Arris said. ''But I killed him.''

''Then I'm right. You're the one.''

''What if I am? Your father must know, and he took me.''

''Sometimes my father is a fool.'' Van looked out over the ears of his horses and did not speak again. Arris shivered as the wagon topped a ridge, and the wind of the hills began to batter at them.

It was late and moonless when they finally stopped and made camp under an overhanging rockshelf in the high, bone-dry mountains halfway to Gama. The horses crowded at the back of the shelter, snuffling and whickering in the cold. Their breath puffed into clouds. Van moved among them, rubbing them down, feeding them small handfuls of warming grain as he picketed them to each other. Danae was oiling the dusty harnesses. Vaessa, after cooking the meager evening meal,

had begun to strum a lute and sing in a pleasant, low alto
voice.

Arris pillowed his head on his cloak against the rock face.
He was cold, even wrapped in two blankets. But he was fed,
and the low fire was comforting, and the music almost made
him forget his fear. He did not know the song, but it had
many verses, and he soon had the melody. He began to sing a
light descant, interweaving it with Vaessa's tune. He made
his voice fuzzy at the edges like hers, instead of the clear
tones he had sung before.

The girl ran more complex harmonies on her lute, and
Arris stayed with them. Her back was toward him, but he
could see her fingers on the instrument and match the changes.
Finally she sighed and stopped.

"That was beautiful, Danae. You've never done it so
well."

"It wasn't me," said the younger girl dryly. "It was
Duan."

Vaessa stiffened and turned toward him. Across the fire,
Senna laughed and said, "We shouldn't give him up to the
Yaighan. Adds something to the ensemble, I'd say. Espe-
cially since I wasn't blessed with soprano daughters."

Vaessa put the lute in its box and gathered the pots and
dishes into a bag to carry to the wagons. On her way, she
glanced down at Arris, her pretty green eyes harsh and accusing. "How can your voice be beautiful after what you did?
Van told me you killed a man last night."

Arris looked over at Terai, but the Yaighan seemed not to
notice. "He would have killed me," he defended.

"On orders from the Prince. Maybe he should have, if
what they say is true."

"Daughter," Senna began ominously, but Terai put a hand
on his shoulder.

"Leave this between them."

"It's true." Arris took a deep breath. "The Prince wants
me dead. And I *am* Arris j'Areyta. But my father didn't kill
the Khalif, and I didn't help him." His voice shrilled with
two weeks' worth of anger. "I wouldn't be surprised if it was
Nievan himself. And Verchaki take the Prince and his orders!"

Vaessa backed away, her face pale. Van threw down his
grain bucket and strode forward. "Don't speak to my sister
like that, you little—"

"Van! Vaessa!" Senna rose ponderously, and his children wilted. "You'll stop insulting our guest. If I'd thought him guilty of any crime, I'd have turned him in in Qadasiya."

They murmured unfelt apologies and retreated into the second wagon, their faces blank but their eyes furious. Arris watched them go, feeling frightened. What would prevent them from telling the soldiers where he was after they returned to the North?

"They're not sorry," Danae said, putting down the harness and coming to sit beside Arris on the rocky ground. "But I am. Don't pay any attention to them, Duan. They're stupid."

"Arris," he corrected with a wan smile.

"Arris, then. What difference does it make? You're just a little boy. You can't have done anything to deserve death."

"I killed the soldier," he said defiantly, resenting being called a little boy by someone not much bigger.

She looked troubled. "You had to, didn't you? He would have killed you. But you're sorry you did it, aren't you?"

He remembered the pain-filled face of the dying youth, and thought of the burned timbers of the summerhouse, and his father's calm blue eyes. "No."

Danae looked at him gravely, then nodded and followed the others to the wagon. She did not seem angry. Arris hoped she was not. He had not thought he had done anything wrong. His mother, at least, would be proud.

"Your children lack diplomacy." Terai spread his blankets out by the fire with choppy, abrupt movements.

Senna shrugged. "They speak their minds. A quality I've noticed in you, my friend, whether or not the occasion calls for it."

"They had no excuse to attack him like that."

"It's my fault, I suppose. I don't usually keep them ignorant of anything this important."

"I made you swear not to tell them."

"Aye. You're a secretive man, Terai."

The Yaighan began to bank the fire. Senna watched him, a tolerant smile pulling at the corners of his bushy beard. Then he turned to Arris. "Again, I'm sorry, lad. But perhaps it would be better if you sleep out here tonight. What do you think?"

They would still be angry. He would rather be cold than have to face Van or Vaessa again. Arris nodded. Senna brought him several more blankets and a pillow and helped him make a bed near Terai's.

He lay there, closely wrapped, watching the flames dying in their dance until they were no more than white coals. Senna went to the lead wagon and did not come back out. The horses were quiet on their ropes. Arris wondered if Terai would feed the fire again or let it go out. The Yaighan sat cross-legged on a rock staring out of the overhang into the night.

The boy shivered and curled himself tightly into the blankets, crossing his arms over his chest. He did not feel like sleeping. After a long time, Terai came back to his bedroll and wrapped himself in its folds. He glanced at Arris, and finally spoke to Yaighan.

"You're just what they wanted."

Arris did not respond.

"I didn't know at first. You seemed like any other child." He shook his shaggy head. "But you startled me last night. Nine years old, and you did what most grown men would shrink from."

"I had to."

"Aye. You're what they want. Strong with their kind of strength, and beautiful, and dark. Dark as the sleeping Goddess herself. Cold as the wings of the Lossiran."

"Have you ever seen the Lossiran?" Arris asked, uncomfortable, unsure what Terai meant by his words.

"A few times. Once it was far away, seventeen years ago, in the battle. When the Khalifate army conquered us, when they put the Lord Areyta over us. The Vulture was far away, and it didn't help us at all. I think it only meant to watch so it could report the outcome to its Mistress."

"My father led that army," Arris said. "But I don't think he saw the Lossiran."

Terai's lined face was still in the shadows. "No. Few did. But it was there, cold and fearless even in defeat. As you were last night."

"Are you angry?" Arris asked urgently. "Was I wrong to kill him?"

The coals of the fire were black and smokeless when Terai answered. "Wrong? No. You did nothing wrong." He sighed. "Go to sleep, boy. Tomorrow you'll see Gama."

•   •   •

But the day wore on to cold afternoon, and the sameness of the hills grated on Arris until he felt raw. For a while he stayed alone in the back of the lead wagon, trying to make sense of the two-necked lute from which Van could wring such plaintive sounds. He picked out a few tunes, but his fingers were soon sore.

"Come up here, lad," Senna called back after Arris had played the same fumbling melody ten times over. "Take a rest."

The boy obediently replaced the lute in its case and secured the straps, then climbed through the flap in the canvas to the board where Senna sat.

"How about taking the reins for a while?" asked the big man.

"Could I?" Arris said wide-eyed. "I've never tried that. There are eight of them. What if I drop one?"

"It won't matter much at this speed. Here."

Arris took the soft leather straps as Senna's fleshy hands enveloped his own and arranged the reins in his small fingers. The horses were tired and plodding, but he could feel the pressure of their bobbing mouths through the oiled harness. He imagined himself the driver of one of the Khalif's war chariots, and wondered how it would feel to go faster.

The novelty was slow to fade, but at last Arris looked away from the reins to Senna's broad, pleasant face. "Why did you take me with you?" he asked. "You knew who I was. You knew the soldiers wanted me."

"Terai told me, when he offered to guide me to the Winter Festival. I've wanted to perform in Gama for years. And he knew that of anyone, I was unlikely to refuse."

"Why?"

"Because your father couldn't have killed the Khalif. General or not, I've never met a gentler man."

"You knew my father?" Arris asked incredulously.

"Aye. Five years ago. I don't suppose you'd be old enough to remember, but the Kwaitl nomads rebelled against some new taxes on their herds. Vizier Nievan drafted our wagons for supply services to the armies. Your father couldn't let us go, but he paid us well for our time. Which was more than he needed to have done."

"Did you like him?"

"He was a decent man. Spoke to me like an equal. You

remind me some of him." Senna chuckled. "Only some. The
rest you must have got from your mother. You don't look
anything like Areyta."

"My brothers do," Arris said wistfully. "Tall and blond
and good at war. Falcmet is fifteen by now, almost a soldier.
Husayn is two years younger, Van's age, and he'll be one
too."

"Good at war? Wouldn't you say that of yourself? Not
many children nine years old have killed a man."

"Terai really killed him. He would have died from his
wound. I just made it quicker. That wasn't war, anyway. It
was just killing."

"I thought you didn't regret it."

"I don't." Arris puzzled over the reins. One of the horses
had begun to drag behind the others.

"Are you sure, lad?"

Arris considered. "Well . . . Terai began it. I probably
should have let him finish it, once he realized it had to be
done."

Senna looked unaccountably sad. "Here, lad. You'll be
getting tired of that." He took back the reins.

Mountains obscured the setting sun, tilted slabs of rock unbalanced from their rest in ancient times. The road had been
high, jolting along narrow ridges where the air was thin and
cold even in the sunlight. Now there was mostly shadow, and
Danae had set the drag brakes on the lead wagon to slow their
descent. It was her turn to drive, and Arris sat beside her,
scarcely able to contain his excitement.

"How far down does this go, Terai?" Danae asked nervously, peering down the steep, gloomy incline.

"Not too far," he said from horseback. "It's the first
defense of Gama. Anyone who tried to descend this quickly
would be in trouble. And even if they got down, the Canyon
Gate would stop them."

Danae kept a tight grip on the reins, hunched forward on
the driver's board. "I hate to travel," she muttered.

Terai laughed. "Then what are you doing in a traveling
company?"

"My father likes it. I don't. But I don't have a choice. I'm
not old enough to marry."

"Will you marry just to stay in one place, then?"

She giggled. "Of course not. I'll marry someone I like. Maybe in Khessard. I think I'd like to live in Khessard."

Terai shook his head. "I don't think you'd like it much, girl. Anywhere in the Khalifate, you'd be kept indoors, veiled, surrounded by servants who are more like prison guards. You'd never see anyone but your husband and maybe some other wives he might have."

"My mother never wore a veil," Arris said. "I don't think my father ever asked her to."

"No Yaighan woman would stand for such treatment, and Arcyta knew it," Terai said.

"How do you know so much about wives, Terai? You don't have one," Danae said. "And how do you know what it's like for wives in the Khalifate?"

"Women get bored." He shrugged. "They take lovers. Men who aren't afraid of the wrath of the Brothers Ylla."

"You?" She giggled. "What would my father say if he knew what you tell his innocent twelve-year-old daughter?"

"Innocent? With the songs you sing?"

"Look," Arris breathed. Danae's retort went unvoiced. Between gargantuan rocks that reared like the close-set horns of an ibex, at the end of the long, deep-shadowed canyon, rose a tall gate. Its dark wood overlapped, and was crossed and banded with iron. It looked as strong as the hills, and was the height of four grown men.

"Come, Arris," Terai said. He reached out a strong hand to help the boy swing onto the back of the short-coupled horse. The wagons halted at his signal.

Arris clung tightly to Terai's waist, trying not to look afraid. The horse trotted forward. "Ho the gate!" the Yaighan called in a powerful voice.

Arris strained to look upward. A helmeted head appeared over the top, paused, and drew back again. Running feet sounded dim behind the portal. Finally it opened a little. A tall, muscular figure clad in riveted leather armor, with helmet and greaves of beaten bronze, stepped out and saluted them. The gate guard was a woman. Arris stared, but Terai did not seem surprised. He returned her salute.

"My lord Terai! We expected you by the main road, and a day later."

"I have the boy, and minstrels for the Festival."

The woman fingered her worn scabbard and looked at the ground. "I'm sorry, sir. I can't let you in until morning."

"What?"

"It's the first night of Winter Festival."

"I know. They're to perform."

"Tomorrow. Tonight is the Ritual of the Yearking. They are foreign. I can't let them in. If you and the boy want to go on you may, but the Northerners must stay at the Canyon Gate."

Terai relaxed. "Arris and I will wait. You're right. It wouldn't be wise to bring them in tonight. But I'm their guide, and when they pass the canyon they'll still have an hour's journey."

The guard bowed. "If you need anything before morning, call for me. My name is Rakeen. May She guide you."

"And you, good officer," Terai said. He wheeled his horse and rode away from the gate as Rakeen went back inside.

"Why can't we go into Gama now?" Arris asked petulantly. "I want to see my mother. And why did she call you my lord? And what is a Yearking?"

"You'll learn soon enough." Terai would not speak any more.

Arris could not sleep for excitement. He wandered around the camp, worrying the horses, plucking aimlessly at the instruments, until Senna caught him and bundled him into his blanket roll. Then he lay quiet and listened to the soft speech of the two men and the rustling of the fire. The other children were long since asleep. He dozed a little, but woke to the sound of his name.

"And Arris? Will you say now why you brought him here?"

"His people are here. His mother and brothers. He'll be safe."

The big man snorted. "This is the first place the Regents will look. No, there's another reason. You and Ruena both are too concerned for him, and far too respectful toward him."

"He's used to respect. He's the son—"

"Of a man you never acknowledged your lord."

"No. Of a woman from the highest lineage of the tribes. It isn't your concern, Senna."

"It is now. Tell me."

"A little, then. The boy is . . . special to them. He has been watched since his birth, and he has the talents they hoped. Now he's old enough to learn to use them."

"Then the rumor he's a witch has some truth to it."

"Some. He can speak to the Messenger . . . to something few can see. They say he'll do well."

"They?"

"The Lady. The Council of Women. The priests."

There was a silence. Arris squirmed in his blankets, wishing Terai would say more. Often he felt he almost understood what they meant, his mother and Ruena and now Terai, but they never said enough.

"Given a choice, old friend," Senna said gently, "would you give him to them?"

"I . . . don't know. What they'll teach him isn't easy. It can be very dark, very cold, for one so young."

"Give him to me instead. He adds to our ensemble, and besides, I like the boy."

"His talents aren't limited to music," Terai said bleakly. "They wouldn't accept that. They'd come to your wagons in the night and take him. Most likely kill you all."

"And you as well, I suppose."

"No. They wouldn't dare . . . forget about him, Senna. But your offer was well made, and I thank you for it."

"You don't have to be their puppet."

"No?" He laughed softly, and Arris shivered. "You are a fool, and I'm going to sleep. Good night."

CHAPTER
5

ARRIS WAITED EAGERLY with Terai before the gate as a dim winter sunrise filtered into the canyon, banishing the deep shadows. They could hear a confused sound from within the walls: murmuring, surprised exclamations, creaking as massive bolts were drawn back. Senna stood behind them with his wagons, while his children busied themselves tuning the instruments and donning their red costumes.

The gate opened. Terai seemed briefly startled. The young man who strode toward them was an artistic figure, his features handsome to the point of beauty. His curly dark hair reached halfway down his back, and his tunic and leggings were silken and sapphire blue. The cloak that swept behind him in the early morning breeze seemed woven of all the colors in nature swirled and patched together. He smiled at Terai and greeted him with a handclasp.

"It's been long, my lord, since you walked in Gama. My Lady would like to see you and the boy before she sleeps. Will you come with me? The entertainers will be guided by Rakeen later."

"The Lady wants to see me? In the White City?" Terai frowned.

"She has requested it."

"Commanded it, you mean." There was barely repressed anger in the leathery face.

"Sir?" The gate guard stepped out beside the silk-clad youth. "I know where the Northerners are to go. They'll be well housed, near the Feast Hall where they'll perform tonight after the hunt. You needn't worry about them."

49

He nodded. "Very well, Officer Rakeen. Give me a moment, young Keri. I'll explain this to my friends."

The youth made a short, ironic bow. Arris suspected Terai had offended him. Perhaps he was used to a grander title than "young Keri."

Senna came forward at Terai's signal. The guide told him the arrangements that had been made, and promised to come by later to make certain they were well taken care of. The big, bearded minstrel held out a hand to Arris and drew the boy away from the others. Then he hugged him tightly.

"If you don't like what you're taught, get word to Terai," he whispered. "There will always be a place for you in my family."

A red-clad figure jumped out of the second wagon and ran to them, still lacing her tunic. Danae's face was flushed, her blond hair tangled with a comb stuck in it. "I was watching," she gasped. "Papa was saying good-bye to you."

"I'll probably see you later, when you perform." Arris was eager to get back to Terai and Keri.

"Maybe. But maybe not. I just want you to know . . ." She stepped forward and kissed him suddenly, then ran a hand through his thick hair. "I think you're very brave. And you sing very well—for a little boy." She ran back to the wagon and climbed through the canvas flap.

Senna guffawed and clapped Arris on the back. "Watch out for the women, boy! You'll break a few hearts, I warrant."

"Come," Terai called. "Mustn't keep the Lady waiting."

Gama had no wall, and apparently no fortifications beyond the Canyon Gate. The broad valley was surrounded by high, jagged mountains that resembled the open mouth of a carnivore. The Teeth, Terai had called them. The sapphire youth led the horse with Arris on its back across rough, short-cropped grasses tended by ranging herds of sheep. Terai waited at the horse's other shoulder.

Where was the city? They passed scattered stone cottages the hue of soft red clay, occasional lone standing stones, and sheepfolds. There was a cluster of low buildings several miles ahead, but Arris saw nothing he would even consider a large town. The cottages seemed to be schoolrooms. Children ran relay races around one, watched by two brown-robed old women. A group of young girls walked slowly in a circle, their faces tense with concentration. Sullen-looking boys a little older than Arris lounged on a porch.

"Soon you'll be among them," said Keri. His smile was wide and disarming. "Does that please you, son of Tauena?"

"You left the cottages yourself only a year ago, for the last Winter Festival," Terai said. Keri turned sharply, and the older man grinned. "Yes, I know who you are. This is the first day of your year. My congratulations, Consort." He made an elaborate bow.

The youth flushed. "No need for that. I only became the Yearking last night."

"I wish you a good year." Terai softened his tone. "But I wonder, Keri. Did you think of refusal?"

He shook his statuesque head. "Sir, you're the only candidate to refuse the Kingship for the past three hundred years. I think you'll keep that distinction. After all, this is the Decade of Preparation!"

"For the Millennium. Aye, I was aware."

Arris was fascinated. Terai had refused to be King. Why would anyone do such a thing? And if Keri was King, why was he guiding them to the city over these dusty fields? And why was he apparently only going to rule a year?

The rose-colored cottages were smaller now, and closer together. They appeared to be family dwellings, but they were empty. The horse walked quickly, ears pricked and muscles tense. It passed a large, windowless building set into the side of a hill. Arris extended his awareness as his mother had taught him, trying to discover if there were people inside. He felt nothing. He had seen no adults in the valley beside the two old women who watched the youngest children.

"Are we in Gama?" he finally asked.

"The whole valley is Gama," Terai said.

"But where are the people?"

"In the hills," Keri said wistfully. "On the Festival Hunt. They'll be back this afternoon."

"Why didn't you go hunting?"

"Too dangerous for the Lady's bedmate," Terai muttered.

"I don't understand."

"You will," said the older Yaighan. "When they feel you're ready to learn. For now it's enough that Keri is the King, and it's important he stays out of danger."

"Oh. Who is the Lady? My mother?"

"No." Terai chuckled. "What made you think that? Tauena is probably here, but we're going to see the Lady. The Queen. The Firemother of the tribes."

"She's wanted to meet you for a long time," Keri said.

The carved door of one of the stone buildings caught Arris's gaze. Leaves intertwined around a stag's antlers, but the antlers rose from the head of a vulture, and caught in their branches was a crescent moon. The boy's skin tingled in recognition. This was a design that held power.

"We're almost to the city gate, sir," Keri said after a while. "My Lady said to ask if you'd like to open it."

"No." The word was angry.

The young King shrugged and smiled. "As you will."

Arris saw no gate, only a well-trodden pathway between two slim, weathered standing stones. Spiral carvings etched the rocks, covering every surface. The horse trotted forward, pulling loose from Keri's guidance. Arris thought it might be possible to touch the pillars, one with each hand, from the animal's back. He spread his arms.

"Stop!" Terai's voice lashed out and the horse skidded to a halt. Arris brought his hands down quickly and steadied himself on the withers, angry at being thwarted in a harmless desire.

Keri moved in front of the stones and turned back with a startled look. "Goddess's blood! It's half-open already."

"The city is eager for him," Terai said grimly.

The King spread his arms as Arris had done, and reached for the pillars. They seemed to lean inward to meet his hands. Now Arris felt the energy in them. They vibrated like trembling gossamer in a breeze, yet there was no wind and they were heavy stones. A humming rose from between them, low and droning as a beehive ready to swarm, and Keri's long black hair uncurled and began to writhe out from his head. A spinning cone of red light appeared above the King, flashing reflections on the stones. Keri's face contorted, and cords stood out on his neck. The stones rocked away from him. The cone expanded, then split in the center and wrapped each half of itself around one of the pillars. They glowed with crimson fire. Flames hissed across them, following the spiral etchings, then vanished.

Between the standing stones appeared a smooth paved road. Now Arris could see the city. Fields and scattered cottages had been replaced by tall white buildings, wide, fair courts with dancing fountains, and a broad avenue lined with polished, heavy-featured statues. Gama. Arris laughed in delight as all the wonder of the word came crowding back into his mind.

Keri grinned. "Isn't it beautiful?"

The boy laughed again as the horse started forward, little perturbed at the change in its road. As they walked, Arris twisted around to look back through the stones. They had become smooth white columns supporting a graceful arch. Beyond them, the same mountains rose over dusty fields. But the grass was long and uncropped, and there were no signs of cottages, children, or sheep.

Terai was in an inexplicably sour mood. Arris decided to ignore him. He was in Gama at last, and he would see his mother soon, and he had seen Yaighan magic at work. Now he knew he wanted to learn anything the city could teach. He longed to feel that crimson fire, and his hair on end, and breathe power from the stones.

The Lady's house was not the palace Arris had expected. It was a small, one-storied cottage in the shadow of the towering Temple of Rehoman, made of shaped stones cunningly joined without mortar, and roofed with a half-dome of slate and clay. They had passed another gate to reach it; there was no sign of the Temple or the little house from the white-polished city. The same valley surrounded them, but it was barren except for two buildings.

Arris could hardly bear to look at the Temple itself. It was beautiful and terrible, a monstrosity of spikes and arches and domes, built of a material that looked like red gold. When he tried to focus his eyes on one part of it to fix the details in his mind, it shifted and wavered and shimmered like a reflection in a lake on a windy day. But its power was familiar: the same power that possessed him when the Lossiran came. He half expected to hear wings, and see the Vulture flapping around the sparkling turrets.

Heavily armed women stepped aside to let them enter the doorless archway of the house. Keri smiled gaily at them, and even the fiercest-looking softened. The King swung out of his motley cloak and hung it on a pair of stag's antlers mounted on the wall. He straightened his clothes and ran his fingers through his glossy hair, then turned and beckoned Terai and Arris to follow him.

The hall was low and narrow, lined with tall, patterned windows set with colored glass. The morning sun shone in brilliant designs that flowed over Arris's skin as he walked. He was filled with a sense of delight that had begun in the white city and fed on each new wonder. He hardly noticed that Terai still frowned, and walked like a bristling badger between a river and a chasm.

There were no doors in the house. The corridor widened and rounded, and soon became a comfortable sitting room with padded furniture of red leather and a fire glowing within a marble hearth. A figure stood before the fire with its back to them, tall and slim and robed in deep red-brown silk.

"My Lady," Keri said proudly, "I have brought them to you."

She held out her hands. Keri kissed them hungrily, then sat in a chair near the hearth. The Lady beckoned to Arris. The boy went slowly, awed, a little frightened. Her face showed little sign of age, but he guessed she was as old as Terai. Her eyes were deep-set and shadowed, black as coals, flickering red in their centers. Her skin was a rusty brown that matched her robes. Her hair fell unconfined nearly to her feet, straight and shining as black silk. She wore no crown or fillet, no belt or ornament. She was beautiful as the night. If he was a man, Arris thought, he would never want any other woman.

"I see now," she said, taking his face in her long-fingered hands and turning it up to meet her compelling eyes. "Look what she has dreamed! He is stunning. Goddess, keep me your Lady ten years more!"

"He would have opened the gate of the White City by himself if we had let him," Keri said. His voice held a hint of jealousy. Arris wondered why the Queen had not greeted her husband more formally before turning to the guests she had summoned.

"Would he have? Did you want to come here so much?"

"Yes," he whispered, shy and embarrassed. He was still covered with dust from the road, and did not understand why she fussed over him so.

"I'm glad." The Lady sat down on a soft couch and patted the cushion beside her. "Come sit with me. I have a few questions for you. I've heard more about you than you might guess, but I need to know what is true and what is . . . well, wishful embellishment.''

Arris sat gingerly. He glanced up at Terai. The guide seemed uncomfortable, even angry, and he stood in the arched entrance as if he wanted to flee the place at his first opportunity.

"Now, Arris, Tauena's son. How many times have you seen the Lossiran?''

He thought. "Seven.''

"Do you see it clearly? As you see me here?''

"Yes.'' He tried not to sound defensive. "No one believed me, but it was there. I guess you have to believe in it to see it.''

"No. No, child. Many who would give their lives for such a chance have never seen it, never felt its presence. I myself have only seen it twice, when I was very young. Does it speak to you? Can you understand it?''

"Yes. And it makes me say things.'' He looked up at her. "Do you mean it never comes here? But it's the Messenger of the Goddess, and you're the Goddess's Lady.''

Her beautiful face was sad. "Even as a child I only saw the Vulture from far away. It never spoke to me. I have heard it will choose only one person in a generation to speak to, although others may see it.''

"Terai said he saw it.''

Her eyes narrowed. "Yes. Terai has seen it, and could again, though I doubt it would choose to speak to him now.''

"And you, Lady?'' Terai's voice was harsh and jarring after the soft, clear tones of the Queen. "Do you choose to speak to me? Or did your new Consort make a mistake in summoning me with the boy?''

"No mistake was made. In a little while, Terai Unannointed, you will be spoken to. Be patient if you can.'' She turned back to Arris and forced a smile. "Your mother told me your hair was long and thick. Did you cut it to disguise yourself?''

He nodded, wary of the edge to her voice.

"A loss indeed.'' The Lady laughed. "Look at him, Keri. His beauty will surpass yours as night surpasses day. Already it tears my heart. But come.'' She clapped her hands lightly. "I haven't finished my questions.''

Arris squirmed under Keri's increasingly hostile gaze, as the Lady ran quickly through her odd list. Yes, he said, he could sense people's emotions and sometimes thoughts; he could not move objects with his mind; he had seen ghosts and did not fear them; he believed in the Crimson Goddess but did not worship her. He did not tell her about the other spirit he had encountered, the bright sword in the Temple that had severed his link with the Lossiran; he suspected it might have been Myrdethreshi, and did not think she would want to know.

"You're a clever boy," she said. "Your mother did not praise you unduly. Indeed, hope rises for the Millennium."

"Lady . . ." he mustered the courage to ask, "where is my mother?"

"On the hunt, of course. Perhaps you'll see her tomorrow." The problem did not seem to concern her. "Keri, my love? You will take this pretty child to the priests for me. But I suspect our gloomy lord Terai will want to accompany you, so wait until I conclude my business with him."

"As you wish." The King went over to a tall standing mirror and began to braid his hair.

Terai stepped forward, anger visible in his travel-grimed face. "I'll be blunt, Lady. Why did you call me here? I swore never to pass the city gate again."

"But you could not refuse my summons." She smiled gently. "It's good to see you here, lord. You should never have made such a vow. The Goddess's chosen belong in her city. You've been outside it for twenty years, Terai." She laughed. "And it shows. You're beginning to look like a real barbarian."

"I refused the Goddess's choosing long ago. And how I look is my own concern."

"But you were so handsome once. How I wept my first year as Lady when I learned you would not be my King."

Terai stiffened as if he had been slapped. "Enough, Maella. Why did you call me here?"

Keri gasped. "Send him away, Lady! He dares to use your name! The priests call him heretic, and worse. Why is he here, anyway?"

"Because I wish it. Be quiet, Keri." She did not seem upset. "If you will remind me of our childhood friendship, Terai, you must expect me to rely on it. To rely on you. You may be the most notorious dissenter of the Yaighan, you may flaunt the wishes of the Council and the priests, but you fight for the cause of our people."

"As I see it. Yes."

The Lady rose and went to the hearth, holding her hands up to the flames and staring distractedly at them. "You've been to Gama a few times recently, if only to the valley before the gate. There are some priests there in the teaching cottages. Do you know what they are whispering? A growing number of priests, and even some of the Councilwomen?"

"No, Lady."

"It may even have gone beyond whispering now. I don't know. Sometimes I feel energies in the valley, new energies I had no part in shaping. There is nothing amiss in the city, and nothing has reached the Temple, but it frightens me."

"What are they doing?"

Her laugh was brittle. "Preparing for the Millennium. So they say. Gathering power to offer the Goddess when she wakes, power to win back our lands, our pride."

"Aren't you doing the same thing? Why else did you want the boy?"

"He is part of the prophecies, part of the traditions." She sighed. "He'll draw his power from fire and air, as servants of the Goddess have done for ages. But these priests, these Councillors, say that not enough can be gained thus. The Goddess has slept too long. She will require the strength they wish to attain. Strength from shadow. From earth. The other path."

Terai's indifference was gone. "That's forbidden," he said sharply. "To walk that road they'd have to call on the shadow powers. The daimons. The strength of her enemies won't help the Goddess."

"Of course not. But they are afraid of the Brothers Ylla, and they have forgotten how strong Rehoman was before she slept. I've made it clear I won't sanction any dealings with daimons. But I fear they no longer accept my authority. They even speak against the Yearkings. They say we'll need a strong leader who has had time to achieve military as well as religious power if we mean to drive back the Ilkharani in ten years." She went slowly to Terai and touched his arm. "I fear them, my lord."

"Why don't you attack them, then? Banish them."

She shook her head. "We are too few as it is. I don't want a war with my own people. But I want to know what they are doing. That's why I asked you here. Do you see what I want you to do?"

"Stay in Gama. Become a priest."

"Again."

"Lady . . ." He took her hands between his. It was not the gesture of an enemy, Arris thought. "Lady, I cannot."

"I'm not only asking you to spy for me. They'll listen to you, Terai. They respect you, for the same reasons they loudly proclaim you traitor and fool. Don't you see? They believe the reason you refused Kingship twenty years ago was that you thought as they do even then. You did not want a post they see as offering only token power. You refused it, and went on to work for the Millennium." She smiled. "They'll probably offer you the new post they want to create. A King who is also a military leader."

"A secular King." Terai glowered. "They would make the realm of the Millennium no different from the Ilkharani Khalifate."

"Join them," she urged. "Steer them away from the shadow if you can. They'll listen to you."

"Because I wouldn't be King."

"They think you meant to defy tradition."

He looked troubled. "Do many believe that? It has always been a tradition that a candidate has the right of refusal. I didn't want to change anything. I had my own reasons."

"Would I trust you if I didn't know that? I even think I have come to understand your motive at last." Her voice was gentle.

"Cowardice," Terai said.

"Love," she countered. "You knew I would be Lady. You did it to spare me . . . to spare me from having to love you, and watch you die."

Keri stared openmouthed. Arris expected Terai to deny her words, but he did not.

The Lady turned to Arris, took his hand, and stood him up beside her. "Look at him, Terai. If you won't do this for me, then do it for him. The priests would cheat him of his destiny. They laugh at the prophecies, at the Goddess's dreams. They say that shadow and steel are stronger than the crimson fire."

"But . . . my vow," Terai argued half to himself. "My work."

"There will be plenty of work for you to do. I'll see to it

that the Council chooses your name to take the post of weapons trainer for our young people. We didn't have anyone qualified until now. And we must begin to form an army if we are to succeed at the Millennium." She looked down at Arris again. "You care for the boy. I can see that. Care enough to ensure that he becomes what the Goddess desires. For him, Terai."

The weathered face broke into a reluctant smile. "All right, Maella. Lady. If you think it's that important."

"Bless you." She kissed him, lightly at first, then hungrily. Her voice shook when she spoke again. "Go now. Was I a fool to see you, even after so many years? Perhaps. Go."

Terai nodded soberly, not looking at her, and took Arris's hand to leave the warm sitting room.

"Lady, please do not shame me so again," came a stiff young voice from behind them.

"Shame you? My love, you mustn't think that. I have other cares, but you are my joy, the sun to my nights."

"For a little while." Keri was bitter.

"Do not think of that. Take the boy to the priests' tower, and know my thoughts go with you."

The tower rose gracefully from the White City, tapering from its wide base to an uppermost story of only one room. Keri led Arris there, not speaking, his handsome face clouded. Terai paced beside them.

The older Yaighan stopped when they were almost at the door. "If I'm to be a spy, I shouldn't walk in straight from an audience with the Lady. Better to wait a few days before approaching them." He touched Arris's shoulder. "Don't worry, lad. You'll see me soon enough. I'll go find the minstrels and see that they're well treated."

Arris watched him leave, feeling forlorn and deserted. He wished he had stayed with Senna. Keri did not like him, and from what he had understood of the Lady's words, the priests did not want him. He had expected to see his mother that morning, and lose himself in her arms, and forget about being brave for a little while.

"Come on, boy," said the young King morosely. Two sleepy-looking men at the top of a wide stone stairway came suddenly to attention. They drew a carven portal aside without a word and bowed deeply to Keri as he passed. Arris trailed behind.

"Well? Come on. What a task for my first day as King. I hope the Lady doesn't mean to turn me into a nursemaid."

Arris stared at the huge antechamber, a great bare room mounted with antlers, and choked back tears. He did not want the King to see him cry. But the room grew filmy and indistinct, and he sniffed, unable to overcome the empty feeling in his stomach.

"What is it?" said the King impatiently.

"You don't like me," Arris choked out. "And they won't like me either, the Lady said so, and I want my mother." The tears flowed. He could not stop them, and he cried harder in shame.

"Oh, sweet Goddess." Keri knelt before him and put his arms around him. "I'm sorry. I wasn't angry at you, child. Please don't cry. I was angry at my Lady, and I shouldn't be. I just didn't understand. Don't cry."

Surprised, Arris looked up. Keri's long-lashed eyes were wet. Arris swallowed hard and hugged the youth back, feeling hard muscles beneath the peacock silk. Soon he had mastered himself again.

"Of course I like you." Keri smiled radiantly as he took Arris's hand. "How could anyone not?"

"The priests won't." He could not rid himself of fear.

"Ah. Is that what you thought she meant? I don't think so. You have a lot of power, and they'll be eager to train you, to use you for their own ends. But there are only a few priests in the shadow faction. Don't worry. Terai will make sure you stay on the Goddess's path."

"What is that?" he asked, frustrated. "What does the Goddess want me for? No one ever explains it. Will you, Your Majesty?"

Keri grinned. "You're the first to give me that title, little one. But you really don't know any of it? Perhaps that's best."

"Please tell me."

"When you're ready, your teachers will explain. But first you must understand our people's history, and the sleeping Goddess we serve." A shadow dimmed his handsome face. "And I think . . . I think the longer you're kept in ignorance, the happier you'll be."

The great tower seemed empty. They walked its stairs and halls, and peered into unlocked rooms. Once they passed a mirror. Keri stared, and grasped Arris by the shoulder to stop him.

"Look," he whispered.

The resemblance between them was uncanny. Arris blinked. He could have been Keri's younger brother, or even Keri himself ten years ago. "We're the same!" he said wonderingly.

"But the Lady is right," Keri said, turning away from the reflections. "You'll be so much more than I am." He smiled slightly. "And yet I don't envy you, boy. I don't envy you at all."

CHAPTER

6

AN OLD PRIEST greeted them at the top of the tower. His sparse gray hair hung halfway down his back, and his knee-length green robe was clean but faded.

"Good morning, Grandfather," said the King. "The Lady asked me to bring this boy to the priests, and since there are no priests here but you . . ."

"They all went hunting," complained the old man. He lay scabbed and mottled hands on Arris's shoulders. His eyes, rheumy and shadowed deep within bony sockets, gave the impression he saw through any object on which he turned his gaze. Arris stood straight and proud, hiding his nervousness. "So this is the lover the Goddess dreamed."

"The boy knows nothing," Keri said quickly. "It might be best for that to continue, Hlaryon."

"Of course." The priest waved his hand in dismissal. "Thank you for bringing him, young Keri. You may go."

The youth's face fell predictably. Arris said with pointed deference, "Thank you, Your Majesty."

Keri favored him with a wry smile and trotted back down the long stairs. Arris shivered. The high room was cold. There was little furniture, and no hearth; only a strange, backward-leaning chair, and a cone-shaped device with lenses, and a glass-enclosed hole in the ceiling. Rolls of parchment, some blank, some written thickly upon, were scattered on the floor along with several inkpots.

"Your Majesty!" the priest snorted. "Tauena should be made to answer for it. Allowing you a year at the decadent court of the Ilkharani."

"My mother didn't want me to go," Arris said. "My father took me anyway."

The old man sighed. "They'll assign you to a class tomorrow. Fifth Level would be your age ranking, but if the rumors about you are true, perhaps they'll put you in Fourth. In any case I can't be bothered with you today. My first opportunity in months for some uninterrupted work." He reached for a used pen with a wilted feather and tore a scrap from one of the scrolls, then wrote something in a crabbed script. "Here. Take this back downstairs to the entrance hall. Show it to the guards. They'll show you where you can bathe, and give you a robe and someplace to stay until the others get back from the hunt."

"Thank you." Arris backed away and almost fell on the open staircase. He turned and ran down the stairs all the way to the bottom.

Another set of antlers, its base crusted with fresh blood, was hung in the entrance hall the next morning. Arris had bathed in a luxuriously empty pool at the priests' bathhouse, and dressed in a short green woolen robe and scratchy openwork sandals. The door guards had shown him to a bare cubicle with a cot and a basin and told him to stay there. Later that night he heard the sounds of wild revels in the streets. He thought of going out and looking for his mother, but he did not want to begin his stay in Gama with disobedience. Besides, he doubted his mother would be among the screaming, singing, chanting voices in the night.

A chubby young priest with a scarred face took the boy from the tower just before midday. His name was Donal, he

told Arris, and he was a teacher of the Fourth Level. He was
going to test him to see where he would be assigned. Donal
led Arris to the city gate, where a middle-aged priest seemed
to be standing guard. The priest opened the gate for them,
then resumed his post. Arris supposed that was how it was
usually done. There had been too few people left in the city
during the hunt to supply a gate warden.

The tests were ridiculously simple. The other Fourth Level
teacher, an ascetic man named Balccir, seemed unwilling to
admit it, but Arris knew he had done well. He told them
when they were lying to him and when they were telling the
truth, what emotions they were masking, what pictures one
was looking at in another room. Soon he was allowed to join
the other new students, who had graduated to the Fourth
Level the night before.

The Yaighan boys were immediately hostile. They seemed
to have heard of Arris, and judging from their attitude they
did not like what they heard. They were all older than he by
at least two years. Some of them were as old as fourteen, and
as large and strong as Arris's brother Husayn. Their talk was
mostly of the Festival. None had gone on the hunt, but they
had attended a feast afterward. Some commented on the
beauty and skill of the Northern girls who sang at the banquet.

Arris wished he had been there to see Danae and Senna
again. Even Vaessa and Van would have been friendlier than
these students. And Terai might have been there. Maybe even
his mother and brothers. His longing for them had settled into
an immovable lump at the bottom of his stomach.

Lessons began that afternoon in a dirt-walled enclosure
outside the large stone cottage. Boys were paired together to
go into the center of the circle and stare at each other. It was
a practical exercise, Donal explained briefly to Arris, on the
techniques of mental attack and defense. The boys' faces
contorted and strained, their muscles twitched as if they
wanted to pick up swords and fence more openly. Occasionally a teacher would step forward and whisper something in
one student's ear, or bark words in a language that was
almost unrecognizable as Yaighan. Arris could feel the power
flying back and forth, but it was contained and bound, weakened by structures he did not understand.

When the teachers chose Arris he stepped into the ring
warily. He did not know what to expect. His partner was a

thin, pinch-faced boy of eleven who was encouraged by grins from his classmates.

"I didn't know they let girls into priest training," he hissed in a voice loud enough for onlookers to hear.

"Silence, Creni," Donal said. "Begin."

Arris raised mental defenses as his mother had taught him, but he was not quick enough. The other boy slid a snakelike attack over the ground between them, up Arris's legs and into his mind. Arris staggered, surprised at the malevolence, the hostility of the blow. The student attacked again. His mental voice was triumphant.

"Creni!" shouted some in the audience in pleased surprise.

Another blow came. It hurt. Anger rose in Arris, fed by the still black place that had grown after his father's death. He would not be beaten by this arrogant youth. While Creni thought he was still reeling, Arris reached out tentacles of awareness and tested his opponent's defenses. There were appalling weaknesses. Abandoning his own safety, he discarded his shielding and blasted a concentrated burst of black power outward from its deep-set source.

He opened his eyes, panting, his body aching. To his surprise, the other boy lay prone on the earth, face down. The students were in an uproar.

"He killed Creni! He killed him!"

The younger teacher stepped forward and touched the unmoving boy. "He isn't dead," he said scornfully. "Just fainted."

Balccir confronted Arris, his thin face scowling. "Goddess's breath, what did you do to him?"

"I fought back," Arris said. "He hurt me."

"I warned you, Donal," said the older teacher. "The boy's talent is wild, uncontrollable. What do they expect us to do with him? I set him against one of our least talented students in consideration of his age and inexperience, and see what happens."

"Inexperience?" The stout man smiled. "Balccir, the boy's been fighting for his life these past few weeks. Hadn't you heard? He held shields against the Lossiran itself for a little while. They're saying he may be the first to be Winged in this century. And you expected him to be challenged by Creni?"

"I expected him to participate in an exercise, not a war. The schoolroom is no place for unmuted power."

"He hurt me, and I fought back," Arris said stubbornly.

"He's a barbarian, Donal. With the conscience of a daimon."

"It was only a mistake. I'm sure Arris didn't mean to hurt Creni. Did you, boy?"

Arris did not answer. He had been angry. Of course he meant to hurt him.

"We knew we'd have extra work with him," Donal said. "His mother's teachings were unbalanced. We'll show him what we mean by muting power, and we won't set him against another student until he learns." He turned to Arris. "Promise me you won't use your mind against another person until Balccir and I tell you that you may."

Arris glanced around the circle of inimical young faces. "Can I defend myself?"

"I won't forbid you shields, but you shouldn't need them."

"Then I promise." He did not feel guilty for what he had done. He did not see why it had been wrong. Creni had not used "muted" power on him.

After a light evening meal the boys were sent up to their rooms. The second story of the cottage was partitioned into thirds, and each room held enough old straw mattresses and wool blankets for ten boys. The timber-reinforced roof hung so low that Arris could almost touch it. Open windows looked out over the valley, and let in cold winds off the mountains.

Arris stripped off the uncomfortable robe and sandals and crawled between the harsh blankets, exhausted. He was miserable. The teachers saw him as a burden, and the students made no pretense of hiding their dislike. He refused to cry. But he longed for the day when his mother would come to take him away to live with her. She must not have heard he had arrived yet, but she would know soon.

There was furtive whispering from the next few beds, and a rustling sound. He did not look. He was almost asleep when his blanket was jerked off and a stick cracked sharply across his bare back. He rolled instinctively, and heard the thud of more blows striking the straw as he gained his feet. Ten boys circled him, grinning. Three held long, knotted sticks they had hidden in their blankets.

Arris backed away, chilled, knowing he had little chance of escape. He was strong for his size, but he would have been small in a class his own age. Here, few of the boys were less than a head taller than he.

Resigned to a beating, he launched himself at the nearest enemy, fists flailing, feet kicking. The others closed in silently. He willed his thoughts away from the pain of the blows and kept striking as long as he could, aiming for noses and crotches and throats. He had the satisfaction of hearing a few groans other than his own, before they caught his arms and legs and held him to the floor.

He found he could expect an attack every few days, whenever the students grew annoyed at his silence and the unprecedented private teaching he received from Donal. He always fought like a wildcat, hoping that if he hurt them enough they might grow tired of their game. He made no complaint. The teachers eyed him thoughtfully and treated the cuts and bruises of the other boys, but they said nothing.

It never occurred to Arris to make friends with the others. He had rarely had friends his own age. At Delronen, there had only been his brothers, when they noticed him at all. At the Citadel there had been Sasha, but Arris would not admit he had ever felt anything but hatred for the Prince.

His mother made no effort to visit him. Two weeks after the Festival, the Fourth Level was given a day's break, and many boys were taken away by their families. Arris waited near the cottage, watching the violent games of those whose parents lived elsewhere, hoping Tauena would have heard of his liberty. He waited and hoped as the sun inched overhead and approached the western mountains.

The night before had been particularly bad. He had feared a few ribs might be broken, but the pain of the banded bruises across his chest lessened as the day crawled on. He grew tired of standing, but his buttocks were tight and welted where they had switched him and he could not bear to sit.

The sun lightened gray clouds above the peaks. His mother would not come. Arris wandered away from the cottage at last, shooing inquisitive sheep from his path with a forked stick. The rough grass scratched his ankles. He was cold, and sore, and angry. Why would Tauena abandon him to the priests?

The students of the other cottages were busy at lessons. There were many groups of girls, and boys younger than he.

He passed the Fifth Level class. Boys his own age looked up with vague envy in their black eyes. But no hatred. Arris wished he was with them. He could have become their leader.

Near the ominous evening shadow of a standing stone that reared more than twenty feet high in the center of the long valley, a group of young men and women was ranged before a row of archery butts. They wore riveted leather armor and beaten bronze helmets, similar to the gear of the gate guard Rakeen. Arris approached, curious. They were not very good. Few of their long war arrows reached the mark. Three of the women were reasonably competent, and two youths. The two stood together and encouraged the archers in accented Yaighan. Their arrows flew straight, but they did not shoot often.

A stocky, green-robed priest with graying hair turned as Arris passed, and grinned. It was Terai. The boy smiled back. His friend must have begun his spying for the Lady.

"That's a day for us," Terai called. "Gather the arrows and go have some supper. I'll see you in the morning."

Scattered cheers arose as the young men and women undid the lacings of their armor and pulled off their helms, shaking out long hair from confinement. Arris stared. The two best archers had golden braids, and square tanned faces with long arched eyebrows. They were Falcmet and Husayn, his brothers.

"Arris!" Husayn dropped his bow and quiver. "Sygathi be praised!" He loped over and scooped the boy into a fierce hug.

"Terai said we might see you soon," Falcmet said, his blue eyes shining with quieter happiness. He reached out long arms and took his little brother into an even stronger embrace.

Arris gasped at the pressure on his bruised ribs. Both youths had grown more than a handspan since he had seen them last, and their leather tunics bulged with new muscle. Falcmet's shoulders were almost as broad as their father's had been, and he looked older than fifteen years. Arris wondered how he had been affected by the news of Areyta's death.

Husayn ruffled Arris's hair and clapped him on the back. The boy winced with pain. Terai stepped forward suddenly.

"Put him down. He's hurt."

"What?" Falcmet quickly complied, and looked anxiously at his little brother's face. "What is it? Terai, you didn't say he'd been hurt."

"I didn't know." Terai knelt and loosened Arris's robe

with gentle hands, revealing the cuts and swellings across his chest and stomach. "You look tender as raw beef. Who did this? Surely not your teachers."

"The other boys," Husayn guessed.

"They should never have put him in an older class," Falcmet said. "Arris won't accept that anyone can tell him what to do just because they're bigger. I should know."

"The teachers should not have allowed this to happen." Terai scowled.

"I didn't tell them," Arris said. "It's nothing."

"Nothing?" Terai said. "What if you were permanently damaged, boy? The Goddess would have no use for you then."

"I can defend myself."

"Obviously not," growled Husayn.

"I'll see that the teachers control their students," Terai said.

"He'd better learn to take care of himself," Falcmet said. "Even if these boys leave him alone, there will be others. He'll always be small and quick to anger. If you don't want him damaged, he should learn to fight."

Terai nodded thoughtfully. "You're right. And there are other dangers, in Gama and elsewhere, for a boy who looks like he does. But with my new work, I don't have time to teach him anything. You boys will have to do it."

"What about our training?" Falcmet said.

"What can I teach you?" Terai chuckled. "Your father was quite thorough. You only discourage the other students. I've spoken to the Lady, and she's agreed you'll both have commands in our motley force."

"Commands!" Husayn exclaimed.

"Why not? If we're to trust you to hold Delronen once we have it, we'd better be sure of your strength." Terai looked down at Arris. "Teach him something of warcraft as well. He may need such knowledge early. But try to keep him from breaking any bones."

"Why?" Husayn asked. Arris remembered his brother had a long record of horse falls and practice wounds.

"The boy is important to us," Terai said. "In many ways." He strode out across the field toward the city gate stones.

"Aye," Falcmet said. "Mother says that, too, and no one

explains any of it. Do you know what in Sygathi's name they're talking about, Arris?"

"The Goddess wants me for something, I guess. But what did he mean about Delronen? The Regents exiled you, and I saw soldiers there. You can't go back into the Khalifate."

"But in a few weeks, Delronen won't be part of the Khalifate," Falcmet said.

"We're going to attack!" Husayn told him. "The Yaighan want their lands in the South back now that Rasul is dead."

"And our father," his older brother said. "They wouldn't move against him because of Mother. But our old estate included some of their holiest places, and they want it."

"And they've promised we can hold it. They trust us not to let the Khalifate have it, after what they did to our father. They're even saying we might be sent to the Citadel later as Yaighan ambassadors, since we know the court and the language."

"Of course, we had to swear allegiance. To their Lady and to their King, in that order. But not to their Goddess, Myrdethreshi be thanked." Falcmet sighed. "Did you know Mother went back to being a priestess? They have her somewhere inside the Council compound, and they say she's taken a vow of humility."

"Humility!" Husayn repeated, outraged. "Imagine, the Lady Tauena!"

"I wondered why she didn't come to see me," Arris said, as some deep muscle unclenched within him for the first time in weeks.

Falcmet stroked his chin where the beard had just begun, and finally said, "Is it true you're going to be one of their priests?"

"I think so."

"Well, then, you'll be a fighting priest," Husayn said.

Falcmet nodded. "Who knows how far you might go among these people, with the blood of Areyta in your veins?"

Freed through Terai's intercession from the attentions of the other students, Arris still found himself stiff and sore most of the time. He spent two hours every afternoon with his brothers. They taught him much as their father had taught them, with no allowances made for his smaller size and lack of previous training. He ran the circumference of the valley,

climbed sheer rock faces with fingers and toes, swam underwater in chill mountain rivers. Falcmet and Husayn wrestled
and sparred with him, taught him archery and javelin throwing, even showed him tumblers' tricks. He was good at those,
and quick at running and climbing, but hopeless when it came
to weapons. His brothers consoled him by saying that he
would grow, and that no one was born with a feel for a
sword—though Arris suspected both of them had been.

Soon, Donal allowed Arris to participate in the mind-attack
exercises. The boy was careful to guard his power, and even
to lose from time to time. But he was vastly stronger than the
others, and soon they all knew it. He took pleasure in this
skill, especially after a difficult afternoon with his brothers.
Balccir frowned and shook his head every time Arris emerged
from the ring, triumphant and laughing, his pleasure in winning taunting the other boys' weakness.

Every morning during breakfast Donal told them another
part of the history of the Yaighan. It was old, oft-repeated
lore for most of the students, but for Arris it was new and
gripping, better than any of the Mythos morality tales. Here
there was no moral, no lesson but the sad truth of power
overthrown.

The Yaighan had once reigned over all the lands between
the Dark Hills and the Endless Sea, excepting only the Deirani
Empire of the far west and the Kwaitl Desert. The Lady and
the Goddess received tribute from scores of minor kings,
among whom the ancestors of the Ilkharani were the least. It
was a dark and bloody time, Donal said with disapproval,
when hundreds of human victims were sacrificed to Rehoman
at the whim of the Council. Though the Goddess required
blood, he said, it should not be unwilling, but consecrated
and freely given.

Almost a thousand years ago, the Five Brothers Ylla had
entered the world. They were gods of a far lesser order than
Rehoman, yet their combined strength was enough to induce
her to relax her vigilance, and at last to sleep. She would
wake when a thousand years had passed, and on that day
would begin the Millennium.

While the Goddess slept, the Brothers Ylla incited men to
rebel against Yaighan rule. It was easily done. The priests
and the Councilwomen were used to relying on Rehoman's
own power, and knew nothing of how to tap what was within

themselves. When they lost contact with the Goddess, they could not defend their cities.

They were driven south, their temples destroyed, most of their population killed. A few took refuge in the old holy city of Gama. Their Yearking, a heroic youth called Rahnisha Tualli, died fighting before the gate, and their Lady killed herself in the effort to remove the White City beyond the plane of the world. The Temple was removed even further, and renamed the Couch of Rehoman, for it was said the Goddess herself slept somewhere within.

It took the people of Gama two hundred years to build a gate back to the world they had fled. When they succeeded, they found a peaceful mountain valley. The Northern kingdoms had broken apart into warring states, and the Southern plains were empty except for a few venturesome Kwaitl. The Yaighan began to spread slowly, while in the North the Brothers Ylla worked to establish the Khalifate.

Only fifty years ago, Yaighan lands had stretched many miles north of Delronen. Rasul Ilkharani's father had pushed them back a little, and the Lord Areyta had almost broken them again. Arris was the object of many hostile eyes during this part of the storytelling.

And now, Donal said fiercely, only ten years remained before the Crimson Goddess woke. What would she find? A beaten people? A people living in fear? No, the priest said softly, no, he hoped she would not find that. He told the boys of the expedition to retake Delronen, and they cheered.

Arris thought what a fine thing it would be to drive the Khalifate into the sea. It would be long-due vengeance for his mother's people, who were once great; it would be his own vengeance for his father's life and for Sasha's betrayal. He pictured Saresha Ilkharani cowering before mighty armies under his command, and he smiled.

CHAPTER
7

THE BONFIRES BURNED like the flaming hearts of captured stars, mocking the struggling new moon in its glowing. Dim, outmatched, the moon was a sliver in a cloudless sky. The scent of fresh woodsmoke rose unhindered to the gods' realm. Arris wondered which of them would be pleased with the offering.

He should not have left the cottage, but the other boys had sneaked out, and he would not have them taste the forbidden pleasures of Spring Festival while he lay alone and unsleeping in the upstairs room. Six months had passed since he had come to Gama, and he knew what the students sought on that firelit night; three months had passed since his tenth birthday, and though he felt none of the desires of the spring sap in the blood, his curiosity was strong.

Spring Festival was an affirmation of fertility, of the Goddess's moon-born power to draw men and women together in blind seeking. Balccir had made it sound holy, awesome, magical; the older boys had giggled, nudged each other, and whispered that the Goddess did not notice whether youth or man. That any woman would have them, not once but many times. Arris had given them pause in the upper room later, wondering aloud whether Balccir and Donal would not attend the Festival too.

Of course the teachers had gone. That was why the boys were able to escape the cottage. They went together, a mass of dark shapes in their black hair and deep green robes, and Arris trailed them just out of sight, but not out of earshot. One of the oldest, a cruel-eyed, beefy youth who had instigated several of the long-past beatings, bragged that he would find the Lady herself and have her in the field, would she or no. This met with general approval and slightly nervous laughter.

Arris could have told him he would not. No one had explained it to him, but he could feel it in the high, cool air, in the moon's crescent smile, in the hungry thrumming of the seedling earth. This night belonged to the Yearking and his Lady, whose passion would make the tough mountain wheat take root where it had no chance of nourishment. The other writhing, moaning couples in the sprouting fields were affected by the Goddess's magic only in the proportion that the boys' water was sometimes flavored by wine.

Arris walked slowly through the fields. He did not stop to join the dancers around the bonfires, or the dusky, naked men and women who sang breathlessly to the moon, exhausted by passion. The flickering darkness and the glow of pleasure made them all seem young and beautiful. Arris walked unerringly, crossing paths and cottage yards until he reached the standing stone in the center of the valley.

In the shadow of the stone, the young King and the ageless Queen seemed in a world to themselves, though there were other couples near. Arris stood in the dimness between two bonfires and watched. He wondered how he could ever have pitied Keri when he learned the fate of Kings. There were few traces of prettiness in the animal form that swayed and thrust with such violent grace. There was beauty, majesty, terror. Shadowed stag's horns twined above the long black curls. The firelight played crimson reflections across the bronzed body, but did not touch the dark antlers.

The Lady was supple as a dancer. Her eyes blazed red. Her hair swept the ground like a living thing as she stood wrapped around the glorious young King, moving with him, gasping with his thrusts. No, Arris thought, his mind whirling; no, he would no longer pity Keri. He would envy him. The King would die in blood and pain, but before his death he would have lived with the power of a god.

Arris had never heard a name given to the Consort of the Goddess. He was the Hunter, who every winter was chased and devoured by his own wolves, and ran again the next day crowned with horns. Now he was flesh, and his lovemaking was becoming frenzied. He howled like a beast. The sight and sound became too much, and Arris fled.

He stumbled over oblivious couples and skirted cheerful groups. Everyone was there. Priestess robes of red-brown, priests' green robes, the everyday attire of shepherds and dry-farmers from the hills, all lay abandoned. Arris wondered if there was a Spring Festival that night at Delronen. His brothers and Terai had driven off the token squadron of Nievan's soldiers, and now waited for real war. Arris pictured Falcmet and Husayn in the fields with a few of their women soldiers, and grinned. They would call it a heretical rite, but they would probably join in.

Sometimes more than two bodies were joined in the darkness, in laughter and amazing combinations. Arris giggled as he passed them, certain he would never feel what seemed to be an uncontrollable urge to be ludicrous. He climbed over the low fence of a sheepfold to avoid a larger group ahead, and stopped on the other side, horrified.

The braggart student, his tormentor, savagely strong, and the woman beneath him crying out in pleasure and lust—it was his mother. Her pretty triangular face was upturned to the moonlight, her mouth open, her eyes wide and exulting.

Arris staggered back as if he had been hit in the stomach. The teachings of the gold-robed priests in the Citadel came tumbling back in a fevered rush: a married woman, a widow, only half a year after her husband's brutal murder . . . it was sin, it was wrong, she was damned. Areyta's ghost would be screaming in torment. Arris could almost hear it.

His mother's breasts were flattened beneath the youth's heaving weight, and her hands clutched his thick buttocks as he drove into her. Arris gagged and ran. Bitch. He saw his father's face in the flames of the last bonfire. Whore. She would not see him, would not send for him, yet she would open her legs for any male in the fields.

Rehoman! He sent up a sick challenge. If this is your power, I defy it. You will never make me lose myself that way . . . never degrade me that far . . .

He ran. Cottages lumbered by like slow oxen. He felt himself moving through darkness as palpable as black cloth. A stone in the path tripped him near the dark Fourth Level cottage, and he fell to his hands and knees. His head spun, and he vomited. Then he wept, angry and betrayed.

The earth pressed against his knees. He could smell its moist heaviness. It seemed to hum with power. Arris held still and listened. No light from the bonfires reached this far, and the moon was distant. He got to his feet and went over to the covered well in the cottage yard, where he washed his face and hands. Then he began to walk toward the power he felt. It was a dark beacon, one that spoke without flame.

The tall stones of the city gate were unguarded. Arris considered opening them, though his teachers had forbidden it. He reached out his hands and found them both drawn to the stone at the left. It was warm, and quivered at his touch. The spiral-carved surface glowed with a vision of the Yearking beside the other standing stone, but this time the Lady wore his mother's face. Arris cursed in Verchaki's name and pushed roughly against the pillar. Somehow he was unsurprised that it moved.

The tunnel descended in a worn flight of stone steps, steep from the wooden hatch set against the root of the standing stone. Then it angled to a gently sloping floor lit with musty rag torches and set with heavy wooden arches supporting the massive weight above. The air smelled faintly metallic, like the scent near the forge of a smithy.

Arris walked quickly, welcoming the growing sense of danger that pressed on his skin. Recognizable threats would be a relief from the thick, congested feeling of rage and betrayal that choked his throat. He wondered if he was drawn to this deep place as to a warming blaze, or as a moth throwing himself into the flame.

He reached out and thrust his hands through a clammy invisible curtain. It parted obligingly, and he was in the room at the end of the passage. He froze. Twelve men and women stood naked in a circle beneath a ceiling ring of candles. His eyes flickered over an altar stone, a sickle knife, a bleating goat trapped in bonds of silver. The sharp scent burned his lungs. He backed away, but the black anger in him yearned forward. Here was more than the priests had shown him. Power to hurt. Power that could be used for revenge.

They turned and saw him. He recognized Balccir and the hard-muscled soldier Rakecn. Both seemed stripped of dignity without clothing. Laughter warred with terror in his mind. The tall, thin teacher was bony and pale, all angles and loose flesh. Yet his eyes held a shadow Arris had never seen. The circle hissed like a pit of snakes and moved to surround Arris. The faces were wild and mad in the candlelight. There were men of all ages and forms, fat and thin, muscular and flabby. There were women who might have been young and beautiful, and a sagging old woman with short white hair. All were painted with streaks of charcoal and sulphur. Their hands reached out like the claws of a circle of kites ready to rend and tear.

Arris stifled a scream as one leapt at him. Ragged nails scratched his shoulders, and hot breath was foul on his face. The man was huge and strong, his massive features a rictus of rage.

"No," said a high-pitched male voice. "Do not harm him."

The speaker was small and wolfishly lean, with black, curled ram's horns bound to his head and eyebrows artificially lengthened to reach his hairline. His hair fell past his waist in tiny braids. The shadows seemed to cling around him like a hooded cloak.

Arris met the burning gaze as steadily as he could. He felt a shrinking sensation in his bowels, and a sudden, violent mental probe left him shaking.

The ram-horned man nodded slowly. "Tauena's son. The Lady's special concern. The dream of the Goddess."

"Our enemy born." The voice of the man holding Arris boomed from a tree-stump chest.

"No." The grotesque old woman moved forward. "Our enemy made, and then only if the Lady has her way. That does not have to be. We've spoken of this before."

These must be the priests the Lady had wanted Terai to spy upon, Arris realized. And Balccir was among them. Perhaps that explained his animosity toward Arris from the beginning.

"He is a danger to us," the big man said. "Now he is within our grasp. I say we use him to call the daimon. A virgin boy instead of a goat will increase our power a thousandfold."

The old woman laughed scornfully. "We may seek power where it is strongest, and defy the will of the Council and the traditionalist priests. But remember our goal, Itain."

The horned leader assented. "We desire to become more powerful than the Lady and her faction, so that when Rehoman the Destroyer wakes she will ally with us in driving back the

Khalifate. How would she respond if we killed her dream boy? No. He must live, and fulfill what was foretold."

"But it need not be as a puppet of the Lady," said the gate guard Rakeen.

"That," said the leader, "was not foretold." He looked at Arris. The boy tried to disguise his fear. "Well? Have you understood any of this? We can't kill you, but there are other things we could do. Enslave your mind, perhaps, with the aid of the daimon we mean to call tonight. You will determine it."

"Why did you come here?" Balccir said gently.

"I . . . I felt a call," Arris stammered. "I felt your power, and I thought I might be able to get some of it. I didn't want to watch the Festival anymore."

"A call?" The murmur went around the rock-hewn room.

"We sent no call," Itain scoffed, still holding Arris. "This is foolish, Cembra."

"We've only done the preliminary invocation," Rakeen said.

The horned man laughed softly. "What did we invoke? The powers necessary to assist us in calling the daimon. This child might well be one of those powers. Indeed, Itain, the presence of a virgin can aid us, but he need not be the sacrifice. He would be quite as effective on the other side of the knife."

"Cembra is right." The old woman spoke with authority. "And who among you would wish to fall wholly into shadow? I know this is only a means to our end, but it has its dangers. Without the protection of innocence, the hint of sanctity in a boy consecrated to the Goddess from birth, we might have no defense against the daimon. He might see us as his lawful prey, and suck our souls from our marrow."

Several of the circle cried out charms to avert evil. Arris had to smile. Peasants and children had used the same spells at Delronen if they sighted a white-spotted deer or heard a raven cry at dawn.

"Well said, Councilwoman," Balccir said dryly.

"Well, boy?" Cembra bent his horned head toward Arris. "Will you help us?"

"You aren't doing anything . . . against the Goddess, are you?"

"No, though we perform this rite during Spring Festival to

escape the attention of the Lady. She will be too preoccupied to notice the small hole we tear in the earth fabric.''

"We gather power to offer the Goddess when she wakes," Balccir said. "Do you see harm in that?"

The boy shook his head. He knew there was something wrong here, and that Terai and the Lady would be angry with him if they knew; but the Lady's face had become inextricably confused with his mother's in his mind, and a betrayal deserved a betrayal.

"I will help you."

A polished horn was held out, and Arris drank deeply of the purple, heady spiced wine within. Two of the young women helped him remove his robe and loinwrap, and combed through his shoulder-length hair with their fingers. The horned priest, Cembra, muttered words as he walked the perimeter of the tiny room, sprinkling wine in his footsteps and tracing spiral patterns on the walls at every tenth pace.

Arris shivered with delight as power tangible as tapestry began to weave around, below, and above him. The women stepped back and joined the rest of the swaying circle, leaving only one link unformed. The priest sang a snatch of melodic song at the power-curtained doorway, then walked inward. As he passed through the circle he joined the hands of Itain and the old Councilwoman. Then he led Arris to the center to stand over the goat in its silver bonds.

The creature whimpered like an infant with night fears. Its huge eyes were still and glazed with terror. The hobbles that held its hind legs jerked a little, then were quiet as it looked up at Arris. It was young. As young for a goat, Arris thought, as he was for a man.

"Don't try to participate in the chanting," Cembra whispered as he handed Arris the sickle knife. The blade was heavy, and felt strangely warm in the boy's hands. "Keep your mind open to us, so we can channel the twisting of power through you. When I call the daimon's name, perform the sacrifice." He touched Arris's shoulder, and his long eyebrows drew together suddenly. "Cleanse yourself of malice and hatred, boy. The blade has a bloodthirst that may grow too strong if wielded by one attuned to it."

Arris nodded. He dissolved his mental shields that kept out the emotions of others and the attacks of his schoolmates.

Immediately he felt a wave of shadow engorge him, as if a sea gate had been opened into a hollow. His own powers flamed to merge with the current. It twisted, as the priest had said, into a maelstrom of blackness that filled him with spinning force. His eyes seemed to be whirling around their pupils.

Ferocious chanting echoed from the handfast circle, bounced off walls and ceiling, focused on the slight figure in the center. The goat shrilled pitifully. Arris seized on the sound with the part of his mind that was still his own. He let pity for the animal overcome him, driving out the bitterness of anger. The knife pulsed eagerly in his small hands, its dull, dormant spirit waking.

The chanting rose in volume until it no longer contained words, only an uncanny wolfish howling that silenced the goat with frozen despair. Arris felt his body straining at the seams with the expanding whirlpool trapped within. The earth shook and small clods of loose dirt began to hail from the ceiling. The candles sighed and went out.

"Come to us!" voices began to shriek. "Come! Come!"

Tears burned Arris's cheeks, driven from his eyes not through pain or fear but through the intolerable pressure that filled his mind. The thin tissues in his nose began to trickle blood.

"Come!" Cembra's voice howled above the rest. "By shadow and fire, by earth and air, by sap and blood and water, by your own great and terrible name! We charge you, daimon of the earth, eater of men, join with us now!" Then he screamed a word that rose from a low bass roar to a hoarse treble croak and back down.

The sickle leaped in Arris's grasp. The boy felt hatred and anger and bitterness flowing back into him through his fingers, drowning the renewed cries of the young goat. He could not cleanse himself again. The time had come to strike. The spiraling powers in his head urged him on. He lifted the blade and brought it down. There was no resistance as it clove through the neck of the animal and buried itself in cracked bone. Blood leaped like a geyser, bathing his face and hands, running in rivulets down his naked body.

The knife whined thirstily as Arris pulled it out. It twisted and struggled, fed by his own black anger, unsatisfied. Arris looked wildly for another target, but the ram-horned priest grasped him from behind and took the quivering weapon away before it could do more.

The circle was silent. The priest knelt with a horn cup and caught a bowlful of the goat's blood. He lifted it in benediction and drank it in three quick swallows. The earth beside the altar cracked and split with a sound like a mountain shearing away in avalanche. The goat's body sank into the fissure, and a figure rose where it had been. It was insubstantial as smoke, yet every feature was sharply delineated.

For the most part it was man-shaped, though its body was massive with boulder muscles that would never fit beneath a human hide. Its nails were finger thick, short and sharp. Its face was crudely handsome, like a talented child's sculpture of a hero, but its teeth were huge and stained.

Arris staggered back from the gaze of its eyes. They were large and well formed, but their color was a sickening mixture of black and crimson and yellow, and they fastened on him with single-minded eagerness. An obscenely long arm reached toward him.

"No!" The ram-horned priest interposed himself before Arris. "He is a servant of Rehoman the Destroyer, whose fire burns away your shadow. To touch him would be painful to you, O mighty daimon of the earth, eater of men."

"You should perhaps watch your tongue more closely," said the daimon in a surprisingly cultured voice. "To remind me of my chosen food, when all you offer is a goat! Yet I have come. It has been many centuries since I have been called to this world. I had almost forgotten it." It peered curiously around the circle.

"You answered our call, placing yourself under our power," said the priest firmly.

"Out of curiosity," admitted the daimon with a wry smile that showed its discolored teeth. "And for the bait you offered."

"The goat."

"No, the boy." It looked again at Arris, who met its gaze with less fear now that it had acknowledged the control of the circle. "What a meal he would make! More than I have eaten in an age of your years. Of course his Goddess means to consume him herself. While he is still young and tender. If he wished to live longer than that, I could offer him power. Power to crush the paltry godlings who pretend to rule here. I would defer eating him until his natural death."

The priest glanced speculatively at Arris, then shook his head. "We did not offer him. You accepted the goat, and cannot ask for more."

"Of course." It seemed offended. "I honor the rules, human. When the boy has grown, and when he has great need, I will offer to him again. Meanwhile, what is the matter you called me upon? I do not wish to wait here all night. Though earth is between us, the moon pains me."

"We wish to offer you an alliance, O mighty prince of shadow."

"Why do you not call me Aghlayeshkusa?" suggested the daimon. "It approximates my true name, and has a pleasing sound."

"Ehh . . . very well," stammered Cembra, growing more nervous.

"An alliance," Aghlayeshkusa prompted.

"Yes. We . . . we propose this: Over the next ten years, as we Yaighan regain our usurped lands, as we push the Khalifate into the ocean, there will be battles."

"That seems a natural conclusion," said the bored daimon.

"We . . . my circle here, and others sympathetic to our cause, will consecrate each battle to you before it is fought. You will respond to our call and assist us in defeating the enemy. In return you may eat the souls of every man and woman who dies by shed blood. Excepting, of course, ourselves."

"Even your fellow Yaighan, who might prefer to consider themselves sacrifices to their own bloodthirsty deity?"

"Yes." There were nods from the others. Apparently the conspirators had feared the daimon would not accept lesser terms.

"Is the boy included in those I cannot eat?"

"For the time being," Cembra said. "If you . . . offer to him as you said you would, and if he accepts, then of course that would release you from your promise to us."

The daimon grinned. "Is this paltry bit of land so important to you that you would give the very souls of your children into shadow to regain it? You need not answer. It was a rhetorical question. I will accept your alliance. But be warned. If you begin to succeed without my aid and go back on your bargain, my revenge will be most unpleasant."

"That will not happen." The priest was beginning to relax.

"The first battle may be soon. You will come to our call? Without an offering?"

"That was not specified." Aghlayeshkusa frowned. "Oh, very well. I find I hunger less for goats than was my wont."

"Then I dismiss you, and require that you descend once more into your deep fortress. By shadow and fire, by earth and air, by sap and blood and water, and by your name, I command it." The priest took a breath to pronounce the daimon's demanding name.

"I am going," the creature said hastily. "But, small boy?"

Arris flinched as he met the obscene gaze once again.

"Remember I intend to speak to you again. And if these renegade priests and priestesses wish me to respond more quickly, they might allow you to do the summoning."

"I can't pronounce your name," Arris said. "My voice doesn't have enough range." He was beginning to feel strangely flattered by the daimon's interest.

"Only say it as I have: Aghlayeshkusa. That is not so difficult. Come, make an effort." The daimon waited expectantly.

"Aghlayeshkusa," Arris whispered.

"Good! I shall enjoy manifesting in this world again." It saluted the horned priest. "May your people fight many battles!" The huge figure dived back into the earth crack, which shuddered closed. It was gone, leaving behind a musky animal odor.

The twisted cone of power suddenly withdrew from Arris's mind, and the boy collapsed. He could not move an eyelid. He watched dimly as the circle broke into weak, swaying people who left the room without speaking to one another. A pair of bony knees stumbled over to Arris. Balccir's, by their shape.

With Cembra's help, Balccir took Arris in his arms and staggered back through the rock passage, out the gateway beneath the stone, and into the night of the Goddess's Festival. Under the loving gaze of the moon, another naked man wandering was no strange sight. And if he returned with his burden to the Fourth Level cottage before anyone else, well, some poor souls exhausted themselves sooner than others with the fires of the spring.

CHAPTER

8

ARRIS BEGAN TO have nightmares soon after Spring Festival. His father on the wheel, blood-covered, muscles tearing, bones cracking. Blue eyes gazed directly at Arris, full of reproach. Saresha Ilkharani sat and watched the torture in the first dream. In the second, he laughed. Within a week he was turning the levers himself, his boyish face unrecognizable.

Arris woke after the eighth nightmare with his blankets thrown from his sweat-covered body. Black pressure throbbed in his head. He heard soft, shadowy laughter outside the open window of the cottage and lay still, frightened of moving. Though he was awake, he still saw images. His mother's writhing flesh beneath the youth's blows. Her gasps of delight. The vision completed his dream. His father's death, his mother's betrayal. Areyta's unavenged ghost now had even more to bind it to the earth. Yet how could Arris avenge his father's honor upon his mother?

Arris did not think the Goddess's path, the path of a priest, would offer him the power he would need for his revenge. He had had a taste of the earth power in the ritual of Cembra's circle, and though it had frightened him, it was undeniably strong. The daimon had promised to offer him an alliance when he was grown. If that meant he would be able to destroy the Ilkharani who had murdered his father, Saresha and Nievan and Maenad, then he would promise the daimon whatever it required in return.

Delronen was peaceful again. Falcmet and Husayn had set their idle warriors to rebuilding the estate. Even the summerhouse was almost as graceful as it had been, though it was

83

surrounded by black stumps. Arris could see no fortifications or defenses, although Terai's spies had said that Khalifate troops were only two days away. There were a few soldiers in the fields, but they were lounging out of armor.

Priests and priestesses, shepherds and peasants had answered Falcmet's call for reinforcements. Arris was glad the daimon had noticed him; since Aghlayeshkusa had requested that Arris summon him the next time, the high-ranking members of Cembra's circle had contrived permission for the boy to accompany them to Delronen. Rumor numbered Nievan's army close to five thousand men. That was a fraction of the Khalifate forces, but this was seen as a minor problem. The Yaighan could not arm half so many. Yet those who knew of the daimon did not fear the outcome; it had been difficult for those few to keep from appearing too lighthearted in the morose company that had marched from Gama.

Falcmet reviewed the troops from the back of a tall Northern horse that had been left behind by the routed occupation force. He tried to encourage them, but Arris could see he was worried. Less than a quarter of the Yaighan wore ringmail. Half bore swords or spears, but few of those had shields. Most would be wielding pitchforks, scythes, and knives. The handful of horses were untrained mountain ponies and draft animals.

Falcmet's pale blue gaze swept past Arris's small black head and quickly returned. A broad smile spread across his face. "Arris!" he called. "Little brother! I didn't know you were coming."

The ranks parted obligingly as Arris pushed through, took his brother's hand, and swung to the back of the warhorse.

"I'm glad to see you," Falcmet said. "But why did they let you come? We're not desperate enough to need children to fight for us."

"They won't let me near the battle." Arris shrugged, not wanting to deceive his brother. "Some of the priests thought maybe I could help in other ways."

Balccir had followed Arris through the crowd. He had been as smothering and protective as Sasha's old nurse since they left Gama. "He may be able to call the Lossiran to aid us," the teacher said. "This may not have to be decided only in the clash of arms." It was the argument the circle had used to gain the Lady's permission to bring Arris along.

Falcmet frowned. "We'd be desperate indeed to rely on such aid." He wheeled his horse. "Don't spread that among the ranks, sir. Soldiers who expect to be rescued won't risk their lives."

Terai returned late that night with the rest of his band of young men and women, the only trained warriors among the Yaighan besides the Canyon Gate and Temple guards who had remained in Gama. There were fifty of them. Arris hoped their skill had improved since he had seen them shooting at straw targets.

They had gathered up the few farmers and herders that had escaped the destruction of Delronen, along with their animals and valuables, to pull them well back beyond the path of Nievan's army. One young woman admitted to Arris that they were not particularly concerned with the peasants' safety. They simply did not want the enemy to receive any assistance. Since many of the peasant families were of Khalifate stock, headed by men who had come to Delronen as soldiers under Areyta's command, they could not be trusted.

The woman was tired and dusty, and she muttered that she would as soon have killed them as not. But Terai had forbidden even any looting of the abandoned farmsteads. Arris looked at the sullen, pale faces of the blond men and women who herded their pigs and cattle past the manor house. They were frightened and angry at having been forced from their homes, but Arris thought they would soon become accustomed to being ruled by Falcmet and Husayn. They would surely accept Areyta's sons as their rightful lords, even if those sons owed their allegiance to the Yaighan instead of the Khalifate.

"Arris-ka!" Husayn sang, leaping on him as he slept. Arris woke in a wild rage fed by nightmares, but the stronger youth held his little brother's arms down until Arris was fully awake. "Come on," Husayn said. "They won't let you near the battlefield later, so you'd better see it now."

"Oh!" Arris bounced from his bedclothes in the crowded Great Hall, where most still slept. He pulled on his green robe and wished he had armor and weapons like Husayn's. Pleasant visions rose of leaping into the midst of the battle tomorrow, hacking right and left, while all around marveled at the skill of one so young. Actually his hands were as skilled with a sword as Husayn's were with a spindle.

It was a lovely spring day, cool and misty in the filtered dawn light. Growing wheat fields spread lush and green beyond the river almost to the foothills. But nothing had been planted to the north of the manor house; in anticipation of war, the fields were left fallow. Weeds and bushes had grown into a tangle of raised roots and braided branches. The ground had been scraped away around them to trip charging horses and men. Ditches, sharp-edged, studded with chipped stones, had been dug in narrow rows along the northern edges of the fields to cripple the chariots.

"Look!" Husayn's smile was full of perverse pleasure. "This is my own special bit of ground."

Arris kicked at clods of earth. A garden-sized plot in the center of the fallow meadows had been cleared of weeds and plowed with deep furrows. The rich valley soil smelled fresh and moist. "Why?"

Husayn looked down at him. "Some stories say that lands are more fertile after a battle, fed with blood and flesh and bones. I've bet Falcmet that if I plant this field after the battle, it will produce richer crops than the river bottomlands."

Arris shivered. "How could you eat anything that grew in such a place?"

"Haven't the Yaighan infected you with their blood lust?" his brother teased. "Don't you drink your mead from dead men's skulls?"

"That's silly."

"Is it?" There was deep unease behind Husayn's light tone. Arris did not have to use his priest-trained mental senses to feel it. "Did you hear about our fight to take Delronen?"

"Just that you won, and most of them ran."

"Some of them died. I killed three." The youth sounded half proud and half sick. "Your Yaighan friends cut off their heads. They burned the bodies, but the heads are still there. In a pile in the summerhouse."

Arris spun to look at the graceful little building. "In there? Are they still there?"

"Of course. They did something to them so they wouldn't smell bad. I haven't been in to look." Husayn laughed. "They'll have to find another place for the heads from this battle if we win."

"We'll win."

"I'm glad you're sure. I just want to kill a lot of them.
Even if Nievan isn't with them, killing his men avenges our
father. Don't you think so?"

Arris stared at him. "No! One of us has to kill Nievan.
And Maenad and Saresha as well, they were part of it. That's
the only way his ghost will rest."

"His ghost?" Husayn shook his head. "I don't believe any
of that religious nonsense. I just hope I can do something in
the battle tomorrow. Something to get me noticed. Falcmet
and I need to be known as warriors before the Lady sends us
to the Citadel as her ambassadors. The Ilkharani will pay a lot
more attention to us then. And they won't dare enforce the
ruling of exile."

"You really want to do that?" Arris said. "You really
want to become a courtier in the Palace where Father was
betrayed and murdered?"

"I can't hide in Gama all my life," Husayn said, refusing
to anger. "Yes, I want to be an ambassador. It's a good
career for a younger son." He grinned. "And I don't think I
could gain the trust of the court by assassinating the three
highest members of the royal family. It's impossible anyway.
It would be suicide to try."

"I'll do it some day," Arris muttered, kneeling to crunch a
clod of fresh-turned earth in his hand.

"You're going to be a priest, silly." Husayn sighed. "Come
on. We should get back. I've got a lot of work to do."

Arris followed him silently. Husayn did not understand the
necessity of revenge. Falcmet would not, either. They were
oblivious to the pain of Areyta's bound spirit. Arris would
have to do it alone.

The circle appropriated the summerhouse early in the dark
morning before the Northern army was expected. They hung
the grisly trophies around its rafters like drying sausages.
Arris examined them curiously once he recovered from his
initial disgust. The heads were still covered with skin, but it
had dried and pulled against the skulls. Short blond hair hung
lank, bloodstained, like straw. There were no eyes.

The priests had hardly spoken to him. He was no more to
them than another prop of the ceremony, like the wine and
the sickle knife. Arris shivered as he undressed. It was cold in

the summerhouse, and he remembered the hungry look the daimon had fastened on him. He desperately wanted the power it offered, but he feared that it would have no honor. It might simply decide to eat him now without waiting for him to achieve his revenge. Perhaps he should call the Lossiran first, to protect himself. He was sure he could do it. That would make the circle notice him.

"The battle won't begin for hours," Rakeen complained, rubbing her muscular arms against the chill. "Why call the daimon now? We'll have to control it until then."

"If we wait any longer someone might wake up and find out what we're doing," the Councilwoman said. "Our army must not know that their souls will be consumed by shadow if they die today."

"It's time." Cembra stepped forward. "We'll make the circle. When you feel the power built up, boy, call the daimon."

Arris nodded, apprehensive. There was a good chance the earth spirit would decide to eat him. He could not imagine what being eaten by a daimon would feel like, but he was sure it would be unpleasant.

There was less fear in the circle than there had been two weeks ago, and consequently less strength. They were confident of the daimon's acquiescence to their control. Arris allowed the twisting cone of energy to enter his mind, and freed a little of his own power to join it.

He tried to fill his voice with confidence, but it sounded high and frightened. "Aghlayeshkusa," he breathed. "Aghlayeshkusa." He remembered Cembra's words the last time. "By shadow and fire, by earth and air, by sap and blood and water, come to me."

The summerhouse rumbled and shook. The grisly baubles strung across the ceiling swayed. Arris's naked skin writhed with expended power. A dim, pained howling sounded far beneath them. But the earth remained unbroken and the daimon did not come. Soon the rumbling stopped, and the cone of power faltered and emptied.

"Goddess take it!" Rakeen swore, inappropriately. "It said it would come without a sacrifice."

"Untrustworthy fiend. It was toying with us," the Councilwoman said. "Just have the boy speak its name, it said. Not even its name, just a sound that pleased it."

The horned priest said nothing. He folded himself cross-legged on the dirt with his palms flat in front of him. After a time, he silenced the gabble of anger and disappointment. "Tell me, boy. How long has this building stood?"

"A few months. My father's summerhouse was burned by Nievan's raiders. Falcmet rebuilt it."

Cembra nodded. "I can feel the ashes beneath my hands. They keep the daimon from reaching us. What was this place?"

"We used it for picnics, for watching the stars, for games, for lessons . . ."

"Some power guards it against shadow."

Arris reached down for a handful of loose ash. It gritted under his fingernails. Then he remembered. They would not want to hear this. "My father dedicated it to his gods. To the Brothers Ylla. There were little statues of them, and he prayed here sometimes."

"Ahh . . . ." The priest rose and cupped his hands to catch the trickle of dirt Arris spilled from his fist. Suddenly he moved, taking the earth and smearing it roughly on the boy's forehead, shoulders, stomach, and buttocks. Arris stiffened, too surprised to move away from the intimate touch.

"Do as I say, boy. Kneel down on the earth and speak to it. Tell it your father is dead, that you are his son, that it belongs to you now." Arris complied, feeling foolish. The people of the circle stared at him. "Now tell it that by right of blood and possession you absolve it of its allegiance to the Northern gods. Name them and renounce them."

Arris hesitated. It seemed unfair to his father's memory. Yet if the daimon could not appear, Areyta would not be assured of revenge. "Who should I tell it to hold as its liege? The Goddess?"

"No," Cembra said slowly, thoughtfully. "Consecrate it to the shadow. But that will require blood. Hold out your hands."

Arris fought back anger and raised his palms up toward Cembra. He said the names of the Brothers Ylla and renounced them. Then he spoke haltingly, encouraged by cryptic nods from the priest. "I . . . consecrate this ground . . . the ground within these walls . . . to the shadow."

That was apparently enough. Cembra bent down. He had no ritual knife, but he unbound one of the black ram's horns from his head and drew its sharp point slowly across the soft flesh of Arris's hands. The skin parted roughly, and bubbles of bright red welled up in a jagged line that stretched across both palms. Arris whimpered softly.

"Press your hands to the ground," Cembra hissed. "Keep them there until I say you may rise."

Arris bent silently. The trickle of blood was not strong, but the burning sting intensified as he held his palms against the ashes of his father's summerhouse. His anger gave way to vague amusement. He had spilled blood near this ground before, only it had been a greater amount of blood, and not his own.

He felt a subtle shifting in the soil, as deep-buried bits of beams and masonry turned over in their graves. The ground no longer passively received the blood he offered. It sucked greedily from the wounds. He began to feel dizzy, and swayed closer to the soil.

"Enough!" Cembra pulled him to his feet. His hands came away with a slurping sound. The cuts had been drawn wider and deeper, but now they were white and bloodless. The priest examined them briefly, then whispered so only Arris could hear. "I'll see to their healing afterward. It will require some effort. I'm sorry if I spoke harshly to you, boy. That was bravely done." The wolfish features did not soften, but the eyes showed new respect.

Arris ignored the numb, black cold that crept up his forearms. "Will we try to call the daimon again?"

"I assume that was the point of this . . . this abomination," the Councilwoman said furiously.

"Blasphemy," Balccir said. "To consecrate part of our ancient lands to the shadow!"

"We agreed to use spirits of shadow," the old woman said. "But this approaches worship, Cembra. I cannot approve."

"Would you prefer to lose the battle?" the priest said with quiet contempt. "We must have the daimon. If you object, remember that if we break our pact and do not call it to aid us we forfeit our own souls. Its anger will fall upon us, not upon our brothers and sisters whom we have so nobly consigned to destruction. Upon us!" He turned to Arris. "Call again. I'll form the circle."

There had been a strange pleasure in the way the earth had

drunk from him. He felt giddy and powerful, and he no longer had any desire to call the Lossiran. "Aghlayeshkusa," he cried, "come to me! The earth is opened."

A long, low, bubbling laugh rose from the summerhouse floor and writhed up the dainty support poles to dance around Arris's head. The boy felt the gaze of a terrible power filled with curiosity and hunger fasten on the back of his neck. He turned quickly.

One of the shriveled heads had sprouted motley-colored eyes and a long purple tongue. Its tight jaws opened with a rattle of bone and a tearing of dried skin. A young man of the circle shrieked and ran out the door, shattering the cone of power. Cembra frowned and glanced at Arris, then addressed the daimon.

"Welcome, lord of the earth. We have fulfilled our agreement. The battle begins at dawn."

The macabre head yawned expansively. "A minor matter. I came to speak to this delicious child again. Do you like my new looks, little one? Is this not a more pleasing form than that in which you saw me last?"

"It . . . it is certainly . . . more impressive," Arris said carefully.

"Yes. And more appropriate. How this mouth will chew the fallen!" The head gnashed its teeth, shaking itself to free its tangled hair from the rafters. It floated in the air of the summerhouse on a level with Arris's face, breathing out decayed fumes.

"You promised to help us win the battle," Cembra said. "Will you?"

"It will be a bloody victory." Aghlayeshkusa laughed. "For I have been promised the souls of the dead. But yes, your friends will carry the day, once they have been well decimated. How I hunger!" It looked longingly at Arris. "You gave me a taste of your blood. I should like the rest."

Arris stood his ground, trembling. "You promised you wouldn't take my soul, not until I'm a man and can offer it freely. Won't it be stronger, or tastier, or something, when it's older?"

The grotesque face hovered inches from Arris's own. Its brow furrowed in thought. Then it nodded, jerkily, like a bouncing toy on an invisible string. "I remember saying something like that. It is true enough. If I allow you to grow,

you will nourish me more than a twenty years' war.'' Its eyes
narrowed. ''Then you will promise yourself to me? You will
promise to come to me in the end?''

Arris was wary. ''You said you'd offer me power. Revenge.''

''When you've grown strong enough to take it.''

''That's when you'll get my promise.''

The severed head laughed. ''Done. Oh, I do enjoy this
world.'' It flew toward the door in spasmodic hops.

''Stay,'' Cembra said. ''There is another thing I must ask
you.''

The woven door swung outward for Aghlayeshkusa. ''I
already intend to do it,'' it commented. ''The taste of a few
innocents will be a pleasing first course to cleanse my palate
for the meaty fare to follow.'' The head bounced out the
door, grinning from ear to ear.

Innocents? Arris stared after it. What could it mean? He
found the answer leaking into the open cone of the circle.
''My father's peasants! It's going to kill them.''

''Don't be silly, Arris,'' Rakeen said kindly.

''You half promised your soul to shadow tonight,'' Cembra
said. ''If you are serious in that, you will have to get used to
the prices it exacts for its gifts. Come along. I'll see to your
hands.'' He pulled Arris's robe from the pile near the entrance and threw it over the boy. Then he dressed, put an arm
around Arris's shoulders, and led him gently from the
summerhouse.

The Yaighan won the battle, but there were great losses on
both sides. The severed head of Aghlayeshkusa inspired helpless terror in all as it bounced through the fray, sucking the
life force from dying soldiers and attacking living Northerners.
It had eaten everything in the peasant encampment first. It
grew with each soul, and its dried skin moistened and stretched
until it glowed with the vigor of the handsome young soldier
whose head it had been. By day's end it was big as a horse.
The last the Yaighan saw of it, it loped across the fields
after the remnant of the enemy that had managed to run.

They might have escaped if they had been mounted. But
Husayn, early in the battle, had led a few of his warriors
behind enemy lines to slice the traces of the chariots that had
been unable to come onto the field for the ditches. They cut
the harnesses without arousing the notice of the slave chario-

teers. Husayn rode the last pair of horses yelling through the melee, harvesting men with a jagged scythe. The other released horses bolted at the approach of Aghlayeshkusa's head.

The day won, the Yaighan had no stomach to take their opponents' skulls. The fields were burned. The remaining army marched back to Gama, leaving Falcmet and Husayn with their small band to settle the outcome of the agricultural bet.

Balccir was planning to tell the Lady that Arris had called the Lossiran, which had taken the shape of a severed head and carried souls to the Crimson Goddess. The boy would do well with such a tale, his teacher said. He might even be Winged. That was an honor reserved to those who could not only see and hear the Messenger, but command its presence.

Arris felt only fleeting guilt about the deception. He was sure he could call the Vulture if he tried. But he was too tired and sick to attempt it only to prove it to himself. Cembra had bathed his hands in boiling herb-infused milk, which did not hurt as it should have since his arms were cold as death and numb from fingertips to elbows. The priest sewed the gashes together, bandaged them, and drew careful runes on the bandages.

The boy slept for four days and was kept in bed a week after that. He dreamed of slaughter and thought about shadow and fire. He knew there was power in the Goddess, but Rehoman's power was far removed and difficult to reach, and he was not certain it could be used for the purposes he intended.

In shadow there was only mock beauty, but there was deep, ready strength. Arris lay in his father's house and vowed to Areyta's shade that he would not shrink from the daimon's offer. No matter the price that would be exacted someday. Even if the daimon came to claim his soul the moment after he killed his Ilkharani enemies, he would have lived long enough.

BOOK
TWO

CHAPTER

9

"I THINK THE Khalifate will annex the Kwaitl territories," Terai said. "With our spies and their spies, there are more spies than Kwaitl . . . Hlaryon, are you listening to me?"

The ancient stargazer thrust a ropy arm toward the clear glass window in the ceiling. "There, boy! Daria's finger. It's finally descended into the field of influence. Chart it for me . . . vector sixty degrees down east, not more than half an arc from the belt of the Giant."

"Vector, arc . . ." Arris muttered rebelliously. He pulled a red-dyed quill pen from the heavy topknot of his long black hair, where its feather had been providing some decoration. The inkpot beside his left foot was nearly dry. It had been a long night.

He leaned close to the huge, messy sheet of parchment and began to calculate with Hlaryon's rusty compass. The pen scratched another spidery line across the web of star paths. When it reached the resting point of Daria's finger, it sighed and belched out a half inch blot of unexpected ink.

Arris grinned. "Grandfather?" he queried in his unreliable new tenor voice. "What's the magnitude of Daria's finger?"

"Magnitude? On a pattern web?" Hlaryon peered down at his reluctant assistant. "You windy-headed idiot. What use will that chart be to me? You've obscured a third of the field of influence. Now it won't tell me as much as the number of kittens Donal's whey-faced cat will produce this time."

"It never tells you that much," Arris muttered. "I don't see why I have to learn astrology, now that I can call the Lossiran. Its prophecies are clearer." He thought of the bright blue-and-gold wing tattoos that covered his shoulder blades.

He had been Winged just before the last Winter Festival, more than six months ago.

"You have to learn everything we teach you," Hlaryon retorted with a wave of one crabbed hand. "Unless you intend to be as sheep-brained as the Yearkings of the past twenty years. The Consort of the Millennium will need wisdom."

"And if you intend to overthrow the Khalifate," Terai added, "you'd better not rely on the Lossiran. What if you called it on the eve of a battle? No troops would follow a general who had to sleep for three days after every major decision."

"I guess you're right." Arris began to scrape away the offending ink blot with the tip of the compass. "I think I can reconstruct the pattern." There were so many things to learn. Terai hounded him all day, even after the other First Level students were through with their lessons. Hlaryon barked at him all night. He did not really mind. If they were successful he would be the Yearking of the Millennium. Now that he knew what the Goddess intended for him, he no longer needed to seek power anywhere else. He would have the power of a god.

Terai yawned hugely, stretching his short limbs. "Do you astrologers never sleep? Remember, old man, there's more to education than pattern webs. Tomorrow night will be the boy's first Spring Festival. Do you want him too exhausted to do justice to that little maid I've seen him whispering with?"

Arris blushed. Onira was barely thirteen, only a few months younger than he. She wanted him to be her first. They had met on the Winter Festival hunt when both had found themselves in the forefront of the mad chase, weaponless and nearly upon the stag. She was not pretty, except for huge, black-fringed eyes, but her laugh was like the deep tones of a harp. She often laughed.

"Tomorrow is a holiday," he said, resigned. "I can sleep in."

Hlaryon shook his head, smiling. "The night has become too clouded for accurate observation. Go on to bed."

Arris wiped the quill pen and replaced it in his hair. He bowed to his teachers and began to descend the long stairs to the dormitory levels of the priests' tower.

"I'll see you at the baths tomorrow," Terai called after him.

•   •   •

I need to talk to you.

Arris rose, startled, to the surface of the warm, crowded pool. He shook back the dense curtain of wet hair that obscured his face and peered around the steamy chamber. Most minds, including his own, were open at the surface level, sharing the joy and anticipation of the festival morning. There were masses of boisterous students and priests, but he could find no trace of the desperate, fleeting contact. The feathered tattoos on his back tingled as if they had been freshly scored.

Arris looked over at Terai. His friend was busy fiercely massaging an oil-slick old man; his mind was taut with its habitual control. Nothing. Arris dived again, working the last grains of cleansing sand out of his hair, shrugging off his unease with the thought of Onira's hard young body and deep laughter. This night would be the culmination of months of impatience. His body's fires had wakened soon after he was Winged. But there was power to be gained by losing his virginity on this particular night, and he had waited. He had not even accepted offers to partner other boys, though he found them as attractive as he found Onira.

Come with me.

The boy emerged with a shudder from the warm water. Few could touch him so clearly, penetrating through layers of mental guards. He finally recognized the voice. A robed figure stood in the doorway of the bath chamber. Cembra, looking oddly subdued in everyday priests' garb without his paint or his ram's horns.

Quick, boy.

What could he want? Arris had left his circle long ago. The Yearking of the Millennium did not have to seek power from the earth. Arris pulled himself out of the pool and strode past the lounging men and boys, conscious as always of admiring glances. Cembra waved him on into the robing room, where Arris wrapped himself in his clean Festival robe and hung his newly polished ceremonial knife on his belt.

"What is it?" he finally asked as he twisted his wet hair back and knotted it.

"Not here."

Arris followed the priest out of the bathhouse and into the street. The White City gleamed fresh, its paved streets running with the rain that had come the night before. Arris stretched in the mild spring sunshine and wondered again why Gama always smelled so pleasant. Most cities were foul, unhealthy places. "The baths will be open another half hour," he complained. "This had better be important. I was enjoying myself."

"I could see that," Cembra said dryly. "If smiles were coin, you'd be rich. Your nights may be busy after the Festival."

"My nights are busy already, with Hlaryon's lessons." Arris grinned. "But I'm sure I'll find time for other things."

Cembra led him to the city gate, where they waited for the gateward to open it and passed into the valley. The muddy road sucked at Arris's clean sandals and coated his feet.

"What do you want?" he asked in exasperation.

Cembra looked around furtively. There was no one near. "The circle met last night."

"And?"

"Your daimon appeared. Aghlayeshkusa."

Arris stared. "I thought it left when it realized you weren't going to fight any more battles until the Millennium."

Cembra sighed. "It threatened to disrupt the Festival unless we let it talk to you. The Council is more sympathetic now to our position, but they'll be ready to burn us if the daimon makes an appearance tonight. It's too strong to be bound by our circle."

"No," Arris said. "I won't talk to it. Why should I?"

"You must!" Cembra touched his shoulder, and Arris could feel his buried fear. "It offers you tremendous power, boy."

"The Goddess offers more."

"You don't need to accept its offer. Just talk to it. Keep it from disrupting the Festival."

"No."

"If you don't," Cembra said in a low voice, "I'll tell the Lady the truth about that affair three years ago. And about your part in it. Consecrating the earth to shadow, summoning the daimon. You'll never be considered a candidate for Yearking."

"Verchaki take you! You'd do that?"

"Without hesitation."

Arris looked at the muddy ground, his fists clenched. He

could not risk the Lady's anger. He could not even threaten Cembra in return. If Cembra were exposed, he would expose Arris.

"You have no choice," the priest said in satisfaction. "It's in the root cellar of the Fourth Level cottage."

Arris followed him reluctantly. He was stronger now. Maybe he was strong enough to stand up to the daimon. But he doubted it.

The earth was awake and seeking beneath Arris's feet as he crossed the empty yard of the cottage. It briefly touched his mind, and pulled back in pleasure and expectation. The root cellar had a small wooden door with a ring latch. Cembra opened it and disappeared down the ladder into the dark. Arris took a deep breath and did the same.

"Close the door," said the priest. Arris did so, blocking out the morning light. The cellar smelled mildewed and damp. A few dim candles illuminated sausages hanging from the beamed ceiling and sprouted potatoes piled on the dirt floor.

Aghlayeshkusa sat upon an upturned crate. It had resumed its heroic body and refined some of its grotesqueness, presumably as it learned what men found attractive. It had long since discarded the severed head. Arris stopped at the foot of the ladder, confused. His pulse raced with fear, but he was also fascinated. He might as well have been ten years old except for the burning in the wings that fletched his shoulders.

"Good morning," the daimon said courteously.

"What do you want with me?" Arris did not meet its gaze.

The daimon's chuckle was a dry, leaf-rustling sound. "What I have always wanted. It is time to seal our bargain. You are old enough to make the pact, and I have grown weary of the delay. I have had to spend my time serving minor magicians and terrorizing shepherds. I did not dare leave this world, for fear no one would ever summon me back and I would lose my prey."

"I have made my choice," Arris said quietly. "I do not choose to accept your offer." He began to erect a shield pattern in his mind to brace against attack, and wondered if he should try to call the Lossiran.

"You have chosen another source of power," Aghlayeshkusa said, seeming composed. "The Crimson Goddess. I am aware of that. They have made you believe you will be the Yearking in seven years.''

"I will be.''

"What is the attraction in that? You would be honored and flattered for a year, that is true, but in the end you would die the death of blood and fire. For me to take your soul now would be merciful compared to that.''

"I'll avenge my father. I'll kill the men who murdered him, and destroy the Khalifate as well," Arris said. "I'll release his ghost from the Wheel. And I'll have the Lady, and the power of the god. I don't need you.''

Aghlayeshkusa rose, looming like a mountain with the sun behind it. It smiled malevolently. "The Goddess has lied to you if she has offered you vengeance. Your hand cannot release Areyta of Delronen from the bondage of earth.''

"I'm his son. I owe it to him. The Goddess will give me the power to do it.''

"Oh, you could kill your three Ilkharani." The daimon sat on the crate again, its insubstantial flesh blending with the slats of wood. "But your act would have no effect upon Areyta. You know very little, child. The Lady knows. Your friend Terai knows. They have lied to you. They have used your desire to avenge Areyta to keep you following their path. But you can no more release him than I can. Blood must be shed by his kindred blood for that to be accomplished.''

"So when I kill Nievan and the others he'll be released.'' Scowling, Arris brushed back a strand of dripping hair that had fallen before his eyes. "And Terai would never lie to me.''

"You are stubborn. Nothing you do will affect Areyta's ghost. He was not your father.''

"That's insane," Arris breathed.

"I begin to see." Cembra stepped forward, his eyes gleaming. "Go on, daimon.''

"Insane?" The daimon wore a look of strange compassion. "They keep your mother from you so she cannot betray the truth. You are strong enough to take it from her. They know that.''

"What truth?" Arris scoffed.

"The Goddess arranged your conception, of course. She sent her Messenger to tell your mother to observe Spring

Festival seven years after her marriage. Rehoman could not have the blood of her enemies in her dreamed-of lover.''

''No.'' Arris shook his head violently and turned to climb the ladder. He would not listen to this. Shadow lies.

A mass of color and light blocked his path, whirling and twisting around the rungs of the ladder until it coalesced into a picture. His mother and the young student in the field on Spring Festival night when he was ten years old, the night he had first met the daimon. The picture began to shift subtly. Tauena's hair lengthened, her body firmed, her face grew younger. The field grayed and cracked and climbed until it was a cold stone ruin under moonlight in a forest. The adolescent atop Tauena darkened and aged until he was an unidentifiable Yaighan in his prime, full of savage strength and the god's power. He was horned. Arris smelled the man's sweat, heard his mother's soft cries. Her eyes shone with pain and ecstasy. Arris clamped his own eyes shut and shook his head in denial.

''You were conceived that night,'' whispered the daimon. ''The Goddess created you. Your mother betrayed Areyta, and you are not his son. They offer you revenge you cannot achieve.'' It chuckled. ''They probably won't even let you try to kill the Ilkharani. The Goddess's fabrication won't be allowed to endanger himself.''

''Stop it,'' Arris said helplessly.

''They never offered you power. You will be consumed by Rehoman. Your strength will feed her. Your youth and beauty will wither in fire to satisfy her. But that does not matter. You are a dream in the mind of the sleeping Goddess. When she wakes, you may vanish like all dreams.''

''Why are you saying these things?'' Arris clung to the ladder. ''They can't be true.''

''You may have wondered why the Lossiran came to you in the Citadel. Why it made you condemn Areyta to death. The Goddess knew that unless he died you would never come to her. She killed him. He died so you would accept what you were created to be.''

''No.'' He opened his eyes a crack. His mother slept in the arms of the stranger.

''A logical argument,'' Cembra said. ''Though some of it is surely exaggerated. But how can you know these things? Rehoman would not tell her plans to earth daimons.''

"Of course not, friend." Aghlayeshkusa waved its hand. The picture disappeared. "I spoke with one who knows, but can do nothing about his knowledge now. The ghost of the Lord Areyta."

"My father?" Arris turned around slowly.

"Your stupidity is wearying, boy. I will put your doubts to rest. This renegade priest knows the words that can summon and bind a ghost. Call Areyta here. Since you control him, you will be assured I did not invent him to delude you."

"Yes," Cembra said eagerly. "The ghost would know the truth. Arris? I'll need to borrow strength from you. I don't usually try anything like this without the circle."

Arris shrugged assent, too confused to protest. What if the ghost confirmed what the daimon said? This was a worse attack than any attempt to devour his soul.

The daimon moved from the center of the cellar, and Cembra stepped forward to begin his chant. Arris opened one of his surface guards and extended a listless chain of power to the priest, as he had learned in the circle. He felt the deep notes draw upon him, and fed them passively, not trying to meet Cembra's level of effort.

This was not the first time he had seen the pictures the daimon had shown him. They had been part of his nightmares in Qadasiya after Ruena had taken him in. Did that mean they were true?

The spell progressed smoothly. Mists of blood and sweat formed in the room, like dancing wisps of cloud over a high peak. They circled delicately. The priest was howling. Arris felt the tug of the envisioned chain sucking from him.

Surely he would have known if Areyta was not his father. Even as a small child he had been sensitive to other people's minds. He would have known.

There was no decay or rotting smell about the form that slowly materialized. Blue eyes stared at Arris through dripping blood. The limbs were cracked and horribly askew, the skin blackened with bruises and fire.

"Father . . ." He ached with the misery of the spirit. How could an innocent victim be condemned to suffer eternally? The oceanic eyes engulfed him. "Father . . . I've sworn to release you. I'll kill them all. I swear it every night."

The head moved a little back and forth, twitching its jaw.

"You have to command him to speak," the daimon said to

Cembra. "Tell him to answer the boy's questions. You control him."

Cembra drew himself up pompously. "Spirit of Areyta, sometime lord of Delronen, I command you to speak and answer. Do you acknowledge my power over you?"

"Yes." The voice rasped from the mangled throat. Arris fought the constriction of his own throat. He did not want his father to see him cry.

"The youth Arris j'Areyta will ask you questions. You are bound to answer them truthfully." Cembra stepped back.

Arris tasted salt. He could not speak.

"Ask if he is your father," prompted Aghlayeshkusa.

"Are . . . are you?" Arris managed to say in the high, unchanged child voice that still sometimes possessed him.

The form of Areyta shook its head slowly, with great sadness. "I am not," it said. "You are no flesh of mine. It is hard." The ghost looked bewildered. "I had always thought you were."

Arris sank to his knees on the muddy floor. "I'm your son! I love you. I will avenge you . . ." He looked up, seeking the impossible.

The ghost sighed, a deep gust that eddied the mists. "Don't take it to heart, boy." For a moment it sounded like the old Areyta. "It isn't your fault. You were a good son to me. But you cannot release me. Only . . . by my blood . . ." Its voice faded.

Arris clutched his arms to his chest and rocked on his knees. He could not stop tears from flowing silently down his face. The ghost reached out a transparent hand as if to comfort him, then let it fall.

"You may go," said Cembra with a catch in his voice. The mists receded, and the mangled form of Areyta dissolved with them.

"You see what the Goddess has done to you," Aghlayeshkusa said. "Everyone you trusted has lied to you. He was never your father, and you cannot avenge him. What can Rehoman offer now? I can give you power to use against her if you wish. You can use it for yourself, not for any cause or people. Show Rehoman that even her own creations may turn against her. Show her you control your own destiny." It grinned. "You could still destroy the Khalifate if you wanted to. Though it would not release Areyta's ghost, it might make his eternal bondage easier to bear.''

"No." Arris got to his feet, swallowing hard. "No. I don't need your power. I don't need your help. I don't think any of this was real. You made an illusion of my father, and an illusion of my mother betraying him.''

"Still unconvinced?'' The daimon showed its discolored teeth again. "I suppose I admire your loyalty. And I can understand your mistrust. You should trust no one, and certainly not me.''

"Arris,'' Cembra said, "you know the ghost was real. I summoned it with your help.''

"How do I know what a daimon could do? It could trick us into thinking we had done it ourselves.''

"Of course I could,'' agreed the daimon. "That is why I suggest one final test. Confront your mother. She is not as strong as Terai or the Lady. She cannot keep the truth from you.''

"They won't let me see her,'' Arris said.

"You haven't tried to see her,'' Cembra reminded him, "since you learned she had hidden herself in the priestess compound. I think the daimon is right. She is the only one who can be trusted.''

"If she tells me she betrayed him, I don't know what I'll do. I'll want to kill her.''

"Your rage will open your soul to me,'' the daimon said. "You will return. And I will gift you beyond what any man or woman has known.'' It allowed vast amusement to spread across its face. "Go to your mother, little boy, and hear what she tells you.''

Arris fled up the ladder and out into the bright morning.

CHAPTER
10

THE PRIESTESS COMPOUND was separated from the priests' tower by only a few blocks of pilgrims' hostels, bathhouses, and the kitchens that served them both. Arris had often looked down into the compound gardens from the highest windows of the tower, hoping to see Tauena. He thought he had glimpsed her a few times. But he had never been near her, never even touched her mind since that night three years ago.

"I must see her, Clynetra," he said again, fighting to keep his voice steady.

The doorward's face was suspicious. She peered through the curtained opening set beside the door to the compound, taking in his mud-spattered face, the disarray of his hair, his narrowed eyes. Clynetra was the older sister of Onira, the girl with whom Arris planned to spend the Festival night. She was also one of the soldiers Terai had trained before the battle at Delronen.

"That's impossible. Tauena is cloistered. She won't speak to anyone without a command from the Lady." Clynetra sniffed the air and scowled. "What's wrong with you, Arris? You smell of sorcery. You should be helping build the bonfires, not pestering me."

"She's my mother. She'll want to see me. Send for her."

"I don't have that authority, Arris. Go away or I'll summon the watch."

He wondered why Tauena was guarded so closely. The daimon had voiced suspicions he had considered before. Now he was unsure if it had ever been his mother's choice to withdraw from the world. It could have been more of the Lady's scheming.

"Then send her a message." He could hardly unclench his jaws enough to speak. "Please, Clynetra. It's important. Tell her I need to talk to her . . . about a Spring Festival night fourteen years ago. She'll see me. She has to."

He was led through the gardens, past tended lawns and soft fountains scented with dried flower petals, into a small domed building. Its single room was dark except for twelve lit candles set into a stone pillar in the center. A meditation room, Arris guessed. There were similar places in the priests' tower.

He could feel her coming long before she arrived. The link between them had not broken, then, though he had never been able to sense her presence from outside the compound.

Mother? he reached tentatively.

A shallow, guarded touch acknowledged his greeting, then withdrew. He was left with a fleeting impression of fear. Was she afraid to tell him the truth, or simply afraid to face his anger? He did not think she felt any concern for him. If she cared for him, she would not have abandoned him. As far as he knew, she had never even asked his teachers about his progress.

Arris turned as she entered the room. She was smaller than he remembered. Shorter than he, and he was small for thirteen. Her thick hair was shorn above her ears and her eyebrows were shaven as a sign of her cloistered vows. Her hands were folded across her stomach. Her face was still beautiful, set in cold repose. There was no spark of life in her eyes.

"Arris." She glanced briefly at him, then looked down.

"So you recognize me," he said with a bitterness he had not known he felt.

"You've grown even more handsome," she said, disinterested. "And you'll soon be a priest. Your brothers are at the Citadel now, envoys from the Yaighan. I'm so proud of you all."

"You had little to do with it." He clenched his fists against the urge to slap her to make her look at him.

"You asked to see me," she said after a moment.

"You know why. I need to know the truth, Mother, if it won't conflict with your holy vows."

"Have I ever lied to you?" Her soft-featured face, so like his own, was still downcast.

"I think you have. Who was my father?"

She lifted her chin. Her eyes met his, but her mind was suddenly closed to him. He shuddered at the impact of the severence. She had snapped the link between them, abruptly and without warning. Now he faced a stranger.

"That is between me and the Goddess."

"It concerns me too." The papery voice of the daimon whispered at the back of his mind in the vacuum his mother had left.

"You are Rehoman's child, gifted with her power, destined to lead her people. That is all you need to know."

"Who was my father?" he repeated. He wanted to shake his mother by the shoulders, to force color into her lifeless cheeks.

"And you are my child. The child the Lady promised me."

"But not his."

"But not his." Her folded hands quivered a little. "There was no place for his blood in you."

"He thought you loved him." Arris turned away from her on the raw edge of control.

"I did!" she cried suddenly, then swallowed and regained her composure. "I . . . I still grieve for my husband. He was a good man."

"You betrayed him. Lied to him."

"The Goddess called me!" Her black eyes showed some of their old fire. "And I would not have chosen to refuse. It was the Festival. No Yaighan man would keep his wife from the fires of the spring, and children conceived there are most blessed." Her small hand touched Arris on the shoulder. He jerked away. "I couldn't tell Areyta. He wouldn't have understood. I spared him that. Arris . . ." She faltered momentarily. "Arris, you cannot judge me. I trusted the Lady when she forced me to marry Areyta. I wasn't much older than you are now. She said my life had a purpose beyond the cloistered vows I meant to take. You were that purpose. You were the reason for my sacrifice."

"So they used you, and you used Areyta, and they intend to use me." Arris whirled to face her. "They don't care if they have to lie. What did they promise you? A moment for the Goddess that you could forget in your husband's arms? But it didn't fit into their plans for Areyta to raise me as his son, so they killed him.''

"You can't believe that." Her mask was gone.

"Then they promised me I could avenge him if I'd only be what they wanted. But that was a lie too. He wasn't my father. I can't release him. I can't do anything but feel his pain.''

"He is dead," she said. "It's over, Arris. If what I did was a betrayal, he never knew it. He died thinking I was faithful to him by the primitive code of his gods. Let the past lie with the dead. Let it rest.''

"But he can't rest. You must know that. Rehoman teaches that a murdered man must be bound to the Wheel until he is released by blood. Blood shed by his flesh." Arris tried to unclench his fists and could not. "Falcmet or Husayn might release him, but they won't. They can't see his ghost. They'd never believe it.''

Tauena's hand rose to her mouth in a warding gesture. "What are you saying? His ghost? What do you mean?''

"I've seen him, Mother. And if he died thinking you had been faithful, he knows the truth now. He told me I wasn't his son.''

"You called his spirit," Tauena breathed. "Arris, that's forbidden! That's tampering with the earth powers.''

"He'll never forgive you," he said brutally and untruthfully. "Neither will I.'' He shoved past her and ran from the building. He wanted out. Out of the priestess compound, out of Gama.

"Arris!" she called after him, her voice high and frightened. "Arris, come back! What have you done?''

Now she knew he was no puppet of Rehoman, no passive child to be molded to the Goddess's desires. No doubt she would report this to the Lady. Let her.

"Headed for the fields?" Clynetra called as he hurried past. She was rubbing oil into her sword sheath as she sat by the compound door.

Arris slowed, and found himself smiling. "Tell your sister I'll be waiting for her.''

The doorward chuckled. "You'll see Onira at moonrise and not before. If you see her at all. She may reconsider having an untried boy as her first.''

The jibe was ill timed. Arris bolted down the white-cobbled street. Boy. Everyone thought he was only a boy, from Cembra to Terai to the Lady. A soft, malleable boy to be teased and bribed and bullied into compliance. He would not do as they expected. He would make his own choices.

The bonfires were lit at sunset. Every Yaighan man and woman who had managed to reach Gama crowded around the fires, laughing and calling to one another. Arris heard them from the rocky outcroppings of the Teeth where he had spent the afternoon and evening alone with his anger. By long tradition, the eager bodies could not touch until they were blessed by the first rays of moonrise. There would be time for Arris to climb back to the valley to search for Onira and join the pleasure-seekers.

He began to descend. He would join them, but it was not pleasure he sought. It was power. Both Cembra and Terai had hinted at it, the quadrupling of innate strength that could be gained by sacrificing his virginity on this night of the year. Such a ritual was even more potent if both participants were virgins. That was one reason he had wooed Onira.

He might still become a priest, and even Yearking. But he would approach the Goddess on his own terms, as a man powerful in his own right, not a weak and helpless boy.

Arris, whispered the wind in the daimon's voice.

"Go away," he muttered. Aghlayeshkusa had tormented him over the past hours, reminding him of their unsworn pact, oozing complacency and satisfaction.

Its face fluttered before him in the dark, lit from behind by the rising bonfires. "You promised me your soul . . ."

Arris pulled his dagger and slashed at the image, which broke into tattered ribbons that parted to let him pass. A few wisps trailed behind him through the sheepfolds. They twisted around his head, braided themselves into his hair. He shook himself like a wet dog. They clung to him.

"Leave me alone. I've chosen the Goddess."

"That choice was made for you," a strand of hair hissed in his ear. "Only I offer true freedom, true choice."

"You offer a different kind of slavery." Arris reached up with his dagger and cut off the writhing strands. They fell gently with the wind and turned into a two-foot-long black snake when they reached the earth.

"If it is slavery," said the snake, "then it is a slavery to which you are well suited. Feel the anger within you. Feel the way you yearn toward shadow. The bonfires pain your eyes. You are not a creature of light."

Arris whirled and dived. His dagger cut deep in the muddy earth. The snake laughed and vanished down a gopher hole. Arris breathed deeply, willing his rage back under control. He could not gain the power he sought with such distractions. He had to concentrate fully on the Festival's magic, on Onira, on his body's awakening. He knew that. Yet his hands shook as he brushed mud from his robe and sheathed his dagger, and his ears were filled with dull roaring.

The people at the nearest bonfire impatiently waited for the moon. Some gulped great quantities of mead. Others had already discarded their clothing and were stalking companions. Arris declined offers as politely as he could and hurried to the next circle.

The black snake reared before him, hissing his name. He leaped upon it and stamped its head into the ground. It stilled, and turned back into a few lengths of black hair. Arris shuddered and went on.

A rough hand clapped him on the back and he whirled like a baited tiger, expecting to see the daimon's form stretched against the flames. His hand went to his knife.

Terai stepped back. "What's wrong, boy?"

Arris swallowed hard and forced a smile. Terai was another who had lied to him. The smiling, half-drunken face of his teacher only made him angrier. But it was not the time for a confrontation. That would come later.

"I . . . I fell in the mud," he explained. "I hope Onira won't mind much. Have you seen her?"

Terai frowned. "She's with a group of girls at the fifth bonfire from here. Are you sure nothing's wrong? You look like you've seen a ghost."

"I have." Arris hurried away. More seeking hands reached for him, and he found his lips pulling back into an animal snarl. He did not want to be touched. He could feel the glowing of the moon's power as it rose above the mountain crags. It pierced him, filled him like the summer anger of a hot sun. His body began to respond to it, and to the laughter and small moans of the first couples to come together in the waiting fields.

Onira saw him coming and ran toward him. She had twined flowers in her hair, and the moonlight and the light from the bonfire made her broad, cheerful face almost beautiful. The nervous group of first-time girls laughed and called encouragement. Nearby, the first-time youths watched silently. They were Arris's age, but most were several levels behind him in their training.

Onira took Arris's hand, and he burned at the touch. "What took you so long?" she said breathlessly. "Clynetra said you'd be waiting in the fields."

Arris tugged her away from the bonfire's pool of light toward the darkness of the empty sheepfolds. "I couldn't find you," he said softly. "You look lovely in the moonlight, Onira."

She halted. "Don't try to flatter me so I won't see! You're all muddy, and your hair's messed up. Have you been with someone else? Before me? Couldn't you even wait for moonrise?" Her voice rose above its usual low tones.

"Shh," he soothed, putting an arm around her shoulders. "Of course I waited for you. We promised each other. I was rock climbing, and I lost track of the sun. I'm sorry I didn't clean up, but then I would have been even later."

"Oh." She seemed satisfied, and snuggled closer to him. "Well, I'm glad you're here at last."

He kissed her cheek lightly. "Come."

"Where are we going?" She twisted around to look back at the bonfires and their circles of people.

"Where we can have some privacy." He opened the low gate of one of the abandoned sheepfolds. The sheep were high in the mountains in summer pasture, and Arris thought the valley's smell much improved.

"Privacy? On the night of the Goddess?" Onira chuckled and pointed at the moon. "She'll be watching, at least."

Arris could not suppress a shudder. "Let her watch." He took Onira's muscled body in his arms and kissed her hungrily on the mouth. The anger within him receded under the pressure of desire, under the power of the Goddess.

Onira returned his kiss with unpracticed fervor. Her strong hands stroked his shoulders, tangled in his hair. Arris traced the lines of her form with his fingertips, lightly caressing through the harsh wool of her student robe. He let his hands stray to the twisted knot of her belt. It loosened easily. He let the belt fall. The weight of the ceremonial knife on it made a soft thump when it reached the ground.

Onira opened her eyes wide and looked at him. She seemed suddenly frightened and unsure. Arris smiled gently. He was a little nervous himself, but he was intoxicated by the fresh, damp smell of the night and by Onira's scent, a combination of the delicate flowers in her hair and a warmer, darker note.

As he watched her face she grinned suddenly, shrugging away her shyness. With a strength that probably equaled his own, Onira pulled him down onto the grass. Arris landed hard on top of her. She giggled, and fumbled to unfasten the belt of his woolen robe.

Arris reached down to help her. His fingers closed over hers, and when the knot released he pulled the braided rope free, careful not to bruise her with the knife sheath. He laid it just out of reach.

He had thought about what he should do that night, about going slowly to avoid frightening her, about waking each part of her body to his touch before doing anything else. But his need was growing more urgent, and the moonlight made his robe unbearably hot. He rolled off Onira and shrugged out of his garment. It seemed to leap over his head. Onira watched, her face shadowed. She made no move to do the same.

Arris looked at her uncertainly. "Am I going too fast? I don't mean to frighten you."

She smiled. "I'm not frightened. I'm as ready as you are . . . the moon is so strong . . ." She gazed at him, and added with less assurance, "But you're so beautiful, Arris, and I'm . . . I'm just Onira. No one ever looked twice at my body."

"I did," he reminded her. "On the Winter Festival hunt, remember? You have wonderful legs, especially when you're running." He trapped her shoulders against the ground with his hands. "You're very beautiful, Onira. Why else would I want to spend tonight with you?"

"Don't men like women . . . well, softer, and more graceful, and not as strong as they are?" she said wistfully.

"Your sister would be surprised to hear that," Arris said with a grin. "She had every man in warrior training after her. My brother Falcmet was infatuated with her."

"Really?"

"Really. Now won't you let me see some more of your body besides your legs?" he pleaded.

She laughed and sat up, and helped Arris remove her robe. He sat for a moment, marveling. He had seen nude bodies before, at other Festivals, at the baths. He had been attracted to many, of all shapes and ages, over the past few months. But this was different. This body he could explore, taste, caress. Even in the moonlight, he thought he could see more than he had ever noticed. The way Onira's small breasts cast long shadows across the hard curve of her stomach. The tiny, fragile-looking hairs that crept along the inner surface of her thighs. The graceful way her muscles flowed together as she lay back again, beckoning him down.

He leaned over and kissed her briefly, then began to explore her with his mouth and hands. He kissed down her body, playing with her breasts. His need was fierce, but he knew that if she was not ready he would hurt her more than was necessary.

Take her now. Show her you are a man, not a fearful child.

Arris stiffened and raised his head. The huge man-shape of the daimon loomed against the clear stars only a few feet away.

"Get out of here!" He leaped up, scooping his discarded belt from the ground. He jerked the knife from its sheath and brandished it at the indistinct form. "Leave us alone!" The daimon laughed softly and vanished.

He stood gasping with rage. Onira rose to her feet and touched his shoulder tentatively. "Arris, what is it? What's wrong? Who were you shouting at?"

He pulled her into a protective embrace, hoping her warm flesh would calm his shivering. "Did you see it?"

"See what? I just saw you yelling at the darkness. What's wrong?" She pulled away. "You drew your knife."

He could not explain. What was he to tell her? That a daimon was tormenting him? "I . . . was surprised," he finally ventured. "It was . . . another couple, and I wanted us to be alone."

"Another couple? Arris, that was rude of you, they were probably going to ask if we wanted to share." She sounded disappointed and confused. Arris did not blame her. His explanation only made his behavior less excusable. He wished it had been another couple. He might have been interested in a sharing. He had spied on enough of them in Festivals past.

"I'm sorry." He forced himself to calm his breathing. "I

didn't mean to be rude. I guess I just wanted us to be together the first time, away from everyone else.''

"All right," she said generously, pulling him back down to the soft grass. "But you're going to have to start over again. I liked what you were doing." She patted his behind. "Isn't it funny how no one wears a loinwrap on Spring Festival day?"

"It was too hot," Arris said soberly, relieved. He had feared she would be too upset to continue. Or that she would not trust him anymore. He knelt astride her and began with her breasts. Then he moved his hands down, teasing, barely touching her skin, until they were exploring the warm, moist cleft between her legs. She gasped and pulled him closer, caressing him with long, urgent strokes.

He meant to prolong his teasing, to bring her to a fevered state before he took her. But the moon was strong. He was no longer certain it was only the moon. The valley, the bonfires, the Festival seemed unimportant. All that mattered was Onira and himself.

"I don't want to hurt you," he whispered, "but—"

"It's time," she said breathlessly, guiding him down.

She let a sharp cry escape, but clutched him tighter, and he was inside her. He had to use all his mental training to control his body, to force himself to go slow. He stroked in and out, feeling the intensity of sensation overwhelm him. Onira moved with him, matching his rhythm. Her legs wrapped around his, and her head arched back with eyes closed.

Arris began to move faster. Onira's hands on his back gripped him with bruising strength. The salt taste of her lips greeted him as they kissed again. Arris closed his own eyes, surrendering to pleasure. His thoughts ranged ahead to the year he would lie with the Lady herself at Spring Festival. She was sure to choose him. The need in his loins flooded through him, and already he wanted more. The Yearking would have this and the god's power as well.

He opened his eyes. Onira's face was strained, her eyes glazed. For a moment they seemed to reflect yellow in the moonlight. Her legs crushed him like a vise as he thrust. He cupped her head in his hands and bent to her, his mouth open and seeking. Her soft lips parted, and her tongue flickered out.

It was forked.

Arris fought against steel muscles. He could not escape. His body betrayed him, erupting in ecstatic spasms as he stared in utter horror at the obscene face of the daimon superimposed on Onira's broad features.

Power flowed into him. The power of the first time under the Goddess's moon. But it was twisted, twined with threads of darkness. He gagged on the smell of earth.

The daimon kissed him. Its lips tasted foul. Arris bucked and writhed in its grasp; suddenly they were rolling on the ground, still locked in the fierce embrace.

"You are mine," the daimon whispered.

"No!" Arris's mind was filled with exploding lights. The power blinded and deafened him. He rolled over something sharp in the grass, something that grazed his back. His ceremonial knife. It lay where he had dropped it after the daimon's first taunting appearance. His right hand was free. Arris lunged for it and grasped its hilt.

The daimon was laughing. Arris was still inside it, so tight was its grip. Arris strained to raise the knife. The low, mocking laughter stopped, and the hold of the daimon relaxed. Arris could move. He arched upward, still half-blinded by the burning in his mind, and stabbed down with all his strength.

There was a rending, agonized scream, and the smell of hot blood. Arris slashed again and again. The screaming stopped, but the valley still echoed.

The daimon laughed again. From behind him. Arris's vision cleared. The knife fell from his nerveless hand. Onira's blood spurted across his face and chest from the raw crimson gaping of her throat. Her head was half-severed.

"Onira?" Arris breathed, thinking this another illusion of the daimon. She did not answer. Only the echo of her screams remained. Her black eyes stared upward in unseeing horror.

Arris choked and vomited into the grass beside her. He looked again. She was dead. Her blood drenched both of them. She looked oddly small and helpless, lying naked under the moonlight.

"A fitting offering to the Crimson Goddess," said the daimon.

Arris leapt up after it. He was unarmed; the wavering form of the daimon only stepped aside to avoid his lunges. "Mur-

derer!'' Arris shrieked, finding the knife again and slashing at
the ghostly shape.

"You killed her,'' Aghlayeshkusa said mildly. "And you
had better pick up your robe and get away from here as fast as
you can, before those people carrying torches arrive. They
heard the screams. You must realize they did not sound like
the usual Festival cries of passion.''

Arris could see the wavering beads of light that had de-
tached from the bonfires. He stared at them, numb, unthinking.

"Come,'' said the daimon gently, in the voice of a father
chiding an errant son. "We have far to go.''

CHAPTER

11

THE TEETH OF GAMA were stark, treacherous peaks, slippery
shards of rock that thrust nearly thirteen thousand feet above
the level of the Endless Sea. The Yaighan did not need to
guard the approaches to Gama that were blocked by the
Teeth. No army had ever crossed them, and few men.

Arris and his brothers had climbed sections of the Teeth
before Falcmet and Husayn were sent to represent the Yaighan
at the Citadel. The boy knew the lower courses of the peaks
well. Better than most Yaighan who had lived near them all
their lives. But he was certain Terai also knew them, and
Terai had to be leading his hunters. Otherwise he would have
lost them long before.

The daimon flitted impatiently ahead of him, locating the
easiest traverses, urging him to move faster. The body of
Aghlayeshkusa provided an eerie, smoky light that illuminated the rocks even after moonset. Arris could climb much
more quickly than his pursuers, encumbered as they were
with torches. He scurried across the slick rock faces on hands

and sandaled feet. His Festival robe was soon tattered. His blood mingled with Onira's, oozing from scrapes and cuts, yet he barely felt his bruises.

He was lost within his own body. In his head contending powers battled, clouding his vision, deafening him. The fragile tissues in his nose and mouth seeped blood. Shocked into a numb, paralyzing horror by what he had done, he could control no more than the climbing motions of his arms and legs. At times even that ability failed. Once he was stuck clinging in a rock chimney, unable to think of what to do next. The daimon had to invade his defenseless mind and take charge of his movement before he began to climb again.

The glowering moon had set, and Arris had outdistanced his hunters enough to search for a hiding place. The daimon led him to a tiny opening in the rock, a cave scarcely the size of Arris's body. Its entrance was half-blocked by fallen stones from an avalanche that past winter. Arris squirmed inside, scraping his skin raw, and crouched there shuddering with exhaustion. The daimon touched him gently, full of proprietary concern, and whispered soft, indistinguishable words. Arris fell asleep.

He woke screaming, enveloped in leathery wings, invaded by the Lossiran. The daimon had vanished. The Vulture's wings clutched him, scraping intolerably against his abraded skin. Its cold, ancient spirit, dark as the bottom of a frozen lake, eddied and waved like tides in his mind. He had no control over it. The defenses he had constructed so elaborately over years of training, the constraints that had enabled him to call the Lossiran at the Lady's command, had been demolished.

"Go back," it screeched, battering at him. "Go back. Go back. Go back."

He could not even speak. He struggled in the coffinlike cave, fighting to regain control over his chaotic powers. Nothing happened. Wings caressed him like a lover. The Vulture would not be denied. He wondered if he had ever really been able to command it, or if it had suited the thing's own purpose to come when he called. Now its ancient will commanded him. He began to crawl out of the cave. Then he stood, leaning as if windblown in the direction of Gama. The valley was full of lights. Far down on the mountain he could see the torches of Terai's party, searching, baffled by the daimon's tricks.

He could not go back! They would kill him. He was certain of it. The daimon had told him so. He could not go back. Perhaps he could face death. He deserved it, for murdering that innocent girl with the laughing eyes. But he could not face Terai, the Lady, his mother, Hlaryon, the shame and horror they all would feel. No. He could not return.

But he was lowering himself over the ledge, searching for handholds on the steep face of the mountain to climb back toward Gama. Arris shook with effort, trying to rebuild his mental walls. The Vulture only tightened its hold on his mind.

"Help me," he managed to whisper. "Help me, Aghlay-eshkusa."

The daimon reappeared. It perched on the cliff edge above Arris and the invisible Lossiran. "What did you say?" It grinned.

"Help me . . . please . . ."

The daimon laughed and leaped down onto him. The Lossiran screeched defiance and joined battle. The shock of their meeting drove Arris momentarily unconscious. He lost his grip on the rockface and slid uncontrollably into a fall. The Lossiran unclasped its wings and dived beneath him to break his descent. To do so, it had to disengage from his mind. The daimon filled the vacant space.

Arris felt great talons catch him and bear him upward. He was deposited on the shelf of the stones outside the cave. The daimon worked quickly to consolidate the power that tumbled through the boy's mind, shaping it, building it into adamantine shields.

Arris could move again. He pulled himself to his knees. His ribs ached where the Lossiran had grasped him. The Vulture perched just beside him, its grotesque head lowered threateningly.

"Won't . . . go back . . ." he gasped.

The Lossiran reached out a tentative probe and recoiled from the shadow-born walls in his mind. The daimon laughed inside him. The Lossiran gathered its strength and began to batter against the walls, much as it had done in the Temple in Qadasiya.

"How do I fight it?" Arris asked frantically as the walls

quivered and bowed. He sensed the daimon could not strengthen him any more without the channels of a sworn alliance.

"You know the ritual," hissed the voice in his mind. "A formal repudiation of the Goddess should do it."

Arris hesitated. Only that afternoon he had decided to accept what Rehoman willed for him. He would be giving up his chance to be Yearking. He would be denouncing his Yaighan heritage. But what had that heritage done for him? The Goddess only wanted him back to punish him for killing Onira. He had already forgone the possibility of Kingship. The walls were crumbling.

He opened his arms in a weak reversal of the invocation gesture. "Rehoman! Crimson Goddess of the Yaighan! Mother of blood and fire!" The Lossiran paused in its attack and looked at him in vague surprise. Its scaly feathers ruffled in the dawn breeze. "Hear me! I am Arris, Tauena's son. I was born to your service, but I will not serve you. I was your worshiper, but I will not worship you. I was your acolyte, but I will not be your priest, or your King." He took a deep breath. "I renounce you. I renounce your crimson fire. I swear never to use the power you gave me. I will seal it deep within my mind where it cannot be reached. I swear this by shadow and fire, by earth and air, by sap and blood and water. I do not see you, I do not believe in you. It is done." His arms slashed downward with cutting force. The Lossiran disappeared.

The daimon flowed outside him again and took the sculptured, heroic form it seemed to enjoy. "It is done," it said sourly. "You've gotten rid of the Goddess, and the Lossiran shouldn't be able to contact you anymore. But why did you include that last bit about never using the power she gave you? The power you were born with? You cripple yourself, boy. I had thought to grant you just enough of the shadow strength to enable you to control what you had and turn it to my purposes. Now I'll have to invest you with a lot more than that."

Arris shuddered with the strength of his oath. The awareness, the sensitivity, the magic he had always possessed was receding. It fled to the farthest reaches of his mind and abruptly cut itself off from him. He knew it was still there, but by the terms of the vow he could no longer use it. Such a vow was not a mere promise, a mere given word. It was a spell in itself, a ritual binding that could not be broken.

He looked up and brushed tangled hair away from his face. He felt giddy with resolve. "No," he said. "I want nothing from you. I am done with power."

Aghlayeshkusa was incredulous. "What? You called for my help back there. You pleaded with me. Now you say you don't want what I offer? Don't you understand? The terms of my offer have risen! I'll gift you with incredible magic. The priests down in that valley have no concept of such power."

"I don't want it." Arris looked steadily at the daimon's face. "I don't want anyone controlling my life. I'll make my own way, without gods or daimons. Like everyone else does."

Aghlayeshkusa began to melt into a monstrous form, a thing with horns and talons and gaping, slavering jaws. It roared. Arris could hardly breathe from fear.

"If . . . if that means you'll eat me now, then go ahead. I don't care." He closed his eyes. It would probably be best this way. The hunters from Gama would find him dead. Onira would be avenged.

The hot breath in his face cooled and lightened. No scaly hands touched his bruised skin. Arris opened his eyes. The daimon had returned to its usual form and was looking at him in bemusement, shaking its head.

"I won't fight you," Arris said. "I don't have any defenses anyway. Don't waste your time."

"No," said the daimon, "I won't. Did you really think I would still desire your soul, powerless and empty as you have made it? No, I will not eat you now." It sighed, an almost human sound. "Someday I'll make my offer again. You will know by then how ill suited you are to the life of a pitiful, weak human being. You will welcome the shadow then."

"I'll never turn to you," Arris said stubbornly, amazed he was still alive. He got precariously to his feet.

"You will. Oh, young Arris, you'll regret this quite soon. You'll beg me to help you, just as you did on the cliff with the Lossiran. Only this time I won't answer. I'll choose my own time to renew my offer. When you finally see me again, you'll be desperate to accept." It bowed. "Until then, little one."

The daimon dived from the mountainside, grew magnificent wings, and flew into the rising sun. Arris watched in

disbelief. He was free. The daimon was wrong, he thought.
He would never regret this.

The high spine of the Dark Hills curved to the northwest
above the sparsely inhabited valleys of Yaighan dry-farmers
and shepherds. Arris followed it at first because he guessed
Terai would search for him in the other direction, on the
roads and trails that led to Delronen and the Khalifate beyond.
Terai would expect Arris to flee to a place he knew, a place
where he had friends.

He moved slowly, traveling mostly by daylight to avoid the
moon's gaze. The hills were kind. The sun shone most of the
time, and if it did not, rain always seemed to catch him where
there were sheltering rocks nearby. Mountain berries were
just ripening, and he knew of edible roots and greens from his
priest training. Once he would have been able to hunt small
animals with his ceremonial knife; he would have sensed their
furtive minds, and performed rituals of Goddess power to
bring them to him. But he was convinced he had done the
right thing in repudiating the Goddess and the daimon, in
trammeling his power with the bonds of oath.

Some vestige of power remained, he suspected. Otherwise
he would have been caught by now. Any priest could have
tracked him by his mind's presence, unless he still had some
guards. It had been more than a week. They must have given
up the hunt.

Each day's travel took Arris closer to the hills of the
Westrange, which held the border between the Khalifate and
the Deirani Empire. He had decided to go to Deiran. What
choice did he have? He was exiled from the Khalifate on pain
of death. He had just committed murder in Gama. The Kwaitl
nomads would soon belong to one or the other of those
countries. Deiran was the only realm left to him.

Fortune brought him up short on the crest of a low foothill
ridge the evening of his thirteenth day of travel. The Dark
Hills were almost behind him now. Notches between peaks
had broadened, smoothed, until he was traversing natural
passes. The old, worn shoulders of the Westrange hunched on
the horizon. But below him in a broad valley to the side of a
well-traveled road gleamed the torches of a merchant camp.

Peak-roofed Deirani wagons encircled a cluster of fires. A

picket line of lean horses shifted comfortably nearby. A path wound down from the hill where Arris stood, beside a small stream that widened to cross the road at a rough-bridged ford.

Arris smiled in wonder. He had been thinking that a merchants' caravan might be the best place for him. He spoke both the Yaighan and Khalifate languages well; surely such a skill could be put to use. He had expected to have to travel all the way to a Deirani city, to beg to be allowed to join a caravan as it moved out for a summer expedition. Now one lay before him, as if some god had been listening to his thoughts. But what god would want to claim his worship? It had to be chance.

He brushed the top layer of dust from his tattered robe and tried without much success to comb through his long, matted hair with his fingers. Onira's blood had long since been buried by dirt on his clothing. He would not look prepossessing, but the merchants would not immediately suspect him of murder unless one of them had priest powers.

He squared his shoulders and started down the hill path. Though his crippled senses could no longer tell him where guards were posted or calm the horses with a thought, he could still move as silently as a tree's breath. His brothers had taught him that skill. He tried not to think of Falcmet and Husayn. They would probably have heard what he had done by now.

Arris glided past the outer pickets, scarcely causing a rustle among the placid horses. He could smell roasting fowl from the fires. His stomach cramped as if in sudden realization of its emptiness. Even if they would not employ him, surely these people would grant him a beggar's right to whatever was left after they finished their meal.

He calmed his eagerness with a priest's practiced control and slipped around the tongue of a wagon to step into the circle of firelight. He raised his hands, palms out, in a gesture of peaceful intent.

Shouts of anger and fear in an indecipherable language greeted him. Arris stood still, smiling, as seven of the leather-clad merchants leapt up and scooped spears from a pile near the fire to brandish at him. They addressed him shrilly in their singing tongue. They looked much the same as the Deirani had in the caravan Arris had once performed for when he was with Senna's family. Smooth, honey-skinned faces under round leather caps, shoulder-length hair in shades of brown and black, slanted eyes.

"Do any of you speak the language of the Khalifate?" he asked in that tongue. "Or the Yaighan?"

"Of course. How else would we speak with our customers?" An unmistakably feminine voice laughed mockingly. "What do you take us for?"

Arris bowed to her, and wished he had taken time to clean himself in the stream. There was beauty in her high-cheekboned, unlined face, though he could not guess her age. "Friendly travelers," he suggested, "who might be interested in the services of a strong, intelligent youth. One who speaks both Khalifate and the Yaighan languages fluently."

"We have no need of a translator," said a heavyset man.

"I could take care of your horses, or drive your carts, or do anything you need." He hoped he did not sound too desperate.

A younger man lowered his spear with a dry chuckle. "You'll do anything for a meal, you mean. Look at him, Sapusa. He's starving. Let's at least feed him before we send him away."

The woman approached Arris, her broad face unreadable. "Yes, look at him," she muttered, then began a soft, rapid monologue in Deirani. The men shifted uneasily. The heavyset one smiled suddenly; the young one who had spoken kindly looked dismayed, and offered apparent argument. Sapusa glared at him and silenced him with a taut-voiced phrase. Arris found that they were all staring at him, their gaze so intense that he had to look down.

The heavyset man turned to drop his spear, then spoke to Arris. "Come, lad, take a meal with us. And tell us about yourself. We may yet consider your . . . employment."

Arris sighed with relief and followed the man to the center campfire. For a minute he had regretted the loss of his power; he could not discern their feelings toward him from their alien gestures and expressions. But they smiled at him now, friendly and relaxed. One handed him half a roasted fowl. He tore into it, scarcely able to control his ravenous appetite.

"So," began Sapusa, her voice making the Yaighan language sound like music. "You would like to leave your Dark Hills?"

Arris nodded. His mouth was full of meat.

"What does your family think of that? Did your parents grant their blessing?"

"I have no family anymore," Arris said, thinking it was true enough. "There is no one left for me in the Dark Hills."

"No friends who know your plans?" asked the heavyset man, speaking the language with more effort. "No one who knows you meant to seek employment with a Deirani caravan?"

"No one knows where I've gone, or cares."

"How old are you, lad?" Sapusa said gently.

"Almost fourteen. I know I don't look it. But I'm strong for my size." He looked earnestly at her. "Do you think you could find some use for me? I'm a hard worker, and I wouldn't be any trouble."

The large man said something in the Deirani tongue, which made two of the others laugh nervously. Sapusa frowned at them. "Perhaps." She smiled, beckoning the youngest man over to her. She whispered a quick command, and the man bowed and hurried away.

He returned with a large skin bag full of a sloshing liquid, and several ceramic mugs. Sapusa took them, poured generous measures, and handed a mug to Arris. "Drink with us, and be welcome."

He smiled. The drink smelled enticing: fruity, sharp, far stronger than the watered mead sometimes allowed the students in Gama. He took a deep sip. It reminded him of the wine of the Khalifate, but it was not made from grapes. He could not identify the fruit.

"Then you have work for me?"

Laughter swung around the campfire. Sapusa only smiled, and Arris thought there was veiled sadness in her brown eyes.

"You will improve the fortunes of my caravan by your mere presence," she said.

Arris woke to understanding in the half-light of early morning. Horses were being hitched to the wagon where he had slept. He still lay between bales of hides and crates of restive poultry, but now he was bound as securely as the rest of the cargo. Manacles weighted his wrists and ankles, padded with rags to keep them tight on his small limbs and to prevent chafing. More rags were stuffed in his mouth, and a tight gag was knotted behind his head.

His head ached from the potent wine he had drunk the

night before. It probably had not even been drugged. He was
not used to strong drink. How could he have been so foolish?
He had forgotten the danger of slavery. The Yaighan kept no
slaves, but the Khalifate and the Deirani Empire were alike in
their dependence upon bought labor.

The Goddess had found him after all. This was her punish-
ment for his killing of Onira. It had to be. It was fitting: just
as he had been rejoicing at his freedom from gods and
daimons, he had been subjugated by men. No doubt Rehoman
was laughing in her sleep.

He would not submit to her irony. He would not lie here
like a trussed lamb, helpless and frightened, awaiting whatever his captors intended. Arris breathed deeply through the
gag and gathered his forces for a spell of displacement that
would send his manacles harmlessly into the stream. Then he
sagged in new despair. He had momentarily forgotten. He
had no power left. If he had, he would never have been
captured. He was no more than any other undersized thirteen-
year-old now. He had no protection. He had renounced the
Goddess and sent Aghlayeshkusa away.

Had the daimon foreseen this? It had promised he would
need what it offered very soon. If he called it now he would
be admitting his weakness. It had said it would not come, but
perhaps it had lied. It had told Arris before that he should not
trust it.

Maybe it would come. He would not hesitate now to
promise it his soul. The world was too dangerous for a boy
without power.

"Aghlayeshkusa," he whispered with difficulty, "Aghlayeshkusa . . . by shadow and fire, by earth and air, by sap and
blood and water, I charge you . . . I beg you . . . come! I'll
give you anything you want. Anything." But even as he said
the words, he felt their lack of power. He could not call the
daimon. He did not have enough mental strength to summon
a light breeze from the next hill.

The wagon lurched and began to move onto the road. Arris
could hear Sapusa's soft, gentle voice calling to the horses.
Other musical Deirani voices joined in a chorus of drivers, as
the merchants' caravan picked up speed on the last leg of its
journey back to the Deirani Empire. It was richer by one
unexpected find. One that guaranteed profit, since all that had
been traded for it was a few mugs of heady wine.

CHAPTER
12

THE CARAVAN SNAKED through villages and farmholds, past orchards and rice shallows, in the growing heat of the Deirani spring. It skirted around the southeastern cities to avoid paying the higher taxes charged by city overlords to finance their new garrisons and fortifications. The Emperor Hareku had decreed that Deiran should prepare for war with the Khalifate within a few years. The Regents had grown more and more belligerent and less and less diplomatic as their power grew. The road was crowded with soldiers riding in close formations, featureless and menacing in their enveloping black armor. Their sturdy, compact horses sometimes brushed against the lines of peasants on foot, occasionally knocking down a child or toppling someone into the wet rice shallows beside the road.

Arris attempted to escape the first two times he was allowed to walk beside the wagon with only his wrists manacled. He was caught each time and beaten dispassionately but thoroughly. He would not try again. Sapusa had not said, but he assumed he would be sold to a farmer to work the fields. He would not be expected to work as a field hand in irons. He would escape. His anger had burned down to smoldering coals, to an aching knot in his stomach, which he was determined to control. The more they trusted him, the better his chances would be.

Three weeks after his capture, Arris rode into Khopei, the City of a Thousand Shrines, in the back of the merchant wagon. He saw little of the city's wonders then, though they would grow familiar in the years to come. There were really two cities: the teeming, canal-webbed animal that sprawled around the mouth of the River Vaclav, filthy with poverty and glittering with temples; and the Sapphire Palace, the fragile, low-walled tapestry of roofs, gardens, and terraces that rose above the city on gentle hills overlooking the Endless Sea.

Sapusa's house was tall, walled with featureless stone, set on one of the dirtiest streets of Khopei by the river. Impassive household guards, bare-chested and hugely muscled, guarded the entranceway from the encroachment of beggars or rival merchants. The courtyard was spacious enough to hold the entire caravan, wagons, horses, and men. Sapusa gave brief orders to her servants, then led Arris to a small bathhouse attached to the main residence.

The steam that rose from the bathing pool felt luxurious against Arris's grimy skin. He sighed. "It's been a long time."

The Deirani woman smiled. "For us all, boy. But you shall be first. We'll see if you clean up as pretty as I think you will."

Pretty? Arris thought the word inappropriate. But he waited until Sapusa had unlocked his manacles and left the bath-house, then stripped off his tunic and plunged into the pool. There was scented soap in a basket on the other side. He scrubbed his skin until it burned, and worked through the matted tangles of his hair, pulling it strand by strand from its snarled topknot until it hung wet and heavy down his back to his waist.

When Sapusa returned, she watched as he dried himself, then handed him a short linen kilt that scarcely covered him from waist to knees. "I was right," she said, walking around him and staring. "The Kurontai Roka must be called. I have shown him five slave boys before, and none of them was beautiful enough for a gift to the Emperor. But you are what he has been searching for. If you do not regain the Emperor's favor for him, nothing will."

"The Emperor?" Arris said blankly. "What would an Emperor want with me?"

Sapusa laughed softly. "Surely you can guess. Oh, Roka will be a fool if he does not buy you. You do not have the well-fed house-cat look of most of Hareku's boys. You have a dancer's body, and the face of the god of love. You will make my fortune, boy! And Roka's, too, if he is wise." She looked intently at the lines of his face. "Only a little kohl on your eyes, I think, and a bit of red for your lips. And we'll find some brown paint to cover the tattoos on your back. They're a bit too barbaric even for the Emperor's tastes."

Arris followed her quietly from the bathhouse, inwardly frantic with sudden fear. The Emperor! He was going to be sold to a noble to be given as a present to the Emperor of Deiran. As a catamite, a boy like those on the Streets of Night in Qadasiya. To join a harem of other pretty slave boys. How could he hope to escape from such a situation? The Sapphire Palace would be heavily guarded, and the Emperor's slaves watched. If he was to gain his freedom, it would have to be now.

Sapusa seemed to read his mind. She smiled at him. "Now that I know how valuable you are, I'll take no chances with you." She called two of her burly household guards, who took Arris to a bare stone room on the first floor of the graceful, vine-covered house, where they chained him hand and foot to a massive ring set in the floor. There he waited, lost in despair, more hopeless than he had been even in the moment of first realizing he had been made a slave.

The Kurontai Roka was a nervous-looking young man, handsome in a weak way, with thin features and dark brown hair caught in a short braid at one side of his neck. He wore a bright, color-patched robe that looked ludicrous to Arris's eyes. He spoke neither the Yaighan nor the Khalifate tongue. Sapusa told Arris he had better start to learn Deirani, since no one in the Empire besides merchants or ambassadors bothered to acquire any other language.

Roka was very pleased with Arris, and paid a price for him that would have purchased all the goods in Sapusa's wagons and several ordinary slaves besides. Arris supposed he should be flattered, but he was only miserable.

He was taken through the streets of Khopei and up the hills to the Sapphire Palace riding in a palanquin with Roka, on the shoulders of huge bearers. Roka had exchanged the heavy irons Sapusa's guards had put on Arris for light, gold-toned chains that glowed against the boy's brown skin. The new chains were not as strong as the old, but they were too strong for Arris to break.

The low walls of the palace bristled with spears and pikes in the hands of legions of black-armored soldiers. Arris thought the place poorly fortified, but he knew that no enemy had ever reached Khopei in all of Deiran's history. To him, the masses of guardsmen only meant less of a chance to escape.

The palanquin was left behind at the last of twelve ornamental gates. Two faceless soldiers joined Roka to escort Arris through the inner gardens of the palace. Though Arris grew more and more frightened with each step, he could not help admiring the artistic beauty of the place. The grounds were terraced on the hillsides, sculpted into elaborate labyrinths and rock-edged pools. Flowers and shrubs grew in delicate colors and scents along the walkways. The buildings were low and graceful, with fluted roofs and carved wooden pillars. The innermost palace sprawled over the crest of the hill, but it seemed almost fragile with its filigreed window screens and arched, airy courtyards. It made the stone towers of the Ilkharani dynasty look like the uncouth work of a dour, upstart family of shepherds.

The audience chamber's outer rooms were crowded with supplicants and courtiers. It was a familiar sight, and Arris kept expecting to see the turbaned head of the Lord Areyta moving through the press. The noblemen and women here wore different robes, different perfumes, and different hairstyles than those at the Citadel, but their expressions were exactly the same. Arris could pick out the schemers and the dandies, the somber-faced advisors, the weary, out-of-favor lesser nobles who had been waiting six or more hours to see the Emperor.

The chambers were hung with polished bronze mirrors and sumptuous silken weaves. Arris looked twice each time he saw his own reflection. He was an exotic presence in this alien court. His hair was loose, falling in heavy, perfumed waves to the small of his back. His eyes were rimmed with black and his lips were reddened. A harness of supple leather molded to his bare upper torso, and a jeweled belt supported a kilt of thin gold strips that swung and chimed lightly when he walked. His loins were scarcely covered by a gold-cloth wrap. High strapped sandals bound his calves. He could recognize the beauty of his image, but he hardly knew himself.

Roka was nervous and excited, and did not respond to the shouted comments of other young courtiers as he led Arris forward to ask for admittance to the Emperor's presence.

Arris kept his eyes downcast. His face burned. He did not know the Deirani words, but their meaning was apparent.

Two armored guards listened to the Kurontai Roka, looked at Arris through the eye slits of their black helmets, and whispered together for a moment. Then they bowed and pulled open the great arched doors to the audience hall. Roka strode in quickly, pulling Arris by the thin gold chain that bound his wrists. The hall was lined with spear-bearing soldiers and decorated with soft, delicate statues and mosaics.

The Emperor reclined on a broad couch beside an empty throne, eating a late afternoon meal of fruit and bread from a tray held by a plump, crouching slave boy. Arris knelt with Roka before the dais but did not drop his eyes. He stared at the Emperor. Somehow he had thought the ruler of this ancient, tradition-bound country would be an old man. The thought had consoled him a little. What could an old man demand of him?

Hareku was a warrior in his prime, no older than forty years. His state robes were open in the heat, revealing a scantily clad, lean, muscular body from a painting of Myrdethreshi. His face was hard, lined deeply around the thin mouth and granite-colored eyes. His light brown hair was short and curled. He stretched with the grace of a predatory cat and looked at Arris with sudden interest. The boy felt his whole body flush.

The Kurontai Roka took his feet and launched into a fawning speech. Arris did not understand what he said, but he could guess. Praises of the Emperor, apologies for the temerity of offering a gift to a man who needed nothing, sly allusion to the quality and expense of such a pretty young slave, hopes of the Emperor's continued favor. Hareku was not listening. His stony eyes gazed appraisingly at Arris in admiration and in cool amusement at the boy's discomfort. After a few moments the Emperor spoke expansively, called Roka up to kiss his hand, and dismissed the pleased young nobleman. Roka left the hall without a backward glance at Arris.

Two guards hurried from their places at the wall to grasp Arris roughly and raise him up to face his new master. Arris could not control his shaking. It was unworthy of a Yaighan, unworthy of Tauena's son, but he feared this man. He feared the controlled power of the Emperor's movements, the arrogant brilliance of his gaze. He feared he would not be able to maintain his resolve to fight, his determination to resist to the last. He feared he could not retain his hatred.

Hareku rose from the couch and descended the dais steps. One callused hand cupped Arris's cheek, while the other stroked the boy's hair thoughtfully, feeling the weight of it, the mass of its perfumed waves. Arris stood very still, glaring into the gray eyes. The Emperor smiled in pleasure and anticipation. Then he called a command to his guards, and Arris knew that he was ordering them to cancel the rest of his audiences for that day.

The balcony of the Emperor's bedchamber was high above a strange, half-wild garden balanced between short, twisted trees and terraced falls of rock and water. Arris clutched the railing where he had fled at his new master's approach. He was conscious of the Emperor's slow footsteps behind him. There was nowhere else to run. He did not have the courage to throw himself from the balcony. He wished there was a god he could pray to for protection. He wished he had never renounced Aghlayeshkusa's proffered power.

A big hand fell on his bare shoulder. Arris whirled to fight, knowing that only anger would keep him from tears. He kicked and scratched, but Hareku was too strong. The older man's muscled arms pulled him close, muffling his face against the broad chest. Arris kept struggling. Hareku sighed and began to loop the golden chains around Arris's wrists and ankles until the boy could barely move. Then he picked him up like a child and carried him to the bed.

The Emperor was gentle. He spoke softly in Deirani, stroking Arris as he would a frightened animal, trying to soothe him. It was apparent that he wanted his new slave to find pleasure in his loving. But Arris was too terrified, too humiliated, and his body remained taut and unresponsive. When the Emperor finally took him there was only pain.

The Deirani loosened Arris's bonds before he rolled over to fall asleep. The boy climbed down from the bed awkwardly, bruised, quivering with helpless anger. He crept through the curtains to the balcony and sat there above the sunset beauty of the gardens for almost an hour before he finally began to cry.

•   •   •

He soon learned obedience. There was much to be feared that was worse than the Emperor's rough love. The keepers of Hareku's seraglio were brutal and efficient teachers. They forced Arris's compliance, not through punishments that might mar his beauty, but by starving him until he was too weak to resist. The Emperor would not send for him again until he was fully trained. Once Arris realized this, he determined to learn what they would teach.

The Deirani called it the Dance: the fifty-nine arts of love. There were dances for the most jaded and demanding masters, for men who liked boys, for men who liked women, and for women. Arris learned them all. It seemed he had a talent for it. He also learned the Deirani language as quickly as he could, until at the end of three months he spoke it as well as most of the slaves.

The seraglio was a complex of rooms and gardens below the central palace on the hillside, connected to the Emperor's living quarters by a series of covered walkways. It was guarded by massive, muscular keepers, and housed three separate harems: a soft, overweight, effeminate group of boys who had been trained to this service from early childhood; a collection of beautiful concubines who were sent to entertain courtiers for a night or two as bribes and rewards, but who were never summoned by their master; and Hareku's official wives, who had shared his bed on occasion until one of them had borne him a sixth child, a son and heir.

Arris learned to play the atonal Deirani lyre and was trained to use the warm tenor into which his boyish voice had settled. He exercised with the court dancers and acrobats; he would not allow himself to grow as soft and complacent as the other seraglio boys. If he lost his speed and strength, he would never be able to escape.

He spent most of his time with the female concubines. They were young and beautiful and bored, and welcomed his company. The keepers did not include the seraglio boys in the edict against men within the women's quarters. They did not fear them. Few of the boys even noticed the concubines' beauty. Arris did. He flirted with them and sang to them, and they helped to teach him the arts of love that the keepers did not know.

Arris knew that it might be some time before he had the chance to escape. He would not accept that he would spend his entire youth in the flower-decked rooms of the harem, until he outgrew Hareku's interest and was sold to some other master. However, while he was there, he resolved to gain as much power as he could. The concubines would be helpful allies. Hareku often sent them to attend his nobles, whether to please a courtier or to spy on an intriguer.

The women knew the names and desires of most of the noblemen. They speculated on which among the young court-iers would arise to Hareku's notice; they whispered of those who had fallen into disfavor, and of those who plotted treach-ery; they knew who was suspected of being in league with the Khalifate, and who was in imminent danger of exile or execution.

Theirs was not a hard life, but it was tedious. When they were not required to entertain a patron, they spent their evenings singing, gossiping, telling the ancient stories of Khopei's thousand gods. Occasionally one would become pregnant and be sent away to another part of the palace, or another timid young girl would be given as a gift to Hareku, to be briefly admired and consigned to the harem.

Biteka was one such gift. She was a shy, fawn-pretty girl no older than Arris who had been presented to the Emperor by the city overlord of Khopei, the Kurontai Peroyu. She seemed overwhelmed and frightened by the seraglio. She had not yet been summoned to any noble's bed, but that time would come. On a warm day in early fall, she came running to the garden where Arris sat practicing the lyre alone and away from the games of the women.

"What is it, little one?" he asked, seeing the confused fright on her face. She did not smile. Usually he never failed to make her smile by calling her "little one"; like most Deirani, she was more than a head taller than he.

"Oh, Arris," she whispered, "I think I hurt Tibi's feel-ings, but I couldn't say yes to her, it's a sin against the gods . . ."

"What is?" He put down his lyre and stroked her soft brown hair as she sat beside him.

She looked up, her eyes wide. "To go to bed with her. She asked me to, and I told her no, and she was hurt, I think, but what else could I say?"

Arris sighed. Many of the women comforted themselves in that way, sometimes forming lasting attachments, often falling briefly in love with the intensity of romantic poetry. What was wrong with that? They were lonely. "You might have been flattered that she cared that much about you." He looked out over the garden wall, thinking of the loving priestess couples that often formed among the Yaighan. "My people don't call it sin."

"Your people don't think anything is sinful," Biteka said. "Or else you would never be what you are."

"Now you'll hurt my feelings, little one."

"I'm sorry." She took his hand with a rueful smile. "I probably should apologize to Tibi too. I couldn't agree to what she asked, though. It's wrong. And even if I did try it some day, I shouldn't before I've been with a man."

"Isn't it time for that at least?"

She shook her head vehemently. Arris feared for her. She was a virgin; if she did not accept his offer, her maidenhood would be taken from her by the casual, unfeeling lust of one of Hareku's nobles. Arris knew how to ensure that she felt pleasure that first time. Yet she refused him again and again. He sighed. It was her own fault if she was hurt.

"Arris!" A cry came from behind him. He turned, and Biteka stiffened. Tibi was running toward them, her lush body bouncing in her sheer silks. She was only sixteen, but she was one of the most accomplished and experienced courtesans in the harem. She had four different patrons among the nobles who constantly begged the Emperor to allow them to purchase her.

"What is it?" He rose to his feet, retrieving his lyre from the ground. Biteka stood beside him, not looking at Tibi.

"The steward has come! I'm supposed to entertain that awful General Iyon." Tibi grimaced eloquently, and Arris sympathized. He had never seen the General, but the concubines all dreaded Iyon's triumphant returns to court after routing a band of marauders or leading a successful raid into the Khalifate. He was a brutal man.

"I'm sorry, sweet. Come to me in the morning and I'll help you cover your bruises."

She laughed. "You may not be here in the morning, Arris. The Emperor has summoned you! You're supposed to go let the keepers prepare you. All the boys are so jealous. It's only a week since you finished your training."

Biteka shivered. Arris stared at the lyre in his hands. He

had expected this. He had known he would be called for after he was trained. Yet it was strange. He felt a touch of his old fear, something he had thought he could not feel again after the keepers' teaching.

"Nervous?" Tibi said softly. She kissed his cheek and pulled him by the hand toward the arches of the harem. "Don't be. You're beautiful . . . and you're probably the most talented boy I've ever seen. Hareku doesn't deserve such a bed warmer. But he'll love you."

"You sound so pleased!" Biteka flared, following them. "The Emperor is an evil man. What he will make Arris do is an offense against the gods."

Tibi shrugged, looking sidelong at her. "As bad as what I asked you to do, is it?"

Biteka flushed. "I'm sorry. I can't help how I feel."

"She didn't mean to hurt you, Tibi," Arris said gently.

The courtesan nodded. "I know. And I should have realized she wasn't ready." She smiled at the younger girl. "You can remain a child for a little longer, dear. Until the steward summons you. I hope General Iyon isn't your first." She turned to Arris, her painted eyes sparkling. "I have a wager on you with Dasi."

"What did you bet her?" he asked quickly, grateful for the change of subject.

"That our Sacred Emperor will fall in love with you. You're exactly what he's looking for, little barbarian. A match for him, with strength and intelligence as well as beauty. He'll free you when you're older, of course, out of gratitude."

Arris laughed sardonically. "When the Thousand Gods appear in their shrines, and the river Vaclav runs upstream."

It was an old Deirani saying, and Biteka giggled to hear it on his lips. "The priests say the gods are already there," she said.

"But the river?" Arris met her dark eyes gravely. "I don't think so."

CHAPTER

13

ARRIS SAT CROSS-LEGGED where the keepers had placed him on the Emperor's woven-wood-and-ivory bed, plucking a thin melody from an ornate but ill-tuned lyre. Hareku would soon arrive, and the keepers wanted Arris to provide as artistic a picture as possible. His mass of black hair was piled into an elaborate coronet; wispy, perfumed strands hung about his face, and he had to fight to keep from sneezing. His face was painted and his eyelashes dyed with lampblack. Glittering, heavy earrings depended to his shoulders. He wore a brief kilt of sheer silks in layers of garish color. Instead of covering over the wing tattoos on his shoulder blades, the keepers had traced the fading lines with blue and gold paint to make them appear a new and clever decoration. Arris was not horrified by his appearance as he would have been three months before, but he was decidedly uncomfortable.

The clatter of guardsmen sounded from the corridor outside, and the door opened. Hareku stepped through it in a swirl of state robes, and soldiers bowed as they closed it behind him. Arris remembered what the keepers had told him, and began to sing. The Emperor frowned deeply and waved a hand for silence. His handsome face was cold, his gray eyes hard.

"Only another soft hothouse flower," he muttered. "Like all the others. That is not what I thought I had summoned tonight."

Arris stared at him, forgetting the protocol he had learned. "I didn't choose to be trained in the seraglio!" he said, putting down the lyre and standing up to face the Emperor. "What did you expect them to make of me? A warrior?"

138

Taken aback, Hareku seemed close to anger. Then his features shifted and he laughed. "Well said, boy. I see that you have not changed. And they told the truth when they said you could speak Deirani now. I am glad."

Arris returned the slow smile. Then he lowered his eyes in confusion. Why should he care what the Emperor thought of him? The man had hurt him, raped him. But that night seemed far distant, and he had been hurt and humiliated worse since.

Hareku touched Arris's face gently, then removed the earrings that weighted the boy's ears. "This artifice does not suit you, and it does not please me. Come. My attendants have prepared me a bath. When I am finished, we will wash the paint from your skin. And that sickly scent." He took Arris's hand and led him through a series of luxurious rooms to a small, tiled chamber that held a steaming bath. Small air shafts released moisture and steam above the gardens, and pipes led from the walls with clear-running water, hot and cold, that mingled at the far end of the small pool. Arris had never seen such an arrangement. The baths in the seraglio, like all he had known, were housed separately, and heated by slow-burning fires beneath the ground level.

He helped the Emperor remove the stiff, brocaded robes of state. The clothing was so heavy and elaborate that it stood by itself when they were done, as if there were still a man inside. Hareku sighed and stretched his freed limbs with an audible creaking.

"I hope you can loosen my muscles, boy. They're tight as a priest's purse." He lowered himself gingerly into the warm water. The pool was shallow enough for him to sit at one end.

Arris took a handful of the unscented soap that was mounded into a golden bowl beside the bath and began to work on the Emperor's shoulders. "I learned many things in your harem, Sacred One," he said. "Massage is one of the fifty-nine arts of the Dance."

"And sometimes the most pleasurable," Hareku said. "I need it tonight. I still cannot believe the arrogance of that Ilkharani ambassador. To think I would not see the way he instructed his interpreter to bend and twist the Regents' words so they would not anger me. Nievan Ilkharani does not use such mincing phrases. I know the man. He is no diplomat!

The time old Rasul sent him to me, I almost declared full-scale war with the Khalifate out of dislike."

Though he still hated the Ilkharani as much as ever, Arris tried to keep his voice neutral. "Why don't you use your own interpreter, Sacred One?" he said as he began to wash Hareku's legs. "To be certain of their words."

"No one in my court speaks Khalifate," Hareku said scornfully. "No one bothers to learn that tongue except merchants, and I would not trust a merchant to interpret for me. Too many of them are already Eastern spies."

"I speak the Khalifate language," Arris said. "It was my father's tongue, though my mother was Yaighan."

Hareku looked startled. "Why was I not told?"

"Roka didn't know." Arris shrugged. "The Kurontai Roka, I mean. And I have told no one. It didn't seem important."

"It may well be," said the Emperor. "Do you speak both languages, the Khalifate and the Yaighan?"

"Since I was a baby."

"I did wonder when I was told your name. Arris is not a usual name among the Yaighan." Hareku sighed. "I will think about this later. Not tonight." He rose out of the water, dripping. "It's your turn."

Astonished, Arris submitted as Hareku washed him with gentle hands, and carefully undid the coiled braids and twists of his piled hair. The older man had said he would follow him in the bath, but Arris had not thought the Emperor would bathe him. Hareku washed the paints from his face and began to scrub his back. Flecks of blue and gold floated off toward the deeper part of the pool. Then Hareku stopped, and Arris felt a finger trace the outlines of the feathered tattoos that fletched his shoulders.

"These won't come off," the low voice muttered. "That isn't paint."

"They were covered the first time I was brought here. The Kurontai Roka didn't think you'd like them."

"What are they? I've never heard of such decorations among the Yaighan or the Easterners."

"I was once . . . consecrated to a goddess," Arris said softly. "They are all that is left of my worship."

Hareku helped him from the bath and handed him a drying cloth. "A goddess? The Yaighan Crimson Goddess, I suppose. They say she sometimes appears as a great bird. I'm glad you no longer worship her. There are bloody legends surrounding her name.'' He chuckled. ''Yet I like your wings, boy. They are another reminder of how different you are from my other slaves.''

''It is still hard for me to think of myself as a slave,'' Arris muttered. ''I have not been one long.''

''That was obvious that night, wasn't it?'' Hareku said gravely. ''How you fought me! I still bear some of the bruises.''

''I was frightened.''

''Are you still?'' The Emperor touched Arris's face, his gray eyes thoughtful. ''So many of my boys fear me.''

Arris said slowly, ''You are the Emperor. It would be foolish not to fear you.'' He felt the first stirrings of a desire the keepers had never been able to rouse in him. ''But I must be a fool, because I'm not frightened.''

''I'm glad.'' Hareku led him back to the bedroom.

''Arris!'' Tibi rose to greet him from where she lay on the softest couch of the women's sitting room. She moved painfully. ''You're back!''

''Not for long.'' He laughed, feeling freer than he had for months. ''Not for long. The Emperor is giving me a room in the palace. A room of my own, outside the seraglio. Where I can be closer to him.'' And closer to escaping. Though he had enjoyed the past night, he would not let himself forget that he had to escape.

''How wonderful!'' She kissed him. Arris hugged her happily, then swore to himself when she gave a little cry of pain. He helped her back to the cushions.

''Did he beat you, Tibi? I'm sorry, I forgot you had to attend General Iyon last night. Have you seen the healers yet?''

''They smeared me with ointments,'' she said in distaste. ''I'll be all right, though the court won't see me for a few days.'' She looked up at him, her pretty face tired and drawn beneath its paint. ''Oh, Arris. Never attract that man's attention if you can help it. He's a brute.''

''I'm in no danger.'' Arris sat beside her, stroking her hand. ''How can the Emperor send anyone to him? He must know Iyon gets his pleasure from hurting people.''

''Oh, Hareku knows.'' Tibi smiled thinly. ''The keepers

have complained to him. Damaged slaves, the expense of
healers . . . and there have been other complaints. Peasants in
the border regions, husbands and fathers. Once Iyon had to
pay a bride-price, because he hurt a young woman so badly
she'll never have children. Even a few noble families have
complained, families whose young sons serve with his army
as squires or aides.''

''I can't believe the Emperor would let it continue.''

''You don't know our master yet, Arris. I'm sure he was
kind to you last night, or you wouldn't be so pleased with his
favor. But never forget you are a slave. You're only a body for
him to use. An object for his pleasure. If it would strengthen
his power to give you to Iyon for a night, he would do it.''

''That can't be true.''

''You'll learn.'' She sighed. ''I don't mean to frighten
you. But avoid the General, Arris. Don't catch his eye.
Promise me.''

''I'd go to him every night if it meant he'd never hurt you
again,'' he said fiercely.

Tibi brought his fingers to her lips. ''You're such a sweet
boy. I don't think you mean that, but it was wonderful to
hear.'' She sat up, wincing a little, and propped herself
against the cushions. ''If you don't have to go back to your
new room in the palace right away, could you stay here and
sing to me? We'll forget about General Iyon.''

''I would be honored.'' He bowed to her and went to find a
lyre.

Arris lay in the circle of Hareku's strong arms, exhausted by
the dance. It was the fifth night in a row that the Emperor had
summoned him. The seraglio was mad with jealousy. Hareku
asked for many of the acts the keepers had taught Arris, but
somehow it was not degrading to do them for him. He did not
ask out of a desire to humiliate or punish, but out of a
straightforward, simple need. Sometimes they truly seemed to
be lovers, equals, and nothing intruded to remind them they
were master and slave.

''No boy has ever aroused me as you do,'' Hareku whispered. ''Or satisfied me as fully. Why is that, I wonder?''

''Magic,'' Arris suggested with a sleepy chuckle. Though
of all possible reasons, it could not be that. He had none.

''I think it is your strength.'' A warm hand stroked his

shoulder. "This is what the joining of men should be. Like to like. Though I am somewhat stronger."

"I'm only thirteen years old," Arris said. "What do you expect?"

"No more than you are," the Emperor said.

Arris smiled, and settled deeper into the embrace. Biteka was wrong. This was no sin. And Hareku was not evil.

"Did you know that Roka has been asking about you?" the older man said. "I fear I've ignored him these months you were in training. He thinks his present has done him no good. I shall have to reward him, now that I know your true value. I'm going hunting next week with my daughter Kakima and a few of my court. Perhaps I should ask Roka along."

"I'm sure he'll be honored," Arris murmured.

Hareku suddenly laughed. "I'll take you as well."

"What?" The boy sat up on the bed.

"Yes. It will be a triumph. Overlord Peroyu has been bragging about some of his slaves, but there is no boy in Khopei to match you. He'll be jealous." He grinned in anticipation. "They'll all be jealous. I will have them fawning on me for months to come, setting aside their little intrigues, betraying their friends for a kiss from your lips."

"You would give me to them?" Arris said incredulously.

"Only for a night or two, to bind them closer than ever to my interests. You're a prize, boy! You don't have the softness of my seraglio slaves; you'll be attractive to both sexes. And the keepers tell me you have no aversion to women. I'll show them that I honor you, and make them think they can influence me through you. It has been a long time since I've openly had a favorite. My courtiers have almost given up trying to reach me through my slaves." He looked sharply at Arris. "Don't look so somber, boy. They'll shower you with gifts. You're talented enough to make half of them fall in love with you. I will have to work to keep your heart."

Arris yawned, rolled over, and pretended to be close to sleep. His fists clenched and unclenched beneath the bed-clothes. His heart! He would never give his heart to a man who would use him thus. He would not allow himself to forget again. He could not relax, he could not accept any of it. He had to escape.

.   .   .

The court would not be so easily won. Arris watched cautiously from where he rode at Hareku's left. He suspected that the courtiers invited on the hunt were insulted by his presence among them. Only Roka seemed pleased, and that was because the Emperor had given him a grant of land that would more than outweigh the money he had spent to purchase Arris.

General Iyon rode at the fore of the hunting party, urging on the foot-slaves who were attempting to beat game from the bushes and grasses of the royal hunting preserve. Iyon was a charming and handsome young nobleman of twenty-five years, a brilliant soldier, respected and liked by almost everyone. It was hard to imagine that he was the same man who had torn Tibi's lovely back with a whip.

Hareku seemed oblivious to the whispers and venomous glances of many of his nobles, though Arris knew he saw more than he appeared to. He laughed and talked with his favorite daughter, Kakima, and the young widowed noblewoman who chaperoned her, the Kuronta Shichal, and drank constantly from a jeweled leather flask of Deirani wine. He rode well despite the drink. Only he and Iyon of the hunting party seemed capable of handling their high-bred horses. Arris had rarely ridden before, but he was better at it than the rest of the nobles.

"Where are the animals, my lord Father?" Kakima said petulantly. "Perhaps if we beat the slaves they would search harder."

"They're doing their best, child," Hareku said genially. "Iyon has them well in hand. We may not see much game; there are many of us, and the animals are wary. Someday I will take you in my war chariot to hunt the lions of the Western plains. That is true sport."

"When?"

"Someday." Hareku reached over to touch Arris's wrist. "I'll take you as well, boy. You ride your horse easily; I imagine you could handle the reins of a chariot."

Arris smiled at him, pleased at the thought. His eyes met Kakima's as he did so, and the Princess looked quickly away. She intrigued him. She was sixteen years old. In Gama she would be married, or a priestess, or both. Here she was a child, a tiny creature of fragile, shielded beauty, whose pale skin was kept from the sunshine by a broad hat, whose hands were nervous and unsure on the reins of her gentle mount.

The Kuronta Shichal was not so demure. She stared at Arris with a predatory look on her thin, artfully painted face, and finally spoke admiringly to the Emperor. "Sacred One, where did you get him? I have never seen the like."

Hareku grinned. "The Kurontai Roka gave him to me. Is he not beautiful?"

"You are surrounded by beauty, Sacred One," said a fat man with a slick, greasy face, who had been riding nearby hoping to be noticed. "Nothing else would be fitting."

"I am surrounded by fools," Hareku muttered. Kakima giggled softly as the Emperor turned around to face the speaker. "Admit that I have beaten you, Overlord Peroyu. No boy of your collection can approach my new slave's beauty."

"He has a certain rough grace," the Khopei lord said dismissively. "When you tire of him, give me the chance to purchase him, Sacred One. He wants the refining touch of paints and perfumes. And that mane of hair is really an extravagance. I would certainly never put him on horseback. He does not ride like a slave. His arrogance is unbecoming."

"Did you hear that, Arris?" the Emperor said thoughtfully. "You are arrogant." He reached over and slapped Arris across the cheek, hard. The boy blinked in surprise and anger, and the Kuronta Shichal gasped. "There. The slave has been punished. Are you satisfied, Peroyu?" His voice took on a dangerous undertone. "Do not presume again to question my taste."

"Of . . . of course not, Sacred One," the noble muttered, as if he had been the one who was struck. He bowed over his horse, and Arris saw a flash of hatred in his eyes. "I think I will ride ahead and question the General on the progress of the hunt."

"Do so." Hareku laughed as the man nearly lost his seat in kicking his mount to a ragged lope.

"That man disgusts me," said Shichal with a refined shudder. "One would think he could learn to behave in polite company."

Arris gazed at his horse's withers. His cheeks flamed. Hareku had no reason to hit him, beyond mocking the annoying courtier. Tibi was right. He was only an object to the

Emperor, a thing to be used for whatever purpose suited his master's pleasure.

"Never marry me to anyone like him," Kakima said.

"You need not worry, daughter. He is a fool. Though he does have an eye for beauty. He presented me with the most exquisite slave only last month, a girl named Biteka. I may send her to Roka as part of his reward for giving me Arris." He smiled down at the boy, then frowned. "Did I hurt you badly? I didn't mean to bruise you." He touched Arris's cheek gently. "Don't be angry, little hawk."

Arris felt his hurt fall once again into confusion. Hareku had begun to call him by the pet name because of the wings on his shoulders. He smiled halfheartedly. The Emperor looked relieved, and turned back to Kakima.

"You're too young to think of marriage, girl."

"I'm sixteen years old, my lord Father," she said softly. "If you wait much longer to decide who I'm to marry, no one will want me."

"You are my daughter. It would not matter if you had the complexion of a sow. Everyone would want you."

"Father!" she protested.

"But you are beautiful, and so many worthy courtiers beg me for your hand; how can I choose?" He grinned. "Here comes one of them now. No doubt Peroyu drove him from the front."

General Iyon reined his mount gracefully before the Emperor. Arris did not like to think of the soldier married to the fragile Princess. Yet Kakima blushed and smiled at the General, and Arris could understand the attraction she must feel. Iyon was lean and handsome, and addressed her father with the manner of a respectful equal, not with the fawning attitude of the other courtiers. If Kakima had never heard the black rumors that surrounded his name, she might well think him the perfect husband.

"My Emperor, there is no chance of finding game in these hills today," Iyon said soberly. "Poachers have been at work again. We found the heads and antlers of two deer, and their offal, lying just ahead."

"Oh, how horrid," Kakima said faintly.

"Forgive me, my lady," said the young General. "I did not mean to upset you."

"Poachers?" Hareku scowled. "I thought we had discouraged them sufficiently last winter."

"Apparently not, my lord."

"They can't have killed every beast in my preserve."

"No, lord, but the other game will have been frightened back into the plains. We won't encounter any today."

"I suppose we'll have to turn back," the Kuronta Shichal said brightly. The delicate noblewoman had seemed uncomfortable in her saddle all morning.

"I was finding it all quite tedious," Kakima said with an attempt at Shichal's voice of cool sophistication.

"The Princess is weary," Iyon said gallantly. "Then we must turn back."

"General, I shall expect the same demonstration as before," Hareku said grimly. "Execute all suspected poachers in the central market of Khopei, before the temple of the Just God Chiou-Ro."

Arris wondered what a god of justice would think of such an action. Few of the suspects would actually be guilty.

"And the families, my lord?" Iyon said. "Last year's executions were obviously ineffective."

"As you will. Try to have it finished within a week. I shall be most grateful. I'll have to think of yet another way to reward you, my friend."

Iyon smiled. "I have already thought of what to ask for."

Arris grew cold as the dark, pleasant eyes turned on him.

CHAPTER

14

"OH. STOP IT. Arris," said Kakima at last as she leaned over the balcony of her chambers above the Water Gardens.

Arris stilled the strings of his lyre. He had been playing a complex piece that seemed to intertwine with the soft music of the fountains and pools below. In the three years he had been at the Sapphire Palace, he had taken advantage of the teaching of the many itinerant musicians that came and went in Hareku's court. He was now a competent, if uninspired, lyrist, and none of his patrons ever complained of his singing voice. Hareku encouraged him to develop as many of the arts as he could to add to the boyish beauty he still retained at sixteen.

"I'm sorry that didn't please you, Princess. Perhaps a livelier tune, or a song?"

"No. I'm tired of everything. I'm bored, Arris. Nothing you can do will amuse me today."

"Nothing at all, mistress?" He put down the lyre and rose to kiss her on the cheek.

She stroked his hair absently. "Even your beauty is tiresome. Because I can't have it. Father sends you to dance with everyone in the palace but me. I'll probably have an ugly husband, too, unless he marries me to General Iyon." She sighed.

"Better a toothless leper than Iyon," Arris said grimly.

"I know you don't like him. But he's always wonderful to me. And he must like you, Arris. He asks for you every time he gains Father's favor. Kuronta Shichal says the only reason he hurts you is that you won't do what he wants."

"What he wants, my lady, is to hurt me."

"And anyway," Kaxima said airily, "you're only a slave. I'd be his wife."

"Are you talking of marriage again, my flower?" The deep voice of the Emperor clashed with the peaceful fall of fountains. Arris turned and knelt, hoping Hareku had not overheard his words about Iyon. The Princess bowed. "I've told you why we must wait. We'll soon be at war."

"And everyone will die, and I'll never be married. I'm already nineteen years old. It's probably too late."

"Foolish girl," Hareku said affectionately, kissing her lightly and motioning Arris to rise. "Where is Shichal?"

"I sent her to find me some purple flowers to wear with my gown tonight, at the party Peroyu is giving for the ambassador. There will be Khalifate musicians there, did you know?"

"Yes, the ambassador brought them in his retinue. Peroyu

claims they are very talented." Hareku shrugged. "We will see."

"They will probably be no better than Arris, and his music bores me so. Doesn't it tire you too, my lord Father?"

Hareku chuckled and took Arris's hand to lead him from the room. "His music never interested me nearly as much as his dancing."

Kakima giggled at the indelicacy. Usually the Emperor was careful of his language when she was near. "How would I know that? You never let him dance with me."

"Enough," Hareku admonished, frowning at her until he had closed the corridor door. Then he smiled at Arris. "Come. We must meet with the Khalifate ambassador before this evening's festivities. I will expect an exact translation of his words, but make my replies as politely insulting as possible, will you?"

Arris nodded, half running to match the Emperor's long strides. "What is he here for, my lord?"

"A demand of reparations for the latest of Iyon's border raids." Hareku paused as a train of slaves bearing sweetmeat baskets split in confusion to allow him through. "A paltry raid. Peroyu is spending more on tonight's party than Iyon's troops captured from the Khalifate."

Arris slowed his pace, thinking of the night to come. "Do you still want me to attend the Kurontai Gasu, my lord?" he said in a small voice. "To thank him for his gift of horses?"

"I commanded you to attend Gasu."

"I know . . . but we have not been together for more than a week, my lord. I begin to think you are as bored with me as Kakima is."

"Has it been so long?" The Emperor's features softened. "I didn't realize. If it is so important to you, my hawk, then come to me tonight. Another reward will suit Gasu as well." Hareku turned his face upward with a callused hand and kissed him gently. "I should never send you from my bed. Yet I continue to do so, whenever a courtier presents me with a new robe or a traitor's head. Do you hate me for it?"

"I could never hate you."

"Yet you still do not love me," said the Emperor sadly.

Arris did not answer.

* * *

"I would do anything to escape from here," Biteka said fiercely, peering through the lattice of the alcove into the wine-flushed riot of the party for the Khalifate ambassador. "Wouldn't you, Arris?"

"Of course," he said absently, adjusting a lace streamer that hung from the girl's scant costume. Biteka and other young concubines were to dance for the court; Kurontai Peroyu had promised that the girls would be presented to the nobles who showed the most enthusiasm over their performances. Arris smiled thinly. The Khopei city overlord would gain a few new followers tonight, but their allegiance might not last beyond morning.

"How could you do this to me, little barbarian?" hissed a soft voice at his ear. A hand clenched in his unbound hair and pulled him around. Tibi's pretty face glared inches from his own.

"Do what, sweet?" he managed to say, holding very still. His scalp burned. If she twisted her hand, he would lose some hair.

"Convince your beloved Emperor to take you for himself tonight instead of sending you to Gasu!"

"Convince the Emperor? I have no influence over his whims. Why should it upset you that I don't have to attend Gasu? He's old and sick and smells of stables."

"I will have to bathe all morning to rid myself of him." She released him, scowling. Arris rubbed his head. "The steward told me I'm to take your place."

"A good choice. You're almost as pretty as I am, if a bit heavier. Gasu won't be too disappointed." He ducked under her raised arm and kissed her. The dancing girls laughed. "I'm sorry, Tibi. I really didn't have anything to do with it."

"Of course not," she said sardonically.

"Dancers!" The Kurontai Peroyu shoved his massive body into the crowded alcove. "It is time. Entertain them well, and you'll be rewarded." He noticed Arris. "Oh, there you are, boy. The Emperor is looking for you. Where have you been? He needs a translator to speak with the Khalifate ambassador."

"I thought Shichal was taking care of that." She had probably forgotten. The flighty noblewoman had a genuine talent for learning, but half their lessons ended in lovemaking anyway.

Biteka stopped Arris with a hand on his shoulder. "Will you be attending the Emperor tonight?" she whispered.

"Yes."

"All night?"

"Of course."

"Remember what you said. That you would do anything to escape." She joined the snaking line of dancers as cheers and calls rose from the audience hall. The noblemen were vying for the rewards Peroyu promised, while unattached noblewomen like Shichal urged them on in great amusement. Arris was left with Tibi in the alcove, wondering what Biteka had meant by her words.

"My lord?" Arris said softly as he approached the throne. The Emperor was finishing a bowl of sweetmeats, looking tired and bored. Kakima sat beside him on a padded stool, radiant in a white gown decorated with fresh purple flowers. One of her ladies-in-waiting stood discreetly behind her, a vaguely pretty girl near Kakima's age who was usually eclipsed by Shichal. Arris could not remember her name. The Khalifate ambassador, a thin, balding man who had taken off his turban in the heat, sat uncomfortably on the dais steps.

"Arris," Hareku said tightly, "the ambassador has been trying to tell me something for half an hour now, while you gossiped with my concubines."

A roar went up from the hall as the first girl was awarded. Arris decided against mentioning Shichal. "I'm sorry, Sacred One. Some of the costumes Peroyu gave them were ready to fall apart."

"That was no doubt his intention. I lent the girls to him for the night, and told him to do what he wanted with them. Gods know I have no use for them."

"My lord."

Hareku relented. He smiled slightly and indicated the nervous envoy. "Now will you see what he has to say?"

The Khalifate ambassador was ill and wished to be excused from the festivities, though he understood they were in his honor. Arris repeated the man's message.

"I quite understand," the Emperor said. "I wish I could escape as readily. Tell him he may go, Arris, and wish him a restful sleep."

The ambassador hurried away. The dance was over, Arris

saw. With a touch of humor, Peroyu had awarded one of the concubines to the Kuronta Shichal, who was amusing herself and a circle of courtiers by soliciting advice on what she should do with the girl that night. Peroyu had also rewarded himself for his own enthusiasm. Biteka clung to the overlord's arm, cool and decorative. Arris recalled that Peroyu had originally presented Biteka to the Emperor. Perhaps that explained his uncharacteristic interest in a woman.

"Sacred One!" called Peroyu. "The musicians are ready to perform for you now. They await you in the garden."

"Tell them to begin," Hareku said. "I'll join you presently."

Peroyu bowed and turned with Biteka at his side to lead the revelers into the torchlit garden. A cool night breeze drifted into the audience hall as the doors were opened. It smelled of flowers.

General Iyon strode through the crowd in the opposite direction and saluted the Emperor's dais. He wore severely cut black silk, which set off his dark hair and eyes and accentuated the grace of his slim figure. A sheathed sword hung at his side. Its hilt was set with colorless jewels that caught the lamplight.

"May I have the honor of escorting the Princess to the gardens?" he asked softly.

Hareku waved his hand, seeing his daughter's quick, involuntary smile. "Go on." Kakima took the General's hand and walked down the steps, followed by her lady-in-waiting.

The hall was almost empty now. A few older couples talked quietly at the cannibalized tables as discreet slaves began to take away the remains of the feast. The Emperor's sigh was loud in the silence.

"It galls me," he muttered, "that Peroyu takes such pains to impress our enemies. And that I sit quietly and pretend to enjoy his antics."

"You don't want the Khalifate to know you're planning war," Arris said with a shrug. "You have to be civil to their envoys."

"At least I don't have to play the host," Hareku said. "Come. We must put in an appearance at the musicians' performance. But then to bed, following the example of our worthy enemy."

"He will sleep alone, my lord," Arris pointed out.

"He should have applauded more loudly. Perhaps Peroyu would have given him a girl."

The music that rose from the far end of the gardens was occluded by the hum of drunken chatter, and interrupted by fits of applause, yet Arris strained to hear it. A strange arrangement. The leading voice was taken by a cascade of brilliant notes that had to come from a two-necked lute played by an expert. The lute was accompanied by soft female voices singing in a low register, and a deep range of bass chords plucked from some stringed instrument. The effect was unusual. Arris had never heard anything like it.

"They are talented," Hareku said, walking through the crowd with his arm around Arris's waist. "I did not expect them to be. I'll have them play for us privately before they leave. Would you like that, hawk?"

Arris did not respond. It was Senna's family. Their muted red costumes were torchlit from behind, and fire shadows played on their blond hair. What were they doing here? How could the gods allow such a cruel trick? Arris wanted to melt back into the mass of Deirani, but Hareku walked forward and the musicians' eyes were drawn to him.

They had changed. Senna was older and heavier, crouched over the bass instrument. Van was a soberly handsome young man whose hands were sure on the two-necked lute. Vaessa was lovely, slim and tall. She would be twenty. Danae's face was thin and mobile, too animated to achieve the repose of true beauty. Her figure was boyish, scarcely curved. Yet Arris was mesmerized by the way she swayed to the music, singing without words, delighting in her audience.

Danae smiled at him, aware of his gaze. She did not recognize him. How could she? He was not the short-haired, Goddess-gifted boy she had known. He was the favored catamite of Deiran's Sacred Emperor, a graceful, exotic creature whose magic had faded with the dyes in his wing tattoos.

Hareku led the applause when the piece was finished. The musicians smiled at one another and bowed deeply. They prepared to begin again, but the Emperor held up his hand for silence. "Tell them it was beautiful," he said to Arris. "Tell them I would like to hear them tomorrow."

Arris stepped forward to relay the Emperor's words. Senna grinned. "We would be honored to play for the Sacred Emperor."

"Good. A messenger will be sent to you in the morning." Arris could not maintain the formality of a translator. "That was marvelous. I play the lyre a little, but I've never heard music like that before. Where did it come from? A composer of the Ilkharani court?" He saw Danae's blush, and her shy, embarrassed smile. "You wrote it?"

"My daughter is quite talented," Senna said proudly. "His Royal Highness Saresha Ilkharani has shown her special favor, and we hope he will grant her his patronage when we return to Qadasiya."

"Papa," the young woman said softly, exasperated.

"Your music is lovely." Arris bowed to her. "And so is its composer." He smiled into her bright green eyes and turned to follow the Emperor from the gardens.

"I saw your eyes on that Khalifate girl," Hareku teased. He lay prone across the bed, beginning to relax as Arris's sure hands kneaded the day's tension from his muscles. "Would you rather have spent the night with her?"

"Of course not." Though Danae was fascinating, it would be best for him to avoid her. He wondered why they had come to Deiran. Senna was a friend of Terai's. Had the Yaighan traced him at last, and sent the musicians to find him and bring him back to face Onira's murder? Yet they had not recognized him.

"I'm glad I didn't send you to Gasu."

"Tibi will serve him well. Though she was angry with me."

"Tibi?" Hareku rolled languidly to his back.

"The concubine who is with Gasu in my place. Don't you remember?"

"I scarcely remember half their names," the Emperor admitted, pulling Arris down beside him. "I told the steward to send Gasu a pretty girl with experience, not one of the youngest."

Arris nodded. "Tibi. She's nineteen."

"Kakima's age." Hareku was briefly startled. "Well, she should please him. But she won't be as useful as you, Arris. My courtiers think they can influence me through you. They don't realize that you are my ears, and that you only tell them what I want them to know."

"I've never tried to influence you. I wonder if I could."

"Probably. I can't refuse you, little hawk." He smiled. "How shall we begin tonight? Which Dance would please you most?"

"You once challenged me to go through the fifty-nine arts backwards," Arris laughed.

"Merciful gods! That took us weeks."

"Then let me show you the forty-second Dance, my lord. It begins thus . . ."

Arris struggled to wake from a dream of vulture's wings, cold, decayed, clutching him to draw him back into a gaping mouth. His eyes fluttered open, saw a beautiful and terrifying woman's face, and shut again. After a moment he woke, and sighed with relief at the familiar sight of the hangings above Hareku's bed. An echo remained, a rasping voice from his dreams, a voice he would not name. *Choose*, it hissed. *Freedom or love.*

Arris shook his head to clear it. His naked body was filmed with sweat, though the curtains of the balcony billowed gently in a cool breeze. The doors must have swung open in the night. He could hear the distant play of the fountains in the Water Gardens, and the high, piercing laughter of a woman with the last remaining revelers of the night's party. He glanced to one side. The Emperor lay curled on top of his bedclothes, sleeping deeply, the lines of tension and weariness smoothed on his stern brow. He looked younger in his sleep, Arris thought. Less burdened. He looked like the man he might have been if he had not been Emperor.

The night air was chill. A floorboard creaked out on the balcony. The day had been high summer, and the change in temperature was sharp. Arris sat up quietly, careful not to disturb his sleeping lover. He swung his legs over the edge of the bed and gingerly eased his weight onto his feet. Hareku did not stir. Arris looked down at him and smiled, then walked across the layered rugs to close the balcony doors.

It was the darkest time of early morning, and the torches had gone out in the gardens. Arris began to pull the doors inward, then stopped. There should have been a light from below. He should be hearing the even footfalls of the sentry stationed under the Emperor's chambers. The jingle of chain mail, the rustling of leather on leather. Arris crossed to the railing and bent to look out over the rocky gardens.

A strong arm gripped around his chest, and a cold steel blade brushed gently at the side of his neck. Arris did not move. He could see the sentry lying like a broken doll, his head at a strange angle, his sword still sheathed. His heart beat faster, yet it all seemed part of his dream.

"Make no sound," a familiar voice hissed in his ear.

"Biteka?" He tried to turn his head. The blade drew a shallow cut on his throat.

"Remember what you said. You would do anything to escape," the girl whispered, in a tone he had never heard from her before. "Say nothing and do not hinder me, and I'll take you with me when I'm done. There are two horses waiting at the nearest gate, and guards have been bribed along our path."

"What?" he said stupidly.

"Freedom, little fool. Freedom, or death."

That had not been the choice offered by the vulture in his dream. But Arris relaxed in Biteka's grip, and she lowered the sword. He turned. Her long brown hair was bound up in a black hood, and her face was stained dark. She wore loose-fitting black trousers and a tunic, soft slippers and gloves. Even her short sword was lacquered a dull black. Her eyes glittered dangerously.

"I don't understand," he murmured, staring.

"I'm a Jai-Sohn. A follower of the Shadowed Way."

Jai-Sohn. It meant black sword, which was apt enough. Arris trailed her past the blowing curtains into his master's bedchamber. Hareku shivered a little in his sleep. But he knew he had nothing to fear in the Sapphire Palace, with sentries stationed in corridors and below balconies, with his trusted slave at his side. Biteka moved toward the bed with a sliding, sideways dance like a snake about to strike.

Arris would be free. It would be the end of three years of longing, of plotting and scheming, of waiting for the moment. The moment had come. He would turn away now; he did not think he could watch the black sword bite into Hareku's sleeping body. He did not think he could bear to see that stern warrior's face locked in pain and the effort to wake, an effort that would be useless.

Biteka was almost upon the Emperor. Her teeth bared like a stalking cat's, she raised the dark weapon. Horror rose in Arris as he realized he did not want this. He sprang, screaming for the guard. He saw Hareku's eyes open with instant comprehension as he slammed into the girl's black-clad side and knocked her away from the bed. The sword caught a tasseled hanging and brought it down on top of them.

"Guards!" the Emperor shouted. "Guards! Murder!"

Arris had thought he had forgotten Terai's teachings. But his body moved without thought, blocking Biteka's holds and kicks, grasping her wrists to keep her fingers from his eyes. She fought silently, with a speed and strength Arris would never have guessed she had. The fallen bed-hanging shifted beneath their feet, throwing Arris off balance. He fell. Biteka launched herself on top of him, her sword free.

The door to the Emperor's suite crashed open, and Arris heard the pounding of booted feet. He rolled under Biteka's thrust and sprang into the air in a movement he had been taught by court acrobats. He landed hard on Biteka's back and knocked her forward. She was suddenly still as Arris came to his feet beside her.

He gulped. Biteka crouched unmoving, impaled on her own black sword. Its tip peered from her back, and dark blood welled slowly from her chest. She looked at him dimly, not understanding.

Hareku faced her, flanked by black-armored guards. "Who sent you to kill me?" he demanded. "Who? Was it the Khalifate envoy? You're a Jai-Sohn. Who hired you?"

The girl stared at him. Then her muscles gave way, and she fell to the floor, unseeing. Her blood began to pool on the patterned rugs.

Arris brushed back long hair that had fallen in front of his face, and met the Emperor's granite eyes over the body of the dead assassin. Freedom or love, the Lossiran had said. He had made his choice.

CHAPTER
15

"WHO COULD HAVE sent her?" Hareku said, watching as his guards wrapped Biteka's body in a bloodstained rug to carry her from his chambers. "A Jai-Sohn . . . they were taking no chances."

Arris opened a cabinet and pulled out dark silken robes for his master. He laid them on the bed, keeping his gaze from the girl's still, pretty face. "She was with Kurontai Peroyu at the party," he said slowly. "It might have been him. He gave her to you three years ago."

"I don't remember." The Emperor's hands were shaking.

"She was one of your concubines. Her name was Biteka."

Hareku scowled as he began to don the simple robes. "It must have been Peroyu, then. It takes years to create a Jai-Sohn. He must have known what she was when he presented her." He turned to the nearest black-armored soldier. "Guard! Find General Iyon. Tell him to meet me in the interrogation rooms. Arrest Kurontai Peroyu and the Khalifate ambassador and bring them to me there. And double the guard on my son's chamber, above and below."

"Yes, Sacred One." The soldier hurried from the room, followed more slowly by his fellows carrying Biteka's body. The door shut behind them.

"Surely they wouldn't try to attack your son, my lord. Ekani is only six years old," Arris said, refastening the gaudy kilt he had worn to the party.

"If Peroyu intended to gain the throne, my son's age would not concern him." The Emperor moved forward and lay one big hand on Arris's right shoulder. "You saved my life, little hawk. It was well done. You used some of her own

158

tricks against her. Where did you learn them? If I had known you were half a Jai-Sohn yourself, I would not have slept so easy."

"She offered me my freedom if I would help her," Arris said almost to himself. "She said there were horses waiting, and guards bribed along the path."

"Guards bribed? We will deal with them," the Emperor said grimly. Then he cupped Arris's chin, and brought the boy's face up to meet his gray eyes. "Yet you chose to remain my slave. To risk your own life for mine. Why?"

"I . . . I could not watch you die, my lord."

The older man embraced him with crushing strength. "Perhaps you do love me a little. I will reward you. Your freedom? You will have it."

"My lord?" Arris said in a muffled voice against the Emperor's chest.

"Not tonight, though." Hareku held him out at arm's length, smiling. "I will not give you up so easily. But you won't be a boy much longer. Two more years? Yes. The day you are eighteen years old you will be freed."

Unbidden tears sprang to Arris's eyes, and when he spoke his voice was gruff. "The river Vaclav flows uphill," he whispered.

"What?"

"Thank you, my lord." He laughed softly.

"Though I may still have a use for you when you are a free man."

"I have nowhere else to go," Arris said.

Hareku nodded. "With your command of the Khalifate language, and with the skills I saw in you tonight, you could serve me well. Properly trained, you could be a weapon to strike at the heart of my enemies." He spoke thoughtfully. "You killed a few moments ago. You don't seem upset by it."

"She deserved death." Onira's moonlit face rose in the boy's memory. "I once killed someone who should never have died."

"But you are not afraid to kill if you have a reason. That is the first step along the Shadowed Way. A Jai-Sohn does not usually fail, Arris. A trusted, well-trained Black Sword can be a decisive piece in the game of war." He gripped Arris's shoulder. "You could be a bolt aimed at the Ilkharani. What do you think?"

An old, mossy stone seemed to move in Arris's mind. From underneath it tumbled half-forgotten fear and hatred, betrayal, avowals of vengeance. The memory of Areyta's ghost haunted him. Something the daimon had once said . . . if he could not release Areyta from the Wheel, he could at least make his imprisonment easier to bear. Startled at the intensity of his feeling, Arris looked up at his master. "Yes," he whispered. "I would like to learn the Shadowed Way."

Arris was ill and exhausted by the time Iyon and Hareku finished questioning the Khalifate ambassador. The man had begged for death in the end. Arris had dutifully translated his pleas and his final confession, then watched with undisguised relief as Iyon ended the pitiful creature's life.

The Emperor's voice was harsh and tight with weariness. "There can be no question this was a plot by the Ilkharani."

"I agree, my lord," said Iyon, wiping his long knife clean on a white cloth proffered by a pale slave. "Though Peroyu spoke only of his own ambition for the throne. He was a stubborn man, loyal to the end to his Ilkharani masters."

Arris followed the two men out into the dawn light of the pleasure gardens. The bodies of a hundred men swayed from the delicate trees: every Deirani sentry who had been on duty along the path by which Biteka had meant to escape, and the Khalifate ambassador's retinue. Few of those killed could have been guilty of complicity in the assassination attempt. Another sacrifice to the Just God, Arris supposed. His master could be a bloody and frightening man when he was angered.

"Do you still want the bodies of Peroyu and the ambassador drawn and quartered and impaled on the Khopei city gate?" Iyon asked.

"Yes," Hareku said. "They will provide a fitting triumphal arch for Kurontai Roka to pass underneath when he enters the city as its new overlord."

"I am sure Khopei's new lord will be less ambitious than its old," Iyon said dryly. "Roka is not a stupid man."

"My lord . . ." Arris ventured at last, "have you decided yet about the musicians?"

"I won't kill them, since the prospect seems to upset

you," the Emperor said. "I admit they performed well last night."

"Entertainers are often spies," Iyon said.

"I have need of a messenger to tell the Khalifate what has happened here. I have decided to send the elder musician. I'll keep his children here to ensure he returns with my enemies' answer."

"They haven't done anything wrong!" Arris protested. "My lord, I beg you, don't keep them prisoners."

"I will keep them in honor, as benefits performers under the patronage of an Emperor." Hareku walked faster. "Come. You will write my proclamation for the Ilkharani in their barbaric language. Then you may inform your musicians of my decision."

"Lord, you should reconsider," Iyon said. "If you are to be properly feared—"

"Do you question my orders?" The older warrior turned. "Perhaps you think you could rule better in my place? Do not try my patience, Iyon. There is room for another blossom in this perfumed garden."

"Sacred One, forgive me," the General said quickly, paling. "I meant no disrespect. As a soldier, I urge that the enemy be given no quarter. But the divine grace of my lord tempers slaughter into justice."

"Well said." Hareku chuckled. "I am weary this morning, Iyon. You are the last man I would suspect of treason. I am sorry."

The General bowed, relieved. Arris shivered. If the Emperor had been more angry he could have commanded Iyon be killed, and no one would have protested. Sometimes Arris thought he did not know the man whose bed he shared.

The musicians greeted Arris's words with stunned silence. They had been alone in their tiny ground-floor room all morning, and had had no way of interpreting the screams they had heard. Vaessa and her brother Van sat together on a threadbare couch near the small window, staring at Arris with open hostility. Danae stood with her father, whose expression was bemused and weary.

"How can we trust your Emperor to treat us with honor," Senna finally asked, "after he has killed everyone who came with poor Lord Reyse, from squires to groomsmen? He has broken every law of diplomacy.''

"Your ambassador plotted to kill him," Arris said. "That is not the work of a diplomat." He handed a rolled parchment to the minstrel. "This is the message you are to take."

Danae scowled. "How do we know this isn't a trick, to kill our father in some lonely place?"

"The Emperor gave me his word none of you will be harmed."

"Gave you his word?" Van said contemptuously. "You? A harem slave?"

"And what good is the word of a tyrant?" Vaessa demanded.

Senna coughed delicately. "We are the Emperor's guests," he warned. He turned back to Arris. "I suspect I have you to thank that my children and I aren't hanging in the palace gardens this morning. Your Emperor would never have thought to spare us unless someone spoke on our behalf."

Senna was a perceptive man. Arris smiled slightly, and bowed toward Danae. "Your daughter's music would be a great loss, sir, as would her beauty."

"You're very good at flattery," Danae said, regarding him with suspicion. "I suppose it must serve you well here."

"What does the message say, Papa?" Van asked. "Does it seem authentic?"

Senna spread out the parchment and read it carefully. "Aye. Though written in a lad's hand, these are the words of an angry king. He accuses the Regents of trying to kill him, and demands an apology and reparations. He threatens war if his demands aren't met."

"Arrogant bastard," Van said.

A sentry shouted through the door. Arris called back an answer in Deirani, then turned to Senna. "Your horse is ready, sir. You'll be given a military escort to the border."

"Don't go, Papa," Vaessa cried. "Don't leave us here in this horrible place!"

Danae shot her a withering glance. "'If he doesn't go, we'll all be killed." She stood on her toes to kiss her father on the cheek. "Go quickly, and come back as soon as you can. We'll be all right."

"Of course you will." Senna's voice was uncharacteristically hoarse. He kissed his daughters and embraced his sullen son. "Don't worry about me. The Emperor will keep his word." He straightened his tunic over his massive stomach and hurried to the door to join the waiting soldiers.

"I'll show you to your new quarters," Arris said after a moment. "If you'll follow me . . ."

"To a prison cell!" Vaessa said in alarm. "I won't go!"

"You'll have a pleasant suite near the Water Gardens," Arris said impatiently. "I'll send slaves down later to bring up your instruments and baggage. Come."

"We won't leave our things," Van growled. "Who knows what might happen to them?"

"I'll go with him," Danae said, trying to keep her voice light. "I want to see our rooms."

"Don't be foolish," Vaessa said. "We should stay together. It's dangerous."

"She'll be in no danger from him." Van laughed. "Go on, little sister. Amuse yourself."

Danae seemed determined not to think of the morning's events. She conversed easily as she walked, admiring wall hangings, exclaiming over mosaics, marveling at the gowns of courtiers she passed in the halls. "At first when we came here," she said, "all I saw was strangeness. Now I see that part of your people's strangeness is that you try to make everything beautiful. It is as if every one of you was an artist."

"I'm not Deirani," Arris said. "But you're right. They like to surround themselves in beauty."

"They even dress up their slaves like painted peacocks," she said. "Forgive my curiosity, but Van was right, wasn't he, when he said you were part of the Emperor's harem?"

Arris nodded. "I'm Hareku's favorite, my lady."

"The priests of the Brothers Ylla say that's a sin."

"It's common enough even in the Khalifate," Arris said, remembering the indiscriminate bravo Taifid.

"My people don't keep harems of boys!"

"Perhaps not. But a slave can expect much the same treatment wherever he is." He was glad he had not followed his momentary impulse to tell her who he was.

She looked at him narrowly. Her bright green eyes were at the same level as his own. "You seemed to enjoy it last night. Parading around on the arm of your bloody master. Was there really an attempt on his life, or was that just an excuse to kill everyone in sight?"

"The assassin almost succeeded, my lady."

"Even if that's true, Lord Reyse didn't send him!" she said. "Why did your Emperor have to kill everyone, and send my father away, and make us stay here . . . ?" She was suddenly close to tears. "I never wanted to come to this horrible place. I . . . I hate to travel . . ."

Arris stopped walking, hovering uncomfortably near her but not daring to try to soothe her. It was obvious what she thought of him. Even if she had recognized him, Danae would have despised the creature he had become.

"The Emperor promised you'd be well treated," he said. "And when your father returns, I'm sure you'll be released. Don't cry, my lady."

"Stop calling me that!" she said with a laugh that was half a sob. "My name is Danae, and I am no one's lady."

"Forgive me." He smiled. "Danae."

She dashed a hand across her eyes and began walking again determinedly. "I should be apologizing to you," she said. "I'm . . . behaving badly, I know. None of this is your fault. And you've been kind to us. If Papa is right, you saved our lives. I am grateful, truly." She reached out to touch his hand with a rueful smile. "What is your name? I didn't even think to ask."

"I am sometimes called Tchoran," he said. His hand tingled. It was discourteous, but he could not stop staring at her eyes. They sparkled with the tears she still fought to suppress.

Danae repeated the name until she had the correct pronunciation. "I like it. Tchoran. What does it mean?"

"Little hawk. They call me that for my wings." He turned as he walked to show her his tattoos.

"How beautiful." Her voice was subdued. "I think . . . I think I once heard someone describe such designs to me. I can't remember. It was important once."

"A pretty tableau!" applauded General Iyon, stepping from a shadowed alcove. Arris stiffened and bowed to the soldier, not meeting the amused black eyes. Danae curtsied, staring at Iyon. She probably thought him very handsome. "I can see why you begged Hareku to spare the poor musicians' lives," Iyon said. "Though I would have chosen the prettier daughter."

"I'm only showing her to her family's new apartments," Arris said, grateful that Danae could not understand Deirani.

"A dutiful slave, as always." Iyon smiled at him. "And as such, it will please you to hear that the Emperor has commanded you to attend me tomorrow morning. In the Wild Gardens, where there is no chance we'll be observed."

Arris stared in disbelief. How could Hareku do this to him the day after he had saved his life? And what had Iyon done to be rewarded beyond wringing questionable confessions from Peroyu and the Khalifate ambassador?

"Don't look so devastated, boy," Iyon said after a moment of savoring Arris's reaction. "I'm not going to touch you. Hareku expects me to control my appetites if I'm to marry his daughter. No, this is quite different from our usual play. Hareku wants me to try to teach you the Shadowed Way of the Jai-Sohn."

"You?"

"I've trained many Black Swords. All with more promise than you show. But I can't refuse the Emperor's whims."

"You'll find me more talented than you think," Arris said coolly.

Iyon snorted. "I think you are no more than a pretty slave with a talent for the Dance. You were able to kill a Jai-Sohn last night only because sweet little Biteka had neglected her training while she was pretending to be a harem slave."

"I'll learn whatever you can teach," Arris said.

"We'll see. I fear our noble Emperor is insane in this. I've told him I won't teach you anything if I find you hopeless. Which I fully expect, young Arris." He turned and strode in the other direction.

"Arris," Danae breathed. "I couldn't understand what he said, but he called you Arris. Of course. Terai told us of your wings three years ago when he came looking for you." Arris turned to stare at her. "Why didn't I see it? You're obviously Yaighan, even under all that paint and perfume. So that was why you kept the Emperor from killing us."

Perhaps he should have allowed Hareku to go ahead. He had been a fool to think he could carry off this deception. But he had never thought she would listen closely enough to the Deirani language to pick out his name from among so many alien words. His wings . . . of course Terai had mentioned them. He was the only Winged person among the living Yaighan.

"I . . . owed your family that," he said weakly.

"I should never have believed it was because of my music," she said. "Or because of my supposed beauty."

"I didn't lie when I called you beautiful," he said.

"No? Then you're the only one who has ever noticed." She sighed. "I admit I was flattered. You are quite handsome, even if it's obvious you prefer to be with a man."

"I don't!" he said. "I mean, not exclusively. I have many women patrons, and none of them has ever complained—" He stopped short, embarrassed.

"Do you service the whole court, then?" Danae said bitingly. "Arris, what's happened to you? Do you actually enjoy being a slave? Is it so pleasant here, as the Emperor's catamite?"

Arris winced at the word, but tried to answer her. "I've been here three years. I'm very good at what I do. If I have to be a slave, does that mean I have to be miserable?"

Danae shook her head. "I'm sorry. That wasn't what I meant to say at all." She followed him as he began walking again. "Arris, why didn't you come to us three years ago? Terai didn't say why you left Gama. He only said the Lady was desperate to have you back, and your mother was sick with worry. Why didn't you come to us? My father offered you a place in our troupe if you didn't like it at Gama."

"And that was the first place Terai looked for me," Arris said.

"We'll have to get word to him," Danae said. "He can come rescue you, or buy your freedom."

"He couldn't afford me," Arris said with a wry smile. "No, Danae. I don't want anyone to know where I am. I can't go back to Gama. I don't even want you to tell the rest of your family." She did not know about Onira. Arris wondered why Terai had not told them.

"Why? Surely you don't want to stay a slave?"

"I won't be one for much longer." He wondered how much he should explain. "I saved the Emperor's life last night . . . I killed the assassin. He promised to free me when I'm eighteen."

"How long is that?"

"Less than two years."

"I had forgotten you were only three years younger than me," she said. "You were such a little boy when you were nine. And you aren't very big for sixteen, either."

"You could never be accused of flattery," he said.

"I'm just being honest. I did say you were handsome."

"And painted like a peacock," he said sourly.

"Well, you are." She giggled. "Actually, you look rather like a Temple painting of Kerami I once saw. The priests would say that was blasphemy."

"Your priests are quick to put labels on things."

"They aren't *my* priests," she said as they entered the open doors of the apartments the musicians had been assigned. "I've never believed in any of that, though Kerami is rather a nice god . . . oh, this is beautiful!"

He had thought he disgusted her, and now she was comparing him to the Khalifate god of love. Arris did not understand her at all. She exclaimed with apparent pleasure over the ripe, tasteless decorations of the apartments that had been Peroyu's. Arris watched her rush from object to object, running a hand along a chair's smooth grain, ruffling the placid surface of a fishbowl. The obscene paintings that had been Peroyu's favorites had been removed, he saw in relief. The few times he had attended the Khopei overlord, Peroyu had insisted on attempting to duplicate some of the contortions and sequences in the paintings; then he had blamed Arris for the failure of his own grotesque body to comply with his wishes.

"Come," Arris invited. "I'll show you something better." He thrust open the glass-inlaid doors to the balcony. The fountains of the Water Gardens splashed musically in the sunlight.

"Oh . . ." she breathed. "I've never seen anything like this. To think I'll be seeing it every day—" Then, suddenly, she began to sob again.

Arris helped her to a carved bench. She shook all over, her face hidden in her long-fingered hands, her emerald eyes screwed tightly against tears. "What's wrong?" he murmured.

"How can I be so heartless," she managed to say, "when everyone is dead, and I don't know what's happening to my father, and I'm a prisoner here . . ."

Arris knelt before her and embraced her gingerly. She clung to him, her body heaving. "It won't be so bad," he whispered. "You'll see. He'll be back soon. Everything will be all right. The Emperor promised me." He hoped it was true.

CHAPTER

16

ARRIS RAISED HIS head wearily and looked back over the meadow he had just traversed flat on his stomach with the path of a drunken snake. There had been scarcely any ripple in the grasses even for a trained eye to see.

"Again," Iyon snapped, watching him from where he lounged by a tree.

"Again? I did that perfectly."

"You won't know the Shadowed Way until you've done every exercise perfectly a thousand times."

"It wasn't this hard to learn the Dances," Arris said rebelliously.

"Don't waste my time in argument. Again."

Arris sighed and lowered himself into the sliding cross-step that would take him swiftly to the cover of the tall grass. He eased himself to the ground. His elbows and knees seemed to be pierced with quivers of arrows as he began the crablike walk that enabled him to move quickly, his body almost in contact with the earth at every point.

"Vary your line!" his teacher called. "An alert sentry can see you if you're going straight."

Arris complied, muttering under his breath. The General was a demanding and unforgiving instructor, quick to enforce a command with a blow when he thought his pupil was moving too slowly. Arris's hatred for him had not lessened, though his respect had grown. Iyon knew the Way of the Jai-Sohn from the most minute postures to the broadest, most time-consuming strategies of the assassin. Once he had admitted that Arris was capable of learning, he had taken time from his drills with his troops to spend four hours every morning with the Emperor's slave boy. Thus far, in two weeks, Iyon had taught Arris the rudiments of skills most Jai-Sohn took four months to attempt.

The grasses scratched Arris's face and made his eyes water and his nose itch, but if he sneezed Iyon might keep him at this exercise for the next two weeks. He scrambled across the meadow, ingraining new layers of dirt into his sweat-stiffened black tunic and leggings. He tried to detach his mind from the discomfort of his body. The Jai-Sohn used disciplines of thought that were much like the training Arris had received at Gama. The Jai-Sohn rituals, though, were meant to help gain control over the physical body, not the Goddess-given powers of the mind.

When he had crossed back again to Iyon's side of the meadow, the young officer favored him with a rare smile. "It will take you hours in the baths to be fit to attend Hareku this afternoon," he said. "If you mean to see your little Khalifate playmate as well, you'd better begin scrubbing yourself now."

"May I go, my lord?" Arris asked in disbelief. They had only been working two hours this morning. Though his muscles screamed from the torture of the crab-walk exercise, he had steeled himself to put them through more.

"Go on. I, too, have wooing to do." Iyon grimaced. "In a moment of weakness, I promised to teach Kakima to drive my war chariot. It will have to be this morning, since I'm going out to review the Fengian garrison this afternoon." He looked at Arris thoughtfully. "It might be a good idea for you to learn the chariot. We can't be sure you won't end up in battle sometime, and you'd never last more than five minutes afoot. You're too small. Probably you're too light to handle a team well, but you might be good at the more acrobatic wheel feats. We'll take some of our lesson time next week for that." He waved his hand. "Go on, boy. I'll be down later."

Arris raced away, stretching his cramped muscles, before Iyon could have the chance to change his mind.

"It's Kerami himself," Vaessa said sarcastically when she answered the door. "Danae! Your love god is here."

Arris chuckled. Danae had mentioned to her sister that she thought he looked like that Temple painting; that had been a great mistake. Whenever Vaessa found something that could irritate Danae, she worried at it like a dog at a meatless bone.

"Oh, it's you, Tchoran," Danae said, her voice tight with annoyance. Arris hoped she would not direct it at him. Their friendship was still as fragile as a flower sculpture.

"I brought the deep-toned lyre," Arris said, holding it out as a peace offering. "You said you'd teach me the bass lines of your new music."

"That's Papa's part!" Vaessa said. "Danae, you can't let him take Papa's place in the music!"

"It's unbalanced right now," Danae said sharply. "We need the low chords to keep Van's lute from wandering off into its own private realm like it did last night."

Arris grinned inwardly. He had attended the Emperor at the banquet where the musicians had played for the first time since Peroyu's ill-fated party. Van's playing had been brilliant, but Arris had known from Danae's taut and furious face that her brother was not staying with the music she had written.

"I won't play with him," Van shouted from the balcony, as the cascading notes of his limbering exercises suddenly clashed in discord. "Let Vaessa play Papa's bass."

"Before the Emperor?" said the older girl nervously. "I don't know. I might lose the rhythm, or forget the fingerings . . ."

Danae laughed. "You lose the rhythm most of the time anyway, even when you're only singing. Come, Tchoran. We'll go down by the fountains and see what you can do."

Arris's fingers were stiff from clawing at the dirt in the meadows that morning, but he managed a passable imitation of Danae's hummed phrases. The cool mist of water from the fountains around them was welcome relief from the hot summer sun.

"That's pretty good," Danae said at last. "Can you learn it by tomorrow night? I know you have other things to do besides practice music."

"I can learn it." He smiled at her. "The Emperor really enjoyed your performance last night. He's glad now that he listened to me and didn't kill you."

Danae sniffed. "Van was an idiot last night, so your Emperor is no judge of music. It's just another of the pretty things he likes to surround him. Like that fancy meat sculpture and the dancing girls. And you." She giggled. "I've been thinking of writing a satire on his lack of taste. Perhaps

I'll perform it tomorrow night. Of course, since I'll sing in Khalifate, your Sacred Emperor won't know the names I call him.''

"He will if I translate them," Arris said sweetly.

"You wouldn't!"

"If he commands it, I will. I'm his slave, remember?"

"Couldn't you make up more flattering words?"

"I'm no poet."

"Then you're scarcely an incarnation of Kerami," she said. "Isn't poetry one of the fifty-nine arts of the Dance?"

"One of the lesser arts," he said. "Like music."

"You'd call music a lesser art?"

Arris leaned over and kissed her lightly. "There are greater arts even than music, Danae. You'll find I'm their master."

Danae pulled away, blushing. "I admit I'm . . . intrigued. But right now I want to hear those transition chords again."

"You're as bad as Iyon," Arris muttered, bending over the lyre.

"I can't hold them at this speed, my lord!" Arris shouted, as the reins burned across his palms. The muscles in his forearms and across his upper back were strained and fatigued, and the four-horse team galloped wildly down the track, moving too fast to feel his attempted guidance. The heavy war chariot bounced jarringly on its four thick wheels. The overlapping leather shields that formed a low wall on three sides of the chariot quivered and groaned.

Iyon's strong arms reached around Arris to clasp the reins over the boy's hands. "Can you unwrap them?" he said in Arris's ear. Arris shook his head. The leather straps were bound tightly three times around his wrists and up over his palms, and they were pulling tighter as the horses ran. Tears sprang to his eyes from the wind and the strain on his grip.

Iyon edged his fingers into the spaces between the reins where they left Arris's hands until all eight straps were under his control. He jerked back sharply, bracing his feet against the grooved slats of the chariot floor. Two horses stumbled as they tried to turn too quickly. Arris grimaced with pain as Iyon's fists closed over his for a stronger hold on the reins. He tasted salt, and realized he had bitten his lip. The clattering of the runaway vehicle slowed a little, then Iyon lunged to force the team into a tight arc. Soon they were trotting in a small circle, panting and blowing, their soft nostrils wide and red-edged.

"You can stop them now," Iyon said wearily. "Pull them over to the edge of the track." He released his hands from the reins. Arris gasped as the full strain of the leathers hit his palms again. But he did as the General commanded and drove the horses slowly to the grassy meadow beside the dirt track. He stopped them and pushed the brake lever with his feet. The wheels locked, sliding a little.

"That was a sloppy halt," Iyon muttered, but he did not scold Arris when he saw the blood seeping around the wrapped leather on the boy's hands.

"I wasn't strong enough," Arris said in frustration. "I couldn't keep my grip. I kept losing part of the reins from my fingers." He unwrapped the straps gingerly. They had scored raw lines on his wrists and palms. Blisters he had acquired earlier that week were messy and broken.

"You won't play the lyre with those tonight," Iyon said with a low whistle. "Hareku will be angry with me. He never asked me to teach you to drive a chariot."

"I want to learn," Arris said fiercely, wiping bloody handprints on his kilt.

Iyon reached out and took Arris's hands gently, tracing their lines with his fingers. Arris stood very still, feeling an old prickling of fear. The General's lean face was thoughtful and absorbed. "Such delicate hands," he said. "An artist's hands, and I am trying to make you a warrior. Perhaps I shouldn't try. The gods designed you for beauty, not strength."

"You said I learn quickly."

Iyon looked up and smiled at his student's troubled expression. "So you do." He let go of Arris's hands. "And though you'll never be a swordsman or a battle charioteer, you'll make a deadly Jai-Sohn. Hareku wasn't wrong about that. Your hatred of the Ilkharani seems almost personal at times."

"They destroyed my family," Arris whispered, looking out over the meadow at the palace hills beyond. "They killed my father."

"Ah." Iyon nodded. "And sold you into slavery?"

Arris shrugged. He certainly would not tell the General the complete truth. He did not know why he had said this much.

"Well." Iyon vaulted over the shield wall to the ground in

a smooth, graceful leap. "I'll expect you here again tomorrow morning."

"Here? I thought you said I'd never be a charioteer." Arris climbed out, not wanting to put his weight on his hands as Iyon had done.

"Oh, you drive well enough. As well as any warrior needs to. Well enough to take over if your charioteer is killed; they're the first targets of the enemy, you know." Iyon grinned. "And you have yet to learn the wheel feats. I'm very good at those, and I'll see to it you learn them properly. Some call them flashy, but they can be useful."

"What are they?"

"Leaping out of the chariot to fight alongside, and getting back in, at any speed," Iyon began. "Dropping before an enemy chariot and coming out alive on the other side. Running down the tongue between the horses to clear fouled lines, deal with enemies, or cut loose dead animals." He chuckled at Arris's dismayed expression. "There are others. They aren't much different from your acrobatic tricks."

"But there's no danger of being trampled to death performing with acrobats," Arris protested.

"No. Only the danger of deadly boredom. Tomorrow."

"Tomorrow," Arris groaned.

"I'll never get out of this place," Danae said, throwing her quill pen at Arris and kicking at the sheet of parchment upon which she had been writing the melodic line of a new composition. "And now *you're* leaving."

"If Hareku ever decides it's time for me to go," Arris said mildly, rubbing the side of his neck where the pen had hit. Danae had good aim. "My eighteenth birthday was four months ago, and he says I'm free, but he still insists on waiting."

"Have you talked to him again about letting us go with you?" she said more quietly.

Arris shook his head. Hareku had refused to let any of Senna's family leave the Sapphire Palace. By the time Senna had returned from his messenger mission, they all knew too much of his court and his military organization. The massed troops of Deiran marched to the palace every week for a parade review. The war lay poised and quivering like a drawn bolt, ready to spring alive as soon as Arris's task was done.

The confusion caused in the Khalifate by the sudden deaths of Nievan, Maenad, and Saresha Ilkharani would provide the opening for the Deirani to invade.

"I hate it here," Danae said. "If I'd been at the Citadel these past two years I'd have gained the Prince's patronage by now." She scowled at the parchment. "My music hasn't grown. I need to be where other musicians besides Van are good enough to play what I want to write. I'm tired of always giving the leading voice to the lute."

"I like your music as it is," he said with a smile.

"Just because your Emperor showered us both with gifts when I wrote that song for you to sing to him . . . oh, Arris! I don't want you to go. Now that you're free, and you don't have to . . . to do all the things he made you do, I thought that we . . ." Her bright green eyes looked up at him pleadingly. "I thought that maybe our friendship could grow into something more. Don't you want that?"

"Of course I do. But I haven't changed, Danae." Arris was tired of the familiar argument. She would have to accept him as he was or not at all. "Do you see this necklace I'm wearing?"

"It's beaten gold, isn't it? It's very pretty."

"The Kuronta Shichal gave it to me this morning. After I spent last night with her. And the Kurontai Roka has asked me to come to dinner with him in Khopei tonight."

"But you aren't the Emperor's slave anymore. You don't have to do those things."

"I want to do them. I'm not going to change. Do you understand?"

She stared wide-eyed at him. After a moment she spoke softly. "I can't change either. I'll never give myself to you if I only get a part of you in return. It isn't enough, Arris."

"I'm sorry."

"I can't give you gold necklaces," she said, "and I'm no city overlord, but I think . . . I think I might be able to love you. Obviously that's not what you're looking for." He handed her the quill pen that had fallen on the floor. She glared up at him. "Go on. Go back to your so-called lovers. That's what you want, isn't it?"

"I do want you, Danae," he said quietly. "But I want other people too. I wish you could accept that."

"Get out!" she shouted. "Do you hear me? Leave me alone!"

"No, no, idiot!" Iyon shouted over the clash of meeting swords. The roomful of furloughed soldiers laughed and cheered as Reishan the swordmaster crossed blades with the fierce little slave from the palace. Outside the narrow windows, the stink of Khopei gutters rose to meet the stench of sweaty, unwashed bodies among the soldiers. "Don't fight like a squire trying to uphold his family's honor! You're following the Shadowed Way, not the rules of dueling!"

Arris nodded. The swordmaster knew most of his tricks now, and was forcing him to fight man to man, not giving him any opportunity for misdirection or foul play. Reishan was as tall as Iyon and much heavier, and wielded a longsword. Arris was still lean and small; he had despaired of ever growing any more. His short, black sword was strong enough to withstand Reishan's blows, but it had no reach. It was built for many uses, but not for dueling. Iyon was right.

"Give it up?" Reishan said hoarsely. His shaggy brown hair hung in dirty strands over his cunning, deep-set eyes. Arris lowered his stance still more, watching those eyes. He had thought of a trick, one Iyon had never taught him. It worked in his mind, but would it work in combat?

Reishan shouted and lunged, bruising Arris's shoulder as the youth ducked the blow. Arris shifted his weight back, caught his opponent's blade with his above his head, and sprang up and forward, using the locked hilts of the two swords as a steadying grip. He kicked out with both feet to catch the swordmaster beneath the jaw. Reishan fell like a great oak, and Arris landed astride him, his sword pressed to the Deirani's throat.

Watching soldiers applauded, and Iyon grinned. "If he hadn't been careful with you, that kick would have dislocated your neck," he informed Reishan cheerfully. "He wouldn't need the blade."

"No true warrior needs such trickery," Reishan said as he rose.

Iyon's voice was grim. "No true warrior would survive more than a few days where Arris is going. But there will be plenty like you in his way, and he must know how to deal with them. I thank you for your time."

"Damned acrobats," the swordmaster muttered. He would not grumble much more, Arris knew. He valued the money he was paid for these sessions, even if they bruised his vanity.

"Come, Arris," Iyon said. "It is time." They pushed past the milling soldiers and started down the dark staircase. "The Emperor has decided you'll leave with my border patrol tomorrow."

"Tomorrow?" Arris said blankly.

"You've been saying for months that you're ready."

"I am, but—"

"Our spies say the time is right. The young bravos of the court are getting bored with their current amusements. They've been prowling the streets of Qadasiya looking for novelty. That you can provide."

They stepped over the steaming gutters to the street where sweating, half-naked slaves waited with their palanquin. "I wish I could go as a musician," Arris said forlornly as they climbed into the curtained box.

"You never learned any genius." Iyon shrugged. "The best cover is one that fits your talents. And this will give you a chance to work with Sebian. He's been established in Qadasiya for a long time, and he's one of our most trusted men."

He ran a high-priced whorehouse on the Streets of Night, a center for the depravations of the nobility known as the Silver Cat. Arris sighed. It was hoped he could attract patrons, and eventually gain an invitation to live at the Citadel. From there, he could plan his strategy as a Jai-Sohn. But until then, Arris thought morosely, he would be back in the earliest years of his slavery, forced to cater to the whims of any man or woman who could afford his price.

Iyon looked at him thoughtfully. "Didn't you guess it would be soon? The Emperor asked you to his bed every night for the past week. That should have told you something was about to happen."

Arris nodded. He was too old to fire the Emperor's appetites anymore, he supposed, though he was still boyish for eighteen. The last six nights had been unexpectedly pleasant for them both, though. He would be sorry to leave.

• • •

The patrol waited patiently in the dawn light, drawn up in close formation just outside the lowest eastern gate of the Sapphire Palace. Iyon barked his men through the rituals of checking their saddle leathers and weapons, making enough noise to ensure the Emperor and Arris of privacy.

Hareku had ridden down to the gate with only a small escort. Arris was surprised to see him. They had taken leave of each other quietly in the dark of the morning. Each knew the other's body well enough by now that their lovemaking had become instinctive, natural, easier than conversation.

"I thought it would be time to send you away," Hareku said, his granite eyes narrow with suppressed emotion. "I thought you would have lost your beauty, and I'd have found another boy . . . but there aren't any others like you, Arris. I should never have freed you."

"You're the Emperor," Arris said warily. "At your command I would be a slave again."

"But then you would hate me."

"Probably."

"Ah, my hawk." Hareku kissed him gently, his hands on either side of Arris's face. "This past week was wonderful." He sighed. "But I've flown you to the lure too long. It's time you hunted bigger game. Iyon tells me he has never had such an apt student of the Shadowed Way."

"Iyon said that?"

"He would deny it if confronted." Hareku embraced him strongly, then pulled away, dropping his hands. "I don't see your minstrel girl. Didn't she come to say farewell?"

"We . . . took our leave," Arris whispered. Danae had not spoken to him since their argument more than a week ago. He wished he could have found another way to resolve their differences. He would miss her. She probably hated him now.

"She will pine away for you. Arris . . ."

"My lord?"

"I wonder." He stood forlornly in his simplest robes, looking for a moment very unlike the Sacred Emperor of Deiran. "I wonder. Did you ever love me?"

Arris swallowed hard. "Sometimes, my lord. Sometimes I did." He vaulted onto his waiting horse and trotted to join Iyon's patrol, not looking back.

BOOK THREE

CHAPTER

17

ARRIS HAD WALKED for two days by the time he intersected the Ummass road north of Qadasiya, following the careful, indirect route General Iyon had plotted for him. The garb of a Westrange shepherd, an upland farmer, and a river-fishing peasant all lay wadded in dirty folds in his pack atop his Jai-Sohn clothes and his black sword. He wore the somber, full-cut robes and turban of a minor Ummass merchant's youngest son, the disguise the Deirani spy Sebian had been told to watch for. His long hair was bound in a painfully tight knot beneath the turban. Nothing could change his Yaighan features, but many people of Yaighan descent lived in the Khalifate.

"Clear the road! Clear the road! Move, you fools," shouted a gruff voice. Arris heard curses and shrieks behind him, and turned to see five soldiers on huge warhorses riding abreast down the road toward him. The peasants and travelers who crowded the dusty highway scurried to the sides, pulling curious children and reluctant horses into ditches against the low hedges of the nearby farmland.

A one-eyed peddler with a scarred, dark face and a huge pack that towered over his filthy turban turned to Arris with a wry smile. "Better to move, lad, than to die beneath the hooves of the glorious Prince's bodyguard." The whining man had been pestering Arris all day to join him in conversation. At last the youth was interested in what he said.

"The Prince?"

"Look for yourself after you get off the road." The peddler pulled at Arris's sleeve. Arris shrugged and walked to the hedge as the soldiers passed. One man reached out negligently with a whip but missed Arris's retreating back.

Behind the line of soldiers rode a bright troop of young men. The late afternoon sunlight sparked off the jewels set in their turbans and sword hilts. They were dressed nearly alike in short, knee-length tunics patterned in garish stripes, sheer leggings, and tall, supple boots with heels. All were blond, and wore their hair at shoulder length. Only a few had mustaches, and none had beards. Arris supposed the fashions had changed since he had been at court with his father.

"Which one is the Prince?" he asked the peddler.

"You don't know?"

"I've lived in Ummass all my life," Arris said diffidently. "I've never seen the young Ilkharani."

"You can't miss him." There was dry amusement in the peddler's grating voice. "The one in the center. With the flower garland on his wrist from the admiring maidens of Khessard."

Arris should have guessed. Saresha Ilkharani had been a cherubic child, and he was a beautiful young man. Arris's eyes had already been drawn to him in appreciation. Saresha's sky-blue eyes were set in a delicately chiseled face, framed by a cascade of dark golden curls. His lightly tanned skin was almost the same color as his hair. He was not tall, but he rode with grace and skill, and the unconscious arrogance of royalty was evident from the slight tilt of his handsome head and the tapered angle of his hands on the reins. There was no doubt, Arris thought, that Saresha had the favor of the sun gods whose high priest he would become in three years. If he was allowed to live that long.

"He's been on a pleasure trip with some of his Companions," the peddler remarked. "They were grandly entertained in Khessard. Food and sport, women and drink, music and dancing. They attended the war games, and I hear the Prince honored the master charioteer with an invitation to dine. He fancies himself quite a warrior, they say." He chuckled. It was a strangely familiar sound, and Arris looked at him more carefully. "He'll never know if he's really any good. His Companions always let him beat them at their sports."

"His Companions?" Arris said absently. No, there was nothing about this repellent man that he recognized.

"Only a few of the young men at court, but numerous enough by all accounts. He began to gather them about five years ago. Most are older than he is. They take a vow when they join to protect their Prince. Or their Khalif, as it may well be by the time the war begins.''

The bright train passed. Arris climbed back to the road to walk in the dusty hoofprints. If Saresha had not betrayed him as a child, he might be one of those favored Companions now. Instead, he would be the Prince's death. ''Do you expect war?'' he asked as the peddler joined him.

One black eye looked at him shrewdly. ''Don't you?'' He shifted his heavy pack and bent a little more. ''I've seen the shipyards of Khessard and Rillath. They say the new warships they're building are capable of surviving the trip around the Deadly Horns to attack Deirani cities from the sea. And the musters in Trevena and the Gharin Emirate and every other province only match the troop buildup everyone says is going on in Deiran.''

Arris belatedly remembered he was supposed to have been living in this country. He nodded. ''Well, of course I knew all that, but I never really thought . . .''

The peddler chuckled again, a deep sound that made Arris shiver in the heat of the failing day. Where had he met this man before? ''It may not be too bad,'' he said. ''They say the Yaighan may fight with the Khalifate against Deiran, now that there's friendship between the Citadel and Gama. What do you think, boy?''

''I suppose it's possible,'' he said weakly. Friendship between the Citadel and Gama? When he had been in priest training, the Ilkharani court had barely tolerated the presence of his brothers as Yaighan envoys, and then only because they were still unsure what had really happened at Delronen.

Now that Arris deigned to talk to him, the peddler seemed to suddenly remember his profession. ''Listen, young master . . . seeing those fine noblemen put me in mind of this . . . silence me if I offend you, but your turban . . .'' His voice whined again.

''What about it?''

''It is far from the latest court fashion,'' the one-eyed man said. ''Now, I have one in my pack, not as fine as the jeweled ones worn by the Prince's Companions, but you'd find it quite adequate. An ample length of varicolored silk, of the sort worn by the very best people.''

"I'm going to Qadasiya to conduct my father's business," Arris said. "Not to observe courtly fashions."

"Quite so," said the peddler. "And you must take care to impress everyone who sees you with your sobriety and trustworthiness. I can show you a handsome case for your papers and goods to replace that dusty pack you wear . . ."

Arris was too weary when night fell to consider walking the last ten miles to Qadasiya, and his latest disguise required that he sleep in a roadhouse instead of a ditch. He allowed the friendly peddler to direct him to an inauspicious-looking inn that was the showplace of a poor village with no name. He had yet to buy any of the peddler's goods, but the man was an amusing companion, and something about him both intrigued and disturbed Arris. He wanted to find out what it was.

The inn was almost full, and Arris agreed to share a tiny upstairs room with the peddler. There were two dirty straw pallets covered with worn blankets on the plank floor. Arris threw his pack down on one of them and went to open the shutters of the narrow window to try to get some air into the stuffy, foul-smelling room. The peddler lay down on the other mattress, fully clothed, still wearing his filthy turban and the wide band of black cloth that covered one eye.

Arris was not going to sleep in his turban. He did not know how the Khalifate men could stand to keep their heads wrapped in such heat. He pulled it off and sat back down on his pallet, loosening his heavy fall of hair from its topknot. He was not going to present himself at the Silver Cat with his hair matted and tangled. He pulled his comb from a side pocket of his pack and began to work.

"That's definitely not in fashion at court," the peddler said in an amused voice that no longer whined or grated. Arris finished the last snarl, tossed his hair back over his shoulders, and turned to stare at his companion. The peddler had propped himself up on his elbows. It was not only his voice, Arris thought. His face, too, seemed familiar, though it was hard to see in the gathering darkness. "Nor is it in fashion in Ummass or any other Khalifate city. Careless of you, boy."

"I don't know what you mean." Arris shifted his weight and moved a fold of his robes to clear his dagger hilt.

"Unless you learn more caution, the Deirani won't get much use out of you."

Arris leaped to his feet, drawing his dagger. He did not know how the peddler knew this, but he would not escape this room tonight.

"You'd kill so quickly?" The familiar voice stilled him. "With no daimon spirit guiding your hand or clouding your mind? You've changed, Arris."

"Terai," Arris whispered in defeat. Why had he not realized earlier?

The Yaighan removed his turban. The unnecessary eye strap went with it. His lank gray hair fell just below his ears. The dark eyes in his weathered face met Arris's frightened gaze. He did not appear to have changed at all.

"How did you find me?" Arris lowered his knife. He knew he could not fight his old teacher. "Are you planning to take me back to Gama? Or are you going to kill me here?"

"Kill you? Boy, I've been searching for you for five years. I'll do my best to keep you alive."

"It doesn't matter." Arris sat back down on the pallet. "Here or in Gama, it doesn't matter to me."

"No one wants to kill you," Terai said sharply. "Except, perhaps, Clynetra. She never agreed with the Council ruling that her sister's death wasn't your fault."

"I killed Onira."

"Cembra finally came forward and explained about the daimon, and the foolish chance he took in calling up the Lord Areyta's spirit. He paid for Onira's death on the altar of the Couch of Rehoman."

Arris stared through the dusk. "I thought—"

"You thought you'd have to face the Lady's wrath." Terai sighed. "She was angry, but not at you. At all of us, especially your mother and me, for not telling you about the Goddess's hand in your birth from the beginning. She was afraid we had lost you forever."

"You lied to me when you said I could avenge him," Arris said. But the hurt that went with those words five years ago was no longer there.

"Believe me, Arris, I regret that. If for no other reason, for the years I've spent searching for you, exiled from Gama and the Lady's presence. Thank the Goddess for the greed of spies. I went to him seeking information for my own plans, but Sebian put me on your trail at last."

"What? He told you who I was?"

"And the route you'd be taking from Deiran."

"I can't believe it. Iyon called him one of his most trusted people. He was well paid to keep silence."

"I paid him better to talk. I had to know if my information was true, that a trained Jai-Sohn was coming to Qadasiya with orders to kill the Regents and the Prince. It would ruin one of my own pet schemes to gain back the favor of the Lady and the Council." Terai grinned. Arris could see the gleam of white teeth in the darkness. "Even with the name, I wasn't sure it was you. But then I met Danae, and it fell together."

Nothing could surprise him now, Arris thought. "Danae?"

"Didn't you know? She reached Qadasiya yesterday."

"She must have taken the direct route from the border. If anyone recognized her—"

"She could have endangered your mission. But I'm certain no one noticed her. She seized the chance to get back to the Citadel and try once again for the Prince's favor. If she succeeds, she could be of help to us."

"To us?" Arris said warily.

"We may be able to work together on this," Terai said. "You can't establish yourself at the Silver Cat now that Sebian has proven untrustworthy."

"I never wanted to go there," Arris said. "But Iyon insisted it was the only way I could gain quick access to the court."

"There may be another way. Listen, boy. I don't care if you kill Nievan and Maenad. They are enemies to the Yaighan as well as the Deirani. And Saresha Ilkharani's death will be an important offering to the Goddess when she wakes. He is the pawn of the Brothers Ylla, just as you were intended to be Rehoman's pawn."

"Then you won't oppose me?"

"Oppose you? No. Though I'd like to change your plans a little. You can still fulfill your oath to your Emperor, and serve your own people at the same time."

"How?" Arris asked, suspicious. He would not return to the Goddess's plans for him. He would not!

"I can get you into the court, with the help of your brothers. We'll present you as a Yaighan princeling sent by the Lady to learn the ways of her trusted allies. You'll gain the Prince's interest, perhaps even join his Companions."

"I don't want to pretend friendship for him," Arris protested. "I only want to kill him."

Terai continued. "You'll get close enough to the Prince to be with him on Winter Festival night, and to ensure that the assassin sent against him doesn't succeed."

"What?"

"That assassin will be a young man named Weida, the current Yearking of the Yaighan. You will make certain the Yearking dies by Saresha's hand. The Lady herself will come in disguise to the Citadel; you will see to it that she shares the Prince's bed at least once."

"Making Sasha the next Yearking. Why?"

"He is the favored child of the sun gods," Terai said. "His death on the Temple altar at the moment the Goddess wakes and the Millennium begins will be the first blow struck in our holy war." He chuckled. "And I'm certain no one will mind if you're the one who wields the sacrificial knife."

Arris shook his head. "No. That would make me Yearking of the Millennium. That's what I ran from years ago."

"I thought you ran from the consequences of murder." Terai leaned across and touched Arris on the arm. "The Goddess still wants you, boy. The Lady wants you. That's why I've been searching for you."

"I'll help you in your plan for the Prince," Arris said finally. "And as soon as Sasha is safely on the way to Gama, I'll kill the Regents. But I won't be Yearking. I swore I'd never accept anything from your Goddess again."

"My Goddess?" Terai said mildly. "Surely she's yours as well. She created you."

Arris flinched. "I never asked to be her creation. I won't change my mind, Terai. I agree your plan is better than General Iyon's for getting me into the Ilkharani court. And my revenge will be sweeter if I gain Saresha's trust and then betray him, as he betrayed me. But I won't be Yearking."

"I won't argue with you. I refused that calling myself. But the Goddess and the Lady may have something to say about it."

"My life is my own," Arris muttered.

"As much as any man's."

The darkness outside the narrow window of the upstairs room had thickened and grown until it was black night, with only a few stars showing. Arris stared out the window, glad he could see no moon. "Tell me about your plan," he said. "Can my brothers be trusted to go along with it?"

Terai laughed. "No. They've been useful ambassadors, and they've lulled the Citadel into a false sense of friendship with Gama, but that's because they don't know about the Millennium. They would never go along with a plot to kill the Prince. Husayn was one of the first to join Saresha's Companions. They're both very close to him."

"Then how do you expect them to help us?"

"They won't know who you are. We'll tell them the same story we want them to tell the Prince. They'll be glad to help you gain his trust."

"They're bound to recognize me. Don't be foolish, Terai."

"I don't think they will. You've changed more than you know." Terai spoke softly in the dark room. "The last time Falcmet and Husayn saw you, you were eleven years old. I last saw you when you were thirteen, and if I hadn't had descriptions from Sebian and Danae I wouldn't have known you." He paused. "It isn't just that you've grown, Arris. It's the way you walk, the way you speak. You have the grace of a Deirani who dances both ways."

"Is it so obvious?" Arris said, startled. He wished he could read Terai's expression. Was his old teacher disappointed by what Arris had become?

"And there's something dangerous about you," Terai continued. "I can feel the power bound within you, and that's part of it. But I think even the most shallow noble of the Citadel would fear you a little, even as he was drawn to you."

"I'm a Jai-Sohn," Arris said uncomfortably. "Maybe that's what you feel."

"Maybe. I wonder what Karillos will sense from you. He may be a problem."

"Who?"

"Karillos. A priest of the Five Brothers, a very influential man at the Citadel. Perhaps the only Khalifate priest I've ever encountered who truly seems able to speak with the gods he serves. You'll have to be wary of him."

"I could assassinate him before he becomes a danger."

"And tell the whole court they have a Jai-Sohn in their midst? No. Though you had better kill Sebian as soon as you reach Qadasiya, if you don't want to be betrayed again."

Arris nodded. "He would have to die in any case, for me to follow your plan instead of General Iyon's. This way I can send word of his betrayal to the General, and tell him I'll have to infiltrate the court another way. And I'll need Sebian's records of contacts and informants."

"I'll help you if you want."

"I don't know. It might be better for me to act alone, to keep Iyon's trust." It would be the first true test of his Jai-Sohn training. If he could not assassinate an unguarded merchant and steal his records, he would be foolish to attempt to kill the three Ilkharani.

"He keeps his records at the Silver Cat," Terai said. "It would be best to kill him there, too. No one is ever much surprised by murders on the Streets of Night."

Arris stretched out on his pallet in his long Ummassid robes, trying to get comfortable with his pack as a pillow. It would be much more enjoyable to be a Yaighan princeling than an exotic courtesan in the Silver Cat. And Danae would also be at court. Perhaps they could finally work out their differences. If she did not learn why he was really there.

"Terai?" he said hesitantly. "Danae . . . she knows I was training to be a spy for the Emperor. But that's all she knows."

Noises from the other pallet indicated Terai was also getting ready to sleep. "She doesn't know you're an assassin?"

"No. If she did, she would probably turn against me. Our friendship doesn't extend that far." Arris sighed. "I wish she had stayed safely in Deiran."

"If you can keep her trust, she should be useful. A musician can move more easily through the different levels of court society than a Yaighan princeling can." Terai yawned audibly.

"I suppose so." Arris lay back thoughtfully. He would have to be careful. His brothers could not learn who he was, or they would suspect he had come to kill the Prince. He had sworn to Husayn once that he would do so. Danae knew who he was, but she could not know why he was really at the Citadel. And the priest Karillos . . . without his Goddess power, Arris could not defend himself against the man if Karillos had been granted power by his own gods. He would have to avoid him.

"Arris," Terai said after a long silence. "If you would

rather I leave you alone . . . that I don't draw you back into the schemes of the Goddess and the Lady . . . I would understand. I don't have to tell them I've found you.''

"They would have found me eventually anyway," Arris said. "This way, at least I know enough of their plans to keep from getting too entangled. But thanks for the offer.''

Terai sounded relieved. "It will be good to be able to get into the White City again. My earlier exile was my own choice, but this was different. The gate was shut to me, and the Lady refused to see me.''

"Will you go back right away?"

"First I'll get you well established at court. And make sure Sebian is cleanly eliminated.'' He laughed softly. "I've never worked with a Jai-Sohn before, Arris. Maybe even at my age I can learn something new.''

"I'm glad you found me, Terai," Arris said impulsively.

"I am too, boy. I am too.''

CHAPTER

18

THE CALL TO midday prayer shrilled through the hot summer air as Arris and Terai passed under the northern arch of Qadasiya's weathered city wall. Arris squinted against the sun and looked up. The huge Temple loomed over the warrens of the city, impossible to ignore. He felt a chill of memory at the sight. The terrifying day when the Lossiran had attacked him in the cool, whitewashed hall was still vivid in his mind.

"Not much like Khopei, is it?" Terai commented, serenely dodging a beggar's outthrust bowl and sidestepping a stagnant pool of waste where refuse had dammed the gutter.

Arris laughed. "There aren't any beggars in Khopei, at least. The Overlord's guardsmen make certain of that. They

armor to get out of the palace. No one can tell who's underneath that black armor. I left his armor in Khopei where he could pick it up later, and bought a horse and a black wig, and darkened my face. I rode straight through to the border in three days, because I knew I didn't speak Deirani well enough to fool anyone if I stopped at a roadhouse.''

"How did you get past the border patrols?"

"That was harder," she admitted. "But once I was in the Khalifate I didn't have any problems." She looked him in the eye. "I couldn't stand to know you were here and I was stuck in Deiran for the rest of my life. It wasn't fair! And I was so tired of playing with my family. I needed a change."

Arris nodded. "When I send word to General Iyon that I've arrived, I'll say you're with me. And that you'll help me at court. Maybe that will keep them from being too hard on your family."

Danae's eyes widened. "They wouldn't blame them, would they? No one knew I was going. Papa would never have given me his permission. Do you think they'll be in any danger?"

"Probably not. If the Emperor is in a reasonable mood, and doesn't listen to General Iyon."

Danae looked subdued. "I did think of that," she said in a small voice. "But I was already halfway here. I couldn't turn back."

"Enough chatter, girl," Ruena said with a smile. "I'm sure these two men are hungry after their journey. Do you want the meal we worked so hard to prepare to sit in the back room forgotten?"

"I'll get it," Danae murmured. She hurried through the hanging beadwork that separated the two rooms.

"I'll mention Arris at my meeting with the brothers j'Areyta," Terai said, sitting on the stool Danae had vacated. "We'll give them a few days to prepare to welcome him. You'll need a new name, boy. What would you prefer?"

"I've already told them he is coming," Ruena said with an air of satisfaction. "And I've told them his name. Rahnisha Tualli, the hope of his people."

Arris stared at her. It was the name of the doomed Yearking of legend who had been the last to fight for the Goddess at the gates of Gama. "A name of ill omen, lady."

"It will mean what you make of it," she answered.

"If she's already told it to Falcmet and Husayn, then Rahnisha you'll be," Terai said. "We'll plan to introduce you at court in a week's time. Meanwhile, you can take care of Sebian and his records, and buy clothing and jewelry suitable for a prince. I have enough funds at my disposal to see you well outfitted."

Ruena smiled warmly. "You will make a good prince, Tauena's son! You've certainly changed since I saw you the first time. Where is the frightened little boy blazing with untrained power who ran to me nine years ago?" She shook her head. "All clouded, bound in the net of an angry vow. But don't worry, child. What the Goddess allows to be done, she can undo. You'll have your power again, and more besides."

"I don't want my vow undone," Arris said, half-angry. "I'd be happy never to see the Lossiran again, and I have no desire to be with the Goddess when she wakes. Can you understand that?"

She shrugged. "As you will. Where is that girl? I must have sent her hours ago."

The aroma of spiced rice and roasted fowl steamed from the trays Danae carried into the front room of the shop. Ruena cleared a shallow bowl, cards, and a cloth from a small table she used to do future readings for clients. "Pull your stools over here," she ordered. "Dear Goddess, but you're both filthy. I should make you go to the baths before you eat."

Terai pulled a leg from the fowl and took a deep bite, smiling through the grime that had been part of his peddler disguise. "We would have fainted away with hunger in the heat. But don't worry, my lady. We'll go this afternoon. We have to begin to make Arris into a prince. And I need to look like a respectable Yaighan messenger when I meet with our ambassadors." He glanced at Arris. "Your brothers know me as a weapons teacher and a priest, but not as a spy. They don't even know I'm not allowed in Gama anymore."

"The Lady had every right to exile you," Ruena said, "after you lost her Winged boy. Now that you've found him, she'll welcome you back."

Terai sighed. "Yes, they'll let me into Gama again. But they won't want to hear that the boy I've found refuses to fit neatly back into their plans."

"What plans?" Danae said, pausing with a lump of rice halfway to her mouth.

Arris spoke quickly. "They wanted to make me a priest."

"A priest!" She burst into laughter. "You? The darling of the Deirani court?"

He was confused for a moment, until he remembered that priests in the Khalifate were supposed to be celibate. Danae evidently believed Yaighan priests were the same. He grinned. "You can see why I refused."

"I'm not sure about this, Terai," Arris said, standing in the alley behind the Silver Cat three nights after his arrival in Qadasiya. The music of wailing flutes and low drums cut through the stonework of the three-story building, calling to any traveler of the Streets of Night who had enough money to enter. "I'd rather kill him as a Jai-Sohn, quietly and in secret."

"This way you can steal his records and eliminate him the same night, with no suspicion or accusations later," Terai said. "And with no danger of someone seeing you on your way back to the inn in your black clothes. Besides, I've already told him that Rahnisha Tualli plans to sample the delights of the city before his presentation at court. He'll wonder if you don't appear."

"You've forced me into this, Terai. I hope you're right." Arris adjusted the pleats of his newly purchased robe. He had decided against wearing the latest court fashions, but he would present an impressive figure nonetheless. Atop his tunic and leggings of deep crimson silk, he wore a skirted overrobe of dark gold with slashed sleeves revealing green velvet inserts. His wide belt was beaded in a swirling tapestry design, and supported an exquisite emerald-hilted dagger he did not expect to use. He wore no turban, since he did not mean to pretend to be a follower of the Brothers Ylla. His hair was tied up in a high, flowing tail, and his lobes were heavy with massive golden earrings. His boots were heeled, of supple and delicately tooled red leather.

"You should enjoy it," Terai said dryly. "Remember to direct pursuit my way." He turned and glided back into the shadows.

Arris nodded, took a few deep breaths, and left the alley to climb the wide, inviting staircase of Sebian's establishment.

He knew the merchant would be there tonight. Terai's planning had been thorough. It depended upon his ability to carry off a charade that would be simple to one used to the deceptions of the Sapphire Palace.

He knocked lightly on the dark wooden door and smiled with assurance at the burly house slave who answered it. "Your master expects me," he said, allowing a soft Yaighan accent to color his speech.

The slave was head and shoulders taller than Arris. His bulk nearly filled the doorway. He looked at Arris's finery and bowed slightly. "Whom shall I announce?"

"Rahnisha Tualli, Prince of the Yaighan." It sounded ridiculous to Arris, but the slave nodded gravely and motioned him inside.

"If you'll wait in the anteroom, Your Highness, my master will be out to greet you directly."

The Silver Cat was well appointed as bordellos go, Arris thought, trying to fall more easily into his role. It was obvious from the friezes and mosaics on the walls that it did not offer the usual Qadasiya pleasures, either. The artwork was ostensibly religious, but the lines of handsome young cupbearers attending the portrayed figures of Kerami and Myrdethreshi were not there to pour wine. Other pictures showed pretty children of both sexes, and exotic dancers in painful-looking poses. No wonder Iyon had thought Arris would do well as a courtesan here. Instead, at least for tonight, he was a customer. He heard a bustle of movement behind the nearest curtains, and quickly composed his features into the mixture of eagerness and arrogance he felt Rahnisha Tualli would project.

"Most Royal Highness!" exclaimed the overweight and overdressed man who bustled through the curtains. Sebian's face was not unattractive, but the regular features seemed slightly askew, the nose and mouth not quite in proper relation to one another. An odd face.

"You may address me as "my lord,' " Arris said lightly. "You are the master of the house?"

"Your servant, my lord," said the man in a fawning tone. "My name is Sebian. I am most honored by your presence, most honored."

"I am sure of that." Arris followed the Qadasiyan through the curtains toward the wailing music. A wide corridor set

with rows of closed doors led toward a crowded hall. The
sickly sweet smell of rapture smoke crept from some of the
rooms; few Deirani enjoyed its excitant effects, and Arris had
forgotten how widely it was used in the Khalifate.

"I was fortunate enough to hire rarely talented musicians
and dancers for my entertainment tonight," Sebian said. "I
hope my lord will enjoy my humble efforts. Or if my lord
does not wish to join the gathering, you have only to tell me
what would please you in a companion for the evening, and I
will provide for your desires."

"Later, noble Sebian. I want refreshment first, and music."

"Good, good. You'll be pleased to hear we have been
blessed tonight. Three noblemen of the Citadel court have
chosen to join my gathering. As my lord has yet to be
presented at court, perhaps I could point them out to you?"

"Please do." A nearly naked girl, younger than he had
been when he was first made a slave, approached to offer
sweetmeats from a lacquered tray. He accepted a honeyed
cake and glanced around the hall. Lanterns hung from the
high ceiling, strung with bright ribbons and glittering with
glass gems. On a low dais, three young boys playing shrill
flutes and two girls with deep-toned drums swayed and pos-
tured teasingly as they performed. A narrow, curving staircase led upward from the far end of the hall. Terai had said
that Sebian kept his accounts and records on the third floor of
the bordello. The people appeared to be mostly local merchants. He could see the three young courtiers among the
press of dancers and painted youths.

"My lord Taifid!" the master of the house shouted to a
slim nobleman dressed in the short robe and tall boots of one
of the Prince's Companions. Arris stared at the man as he
approached. Taifid's face was still attractive, though without
the heavy-lidded softness of his youth the Lord Collector's
son had no claim to beauty. He was the same man who had
indirectly helped Arris escape the Citadel nine years earlier.
"My lord," Sebian said, "it pleases me greatly to introduce
to you His Highness Rahnisha Tualli, on his first, and, Kerami
willing, not his last, visit to my most favored house."

"The Yaighan Prince we've heard about from Husayn?"
Taifid peered at Arris with wine-fogged interest. "Really,
Sebian, you should have introduced us the other way around,

with the Prince named first. Protocol, you know. Dear gods, he's pretty."

"My lord," Arris said, trying to disguise his amusement.

"No offense meant, of course," Taifid said, beckoning Arris to follow him. "But we should talk. We really should talk. Y'r Highness . . ."

"Rahni," Arris said with a flirtatious smile. It would not hurt to gain the friendship of this particular Citadel noble right away. And Taifid was undeniably attractive.

"That's right," Taifid said, pleased. "Don't stand on ceremony at the Silver Cat. And call me Taifid, of course." He grinned at a half-clad boy who wriggled past them bearing goblets of wine. "Not many from the court come here, you know. Afraid of the priests. The Temple raids about every month, but we pay them off. They say this is all sin and heresy. What do you think?"

"I don't follow the Khalifate religion," Arris said. "The Yaighan have no rules telling them whom to love, or when, or how."

"Enlightened people," Taifid whispered in his ear. "Come, young Rahni. I'll buy you a drink."

Less than an hour later, feigning drunkenness, Arris reeled upstairs, ostensibly in search of the house's earth closets. The music and laughter had risen to a floor-shaking noise. He was sure nothing would be heard. As he had surmised, a guard stood at the top of the staircase on the third floor. A key hung at his belt. Arris staggered upward.

"The closets are on the second floor, young master." The guard was tall and thick-bodied. He looked quite strong, but was apparently unarmed. Arris glanced back at the stairs to be certain no one had followed him. He had tipped one of the flute-boys to distract Taifid, who had become more and more solicitous.

"What've you got back there?" he inquired fuzzily.

The guard moved back a few steps to stand in front of a closed door. "Forgive me, sir. You'll have to move off. Customers aren't allowed here." He pushed Arris lightly with his hands, and the youth reeled back a long step to the landing.

"No right to treat a prince that way," Arris muttered. The guard relaxed as he began to turn away. He crouched and leaped in one blurred move, kicking high with a heeled boot, catching the unprepared guard in the throat and knocking him back against the door. The guard gave a muted cry as Arris landed astride his chest. His voicebox was probably crushed.

Arris lunged for the guard's flailing wrists and took a heavy blow on his lower back that made him gasp with pain. But Jai-Sohn training allowed no time for thought, and his hands slammed a sharp blow to the prone guard's chin. The big man went limp, his neck dislocated.

Arris pulled the key from the guard's belt, unlocked the door, dragged the guard through it, and closed it again as quickly as he could. Verchaki take the man, that had hurt. Iyon had never hit him like that when they practiced that maneuver. He would have bruises for weeks.

A little blood trickled from the dead man's nose and mouth, but not enough to stain Sebian's floor. Arris strode briskly to the wide marble table in the tiny room, noting a window that could be opened above the alley where Terai waited. Huge account books lay on the table, but Arris assumed any records of Sebian's spying would be better hidden. He began to search.

"Murder! Murder!" Arris clattered down the stairway a few minutes later, fastening his elaborate belt with fumbling hands. His wide-eyed shrieks attracted amused attention from most of the revelers, but Sebian crossed quickly to him and was soon convinced his noble young patron was serious. He climbed the stairs behind Arris, pale and breathing hard.

The corpse of the guard lay in the open doorway, and a thin wreath of smoke drifted from the room beyond. Arris glanced at Sebian, and was gratified to see the sweat start from the obese merchant's brow.

"Dear gods," the man breathed, clutching the stair railing.

"I was just coming out of the earth closet," Arris said in a frightened tone. "I saw that man lying at the top of the stairs, then someone dragged him away. I went to look. Someone was climbing out the window with a bunch of papers in his hand. And there's a fire on the table." He had set fire to all Sebian's spying records he did not need. The papers he had come for were folded tightly in his boot.

"A fire? My papers!" Sebian rushed into the room. The small blaze was well contained on the wide marble table, but his books were already ruined. He leaned out the window. "Lost. I'm lost . . ."

"I saw the direction the thief went," Arris said helpfully, slurring his strong Yaighan accent.

"Your Highness . . . my lord . . . I thank you. You must believe me, this sort of thing does not often occur at the Silver Cat, it's most unusual . . ." Sebian brushed past Arris and bellowed down the stairs for a slave to come put out the fire.

"If you go after him quickly, you might catch him."

Sebian eagerly grasped the idea. He ran down the stairs and past the curious crowd, followed by Arris. He sent his remaining guard slaves into the alley in the direction Arris gave them, and rummaged inside a brass-bound cabinet until he found a sheathed sword. "You must come with me, my lord," he urged. "You can identify the murderer."

Arris kept himself from smiling with an effort. They hurried into the alley. Sebian stumbled twice in the unaccustomed darkness. Then they heard a cry from several streets away. The guard slaves had seen Terai running.

"Quick," Arris cried. "He's headed north. We can intercept him." He led the panting merchant on a tangent through the maze of the Streets of Night.

"Must . . . rest . . ." Sebian finally gasped, only seven alleys distant from his bordello. Arris halted. It was dark behind the tall, decaying buildings that held far less luxurious cribs than the Silver Cat. It would do.

He whirled to meet the lumbering man, and reached out to draw Sebian's sword from its sheath. He pressed it softly into the folds of fat over the would-be spy's ribs. "Did you think," he whispered, "that the Emperor would not know? You betrayed him."

"No . . ." the merchant pleaded. "Oh, gods, you must be the Jai-Sohn. Please . . . please, I can help you still, you'll need me to make contact with Deiran—"

Arris thrust sharply with the long sword, standing well back so no blood would mar his princely clothes. Then he dropped Sebian's sword on top of his body and turned back toward the Silver Cat. It would look suspicious if he did not return with the rest of the searchers. Perhaps he would even take Taifid up on his offer for the night. He might as well enjoy his new identity.

CHAPTER
19

"FALCMET AND HUSAYN will meet us at the gate," Terai said as they rode under the last shadows of the leaf-laden trees in the summer forest. "Remember who you are, boy. Rahnisha Tualli, Son of the Lady, Son of the Tribes, Prince of the Yaighan."

"They know there aren't any titles in Gama," Arris said uneasily.

"The sons of the Lady would be princes in the Khalifate. I've explained to them that your mother felt you should have a title to gain quicker acceptance at the Ilkharani court."

"I still don't like it," Arris grumbled. He spread the skirts of his gold overrobe so they would fall more gracefully over his saddle. He wore the same clothes he had worn at the Silver Cat. The rest of his newly purchased wardrobe rested in a heavy trunk strapped to the back of Terai's sturdy pony. Terai was to play his manservant in the Citadel, at least until Arris was well established.

The Palace brooded over its long moat, rising up over the forest road like a stark canyon wall. It had better fortifications than the rambling hillside courts of Khopei, and held an even vaster array of gardens and courtyards and fields inside its massive walls. Yet it could not compare to the Sapphire Palace for artistry. Arris wondered how Rahnisha Tualli, used to the grace of the White City, would react to the Palace and the Citadel. He decided he would be awed by its size, and by the oppressive weight of its somber stones.

Falcmet and Huṣayn sat tall warhorses outside the open gates. They were grown men now, of impressive height and strong build, with reputations as matchless warriors that had grown since the one-sided battle at Delronen. They no longer wore their shoulder-length blond hair in braids; it waved thickly back from their broad foreheads in the style favored by the Prince's Companions. The short robes and tall boots of court fashion looked oddly out of place on two such soldiers.

Arris wanted to discard his disguise and gallop up to them, to see the delight on their familiar faces when they learned who he was. He looked down at his slim, delicate hands on his reins, and suddenly wished he was at least a foot taller and a hundred pounds heavier.

"Be careful, boy." Terai looked sharply at him. "Remember to change your speech patterns as much as you can, and use a thick Yaighan accent. If you're ever too much at ease, there's a chance your brothers will recognize something about your speech or your mannerisms."

"I know." He straightened. "I just wish we trusted them enough to tell them the truth."

"Their friendship with the Prince is too strong."

"And I'm to make them dislike me if I can." Arris spoke softly now. They were almost in earshot of his brothers. "I don't want to do that, Terai."

"They don't have to dislike you. Just be uncomfortable around you. The further they stay away, the easier your disguise will be. You'll only need to give them an idea of the sort of pleasure you enjoy, and take care to be seen with Taifid from time to time. If I know Falcmet and Husayn, they won't judge you harshly, but they'll be uninterested in friendship."

"None of that will be feigned," Arris said unhappily. "Even if they knew who I really was, they probably wouldn't like me."

Terai shrugged and urged his horse out onto the narrow thrust bridge over the moat. Arris followed. Falcmet and Husayn rode toward them, smiling, to meet them in the center of the bridge.

"My lord Prince," Falcmet said gravely. "Please accept my welcome. I am Falcmet, Lord of Delronen, First Ambassador of the Yaighan, and this is my brother Husayn, Second Ambassador."

"Terai has told me so much about you, I feel I know you already," Arris said in an atrocious Yaighan accent. He had decided Rahnisha would have a fluent Khalifate vocabulary but horrible pronunciation. "I am so glad to meet you at last."

"We are honored," Husayn said. His voice was husky, and high for such a big man. His wide grin at Arris was familiar.

Falcmet fell in beside Arris to ride into the palace yards. Husayn and Terai followed, speaking quietly. "The Lady is your mother, I hear," Falcmet said. "I met her only once, but she is a beautiful woman."

"Thank you," Arris said. "She has told me how pleased she is with your work on our behalf." He glanced pointedly at Falcmet's costume. "But I am curious. I know that both of you are Companions to Prince Saresha Ilkharani. I wonder how you reconcile your oath to defend the Prince with your vow of loyalty to my people." And with the knowledge that the Prince was one who murdered your father, he did not say.

"His Highness did not require any such oath from us," Falcmet said. "He realized it would not be correct. And I hope there would never be a reason to have to choose between the Yaighan and the Khalifate."

"Let us hope not," Arris said lightly. "Forgive me, I did not mean to accuse you of disloyalty. I will have to meet your Prince myself, to see what is so compelling about him. I have met another of his Companions, a man named Taifid. A pleasant sort. He spoke very highly of Saresha."

"Taifid spoke of meeting you," Falcmet said in a voice that was carefully neutral. "He has promised the Prince that he'll like you." He looked sidelong at Arris. "Taifid didn't say where he'd met you."

"At a party," Arris said, reining his horse to follow Falcmet around a patrol of soldiers drilling in the yard. "In Qadasiya."

"The Silver Cat?" Falcmet asked softly.

Arris nodded, smiled, and sat back on his horse, noting with somewhat bitter amusement that Falcmet did look uncomfortable. Perhaps that was all that would be necessary to keep his brothers away.

Falcmet and Husayn slipped inside the audience hall to wait to announce him, and Terai took his trunk and other baggage to the rooms in the east tower that he had been assigned by the Citadel steward. Arris suspected Taifid had arranged to have the rooms near his. The courtier was eager to keep his friendship. Arris had not used any of his exotic Deirani dances, but he was probably still a better lover than the meek and frightened boys Taifid was used to.

A tall, slim minstrel with long brown hair and sharp brown eyes paused in his stroll near Arris, as the veiled girl on his arm suddenly disengaged herself and muttered a few words. It was Danae. She looked beautiful in her bright, ruffled court gown and sheer headpiece. Her green eyes sparkled as she came over to Arris and curtseyed.

"You look lovely," he said softly.

"So do you, Arris."

"Shh," he hissed. "Rahni. Remember to call me Rahni. Or my lord Prince, if anyone can hear."

She giggled. "I'll feel silly calling you that."

"Danae, please. You told Terai you'd help me."

"I will. I've already learned a lot. There's one general, for instance, who fought with your father, and Nievan's people are trying to get rid of him. They claim he's lost his courage. One of them challenged him to a duel, can you imagine?"

"Did he accept?"

"Yes. And he killed the younger man at the first pass. Now they're saying his blade was poisoned."

The slim minstrel's gaze was decidedly hostile. "A friend of yours?" Arris asked.

"His name is Pellen. He plays a wonderful reed flute." She smiled mischievously beneath her veil. "I told him I knew you when my family and I used to perform in Gama, but he's jealous anyway." Her voice lowered. "Don't look so surprised, my lord Prince. I made it clear to you how I felt. If you want to spend your time with people like Taifid, you can forget spending any of it with me."

"Danae—" he began. She turned and glided away to take Pellen's arm. They were soon out of sight behind stone pillars.

"My lord Prince," Falcmet said, looking flustered. He had returned from the Audience Chamber. "The Regents are occupied with another matter. An accusation of an attempt on the life of Vizier Nievan's youngest son, Komor. They won't be able to greet you formally. The Prince is in the Garden Court, though, and if you'll come with me I'll introduce you to him."

"This is the first time a son of the Lady has come to the

Citadel,'' Arris said, slipping back into the accent he had not used with Danae. ''I would have thought they would make time to receive me.''

''I'm very sorry, my lord. There are times when courtesy must be set aside. Will you come with me?''

Arris shrugged and followed him. ''I'll try not to be angry,'' he said generously. ''It is not your fault, good Ambassador.''

Husayn hurried to join them as they walked through the pillared corridors that circled the perimeter of the great hall. ''Saresha has been cornered by Karillos,'' he said to his brother. ''They're arguing some obscure theological point. But I think the Prince will welcome being rescued. He has the look of a deer in a trap.''

''I would not want to intrude,'' Arris said quickly, remembering Terai's warning about the priest of the Brothers Ylla. ''Perhaps I should go up to my rooms and help Terai unpack.''

''No, my lord Prince,'' Falcmet said. ''You must allow us to introduce you to His Highness. He truly wants to meet you, and he will make up for his uncles' lack of welcome, I promise.''

Arris shrugged. ''Very well.'' He wished he could control enough of his trammeled power to erect shields.

The Garden Court bloomed with bright plants set in unimaginative geometric designs. It smelled pleasant, but with none of the subtlety of Deirani perfume gardens, where flowers and herbs and scented shrubs were mingled to create carefully monitored fragrances. Ladies of the court, veiled but no less active in the intrigues and scandals than the ostensibly freer women of Deiran, clustered in ornate groups and watched their more adventurous companions toying with inflated balls of treated silk. One of the balls flew toward Arris. He caught it and tossed it back with a bow and a smile, and watched the fluttering that ensued.

''There they are,'' Husayn said.

Karillos faced their direction, arguing with a short, slim, elegant youth with dark gold hair and a ruby belt. The Prince. Arris felt his pulse begin to race. He had seen Saresha from the roadside a week ago, but now they would be face-to-face. It would require a great effort to disguise his hatred.

Karillos looked somehow familiar. The gold-robed priest was tall and skeletal, with pale, ice-blue eyes. Arris recognized him. He was the priest who had called Myrdethreshi to drive away the Lossiran in the Temple of the Sun nine years ago. Terai had been right to warn against him. He could be truly dangerous.

Falcmet stepped in front of Arris and tapped the Prince on the shoulder. Saresha turned. His tanned face was open and smiling under his burnished hair. His sky-colored eyes were bright with interest. He looked at Arris, and for a moment Arris wondered how he could ever bring himself to kill something so beautiful.

"Royal Highness," Falcmet said, "may I present to you my countryman, my lord Prince Rahnisha Tualli, son of the Lady of the Yaighan."

"Your Highness." Arris bowed, grateful for a reprieve from those startling blue eyes.

"Your Highness," Saresha said, bowing in turn. Then he laughed, the same infectious, musical laugh he had as a child. "No, we can't have that. We'll have to call each other by our first names from the beginning. Do you mind? Is Rahnisha your first name or your last?"

He was charming. Arris forced a smile. "Call me Rahni, if you will, and I will call you Saresha."

"Done!" The Prince reached out to clasp wrists with Arris, and Arris realized with a start that they were of a size. Their eyes were on the same level, blue and black; their forearms were the same length where they greeted each other; their shoulders were the same width; their stance nearly identical. When they were children, the Prince's father had once called Arris his son's "shadow twin." It had not changed. He wondered if Saresha had noticed.

"Highness," said the thin priest in annoyance.

"Oh, Karillos, I'm sorry. I forgot to introduce you. Rahni, this is one of the most intelligent men in the Khalifate, and one whose advice I intend to rely upon when I become Khalif. Karillos is the high priest of the Qadasiya Temple."

"An honor," Arris said warily.

The priest's gaze was sharp and measuring. "My lord Prince. Perhaps you can help resolve an argument that has been troubling His Highness and myself. Would you say that the worship of Kerami implies an acceptance that the pleasures of physical love are sanctioned by the Brothers, or that the meaning of Kerami is a different thing entirely, a matter of philosophical and moral questions?"

Falcmet shifted uneasily. Arris laughed, and said in his heavy Yaighan accent, "Forgive me, good priest. But I understood less than half of what you just said, and I know very little about your gods anyway. I fear I cannot add much to your discussion."

Karillos nodded. "Your gods," he repeated. "Do you have different gods, then?"

Arris decided to be haughty. "I am a son of the Lady. Do you think I would worship the Brothers Ylla?"

"It is as I feared," Karillos said coldly. "You are a follower of the daimon Goddess."

"Karillos," Saresha said lightly, "he is our guest."

"Your so-called religion is forbidden in the Khalifate," said the priest. "Were you not aware of that?"

Arris raised an eyebrow. "I am breaking your laws by my presence here? Forgive me. I had thought there was friendship between our peoples, and tolerance. It appears I was misinformed. My good ambassador, if you would show me to my rooms, I will direct my servant to pack my trunk again."

"Please, my lord," Falcmet said. "Don't be offended. I'm sure the priest did not mean—"

"I meant you are unwelcome here," said Karillos loudly. A lady of the court, running near them to retrieve a ball, stared at him.

"You will apologize, Karillos. Now." The Prince's voice was firm.

"I want to be certain he understands me. Your Goddess is an abomination, one that should have been cleansed from the world a thousand years ago. That you worship her means you are also unclean."

"Come," Arris said in brittle Yaighan as he turned and stalked away. Husayn hurried after him.

"My lord Prince!" He stopped him with a hand on his shoulder.

Arris reached up and lifted his brother's hand off. He hoped he was not overplaying his role. "If it is true that one can judge a ruler by his counselors," he said in Yaighan, "then your Prince is not one who should command your loyalty, Ambassador."

"Please do not judge him so," Husayn said in Yaighan

that was rough with disuse. "Please do not leave! You are the first indication we have had that the Lady is serious about establishing a friendship with the Khalifate. You must not leave!"

"It would reflect badly on your diplomacy, Ambassador, would it not?" Arris looked back, and saw Karillos striding away, and Falcmet and the Prince coming in his direction. The chatter of the women was silenced. He decided to let himself be swayed. "Very well. I will give him a chance to make amends."

Saresha's handsome face was deeply concerned. "Forgive me, Rahni, please. I had no idea he would behave that way. I had forgotten what Karillos was like on the subject of the Yaighan."

"He is intolerant," Arris said mildly. "There are those in Gama who are the same way about the Ilkharani. You must forgive my quickness to take offense. Ambassador Husayn has convinced me I behaved rashly."

"You were wholly justified," said the Prince. "Karillos is usually a worthy advisor. I have asked that he withdraw to his Temple for a few days to consider making a formal apology to you. I expect he will do so."

"Your Highness?" Falcmet said. "Do you still intend to invite my lord Prince to the Companions' war games this morning?"

"Of course." Saresha grinned at Arris. "If you want to go. They aren't as elaborate as the ones just held in Khessard, but they can be entertaining. Husayn is going to be a judge, and I'll be participating. You can too, if you like. Maybe we can show you the welcome you have yet to receive."

"It sounds intriguing," Arris said. "I've never seen war games."

"I'm afraid I won't be joining you," Falcmet said. "The midsummer accounts from Delronen have arrived, and I have to check them over and get them back."

"Sometimes I don't envy you your responsibilities, brother," Husayn said with a chuckle.

"Enjoy yourselves." Falcmet hurried away, leaving them to walk through the Garden Wall gate in search of horses to carry them to the practice fields inside the walls of the north palace.

•   •   •

"Husayn says you're here to learn about the Citadel court," Saresha remarked as they pulled their mounts up at the edge of the first field. A cluster of Companions in leather tunics and greaves over their short striped robes did not seem to notice them. The clatter of swordplay came from within the ring of men. "Well, this is by far the most interesting thing any of us here ever does. And if there is ever a war, it could be useful. We have sword bouts this morning. There will be wrestling later, and mounted battle, and perhaps the charioteers will perform for us."

Arris tried to look eager. He had never really enjoyed martial spectacle. The only fighting techniques he was any good at were classified as beneath the interest of noblemen in the Khalifate. Archery was the province of the lowborn infantry, and the charioteers Saresha had mentioned were most likely slaves. Jai-Sohn tactics in swordplay and unarmed combat would be considered horribly unfair, the tricks of street fighters and criminals. If he allowed the Prince to drag him into any contests, he would not do well.

Taifid noticed them from where he hovered, apparently bored, at the edge of the crowd. He hurried over to them, his handsome, sagging face beaming with pleasure. "Rahni! I heard you'd arrived. And that the Regents refused to allow you to be presented, and that the high priest told you you were breaking the religious law of the Khalifate. What an accomplishment! In your first twenty minutes here, you're already everyone's topic of conversation."

Saresha Ilkharani smiled. "That's a little exaggerated, Taifid. My uncles had important matters to concern them. A scorpion was found in Lord Komor's cradle."

"Will the Vizier accuse all the usual suspects?" Taifid said. "A scorpion! I've found any number of them in my bed. Doubtless put there by jilted lovers. Perhaps I should bring it up to the Regents."

"Aren't they rather common here?" Arris ventured.

"My dear boy, they are everywhere. In insect and human form." Taifid turned back to the Prince. "My lord, you can't tell me the gossip about Karillos is exaggerated. It sounds so like him."

Saresha sighed. "It's true. He'll apologize, once he realizes my request that he consider it was really a command."

A husky young nobleman with a pocked face joined them

briefly. "The sword bouts are almost over, my Prince. They want you to test the winner."

"I'll be there soon, Stenn." Saresha grinned at Arris. "Someday the winner of the sword bouts will beat me, and my Companions will no longer believe my divine right to rule makes me impossible to defeat. Of course, I had better teachers than they did. Your ambassadors Falcmet and Husayn taught me swordplay, you know. Will you come watch me fight?"

"He'll be there in a moment," Taifid said. "I'll see to it he gets a good view. Go on, my Prince. Show them how it's done."

Saresha laughed softly, and trotted with Husayn and Stenn toward the knot of spectators and fighters.

"The reason he always wins," Taifid said, "is that everyone lets him win. He would be crushed if he found out. Never tell him, eh, boy?"

Arris chuckled. He had wondered how anyone as small as Saresha could possibly defeat all those tall, muscular warriors. "It's good to see you, Taifid."

The older nobleman squeezed Arris's shoulder and began to walk with him slowly toward the games. "Is it true you had a run-in with Karillos? Already? Was it really about your religion?"

"I think so. He seemed to dislike me on sight."

"It might have been something else." Taifid's heavy-lidded brown eyes were troubled. "He has an uncanny sense for anyone who . . . doesn't let the teachings of the priests limit them in their choice of pleasures. I've had countless confrontations with him. He's threatened to have me tried for heresy. I'm certain he can't achieve a conviction. He'd only be able to produce boys from the Streets of Night as witnesses, and their testimony would be inadmissible."

"I'll try to avoid him," Arris said. This Karillos could be his enemy on many levels. The matter of his sexual diet would be trivial compared to his presumed worship of the Goddess. And that would be nothing if Karillos guessed his true purpose in coming to the Citadel, and his true identity. The priest's hatred of the Yaighan probably came from that day he had faced the Lossiran in the whitewashed Temple, and had been unable to apprehend the Yaighan boy who was the cause of the disruption.

"Do so," Taifid said. "And I would suggest you keep your . . . interests . . . secret from my Prince as well. He has never believed the scandals spread about me, because he's known me all his life. But he is influenced by Karillos, in this more than many things."

"I'll try to be discreet. Come. Let's watch your glorious Prince defeat another of his indulgent warriors."

"One way I entertain myself at these games," Taifid whispered as they approached the knot of Companions, "is by trying to see when the Prince's opponent deliberately throws his form or skews a thrust."

"It sounds amusing," Arris said dryly.

CHAPTER

20

THE EARLY AFTERNOON sun had become oppressive, shortening the shadows of the nearby Palace walls and heightening the scent of the wild grasses on the practice fields. Or perhaps Arris smelled the grasses more because he was closer to them. The wrestling match he had finally been talked into was not going well at all. The Companions cheerfully shouted encouragement and suggestions, and his opponent, the big youth Stenn, went out of his way to be courteous, stepping back after each throw to allow Arris the chance to get up.

Arris could easily have killed Stenn, but he did not know the Khalifate rules of wrestling, and the Jai-Sohn Way was not concerned with defeating opponents without injuring them. He wondered if any of the tricks Iyon had taught him would be legal in this bout. He knew how to turn an enemy's larger size and weight against him. But each time he instinctively reacted with one of Iyon's moves, he had to quickly disengage his hold to avoid hurting Stenn.

"Come up from beneath him," a nobleman muttered close by. "He's vulnerable at that angle. Not that you have much choice." Others laughed.

Arris nodded thanks and dived into a headfirst roll to come up between Stenn's widely planted legs. He heaved, felt the heavy weight leave the ground, and staggered forward as Stenn fell behind him. Arris whirled and leapt onto his opponent's back, attempting to grasp an arm and twist it around to hold Stenn there. But the big youth shrugged him off like a gnat, leaping back up to his feet and knocking Arris off with a sweep of his arm.

He hit the ground hard, off his form, and heard his brother Husayn's voice yelling, "What's the matter with you? Didn't Terai teach you anything? Show them how a Yaighan fights!"

Arris rolled beneath Stenn's lunge, and glared at Husayn. Very well. He would use his Jai-Sohn techniques, but he would try to modify them. He gathered himself and sprang into a feetfirst leap for Stenn's chest, striking him hard and knocking him down. But Stenn grabbed his legs and threw him overhead as if Arris had been one of the inflated balls in the ladies' game. The Companions shouted approval. Of course the move had failed, Arris thought sourly as he gathered himself again. Usually that leap went for the enemy's throat, and a man hit that hard in the throat did not fight back.

"Well done!" the Prince called, grinning at him. Arris wondered how long people usually lasted with Stenn. For a big man, he was quick and smart.

Stenn reached around him to grasp him from behind. Arris's balance was right; he instinctively gripped Stenn's thick wrists in one of Iyon's favorite moves and leapt into a backward flip, using his opponent's arms for leverage, arcing high in the air over Stenn's head to land atop the big youth's shoulders. His legs scissored around Stenn's throat, cutting off the blood supply to his brain. He almost let go immediately, afraid of hurting the Companion, but then he realized this was not a permanently damaging hold. It might work.

Stenn reached up and pulled at him, but Arris clung doggedly. Unconsciousness would come within ten seconds of applying this hold; dizziness would come sooner. The Companions shouted as Stenn fell to his knees. Husayn, who was acting as judge, ran out to examine the hold.

"Enough," he barked. "Release him."

Arris untangled his legs and stepped down, feeling his pounding pulse begin to slow, his many bruises begin to ache. He reached a hand to his bleary-eyed opponent. "Well fought," he said politely.

Stenn took his hand and heaved himself to his feet, smiling weakly. "Thought I had you . . ." he said.

"I thought he did, too," Saresha said, clapping Arris on the back. "But you had some tricks I've never seen before. If that last move was done in battle, how long would it take the man to die?"

"That isn't a killing strangle," Arris said. "But in battle you'd have a weapon to finish the enemy with."

"Assuming the enemy allowed you to climb onto his shoulders, or the melee granted you enough room for an acrobat's tumbling," a dry voice said from above them. Arris went cold, and did not turn with the others. He knew the voice, the sibilance of its phrasing, the annoyance it always seemed to project. The last time he had heard it he had been hiding behind a tapestry in his family suite.

"I'd like to learn it anyway," the Prince said. "It's good to see you, my lord Uncle. Have you come to watch the games?"

"No, Sasha. I have something to tell you before it becomes common Palace knowledge. But first, introduce me to this energetic young man. I feel I already know who he must be."

Arris took a deep breath and turned. Nievan sat on a tall warhorse, his balding head bound by an elaborate circlet, his puffy fingers laden with rings. He was a little more stout than he had been. Three palace guardsmen on matching black horses waited a short distance beyond. Arris met Nievan's pale eyes. This man would be easy to kill. He would feel no remorse.

"The most royal Regent, the Vizier Nievan, my uncle," Saresha said formally. "Prince Rahnisha Tualli, son of the Lady of the Yaighan."

"A pleasure, lord," Arris said.

"Your Highness." Nievan smiled warmly. "I hope your visit to the Khalifate will result in even closer relations between our peoples."

"That is also my mother's hope," Arris said, falling belatedly back into his role.

"Soon we may stand together against a common enemy,"

Nievan continued. "We will combine our strength in arms. And perhaps the world will finally learn the secret of the battle for Delronen, in which your Ambassador Husayn distinguished himself so."

"Perhaps, my lord Regent," Arris said.

"In any case, we welcome you." Nievan turned back to his nephew, his elastic face becoming somber. "I did not want you to hear this from anyone else, Sasha. You have been most commendably loyal to your father's old retainer, General Fallayan."

"I have," Saresha said, folding his arms over his striped tunic. "He hasn't done anything wrong. No matter what my uncles may believe."

"He has confessed," Nievan said.

"To what?" shouted a lanky, brown-haired young man standing next to Husayn. Arris saw his brother react quickly, putting a restraining hand on the Companion's shoulder.

"Quiet, Jakim," Husayn muttered. "Don't draw attention to yourself."

"To murder and attempted murder, young jen Fallayan," the Regent said. "To using poison in the duel with Murin. And to placing a scorpion in the cradle of my youngest son. His purpose was to begin an insane program to eliminate all of Ilkharani blood."

"Poisoned blades?" Saresha said in disbelief. "Scorpions? No reasonable man would believe such charges."

"He has resorted to desperate measures for a man with such a distinguished record of service to our late Khalif. There are suggestions that the recent acts of sabotage committed against our newly built warships may also be attributed to this bitter man."

"Suggestions?" Jakim cried. "Whose suggestions? Yours and Emir Maenad's? My Prince, this is a travesty. You cannot believe—"

"I don't believe any of it," Saresha said.

Nievan shrugged. "You'll be Khalif one day, Nephew. You'll learn that a ruler may not always trust his feelings. Fallayan is a dangerous criminal."

"Let me see the General," the Prince said harshly. "Let me question him for myself."

"That would not be wise," Nievan said regretfully. "You will, of course, be allowed at his trial, where you may hear the evidence against him." He frowned. "You may also wish to consider whether you should retain Jakim jen Fallayan as a member of your Companions. If his father is convicted, which seems likely, he may feel compelled to vengeance."

"The choice of my Companions is one area in which I have some authority," Saresha said, his fists clenched at his side, his face burning beneath its tan.

"As you will." The Vizier nodded. "I will expect you for dinner tonight, Nephew. Clean, and in attire becoming the Crown Prince of the Khalifate." He reined his horse around and trotted away, his retainers closing ranks behind him.

"They'll soon be rid of everyone I can trust," Saresha said quietly, fighting to control his anger. "Husayn? I know that some of your Yaighan people live in Qadasiya. Will you take Jakim and hide him there?"

"Don't send me away, my Prince," Jakim pleaded.

"They may decide to accuse you as well. Husayn?"

"Of course, Your Highness. And if it becomes necessary, we'll find a place for him at Delronen."

"Good. If any of the rest of you can think of anything, you can find me in my exercise room with Rahni here, trying to learn that acrobatic move of his." He began to walk toward the tethered horses.

"That can wait," Arris said, running to keep up. "You have other matters to concern you now."

The Prince shook his head as he took the reins from his servant and mounted. "I need something to do. Something to keep me from thinking about my . . . impotence . . . when a man's life is at stake." He looked uncertainly at Arris. "But forgive me, Rahni. I didn't even ask if you were willing to teach me."

"It will be an honor," Arris said. Terai would be pleased, he thought, at how quickly he was gaining the Prince's friendship.

"My Prince." Taifid trotted his mount up beside them. "You should speak to Oella. We know she is a reasonable woman, for all she's Nievan's wife. She ought to have some influence over him after six years. And her child was the one threatened by the scorpion. If you could get her to speak on the General's behalf . . ."

"Good," Saresha said, frowning. "It must be approached carefully. Nievan mustn't know it isn't her idea. Send one of your servants to her, Taifid. Then get her to my suite unseen, if you can.''

"Nothing simpler, my Prince.'' Taifid saluted lightly and put spurs to his horse to gallop ahead of them.

No longer a boy in the nursery, Saresha now occupied most of the second floor of the south tower. He led Arris quickly through his rooms, speaking lightly on any topic but the day's events. There were rooms for his body servant and attendants; a large, well-furnished bedchamber and sitting room; a bare wood-floored room with a rack of weapons against one wall, where he was trained each day by the Citadel swordmaster; and a library complete with shelves full of parchment scrolls and bound books.

"I enjoy reading,'' Saresha explained, pushing the library doors open. "Especially histories. Karillos allows me access to the Temple archives, and even lets me bring things back here to study . . . oh. Good day, my lord Uncle. Karillos.''

Arris stopped on the threshold. The gold-robed priest sat in one of the library chairs, leafing through a leather-bound volume, his youthful face suddenly changing from serene to tense. A thin, aging man whose flesh hung loose and whose eyes were sunk in calculating folds waited with him. Emir Maenad had changed considerably in the nine years since Arris had seen him last. Perhaps ruling the Gharin Emirate and sharing the regency with Nievan was too taxing. On a second appraisal, Arris guessed it was a disease that was wasting him so. The man would probably welcome assassination.

"Your Highness,'' said the priest nervously, glancing at the Regent. Maenad nodded greeting to his nephew.

"Excuse me a moment, Uncle,'' Saresha said with strained politeness. "Karillos, I asked you to return to the Temple this morning to consider your apology to our honored guest.''

"Though you will be Khalif and head of the church when you are twenty-one, Saresha, that time has not yet come,'' Maenad said in a scolding tone. "You commanded Karillos to leave the Palace for speaking his mind. Rightly, he came to me. I cannot believe you would so disregard my teachings on tolerance for all views.''

"I don't think you understand, Uncle,'' Saresha said defensively. "Do you know what Karillos said?''

"I understood it was a religious dispute," Maenad said.

"He insulted Prince Rahnisha Tualli. I felt his presence at court would only create unneeded tension. I requested he leave. I did not command. But Karillos has always acceded to my requests before."

"I would have done so again, my Prince," said the priest softly. "But this matter cannot be left unresolved. The Yaighan is a danger to you, to all of us. I sense it. He must not remain here."

"Is there a reason for your dislike of me?" Arris said coldly. "I would hate to see the friendship between our peoples marred by such a triviality."

"The friendship between our peoples?" Karillos said. "That will not last long, son of the Goddess's whore. And it will not be broken by the Khalifate."

Arris stared at him. Did the priest know of the Millennium? "You are irrational, priest," he said. "I cannot excuse your insulting reference to my mother the Lady, but unless a formal apology is presented to the Yaighan Ambassadors, I will indeed leave this place. I will explain to my people that an alliance with the Khalifate is impossible."

"There will be no apology," Karillos muttered.

"Is this the sort of thing you were saying this morning, Karillos?" Maenad asked in a strained voice. "Young Prince, he speaks with the voice of religion. I speak for the state, in saying that the Khalifate values its alliance with the Lady of Gama, and hopes its ties with her people will strengthen over time."

"And the apology, Uncle?" Saresha prompted.

"Will be in the hands of the Yaighan ambassadors no later than tomorrow afternoon. Come, priest." He rose, inclined his head, and stalked from the room.

"Karillos," Saresha said as the priest rose to go. "You strain our friendship to the breaking point."

"You have always trusted me before, my Prince," he said unhappily. "I wish you could now. I tell you this is vitally important. I fear terrible things will happen if you allow this young viper to remain near you." He pulled his robe in to avoid brushing against Arris as he passed.

"Perhaps it would be best if I left," Arris said heavily. "I don't want you to lose the support of his Temple."

"Karillos will come to his senses," Saresha said in a

troubled voice. "He's usually too intelligent to be so swayed by an emotional response. He'll realize his error."

"I hope you're right." He doubted the priest would give up. Karillos did not yet know why Arris was here, but he was on the right trail. Arris wished he had at least some of his old power, enough to shield himself from the priest. Perhaps Terai could shield him.

"I want to learn that hold of yours," Saresha said briskly. "Show it to me."

"It may take some time to learn," Arris warned as they walked back into the exercise room. Saresha shrugged off his tunic and stood there in leggings and boots, a breathing incarnation of a sun god. Arris swallowed hard, and told himself sternly that if he was to be an objective teacher he had better ignore his pupil's beauty. "I don't know how much experience you've had of tumbling," he said, pulling his own grass-stained and torn robe over his head and tossing it across a sword rack. "That's what it's based on, of course. An acrobat's pyramid techniques."

"I'll learn quickly," Saresha promised. His smile was guileless as an infant's, though his sapphire eyes were troubled still. It was a compelling combination.

"Your Highness?" A deferential old man in the livery of a servant entered the room. "A lady requests an audience."

"A lady? Who?" Saresha asked irritably, drawing off his boots in preparation for wrestling.

"Your Highness, she will not say. She is heavily veiled."

Arris raised an eyebrow at the Prince, whose expression suddenly sharpened. "Ask her to come in, Ulan. You and the other servants may have the afternoon free."

"Your Highness," Ulan bowed low and hurried away.

"Nievan's wife?" Arris guessed. "Should I leave, Saresha?"

"No. Of course not. Stop continually asking if you should leave. I'll tell you when I'm tired of your company," the Prince said. Then he smiled ruefully. "That sounded terrible, didn't it? I'm not quite myself this afternoon."

Arris inclined his head gracefully. The Prince was charming even when he was being arrogant.

A slim, dark-robed figure glided into the exercise room with the small, mincing steps Khalifate men supposedly prized in their women. Her robe of brown silk brocade had an attached hood, from which at least four layers of veils depended. Her eyes were brown and lively.

"My lady," Saresha said, rising to bow over his discarded boots. "I am grateful you could come."

She lifted the heavy veils and tossed them back, revealing a plain, ruddy-cheeked face incongruously ornamented by filigreed earrings and an elaborate golden collar. She was quite young, Arris saw with some surprise. No more than twenty-four, he guessed.

"Such secrecy!" she said lightly. "I felt I was being spirited off to some forbidden assignation with a castle guardsman."

"Did Taifid's servant explain?" Saresha asked nervously, in no mood for banter.

She nodded, immediately serious. "I was astonished, Sasha. I knew my husband suspected that someone had deliberately put that scorpion in Komor's cradle, but I didn't imagine he'd accuse the General."

"Please come into my library, Lady Oella," Saresha said, beckoning her forward. "I value your advice in this matter."

"And you hope I can influence my husband on Fallayan's behalf," she said.

"You can be more clear-sighted than my uncle. I'm certain you'll understand when I tell you this accusation may only hurt him in the future." He glanced at Arris. "Come with us, Rahni. Perhaps you can help. You must be used to the sort of intrigue that surrounds an heir to the throne."

"Fortunately, in Gama the sons of the Lady don't succeed to the Kingship," Arris said in private amusement.

"Fortunate indeed," Oella said with an indulgent smile. "It would be pleasant to be a Prince if one could continue in that role. That young composer who has recently come to court . . . Danae, isn't it? She told me you quite enjoy your lack of any responsibility."

"I have the freedom to do as I like," Arris said. "But that brings with it the burden of thinking of something to do." He took her arm and seated her in the largest chair of the library.

"Oh, Sasha, thank you for sending her to perform for me," Oella said. "I see what you find so unusual about her music. That duet for reed flute and soprano was remarkable. Lovely. If you ever decide to drop your patronage of her, I'll support her myself."

"I'm glad you enjoyed it," Saresha said.

"Wouldn't you say she is talented, Your Highness?" Oella said to Arris.

"Yes, very talented," he muttered. A work for reed flute? That minstrel he had seen her with, Pellen. He was a flutist. She had already written a piece for him. He should not feel jealous; he had been the one who had rejected Danae. He should not begrudge her a new love.

Oella nodded slightly. "You're quite right to be uninterested in such gossip, when the General is in danger. I'll do what I can, Sasha, but what shall I say to the Vizier? I can't simply insist that Fallayan isn't guilty."

"Mention to him how this will look to my supporters in the Consulate," Saresha said. "To those who already suspect my uncles of plotting to deny me my inheritance."

Oella looked at him sharply. "Of course you don't believe this."

"I know the Regents are working for the good of the Ilkharani line," Saresha said carefully. "If they meant to depose me, why would they be such demanding teachers? But my followers will believe they are trying to get rid of everyone who might defend me if they attempted a coup."

"Fallayan has always been adamant about his loyalty to you and your father's memory," she said thoughtfully. "Even to the extent of protesting my marriage to the Vizier. He felt there were plenty of children of Rasul's line to ensure the succession, and that it was a plot by Nievan to put his own children on the throne."

"The General is very conservative," Saresha said. "He also opposed what he felt was the overly quick election of the Regents after my father's death." He sighed. "You can see what I mean, my lady. My people will accuse the Regents of taking the opportunity to get rid of a thorn in their sides."

"My husband can be vindictive toward those he feels are his enemies," Oella said. "His dislike of Fallayan is a personal matter. It has nothing to do with your succession. Only last week, the General was loudly protesting the priority of the army's budget toward shipbuilding rather than toward border fortifications against the Deirani." She smiled. "I actually agreed with him there. Those ships are Maenad's pet scheme. I don't think my husband is entirely convinced of their value. But Fallayan did openly oppose the Regents in the matter.''

"Will you try to convince Nievan to drop the accusations?'' Saresha said quietly, looking down at his hands resting in his lap.

The plain young woman shrugged. "I'll try presenting it to my husband as you suggest. I don't know what good it will do. Of course your General is innocent, and of course you're right about the political danger of accusing him, but once Nievan is set on a course he isn't likely to change his mind. I can't influence him that much.''

"He loves you,'' Saresha said, leaning over to kiss her on the cheek. "Maybe you can help. Even if you can't, I'll be grateful for the effort.''

She rose and hugged him, then gathered her veils in her hand to replace them across her face. "Grateful enough to leave your Companions and come visit my children one day soon? The boys don't see enough of their cousin.''

Saresha grinned. "I'll take them along the next time I go to the stables, and give them a ride in my chariot. The driver can keep it slow. How old are they now? Four and six? They'd be safe enough.''

"They'll worship you even more.'' Oella's eyes smiled over her veil. "If it won't be too much trouble.''

"They are my declared heirs, until I father children of my own,'' Saresha said. "I should spend time with them.'' He linked his arm with hers to walk her to the door of his suite.

Arris watched them from the library threshold. He had never thought that the deaths of his victims would affect others. When he killed Nievan, Oella would be widowed, their three sons without a father. When he killed Saresha, Oella's oldest son would be Khalif. When he killed Saresha. The old dream had lost its savor in the space of one day. It was still his duty to Areyta's memory, to the Emperor, and now to Terai. But he feared it would be an unpleasant task.

CHAPTER
21

"KARILLOS WAS HERE," Terai said quietly as Arris entered the spare, stone-walled room he had been given in the palace. The older Yaighan sat at a heavy carved desk in a massive chair, wearing his manservant garb. The elaborate clothing Arris had purchased in Qadasiya lay neatly folded in an open chest at the foot of the narrow, padded bed. A brocade sitting bench by the high window was the only other furniture in the room, which was typical of the residences of high-ranking members of the Citadel court. The meanest provincial clerk in Deiran would be insulted to be offered such a room in the Sapphire Palace.

"What did he want?" Arris closed the door and barred it behind him. After Oella had left, he and the Prince had worked for two hours on basic tumbling exercises; that, added to the wrestling earlier that day, had exhausted him. He sat on the bed to peel off his sweat-stained silks.

"He's convinced you're dangerous, though he doesn't know why. He tried to bribe me into telling him."

"What did you say?" Arris was amused at the thought of anyone trying to bribe Terai.

"Nothing. I played the loyal servant." Terai's voice was uncharacteristically tense. "He didn't accept that. He tried to probe me mentally. Clumsy, but powerful. If his lack of subtlety hadn't warned me what he was attempting, he might have gotten through."

"If he has that kind of power, why didn't he try it on me?" Arris asked. "Surely he would have succeeded."

"He may have already tried." The older man looked somewhat embarrassed. "I haven't told you this before. I didn't

222

think you'd want to hear it, and it wasn't likely to be necessary . . . but you are still shielded, Arris. Those patternings have only been strengthened since that night you forswore the Goddess's power."

"That's impossible."

"Otherwise, we would have found you in Deiran long ago." Terai shrugged his shoulders. "I don't know who or what is supplying them for you. It could be your daimon Aghlayeshkusa, or it could even be the Goddess. In any case, you should be safe from any attempt by Karillos to probe your mind."

Arris supposed he should be relieved, but he was frightened. After all his efforts to escape, he was still an unwitting pawn of some power. He almost preferred that it might turn out to be the daimon rather than Rehoman. If the Crimson Goddess still controlled him, then it could be he had never had any choices in his destiny.

"How did you fare today with the Prince?" Terai said more lightly. "I spent my time with the servants, and most of their conversation was of the accused General. Which gave me the beginnings of a plan . . . but first, your day."

"I gained his respect, I think," Arris said, forcing his thoughts away from Karillos and the Goddess. "And the beginnings of friendship." He told Terai what he had learned of the Companions, of the Regents, and of Oella.

Terai smiled when he was finished. "Then it's true what my contacts insisted, that the Prince would do anything he could to free Fallayan?"

"He can't do much about it."

"Perhaps we can." Terai folded his hands before him on the desk and looked at them thoughtfully. "Let Oella try to change her husband's mind. When she fails, you and I will offer to Saresha to rescue the General ourselves."

"Rescue him? From the Black Masks? That's insane."

"Difficult, perhaps. But it can be done. And if we succeed, you will have gained the Prince's absolute trust."

"And annoyed the Regents in the process." Arris shook his head. "If we don't both get killed."

"You're a trained Jai-Sohn. I'm an experienced spy, and a priest of the Goddess as well. I would say our chances were better than even. We'll have to move quickly, before the Regents have time to torture Fallayan into a real confession.

If we don't reach him by tomorrow night, he won't be fit to travel. But if we can get him, with the help of a few Companions on the outside, and Fallayan's son Jakim in Qadasiya, he could be safely hidden at Delronen within the week. And the Prince might be impressed enough with you to offer you Jakim's place in his Companions.''

Arris nodded finally. "It could work. I'll trust you to arrange whatever is necessary." He pulled fresh garments out of the chest at the foot of the bed and began to dress again.

Terai frowned at him. "You should be well rested tomorrow night when we go after the General. Don't you think you should send me to politely decline Taifid's dinner invitation tonight?"

Arris grinned. "I haven't had a good night's sleep for the past five years, Terai. My body isn't used to it. Don't worry. I'll be ready."

The veiled slave woman approached Arris the next day in the gardens, where he lounged with apparent indifference, studying the patterns of the guards who walked before the ornate black gates that held the first entrance to the underground dungeons. The woman startled him, quietly padding up beside him on slippered feet. Her brown eyes were lowered and demure, though the slight movements of her gloved hands gave away her nervousness.

"My lady wishes to speak to you," the woman said softly.

"Indeed?" Arris remarked, assuming his accent again. "And which lady might she be?" He had no time to pay court to some maiden who might have seen him while she played ball the day before.

"The Lady Oella," the slave said almost inaudibly. Her opaque veil barely quivered with her breath.

Arris blinked, then forced himself to betray only mild interest. "The wife of the Regent Nievan? I have not had the opportunity of meeting her as yet, though I have heard she is a most noble and praiseworthy woman."

"If it would be convenient for you, Your Highness, would you follow me?" the slave said impatiently.

"Certainly." He had to lengthen his stride to keep up with the woman, who did not affect the mincing steps of her mistress. Why would Oella want to see him? To remind him that her visit to the Prince the day before had been secret?

Perhaps her husband had accused her of speaking someone else's words when she argued with him about the General, and she did not trust Arris not to accidentally mention her conversation with Saresha.

The light, frolicking music of a group of string players sifted through the walls of Nievan's large suite in the north tower. After a moment, Arris recognized it as one of Danae's compositions from Deiran, though the once-mournful melodic line had been broken into a series of playful variations, and the leading voice was passed from instrument to instrument until a low harp plucked it out in an almost humorous echo at the end. Arris did not know if he liked it better than the original version, but he could hear the growth in Danae's skills. She had probably been right to seize the opportunity to come back to the Khalifate.

"My lady will receive you within," said the woman, who opened the door before hurrying away.

Arris sighed and stepped through into the suite. It was lovely, furnished richly but with a sense of restraint and balance he did not think Nievan possessed. Even the tapestries on the high walls were woven of subtle, abstract bands of muted hues, instead of the usual bright, complicated scenes of hunting and warfare. Even a noble of Khopei might consider Oella's decorations aesthetically pleasing.

The Vizier's young wife sat on a low stool facing the musicians, who busied themselves tuning their harps and lyres after the deceptively taxing number they had finished playing. Danae was not among them.

Oella turned to see Arris, and rose to greet him, curtseying formally. "I am so glad you could come to meet me, Your Highness," she said with no trace of recognition from the day before. "My royal husband spoke of you yesterday, and I am most eager to hear you tell of your people and their customs. If you would follow me, we may speak privately in my sitting room. I have had refreshments brought."

Arris bowed, conscious of the interested but carefully neutral expressions of the minstrels. He was not certain it was within the bounds of Khalifate etiquette for a married woman to meet with an unrelated young man alone, but Oella seemed quite confident in her request. He followed her without speaking.

When they were alone, she shut the sitting room door

firmly behind them. There were small cakes and pitchers of scented water on a low table, but she did not offer him any. She turned to him, all lightness gone from her face. It was sharp now, its plainness severe. "Do you know why I asked to speak to you?" she asked, motioning him to a cushioned chair.

"My lady, you need not worry that I will ever speak of your conversation with the Prince," he said as she sat across from him.

She nodded dismissively. "I have no doubt of that." Her short fingers tapped on the table beside her, rattling a water pitcher. "Karillos spoke to me for some time this morning." She smiled slightly. "Of course, I discount his accusations against you. They are farfetched even for a priest to believe."

"I am glad my lady thinks so," Arris said carefully.

"Yet there are other matters. Matters I fear you have unknowingly become involved in." Frown lines appeared between her brows as she looked at him. "This is difficult to explain," she admitted. "And I do not wish to offend you. The customs of your people are different from ours. It may be you do not realize the danger you place yourself in. And you do not only endanger yourself."

"You bewilder me, lady," Arris said in his thickest accent, growing more and more uncomfortable.

"I'll try to be more clear," she said, discarding some of her formality. "Since Karillos became the high priest of Qadasiya, only a few years ago, the Temple has suddenly become much stricter. Especially in enforcing the moral standards of the Mythos. It may be that Karillos is very young. He isn't as forgiving as a more experienced man might be. He . . ." She looked down at her lap. "He is very concerned about this . . . enforcement."

"I think I may already have been warned of this, my lady," Arris said quietly.

"Yes. I know Taifid spoke to you of it." She met his eyes again. "My family and the family of the Lord Collector have been closely linked for many years . . . Taifid, no matter his faults, has been an older brother to me. Karillos knows this." Her voice lowered to a hoarse whisper. "He threatened this morning to have Taifid tried for heresy. He has witnesses, he has proofs . . . how can he help but have them, when Taifid

has been so indiscriminate? If it goes to trial, Taifid will be
convicted. And he'll be killed.''

Arris shivered at the fear in her voice. "Why did Karillos
threaten you with this? What did he want from you?"

"He wanted my help in snaring you on the same charges
he'd bring against Taifid," she said in a rush of words. "If I
could produce witnesses that the two of you had been together
. . . he promised me you'd be cast as the seducer, that Taifid
would get off with a light penance and censure from the
Consulate.'' She looked at him helplessly. "Why is he so
afraid of you? He has threatened Taifid before, but he has
never been so serious. We thought it was because Taifid is so
close to the Prince. But now . . .'' She sighed. "I could give
him the witnesses he wants. I keep close track of Taifid's
actions, hoping to protect him. I know he spent a night with
you in Qadasiya, and last night, and probably more.''

"Did you tell this to Karillos?"

"No.'' She forced her drumming fingers to be quiet. "I
may fear for Taifid, but I also know that my husband's
interests would be ill served if the visiting Yaighan Prince
were tried and executed for crimes against Khalifate gods.''

"I don't think the alliance between our countries would
benefit from such an action,'' Arris said dryly.

She almost smiled at that. "I'm afraid Taifid may have to
leave the court for a time, which will be hard on him. And
I'll miss him terribly. But if he is out of the jurisdiction of the
Qadasiya temple, he's unlikely to be in danger. Perhaps I can
get him a job in the bureaucracy in Khessard.''

"I'll miss him too,'' Arris said honestly. "I like him.''

"That's obvious enough,'' she snapped. "Now that you're
warned of the extent of Karillos's hatred for you, young
Prince, you had better be more careful. The priest will learn
nothing from my people, but there are other spies in the
Citadel. And he will be watching you. You may not believe
in the Five Brothers of the Sun, but unless you conform to
their laws while you are here, the Lady will have one less
irresponsible son to worry about. Do you understand me?''

Arris nodded gravely. He had underestimated Karillos; the
priest had worked faster than Arris would have thought possible. "I'll be careful.'' He rose and bowed over Oella's
graciously outstretched hands. "I thank you for your warn-

ing, lady." He looked at her strong, unlovely face. "And I hope your royal husband values you as much as you deserve."

"Perhaps he does, in his own way," she said quietly. "Perhaps he does . . . good afternoon, Rahnisha Tualli."

"Good afternoon, lady." He bowed again and went out.

Even if Karillos had spies watching Arris, he would have no news of this night. Arris and Terai wore dull, deep black and a shadowing spell that would hide them from anyone who did not look directly at them. General Iyon would have said that a true Jai-Sohn did not rely on magic; Arris would not rely upon it, but it added an edge to his confidence.

The Companions had managed to have one of their own stationed with the guards at the dungeon gates. Most of Saresha's friends held honorary titles in the army for their bloodlines and their fathers' prestige, but unlike others of the young nobles, the Companions occasionally served short terms of duty. Tonight Stenn, the big wrestler who still regarded Arris with bewilderment whenever he came near him, had volunteered to take the place of an unwell guard. It would mean that Stenn would have to accompany Fallayan and his son to Delronen, and give up his place in the Companions when the night's work was done. His post was the only one in the escape plan that the Regents were sure to discover. Stenn had insisted on volunteering. Saresha, of course, had promised to reward him when he became Khalif.

Arris slipped through the cool night air like a swimmer underwater, feeling the breeze only on the exposed skin around his eyes, feeling the silent grit of courtyard earth beneath the soles of his gloved feet. Terai's movements seemed an extension of his own thoughts. They glided in alternating patterns, one leading at first, then halting, pressed low against the dark, mossy stones while the other passed and repeated his motions. Iyon had made Arris do this perfectly a thousand times. It was as natural to him now as any other mode of walking.

They could see Stenn ahead of them with the other guardsmen, big and deceptively awkward in his uniform. His shadow, cast by the globe lantern he carried with his spear, loomed jagged against the high, barred gates. Far above them, a sentry walked a circuit of the Women's Wall, his own globe of light moving in the darkness. They had timed their actions by that sentry's path. Now if Stenn only thought to look up, he would know that Arris and Terai were nearby, and it was time to begin.

Arris hoped they could trust Saresha's young Companions to fill their parts in the plan reliably. They had all been eager and excited about a chance to test some of their game-acquired skills. Arris was not sure they understood that this was not another game. Saresha had understood. The Prince had been reluctant to attempt Arris's scheme, until word had finally come from Oella that she had not been able to sway Nievan. The General's trial was set for the morrow. And there were rumors among the servants that Fallayan had been tortured already.

Stenn was moving only a little late. The gate opened slightly, as the Companion and one of his guardsman friends decided together that they could be absent from their post for a moment, while they brought a bottle from the guards' room on the dungeon's first level. The other guard remained looking outward, assured that he would have his chance at the wine when the other two returned.

Arris had not moved an eyelash since he had settled into his last position just beyond the sentry's pool of light. Terai had shifted his weight a few times, less comfortable with the crouched stance than he would have been as a younger man, but skilled enough to make his movements imperceptible. They had not been detected. Arris pressed his folded hands together lightly, summoning speed in his Jai-Sohn trance state. The gate would not be open long. He felt the calm serenity one might feel in meditation in a quiet garden. Iyon was a better Jai-Sohn master than most; he had paid attention to his student's mental state as well as his physical training. This calm was vital, whether one was waiting within sight if the enemy turned to look, or launching a ferocious attack to take out a sentry.

Stenn urged his companion through the gate with a hand on his shoulder, telling a ribald joke that distracted the other guard as well. Arris gave a short nod, knowing Terai had seen, and crept forward with long, low strides, bent nearly double, close to the ground. The gate was still open, though Stenn and the other were through. Arris entered the pool of light cast by the torches, remembering Iyon saying that an enemy used to seeing in torchlight would not likely have the night vision needed to pick out a black form against dark stones.

Now. Moving with a smoothness that made it appear he was going slowly, he raced past the angle of the open bars and ducked into a low alcove just beyond the gate as Stenn and the guard passed him with their torches encased in pale globes. He felt the brush of Terai's hand on his shoulder, behind him in the alcove, and smiled beneath his mask. They were inside. He peered out of the alcove at knee level, knowing that even if someone was looking in that direction they would not expect to see a head that far down. The low-ceilinged corridor was dark. The glow of the sentry lamps dimmed as Stenn and the guard turned into a room at the side.

Terai moved ahead to lead. He knew the plan of the Citadel dungeons, though he had not told Arris where he had found that knowledge. They passed the open door of the guardroom snaking on the floor, then rose to hurry on. They would have to be quick. Stenn had orders to see the gate open again when the sentry on the wall had made another half-circuit.

There would be other guards deeper in the maze, though how many Arris did not know. The corridor sloped steeply downward. The dungeons were part of the oldest burrows of the Citadel, far older than the Ilkharani dynasty. The dank smell of mildewed stone seemed sharpened by the misery of the men and women who had been held here over the centuries. Arris was glad he no longer had his Goddess-given sensitivity. If he had that awareness, surely he would sense a lingering trace of the Lord Areyta's death here at the hands of the Black Masks.

The corridor ended in a wall of blank stone. A narrow iron ladder led downward from a hole in the floor. There would be a small guardroom below, where the prison keepers came sometimes to eat and sleep.

"I'll watch above," Terai said very softly. "I'm too old to go down a ladder headfirst."

Arris nodded. Iyon had taught him this skill as well. It was vital when descending into a room where enemies might be. They could not be allowed to see you before you saw them. He drew his dull black sword and hooked it by a ring on its hilt to a clasp built on the outside of the sheath for that purpose; it would come away with a tug. It hung, point downward, toward his face as he hoisted himself onto the top rungs of the ladder, his legs wrapped froglike above him, his toes in his divided slippers finding a firm grip on the iron supports. He began to inch downward like a spider on a filament of web.

He smelled the dungeons before he reached them. The stench of a prison did not change, whether that prison was Emperor Hareku's or the Citadel's. The smell of men helpless in their own filth, of fire and heated flesh and blood, it would bring fear to the bravest prisoner who was forced down into the long ladder tunnel.

Wall torches guttered in grimy sconces in the guardroom below him. One guard slept on a pallet of rushes in a corner. Other than that, the room was empty. A trio of heavy locked doors led from the central room to the cells. Another door behind the ladder led to the torture rooms. On the opposite side of the room, another ladder descended still farther into the deeps. Terai had guessed that Fallayan would be held in an upper-level cell to await his trial, though. Arris hoped that was true. He had no desire to go deeper.

He could not turn around in the narrow tunnel. He descended slowly, still headfirst, until he was not far from the floor. Then he released his legs and landed lightly beside the ladder. The sleeping guard did not waken. The prison was not really well guarded. The Ilkharani considered the fortifications of their Palace and Citadel proof against their enemies. They had obviously never had to deal with rescue attempts from within the Citadel itself.

Arris pulled his sword free and walked slowly over to the guard. He had heard that some Jai-Sohn found pleasure in this sort of killing. To him it was a necessity to be regretted. But that would not make him hesitate. He bent and slit the guard's throat with practiced efficiency. Then he searched the soldier's belt and took his keys.

Terai had come down the ladder so quietly that even Arris had not heard him. His black eyes narrowed a little over his face mask when he saw the guard, but then he seemed to shrug slightly, and moved to the nearest cell door. Arris hurried to unlock all three doors. Each door guarded a short tunnel lined with cells. Terai took the first tunnel and Arris the second.

They did not want an outcry from the other prisoners, so

they tried to keep their presence unknown. The heavy, iron-bound doors had small openings near the floor through which food could be passed. Arris crept along the floor, looking into each opening only briefly. Most of the cells were empty. He saw one half-naked, shivering slave who had been whipped and would probably be released soon. Farther down, a fully dressed, middle-aged laborer slept soundly on the floor of his relatively clean cell. He had not been there long.

"Come," he heard Terai hiss from behind him. He turned to see the Yaighan at the tunnel entrance, beckoning. He must have found the General.

Fallayan was in the first bank of cells, their only occupant. He was worse hurt than rumor had suggested. He was conscious as they entered his cell, but his eyes were glazed with pain. The bones in both his lower legs had been shattered, as if crushed in a vise. His legs were swollen horribly and caked with dried blood. Blood was pooled beneath him. Arris turned to meet Terai's gaze with dismay. How could they get him out?

Fallayan was a tall, well-muscled old man whose long beard and mustache had been the Citadel fashion when Arris was a boy. His pale skin was mottled with bruises from a day-old beating; his legs had been crushed that morning, if Arris could judge the state of the swelling. His bright green eyes stared up at them defiantly.

"The Prince sent us," Terai said quietly. "We've come to get you out of here. We'll have to lift you. Can you remain silent?"

"Better . . ." the old man whispered, "if you gag me first . . ."

Arris tore two long strips of black cloth from the hem of his tunic. Working quickly, he wadded one strip and pressed it into Fallayan's opened mouth, then bound the gag with the other strip and knotted it behind the old man's head.

The General gave a muffled cry as they raised him from the floor, but the gag made it almost inaudible. Arris was amazed at Fallayan's courage. He suspected he would have given up to unconsciousness long before. He wondered if such a man could live long as a cripple. The legs would have to be amputated when they got him to a healer. Only the very lucky, or the very stubborn, survived such an operation.

They tied Arris's sword belt beneath the General's arms to

haul him up the ladder. There was not enough room in the tunnel for either of them to carry him. Terai went up first and pulled the General's weight, while Arris tried to guide him from beneath and keep his legs from scraping on the passage.

Had they taken too long? Arris climbed the last rungs of the ladder and helped Terai lift the General to his back like a child. Fallayan wrapped his arms firmly around Terai's neck and clasped his wrists before him. Terai's arms linked beneath the old man's knees. Arris pulled his sword belt tight around them both. There was no need for him to sheathe his sword now. He would have to fight for both himself and Terai.

They ran through the corridor, abandoning stealth. Now it was a matter for speed and surprise. Arris loped ahead of Terai toward the shrouded light at the gate. Stenn had just gotten it open, and now his two erstwhile companions were staring at the longsword he had drawn. Arris crashed into one of the bemused guards and drove him from the gate, leaving room for Terai to run past with his burden.

The guard only managed to get his sword half-drawn before Arris killed him. The sharp black Deirani steel slipped through the ring-and-leather mail coat with only a slight hesitation. The stroke was precise. Arris pulled his sword back in the same movement and turned to help Stenn.

The big Companion was staring stupidly at his dead opponent. His longsword had caught the guard with the surprised expression still on his face. Arris grabbed Stenn's sword and pulled the young nobleman stumbling after Terai and Fallayan.

Two dark-cloaked Companions awaited them in a pavilion at the edge of the garden. A hole had been dug beneath an uprooted flagstone of the pavilion floor. Arris and Terai stripped off their Jai-Sohn clothes and stuffed them and the two bloody swords into the hole to be recovered later on some moonless night. The two Companions bundled the General into an enveloping cloak, then drew him up to support him on either side. The cloak reached past his feet, so although he was being carried it might appear he was walking.

"Go on," Arris said in a harsh whisper to Stenn, who stood numbly watching. "They need your guard uniform to get them through the gates. You aren't finished yet."

"I never . . . killed . . . anyone before," Stenn said miserably, staring at his weapons-skilled hands as if they were new to him.

"Think about it later, lad," Terai said. "When you're safe at Delronen. Now move."

"Those guardsmen . . . they didn't have anything to do with this . . . none of it was their fault, and now they're dead," Stenn continued.

"You served your Prince well," Terai said, pushing him toward the door. "Remember that. And remember Jakim waiting for his father south of Qadasiya."

"The hardest part is over, Stenn," Arris said. "Are you going to let Saresha down now?"

He shook his head. "I guess not. But, Rahni . . . I still don't think that was right. I won't ever think it was right." He hurried to catch up to the three indistinct forms of his fellow Companions and the General. Terai and Arris watched him go. By the time he had fallen in ahead of the others, he walked with the measured stride of a guardsman again, only a little more quickly than necessary.

"Can we trust him to finish this?" Arris asked quietly as he and Terai walked back toward their quarters in the court clothes they had been wearing under their black.

Terai nodded. "I think so. And he'll make the best kind of officer when the war comes." His voice was approving.

Arris shrugged. He had killed his first man when he was nine, and he had been proud of himself, not sick and guilty like Stenn. Yet Terai seemed to think Stenn was right to feel the way he did. Arris sometimes wondered if there was something wrong with him. The guards he had killed tonight would scarcely remain in his memory by tomorrow morning, he knew. He was sorry they were dead, but it had been necessary. Terai must have killed many men in his life; did he feel differently about them? Arris did not know.

CHAPTER

22

THE COMING OF winter in Qadasiya and the Palace was not like
the brutal clamp of snow and cold that sometimes paralyzed
the Dark Hills. The leaves of the garden trees in the courtyards and hedgerows crisped and furled as if they were
roasted in a slow fire, until they released their hold on life
and left the trees bare. The court emptied for a time, then
refilled, as every nobleman who owned land returned home to
supervise the harvest, then rode back to winter in the com-
forts of the Citadel.

Saresha Ilkharani celebrated his eighteenth birthday in the
last cool week of the harvest month. His Companions joined
together to give him the ten concubines that the Yllan religion
allowed a Prince of that age; Saresha would now be expected
to send for the girls regularly to begin his task of fathering as
many children of royal blood as was possible. One of the ten
concubines immediately became the Prince's favorite. Arris
had chosen her. Though she was of Northern blood and very
young, she bore a resemblance to the Lady of Gama. Her
dark brown hair was smooth and straight, and fell her entire
length. She was tall and graceful. It would not be difficult for
the Lady to impersonate her when the night of Winter Festival
came.

Arris was careful to give Karillos no grounds for suspicion.
With Taifid overseeing his father the Lord Collector's men in
Khessard, and no more trips to the Silver Cat, Arris led the
life of an ordinary young nobleman. He took his lovers from
among the daughters of minor court functionaries and the
dissatisfied wives of uncaring Consuls. Falcmet and Husayn,
revising their initial judgment, had decided that the Prince of

their mother's people was worthy of their respect. Even Danae, not knowing the source of Arris's prudence, began to see hope that he might eventually change into the constant, trusted lover she desired.

Saresha was rarely seen without his new Companion. He had been immensely grateful to Arris for rescuing General Fallayan, though no one was certain if the General would live long after his legs were amputated at Delronen. More important, Saresha had never had a Companion his own age before, one whose apparently equal rank placed no barriers between them. He had fallen into an easy, open friendship with Arris. The whole court remarked upon it, saying if they did not know better they would think the two had been lifelong friends.

Terai had gone to Gama in early fall. He would soon return with the disguised Lady and her current Yearking, Weida. At Winter Festival, Arris would ensure their success. And his betrayal of Saresha would be irrevocably begun.

"If you hold your stance that way," Arris said irritably, "any taller opponent can come in over your guard. And your feet are set on the same line again. One foot behind the other, remember? Or you'll lose your balance in a lunge." The night had come, moondark and quiet, and his nerves were edged sharper than the long Khalifate rapier he was using to spar with the Prince in the wood-floored exercise room.

"The swordmaster taught me this guard," Saresha said. "If I raise my sword higher, I'll break my body line."

"I'm trying to teach you to ignore those rules," Arris reminded him. "I never follow them, and I beat you every time. Look." He swept down with his sword and slammed Saresha's blade to the floor. "With your sword caught like this, my knife hand can dart in and slit your throat. You either have to drop the sword to block my knife, or be killed."

"But if I drop my sword I'll be killed anyway," Saresha said thoughtfully, his blue eyes examining the position of the two blades. "What if I did this?" He stepped slowly to demonstrate, dropping to his haunches and taking a sliding cross-step to the right, freeing his sword from beneath.

"Good. You'd throw me off balance if I tried to reach you with my knife now. Let's repeat that faster."

They duplicated the sequence of moves again and again until Saresha was escaping the danger easily. Then, with a dry smile, Arris changed his part of the movements. He slammed the Prince's sword down and lunged upward with Jai-Sohn speed, stopping when the tip of his blade pressed against Saresha's bare chest above his heart.

"That wasn't fair!" the golden-haired youth exclaimed.

"Fair?" Arris echoed.

Saresha laughed. "'I know. There aren't any rules. All right. Are you going to show me a way to defend myself against that?"

"You can't," Arris said, leaning on his sword while he regained his panting breath. "The point is that you can't let yourself be caught in that situation to begin with." It was hard to concentrate on his informal training of the Prince tonight. Outside a tall, lattice window, darkness lay like a smothering blanket on the Palace. The Goddess's darkness, as she enfolded them in her sleeping arms. The Lossiran was nearby, and through the day the pressure in Arris's head had grown to a painful throbbing as awareness bound deep within him woke and clamored to be freed.

Saresha lay down his sword and began to stretch his cramped muscles in a fencer's graceful moves, the short tunic he wore baring sinewy legs. Gods, he was gorgeous. Arris tried not to notice.

"It's late," Saresha said, looking out the window. "I hadn't realized. Even the sentry globes seem dim tonight, don't you think so, Rahni?"

Arris shivered. The crier on the Garden Wall had begun to call out midnight. It was time, and Saresha would have to be armed and ready to meet his intended victim if Terai's plan was to work.

"What do you say to a short duel?" he asked, smiling. "By your swordmaster's rules. I've humiliated you enough for one evening. Ought to give you a chance to get even. Besides, I've never figured out why you always beat me in the formal patterns."

The Prince frowned. "I always beat everyone at whatever we're doing. It makes me wonder, Rahni. Does some kind of spell come over my other Companions that makes them weak-kneed every time they face me?" His sapphire eyes were amused. "I appreciate your honesty, Rahni. I don't mind losing when we fight."

"Just a short bout. Or are you too tired?"

"Of course not." Saresha sighed. "All right. Guard yourself, vile enemy of the Ilkharani house."

Arris blinked at the label, and took a formal fencing stance.

Saresha laughed. "That's what Karillos called you yesterday, if you want to know. He still thinks there's something sinister about you." He half-danced forward in a swinging pattern of flashy sword moves. Arris parried without enthusiasm. "I wish the two of you could get along. He really is one of my most loyal advisors. He just doesn't like the Yaighan." He bounded to one side and pressed his rapier tip in under Arris's guard, touching him on the breastbone. "One!"

Arris made the bow of acknowledgment required of the loser of the pass. The two youths resumed their stances, and Saresha moved forward again. Arris could not concentrate on the duel anymore. The wing tattoos on his back tingled and burned beneath the soft cloth of his tunic, as if rustling their inked feathers. He listened for sounds in the outer rooms, and tried to remember what Terai had shown him he must do.

This time the tip of the Prince's sword pinked him in the upper arm. He looked up in surprise at the sharp prick. Saresha scowled at him. "You aren't concentrating, Rahni. That was sloppy."

He smiled sheepishly. "Again?"

"If you think you can avoid stumbling into my blade."

The graceful ritual began once more, but Arris's thoughts were still more distant. Now he heard the soft padding of the assassin in Saresha's bedchamber. There had been no outcry from the sentries. Terai had taken care of them, with the help of the Lady's magic.

He reflexively ducked under a swing and thrust up, his rapier touching the Prince's right leg above the knee. Saresha shook his head. "Not a legal hit." They engaged again.

Darkness rushed in on Arris, and he turned just as the cloaked and masked Yearking thrust aside a door hanging and leaped into the room. His dark clothes smelled of the highly inflammable oils in which they had been soaked. He bore a long, slim sword blackened at the tip with a gooey substance Arris knew to be harmless.

"Stay back!" Arris shouted to the Prince. "You can see

his sword's poisoned.'' He rushed forward to engage Weida in the charade.

Their swords clashed with impressive force, as they began the sidling moves and leaps and fast disengages that were the mark of Yaighan swordplay. The combat had been choreographed by Terai, working separately with each of them. As long as both players remembered their moves, they were in no danger from each other. Weida chanted under his breath the ritual words of consecration of the sacrifice. Those words would usually be said by the slayer, but that was impossible in this case. Arris shuddered when he met his opponent's black eyes. They were clouded with terror and bitter resolve. Weida had not been given the herbal drugs usually granted to the doomed Yearking; they would have slowed his reflexes.

"Get away from him," Saresha shouted. "He's too good. Rahni, you'll be hurt!" He yelled for his guards, but there was no response.

Arris pretended to slip, and fell. Weida brought the haft of his blade down hard on Arris's skull, a blow that had to be real to be convincing. Darts of pain exploded before Arris's eyes. He nearly lost awareness, but he fought to see through the fog.

"Kill him . . ." he said hoarsely. "Kill him, Saresha, or he'll kill you." He hauled himself to his knees and watched the blurry combat.

Weida's slim blade flashed in and out, disdaining split-second openings in the same way Saresha's Companions fought. The Prince panted with scarcely controlled fear. He had never fought for his life before. He was sloppy, but his terror-born fierceness compensated for his lack of grace.

The heavy sound of the combatants' shifting feet echoed in Arris's head with the clash of their swords and the beating of wings. The Lossiran was here, mercifully invisible. The fighting grew more frenzied. For a moment, Arris thought that the Yearking had decided to defend himself rather than offer the sacrifice. But then Weida made an off-balance lunge at a moment when Saresha's rapier was slipping in low from the side.

The outcome had been sure from the beginning. The rapier plunged deep into the Yearking's stomach. Weida fell to his knees with a gasp of pain, forcing the sword to slice upward in the ritual cut. Saresha dropped his weapon and stepped back in horror. The Lossiran's dim form enveloped the wounded Yearking as a glowing light appeared in Weida's hand. A piece of burning coal, Arris supposed, but the flame it touched off in the Yearking's oil-soaked clothing had a crimson in its depths that was only seen on Winter Festival night. The death of blood and fire. Weida writhed soundlessly in the enveloping flames. His crisping flesh smelled of pinesmoke and moss, with only a faint undercurrent of humanity. The power of the Hunter, Rehoman's lover, filled him still.

"Stay clear of the fire," Arris shouted, forcing himself to get to his feet. "I'll get a blanket to beat it out." He staggered into the Prince's bedchamber. Saresha could not follow him. He was trapped on the other side of the flames, against the stone wall of the exercise room. His handsome face was twisted with horror.

The Lady stood beside the Prince's bed. Arris could scarcely look at her. The Goddess possessed her, and the expression in her beautiful, ageless face was cruel, exultant, terrifying. "It is arranged?" she whispered in the most seductive voice Arris had ever heard. "I will sleep with him tonight?"

"Yes," he breathed. "But you . . . you must leave now, and come back later, when the other girl would come." How could he tell the Goddess what to do? He turned from her and jerked a heavy wool blanket from the Prince's bed.

"I will do that," the impossible voice said from close behind him. Long-fingered hands touched his shoulders and turned him with irresistible gentleness. Arris stared up into the dark, smooth face. The Lady stood taller than he by a head. Power was around her and within her, and her red-brown eyes were inhuman, the color of blood. "But first, a taste . . . of what I will know when I awaken." She spoke in an ancient, pure form of Yaighan, the language of magic used by Gama priests.

Arris felt his whole body rouse as she bent and kissed him, though the touch burned. He smelled spice and honey and pinesmoke, and tasted fire. It was a compelling, almost ecstatic pain, that urged and invited him to be consumed. But only the newborn Yearking with the fire of the god within him afresh could withstand Rehoman's touch for long.

She released him after only a moment and smiled possessively. "Mine," she murmured. "You will be mine, and not only for two nights in the year, for I will be free again. No more dreaming.'' Her hand brushed his cheek, and she hurried for the door.

Arris stood gasping for breath, stunned, unbearably aroused. How could he refuse his destiny? His longing for her was stronger than any feeling he had known before. How could he refuse her? She was a goddess, and she wanted him. He was meant for her.

"Rahni!" the Prince shouted from the exercise room. Arris felt a moment of terrible jealousy at the thought that Saresha would know the Goddess before he would. Then he remembered the flames, and the blanket he still held.

The fire had gone out of itself. Weida's body was unrecognizably charred, as was his clothing. There would be nothing to show he had been Yaighan. Saresha knelt beside the dead form, shivering uncontrollably, weeping softly. Arris stood next to him for a moment, looking at the Prince's shadow cast by the lamplight on the stone walls. It was stag-horned. Behind the brilliance of Saresha's tear-wet eyes rested an ageless presence.

"Who was he?" Saresha muttered, clinging to Arris as Arris lifted him, put the blanket around his shoulders, and helped him into the bedroom. "Who could have sent him to kill me? It was so strange, Rahni, the way he caught fire . . . I could have sworn I saw—no, that's impossible. Verchaki protect us, I never killed anyone before. I didn't think I would feel so strange afterward.''

The strangeness Saresha felt had little to do with the act of killing, Arris knew. Rehoman's Consort had moved from Weida's corpse into the new Yearking. Saresha might never know of his presence. But on at least two nights, tonight and Spring Festival, the Prince's shadow would be horned, and his actions would not be his own.

Saresha sat heavily on the massive bed, still shivering. He looked up at Arris. "Are you all right, Rahni? I saw you go down.''

Arris reached up to feel the back of his head. It was bleeding a little. "I'll be fine. Can you stay here alone for a moment? I'll go find the guard.''

Saresha nodded, and watched him as he hurried from the suite.

•   •   •

Three hours later, Arris sat morosely in the Prince's library with a dozen of the Companions, as a continual stream of sleepy nobles came to swear their loyalty and their ignorance of any assassination plot. He was beginning to fear that the rest of Terai's plan could not be carried out tonight. They would not leave the Prince alone.

Guards had removed the charred body of Weida and the broken forms of Saresha's sentries and manservants who had been found in the hall. Nievan assigned men of his personal guard to walk below the Prince's windows and outside his suite, while Maenad was heard to suggest that the Vizier himself might have been behind the attempt.

"If we stay here much longer, we'll be holding morning court," Arris remarked when the latest nobleman hurried from the room.

"The danger is not yet over," Karillos said, hovering protectively near Saresha, apparently oblivious of the stag's-horn shadows behind the Prince's head. "Foul, evil things are abroad in the Citadel tonight. The winged spirit that attacked me in the Temple years ago has been here, and it left darker things in its wake."

"That was no spirit that attacked the Prince," Falcmet said quietly from where he stood in a corner of the crowded room. "If you have a sense of danger, Karillos, it is because whoever sent the assassin will try again. If you'll take my advice, you'll stop worrying about evil spirits and set your spies to finding out who wants Saresha dead."

Karillos ignored him. "My Prince, allow me to consecrate your rooms again in the name of the Brothers."

"That would take hours," Arris said, trying to hide his alarm. Karillos could control powers that might be able to stand against the Crimson Goddess; if he tried to exorcise Saresha's chambers, the Prince himself would be the one harmed.

"You are not the least of the evils present here," Karillos said to him without thought. "When I cleanse the darkness from this place, you will go with it."

"Silence," Saresha said in a voice of command. "You forget yourself, Karillos. I have asked you never to speak so to Rahnisha Tualli again."

The smooth-faced priest bowed low, spreading his hands in unfelt apology. Arris sighed. For the Prince's sake, they tried to appear tolerant of one another when they were near him. Away from Saresha, he and Karillos never lost an opportunity to argue. Their hatred and mistrust had only grown.

"I appreciate your concern, Karillos," Saresha said after a moment. "But it is very late, and I'm very tired. We'll speak of your fears again in the morning."

"Very well." Karillos glided toward the door. "I suppose you will be safe for the next few hours. Good night, Your Highness."

"You're sure you're all right, Saresha?" Falcmet asked as the rest of the Companions began to leave.

"Of course. Thank you." He motioned to Arris to stay for a moment. When they were alone, Saresha spoke softly. "I want to thank you."

"I didn't do a very good job of protecting you," Arris said.

"You could have been killed." Saresha said. "But you tried to save me."

"I was armed, and I am no coward. I wouldn't just step aside."

Saresha's face was shadowed by the lamplight. "He was one of your people, wasn't he? That assassin."

Arris started. "He was masked . . . I didn't see his face clearly."

"He fought as you do. I'm still not sure how I defeated him. He was much better than I am."

"If he had been better, Sasha, you'd be dead."

The Prince shook his head. "It was all so strange. I still don't understand. A Yaighan tried to kill me. When I stabbed him, he burned up like a torch. He didn't even scream. Perhaps Karillos is right. There could have been magic involved."

"Do you think so?"

"I don't know. Most of the priests say there is no magic except the power of the Brothers. But Karillos has encountered other powers. And I once knew someone else who had," he said thoughtfully. "We were both children . . . he was Areyta's youngest son, Falcmet and Husayn's brother. He claimed to have spoken with a bird spirit like the one Karillos says was here tonight."

"The Lossiran," Arris said, looking away from the Prince.

It was the first time he had ever heard Saresha mention their childhood friendship.

"Yes. That's it. I didn't believe him then, but Karillos has told me it was real. I . . . I wonder if you knew him, Rahni. Falcmet said he was at Gama for a while, before he ran away. They think he's dead." His voice was wistful. "Sometimes you remind me of him. He never let me win at anything."

"I knew him," Arris said. "He said you blamed him for the Khalif's death. You wanted him killed."

"I was only a child," Saresha said. "They told me he was a witch. Of course I believed it. But there was little evidence against him, and less against Areyta. Recently I've begun to suspect my uncle, Maenad, of having a hand in my father's death. There were those who accused him when it happened, but nothing was done about it." He sighed. "It was unfortunate. We lost a good general in Areyta, and our hold on his lands in the South. And I lost the only real friend I ever had." He paused. "Until you came here, Rahni."

Arris felt as if someone had punched him in the stomach. Sasha did not hate him. He regretted what he had done. He still thought of Arris as his best friend. How could that be? Arris had never forgiven him, had never stopped hating him.

Until now. And it was too late. He should never have agreed to Terai's scheme to set Saresha up as the next Yearking. The deaths of Nievan and Maenad would be enough revenge for Areyta's life. But what he had done tonight could not be reversed or changed. Sasha would die in one year.

"I'm trying to say that I value your friendship," Saresha said after a moment. "And I don't want to lose you as I lost Arris j'Areyta. If I tell my uncles that the assassin was Yaighan, you'll have to leave. They'll never believe he was working alone. They'll say your Lady and your Council sent him. It could mean war."

"You aren't going to tell them?"

"No. I don't want you to leave, Rahni." Arris heard the Prince rise and walk over to him. A hand touched his shoulder, and he looked up. "No matter what happens. Promise me you'll stay."

He could not meet the innocence, the open trust of Saresha's blue eyes. "I will stay," he said. "As long as you want me here."

A light knock sounded at the library door. Arris suddenly stiffened. The Lady, possessed by the Goddess. Her overwhelming scent came through the wood. Saresha went to open the door, and smiled sleepily at his favorite concubine.

The illusion was nearly complete. The Lady's hair was brown, her face altered into softer lines. It did not disguise the power within her. "My Prince?" she said in the girl's voice. "I had heard you were attacked, but I thought maybe you'd still want me to come to you tonight."

Saresha laughed, putting an arm around her shoulders. "I won't do you justice, pretty one. But I would be glad to have you in my bed."

When they touched the illusion surrounding the Lady slipped a little, and Saresha's weariness began to fade. Arris could feel the buildup of power within them both. The Prince's golden hair seemed to catch fire, glowing brighter than the lamps in the library. Arris rose quickly from his chair and bowed. "I'll see you tomorrow, Sasha."

The Prince did not even respond. The arrogance and desire of the Consort altered his features, enhancing his beauty beyond a merely human level. The horns twined above his curls were more than shadows now. The Lady slipped her hand in his, and smiled over her shoulder at Arris. He stood confused, aroused, unsure which of them attracted him more.

"Would you fight this destiny?" the Lady said softly in the ancient Yaighan tongue. "In one year's time you will be at my side."

If Saresha heard them, he did not seem to understand. Arris spoke with an effort. "I . . . will not choose to be Yearking, Lady."

"Choose? Your life is already chosen for you." She reached her free hand to touch him; Arris stepped back out of reach. The compelling eyes were unsmiling when she spoke again. "Even if you fear me, even if you oppose me, my dreamed-of one, you will come to me in the end. You have no other purpose. You have no other life."

Arris brushed past the two beautiful figures, half-human and half-gods, and ran from the Prince's suite. Soft laughter followed, and the scent of woods flowers.

CHAPTER

23

THE GOD IN Saresha remained deeply hidden after that night. Arris could almost convince himself that none of it had happened, that he had imagined the Lady's presence and the Prince's possession. He lived his role as Rahnisha with growing ease, traveling with the Companions around the Khalifate, finding he had become much sought after and admired for his rescue of Fallayan and his attempted defense of the Prince. Terai was often gone to Gama, and while he was away Arris went for weeks at a time without thinking of his mission.

But the night of Spring Festival was chaotic. The Horned One deserted Saresha to wander around the Khalifate. The Lossiran was seen in the Temples of the Sun. The full moon seemed to give rise to a strange madness among the peasants, a feverish disregard for all the proscriptions of the priests. Karillos left the Citadel the next day, for the first time in months, to reconsecrate the invaded Temples.

Arris found himself unwatched. Taifid was out of his reach in Khessard, but there was nothing to prevent him from seeking out pleasure on the Streets of Night. Still, something kept him from it. The fear, he supposed, that the Prince would somehow find out and think less of him.

He was glad of his restraint one afternoon, a week after Spring Festival, when he chanced upon Danae and her flutist Pellen in heated argument in the garden of the Court of Dreams. He heard them before he saw them standing at the edge of a grove of new-budded trees.

"My music!" Danae was shouting. "I don't care if he was your teacher, you had no right to give him my music! How much did he pay you for it?"

"Really, my love," Pellen said with maddening calmness, "you shouldn't be so upset. Just think, now the people of Khessard, too, can enjoy your lovely compositions."

"And your friend Vatsya will take credit for them."

"He told me he'd acknowledge you when he performed them," Pellen said as Arris approached. "There aren't very many good works around that give the reed flute the leading voice, Danae. Vatsya was very impressed by your music. That ought to please you."

"Well, there will be no more such works by me!" she said furiously. "I won't write another note for you to play."

"Is there some problem?" Arris inquired mildly in his Yaighan accent. Pellen favored him with his usual glare. Danae turned in his direction.

"Perhaps I'll write a cycle of songs for the tenor voice instead. Would you sing them, Your Highness?"

Arris smiled for Pellen's benefit. "With great pleasure."

"That's nonsense, Danae," Pellen said. "Your work would have been ignored if I hadn't played it. You need me far more than I need your music."

"You are no longer with my players, Pellen," she said icily. "And if I ever see you attempting to transcribe any more of my music, I'll—"

"Do you threaten me, pretty one?" He laughed. "What will you do to me, hmm?" With a bow, he took his leave. "Soon you'll beg me to come back."

Danae stared after him, her fists clenched tight. "How could he?" she muttered. "Vatsya is bound to take credit for my music. And he is an old and respected composer. In time people will think I stole it from him."

"That will teach you to be more wary of a handsome face and a pleasant smile," Arris said dryly. "I could have warned you about Pellen from the beginning."

"Could you have?" She rehooked her filmy veil, which had become unattached with her first angry gesture. Her green eyes glared at him over the sheer fabric. "He gave me one thing you have never offered. He was faithful to me."

"To your bed," Arris corrected. "Not to you. There is a difference."

"And I suppose you're an expert on loyalty?" she said. "You, who pretend friendship to the Prince at the same time when you're constantly sending reports to Deiran and your precious Emperor? And asking me to spy on everyone from chambermaids to stewards?''

"That's different,'' he said. "That's my mission.''

"I didn't think it would last this long,'' she said quietly.

"It will be over in a matter of months,'' he said. "Then I'll be going back to Deiran. I still think you should come with me.''

She looked troubled. "I should, I know. If it's possible to get my family out, at least I should try.''

"Think about it.'' He wanted her along for several reasons. Most of all, because he was in love with her, in his way, and he knew he was close to finally winning her. Also, he feared that if he left her behind after completing his mission, someone would learn that she had known all along he was a Deirani spy. She would be in danger of her life. Of course it was unlikely she would be able to free her family from Deiran. The invasion would begin as soon as Nievan and Maenad were dead, and it would be suicide to try to get across the borders once the war was underway.

"I meant that about writing songs for you,'' she said after a moment. "Would you really be willing to perform them?''

"Of course. It's accepted for noblemen here to make fools of themselves occasionally.'' He grinned. "I would enjoy it very much, Danae.''

"I, too, Your Highness.'' She slipped her arm in his as a group of Companions approached. "Let's join your friends. Maybe I can forget about that traitor Pellen.''

"I could make you forget him better alone,'' Arris whispered. She giggled and pulled him back onto the path, calling out to the nearest Companion about the new songs she was going to write for the Yaighan Prince.

As the time approached, Arris found himself more and more reluctant to act. He taught Saresha one of his chariot wheel feats for the Prince's birthday, and they performed to the awestruck applause of the Companions. For days afterward Arris convinced himself that if he did nothing, nothing would happen to Saresha. But he knew in his heart that he could not prevent it. The Goddess's Wheel would not turn backward. Saresha was Yearking. Whether he was bound to the altar in Gama or surrounded by his Companions in the Citadel, he would die at Winter Festival.

Even knowing this, Arris delayed his move until the last possible moment. It was only a week to Winter Festival. It would take that long simply to journey to Gama. He was ready. He no longer had a choice. He gave in to Terai's insisting and put on his Jai-Sohn black.

The window of his room was open, the latticed shutters hooked back. The darkness beyond was relieved only by the dim glow of the sentry lamps on their rounds. He could smell the dried bracken of the hedges below his window, and the tangy scent of the scattered pine trees beyond. He sat on the marble window seat, cross-legged, his black sword balanced on his knees, his hood, mask, and gloves beside him. Terai had returned from his task of getting their chariot ready in a quiet corner of the gardens, the team harnessed and tied, his own horse picketed nearby. Saresha would be disoriented and only half-conscious by now from the drugged wine Arris had watched him drink earlier. He would not resist when Terai came for him.

"A guardsman told me the Kwaitl are disappearing," he said as he stared out into the darkness. He could feel his pulse slowing, his body relaxing in preparation for the Jai-Sohn state. "I suppose your people have something to do with that."

"Do you remember Clynetra?" Terai asked, buckling his short sword around his waist and settling a long, dark cloak over his shoulders.

Arris flinched at the name. The sister of the girl he had killed. "Of course."

"She and some of the warrior-trained priestesses have been working among the Kwaitl. The nomads have always acknowledged Rehoman as a formidable power, though while she slept they went back to their older spirits of earth and sky. Now they feel it would be prudent to be on her side when she wakes again."

"They're probably right," Arris said. "And I shouldn't go anywhere near her if I'm not going to be her Yearking."

"You'll be safe enough," Terai said dismissively. "It's nearly time for the watch to begin to change. I'll go get the Prince. Will Danae be meeting us in the gardens?"

"She said she would."

"Have you told her the truth yet about what we're doing tonight?"

Arris shook his head. "I'll wait at least until we're out of the Palace. I'm not sure how she'll react."

"Nor am I," Terai said softly. "The Goddess alone knows how this will end. Luck go with you, Arris. I'll see you shortly." He left the room. The door shut behind him.

There was no more time for speculation on what might be. Arris focused his gaze down onto the dull blade of the black sword in his lap, letting his thoughts fall deep within the darkness. His old hatred, his boyhood yearning for vengeance, was buried somewhere in there. His hatred of Saresha had burned away, but if he could pull back the layers of deadening time, he would find his memories of Nievan and Maenad intact. He could still see the visions he had dreamed in Ruena's shop, the pictures of the two Regents presiding at Areyta's torture. The more recent memory of the way Areyta's ghost had appeared to him was strong. The hurt he had felt at learning Areyta had not been his father was unimportant. He brushed it aside, concentrating on the hatred, on his vows. He had promised Areyta. He had promised Hareku as well, and Iyon. Hareku he had feared and loved, Iyon he had feared and hated, but he had sworn to them both to kill the Ilkharani.

The tangled emotions he dragged forth were important. They would provide him strength for his task. But he would have to use them carefully. Too much would force him out of the coolness, the alert, undisturbed state of the focused Jai-Sohn. What he had to do should be done carefully, methodically, without the unpredictable heat of anger.

When he looked up from the sword, every stone of the wall beneath the window seemed to leap out at him. He could see the dust in the cracks, feel the pitted hardness of the polished marble beneath him. He could feel the slow beat of his controlled pulse and the deep rhythm of his breathing. The darkness outside the window was complete, as the sentries on the nearest wall began the pattern of the changing of the watch. The changes would move slowly, a web of darkness and renewed light throughout the Citadel. Arris had studied the pattern and the timing, and knew it well. It would help him.

He sheathed his sword and bound the sheath across his back for climbing. He drew his mask over his nose and mouth, and his hood over his tightly bound hair. His gloves and slippers were sticky with resin to aid him in gripping the stones of the outer tower walls. He swung his legs over the windowsill, turned to look inward one last time, and began to descend.

The stones of the ancient Citadel were jagged edged, flat, wedged together with no mortar but pebbles. They were harsh against his cloth-covered hands and feet. In the night they were as black as his costume. Until the sentries lit their fresh lamps for the late watch, he would be invisible. The night air was cool and damp. Arris hoped there would be rain later to hide his and Terai's tracks as they fled. He did not really expect pursuit, though. With Saresha vanished, Nievan and Maenad dead, and the Consulate bound to argue for days over who should be in charge, there would be no one to command a chase.

Like the pattern of the sentries' changing watch, the habits of his two intended victims were well suited to Arris's needs. Nievan and Maenad had established a nightly conference between them, after the business of the day's Regency was done, to plan and argue and discuss their joint rule. They held these sessions alone in Nievan's study, with guards outside the suite. They would be there tonight, Arris knew. Danae had told him, though she had not known why he asked. Danae, too, would be there tonight, singing for Oella in the sitting rooms across from the study. She had offered to refuse Oella's request tonight, since she knew they would be leaving for Deiran, but Arris had told her to go ahead and perform as long as she left for the gardens at the sounding of midnight. She would ensure that Oella and her children were well occupied, and Arris would be left alone with his work.

The sentries of the north tower were changing their watch. Arris moved from behind the thorny hedge where he had hidden to climb up to Nievan's second-floor study window. The breeze that rounded the corner of the tower touched him only to rustle his clothes and cool the small, uncovered area around his eyes. He reached the sill of the study and drew himself up slowly, his arms quivering with the strain of supporting him. The lattice shutters were open, as Arris had learned was Nievan's habit. The Vizier enjoyed the coolness of the night air.

The two Regents stood with their backs to Arris, beside a large desk piled to overflowing with petitions and documents and compartmented trays of counting stones. Maenad, thinner and less well protected from the chill than Nievan, shivered a little in the breeze. Arris slid over the window ledge and crouched against the dark stone below it as the glow of sentry lamps penetrated the night behind him.

He could hear Danae singing to a soft lap harp, and the off-key voices of Oella's two young sons attempting harmony. With a conscious effort, he blocked the sounds from his mind. He drew his sword very slowly from its cloth-muffled sheath and palmed his dagger. Silence and speed would be vital now. He could not afford to gloat over his victims, or even stop to tell them his name and make his revenge more sweet.

"Even if I am not your son," he said silently to Areyta's ghost, "perhaps this will make you rest more easily."

Luxurious robes rustled as the two Regents moved closer together to look at a parchment scroll Nievan held up to the lamplight. Arris rose like a shadow behind them and struck them both at the same time. The Jai-Sohn sword reached around Nievan's thick neck to slit the Vizier's throat, and the dagger pressed upward from below Maenad's thin lower ribs into the Emir's heart.

A human being is such a fragile creature, Arris thought as they fell. It takes so little to injure one, so little to kill. Maenad crumpled into a silent heap at Arris's feet, his head lolling back on the stone floor. Nievan fell heavily across his desk, his arm brushing papers and counting stones to the floor. The small, round markers clattered from their holders. Arris swore softly. He had wanted this to be perfect, silent and sure. Had anyone heard?

The study door opened and Danae stepped in, smiling, saying, "My lord Regent, your wife sent me to offer you some of this most excellent wine—" Then she dropped the bottle she carried, which shattered and flowed to mingle with the blood on the flagstones, releasing its sweet fruity smell.

Arris ran to bolt the door behind her so no one else would see inside. He turned to face her, hoping irrationally that she would not know him for his mask and hood.

Her hand was clamped over her mouth, and her face was pale with nausea. She stared at the warm, bleeding bodies of the Regents, then looked at him. "Arris," she whispered.

"It was . . . my mission, Danae," he said quietly, moving to touch her shoulder with a gloved hand. "Don't betray me, girl. Shh. That's it. Don't look at them. Can you get back through the Palace without making anyone suspicious?" He sighed. "I don't think so. You'll have to climb down with me. Come. Quickly."

Green eyes as still as painted flowers on a vase watched him, lost in horror.

"Are you coming with me or not?" he whispered. "We have to time it with the sentries' rounds. We can't stay here long. Come on, Danae. Please."

She shook her head with sudden violence. "No. This . . . this was why you came here? This was your mission all along? I . . . I suppose I should have guessed. Iyon would never have spent so much time training you just to send him reports on the ships they're building in the Gharin Emirate."

"I am a Jai-Sohn," Arris said with some pride. "This is what a Jai-Sohn does. You are trained to eliminate your master's enemies."

She stared at him still. "I thought you had changed. I thought you realized now how wrong it was, what they taught you in Deiran. But you haven't changed at all. And you're worse than I ever guessed. Arris, look at yourself! You don't even care that you just murdered two men!"

"If any men deserved death, these two did," he said, feeling cold. It was true he felt no remorse or guilt. And he should. What was wrong with him? Did he lack something other men had? But he had been upset at Onira's death years ago. Or had he only been frightened of the consequences to himself?

"You cannot judge whether anyone deserves to die!" Danae said. "Leave that to the gods. Oh, Arris . . ." She looked away from him, blinking back tears.

"If you don't come with me," he said in frustration, "how can I be sure you won't run to the guards and tell them all you know? I can't stand here and argue with you. Either come now or promise me you'll be silent."

"And if I do neither, what will you do? Kill me too? You'll have to, Arris," she said bitterly. "Because I can't let you do this. I'll go to the Prince and tell him everything. I'll lead them after you myself if I have to."

"You can't mean that," he whispered.

"Do you expect our friendship to save you? After this? You've destroyed everything we've had together, and everything we might have had." She was crying now. "I even thought I loved you. I wish we had never even met!"

She was deadly serious, Arris knew. He had not been trained as a priest, or lived for years a watchful slave, to misjudge the depth of another's feelings. He should kill her. It would be the easiest course. It would be the course a true Jai-Sohn would take.

He could not do that. But he could not allow her to jeopardize his escape. "Sorry, Danae," he said softly, bringing the pommel of his bloody sword down at the back of her head. She groaned and fell. For a moment he hated himself more than he had ever hated the Ilkharani.

Arris knelt, ripped strips of cloth from his tunic, and bound and gagged Danae, tying her tightly to the legs of Nievan's heavy desk. She would be found, but not for some time. Not until someone thought to see why the Regents were closeted so late. He checked to be sure she was breathing freely above the gag. Her eyelids were already fluttering. He had not hit her very hard.

He ran to the windowsill to watch the sentries' globes weave their soft chains of light. The hole of darkness came, and he slithered down the side of the tower to run through the garden to the place where Terai waited with the chariot and the kidnapped Prince.

"Danae won't be coming with us," he said, climbing into the chariot as Terai hung his shrouded lantern on the tongue between the horses to light their way. Saresha lay bound under a concealing layer of dark cloaks on the floor of the vehicle, drugged into near-unconsciousness with some of Ruena's herbs. A bright, gold-fringed overrobe hung on the whipstock. Arris pulled off his hood, mask, and gloves, and slung the garment around him. "There will be pursuit. We'd better hurry."

They had prepared for this night with several recent trips to Qadasiya, where Arris had confined his activities to the houses that offered the more usual pleasures—drink, women, and gambling. The guards were used to seeing them, and should wave them through without question.

Terai mounted his horse and urged it ahead of the chariot at a quick trot. Arris pulled his horses' heads up and flicked the soft lengths of reins over their backs. The Ilkharani court drove lighter chariots than the Deirani, with two horses instead of four. Arris found them easier to control, though they were too light for many of his wheel feats. He would not need any of those tonight.

"She found out?" Terai asked as they stopped at the first gate and waited for the guards to open it.

"I gave her a choice," Arris said bleakly. "She did not choose me."

Terai nodded. They rode silently through the midnight Palace, passing the gates easily. They were over the moat and under the eaves of the forest when Terai finally spoke again.

"Did you kill her?"

"I probably should have," Arris muttered. "You don't have to say anything. I know they'll be after us."

Terai looked at him narrowly. "If you had killed her, that would have been the end of our friendship, boy. We're out of sight of the Palace now. We can move faster." He spurred his horse to a gallop.

With a clatter of axle and floorboards, the chariot leaped to follow. Arris felt the limp weight of the Prince shift against his legs. Saresha would hate him when he woke. Danae already did. Terai was angry that he had even considered killing Danae. When it was over, he wondered if he would have anyone left to call a friend.

They were a night and a day's ride south of Qadasiya when they finally stopped for more than a brief rest for the horses. Terai had traveled this road many times, and knew the places where fugitives could safely hide. He led them to a secluded hollow on the wide lands of a wealthy farmer, where the smoke from their cookfire would be dispersed through a veiling of tall evergreen trees with needles the length of a man's hand. A stream ran through the hidden vale.

Arris unharnessed and picketed the chariot horses, gathered wood for a fire, and began to chop some of the fresh vegetables Ruena had sent with them for their journey. His arms and back were numb from driving, though they had slowed their pace to a walk after the first few miles. He set water to boil in a small pot over the fire for the stew.

Terai untied the Prince from the chariot floor, pulled the cloaks off of him and lifted him out, laying him on the ground to loosen his bonds enough for movement. Then he removed Saresha's gag and helped him stand. Arris could hear the youth's harsh breathing in the evening quiet of the grove. He did not look in that direction.

He had the stew ready when Terai and Saresha returned from a pool upstream. Terai had helped Saresha to bathe and dress again. Arris glanced up. The Prince's wet hair lay flat, close to his skull, emphasizing the pallor of his handsome face and the dark smudges beneath his eyes. His bound hands shook as Terai helped him sit on a flat rock near the fire. He kept his eyes lowered and did not look at either of them, even when Arris handed him a bowl of stew and a spoon.

"We can change horses at Delronen," Arris said, turning away from the Prince's awkward effort to eat. "They won't have any news ahead of us. We'll be safe enough."

"We'll still try to avoid Fallayan and Jakim," Terai said.

"What are you going to do with me?" Saresha whispered.

It had been a year since Arris had imagined he would feel triumphant in this moment. He had not realized how ashamed he would actually be. He did not answer.

Terai spoke gently. "You'll be the central figure in the Ritual of the Yearking, at this year's Winter Festival."

"Yearking?" Saresha glanced up, his brow furrowed. "Do you mean to install me as a puppet king for the Yaighan? To claim the Khalifate lands? My uncles won't accept that."

"Your uncles are dead," Arris said. "I killed them."

Blank shock replaced the puzzlement on Saresha's face. After a moment, he whispered, "I don't understand, Rahni. What . . . what good will that do the Yaighan? And how could you do it? I thought we were friends . . . are you going to kill me too?"

Arris shook his head. "No. But you'll be killed at the Festival. I'm sorry, Sasha." He turned away again.

"You're sorry." The Prince tried to control his trembling voice. "You've betrayed me, and murdered my uncles, and you're sorry? Or are you sorry you won't be the one to kill me too? Why, Rahni? At least tell me why."

"I am working for the Deirani," Arris said. "And it . . . is also a matter of vengeance. I am no traitor, though. I never swore loyalty to you."

"You betrayed our friendship. Or did that mean nothing to you?"

"There was no friendship between us!" Arris shouted, whirling to glare at the Prince's pale and anguished face. "It was all a pretense. Can you understand that? I am not Rahnisha Tualli. I never was. I am Arris j'Areyta. I have hated you since I was nine years old, you and your uncles . . ." He jumped suddenly to his feet and walked away toward the horses on the picket line, tears burning at the back of his eyes. Danae was right. He was cruel, cold, unfeeling. But what was he supposed to say to Saresha? That he was sorry, that he loved him, that he was taking him to his death anyway? That would only make it worse.

"Arris," he heard Saresha say beside the fire. "I should have known. I should have recognized him . . . does that mean Falcmet and Husayn are involved in this too? I trusted them . . ."

"They knew nothing," Terai told him. "They didn't recognize their brother after his years in Deiran. Even if they had, they would never have joined him in this."

Was there someone else here? Arris straightened from his blurry-eyed inspection of a worn piece of harness and stood very still. His Goddess-given sensitivity was still imprisoned, though the bonds had weakened from his contacts with the Lady the year before. This touch was so strong the most dense-headed would feel it.

"Terai!" He hurried back to the fire. "There is something here."

The older Yaighan scowled. "Karillos has found us."

"Karillos?" Saresha said gladly. "Where?"

"Less than a day's ride distant, I'd say," Terai said. "Your brothers are with him, Arris."

"Danae must have gone to him," Arris said. "If she tells him everything she knows, he may guess what is happening. That the Millennium has finally come. How large a force, Terai?"

"Most of the Companions," he said, closing his eyes to block out distractions. "A number of priests as well. They have a string of remounts, and are riding without rest."

"Then we can't rest either. And the chariot will be too slow. We'll have to ride."

Terai nodded. "We can buy saddles and gear at the next village, or steal them if need be." He turned to Saresha. "I'll have to undo your bonds for you to be able to ride. Don't try to escape."

"I won't ride to my death!" the Prince said furiously.

Terai smiled sadly. "Even if you escaped, lad, your destiny would find you. The Goddess has you in her hand already. Better to face her with honor than to run, though the end will be the same in either case."

CHAPTER

24

IT SEEMED ALL of Gama was at the Canyon Gate to greet them. The towering rock walls cast long morning shadows on the steeply descending road, and the massive gates themselves were wide open. A gaily dressed crowd parted before the three plodding horses, shouting greetings to their Yearking at the end of his reign. Children were lifted in the air to touch his stirrup as he rode by.

Arris led the way, with Saresha and then Terai after him. It was the sixth day of their journey, and captors and captive alike were exhausted, hungry, and dirty. Their horses had been fresh when they stole them from Delronen; now they were almost gone. Arris scarcely felt the jolting of his slumped body in his saddle anymore. Terai sat straight as always, but his horse had little guidance. Saresha was sick, alternating fevers and chills. Arris had feared he might be unable to reach Gama. They did not know if the Prince's illness was an aftereffect of Ruena's drugs, or the result of the hardship of the journey; Arris doubted the Prince even realized the crowd's acclaim was meant for him.

Among the Yaighan farmers, priestesses, and students were

a number of Kwaitl nomads, curiously watching the festivities. The Kwaitl were an ivory-skinned race related to the Deirani, known for their quick tempers and their dislike of any authorities. They stalked through the press in hooded robes of white wool, each man hung with an arsenal of weapons. Arris wondered if the Lady really thought they could be trusted as allies. He would sooner trust a tribe of daimons.

The crowd fell in behind them to escort them to Gama. A mounted troop of young soldiers moved in front of them. One youth wearing a serious expression and a sword belt over a priest's robe came to ride beside them. "Any trouble on your journey, my lord Terai?"

"We were being followed for a time, but we haven't sensed our pursuit for days now," said Terai in a gravelly voice. "They probably turned back."

Arris looked sharply back at his old teacher. It was true he had felt nothing, but beyond the first sense of Karillos's probe, he had not been able to. He did not have the power. Terai had driven them hard in the past days, never indicating that the danger from Karillos had lessened. But why would Terai lie to the Yaighan? Perhaps the priest had given up. It was a long road.

"The Lady sensed disturbances in the North," said the soldier. "She feared something might interfere with your mission."

"Disturbances?" Arris repeated. "What kind of disturbances?"

"We believe they are related to the Goddess's emergence, lord. They can explain it to you better in the priests' tower, where you'll be staying. But I can tell you this." The youth lowered his voice cautiously. "I saw the Lossiran above the valley yesterday. More than twenty of us saw it."

Arris met Terai's gaze uneasily. "That's . . . very unusual," he said. The Lossiran. He had forgotten. But of course it would be here for the Goddess's awakening.

"That isn't all. There have been manifestations of the Ilkharani gods. The Five Brothers. Priests have been visited and warned not to support Rehoman when she wakes. And they say the Lady thinks that daimon, the one who killed Clynetra's sister, is still somewhere around."

"Really," Terai said thoughtfully, smiling a little at Arris.

Arris remembered that Terai suspected the daimon of supplying his shields. He shrugged.

"Indeed, my lord," said the young priest, going on to tell them more of the rumors and speculations that surrounded the imminent Millennium. He did not address any of his comments to Saresha. He looked away quickly each time his gaze brushed by the Prince. Arris had a feeling the youth did not approve of the unwilling Yearking Terai and the Lady had created. Either he felt the Yearking should not be an unbelieving Ilkharani, or he thought it was wrong to force the position on someone. Whichever his reason, Arris agreed with him.

They were swept through the standing stones of the gate and into the streets of the White City by the cheering crowd. Arris felt anew the wonder he had known as a child when he saw Gama for the first time. The clean, stone-paved streets, the bright white buildings, the fountains and statues were breathtakingly beautiful. The city even smelled fresh and new. A light dusting of snow frosted the walks and rooftops, though most of it was already melting in the crisp morning sunlight.

Saresha did not show any surprise or even curiosity at the dramatic change in scenery after they passed through the gate. Arris watched him worriedly. The Prince swayed in his saddle like one drunk, riding less well than one of the courtiers of Deiran. His face had been flushed earlier. Now it was drained of color, set in misery.

A delegation of Councilwomen met them before the priestess compound. "We will take the Yearking to the Lady's house," their leader said. "My lord Terai, Arris, Tauena's son, you will be shown to a room in the priests' tower where you may rest before the ceremony."

Terai mumbled a courteous reply. The crowd followed the priestesses and the Yearking, as the leader of the Council led Saresha's horse toward the Temple gate. In a moment Arris and Terai were left with their lone soldier escort. "This way, please," the youth said.

"We know the way to the tower," Arris muttered. The young priest favored him with a quick, indulgent smile, and fell back to ride behind them.

"I hope that Councilwoman didn't mean we're supposed to

attend the Ritual tonight," Terai said quietly to Arris. "I have no desire to see the sacrifice."

Arris shuddered. "Nor I. And I don't want to be standing there when the Goddess wakes."

"That might be unwise," Terai said dryly.

They were shown to a room near the top of the tower, just below the star-gazing chamber. The narrow stairs opened onto only two doors. The young priest bowed and smiled, then left them to themselves.

"What about the Companions and Karillos?" Arris asked after he drained the welcome cup of heady spiced wine that he found on the table in the room. "Do you really think they've turned back?"

Terai waited to finish his own wine before he replied. "No."

"Then why did you tell the soldier they had?"

Terai shrugged lightly, and stretched out on one of the cots by the bright window. "Perhaps I wanted to give them a chance. Offer them a challenge. Let's see if they really can summon the gods they worship. Let's see if they really can challenge the Goddess on her own ground, on the day of her emergence from her imprisonment."

"You don't think they'd succeed?" Arris went to the window, and looked down the glass-smooth sides of the tower. No one could ever enter this room the way he had entered Nievan's study. The walls would be impossible to climb.

"Far from their temples and worshipers? With Rehoman strengthened with the blood and flesh of the sacrifice? No, I don't think they'll succeed. She did not know them well enough when she allowed them to trick her. Now she's had a thousand years to watch them, and to plan what she'll do to them when she awakes." Terai grinned. "No, I think that if they meet tonight, the biggest obstacle to achieving the goals of the Millennium can be removed at the very beginning."

Arris sat on the other cot, looking curiously at Terai. "You're really excited about this, aren't you?"

"I've been waiting all my life for this moment, Arris. It's here! The Millennium. The stalemate will be broken. Everyone will have to choose in the weeks to come, whether to follow the banners of the Deirani or the Yaighan, or remain with the doomed Khalifate. They'll have to choose which gods to support. The time has come. Tonight.''

"The night you were born for, boy," said a dry, scratchy voice from the doorway. Arris turned, and leaped to his feet, unmindful of his leaden weariness.

"Hlaryon!" The old stargazer moved more slowly than he had before. When he reached to embrace Arris, the younger man saw that he was nearly blind. "Grandfather . . . your eyes . . ."

"I may not see the stars as well," Hlaryon said. "But before me now I see a wonderful thing. The new leader of our people, tried and tested, ready to take his place at Rehoman's side."

Arris smiled and shook his head. "I'm sorry, Hlaryon. You must be aware that I'm not interested in being Yearking."

"Terai told me that, when he was here a year ago," the old man said. "He told me a great many things. You say you will not be Yearking, Arris? What else will you do? Go back to your Sacred Emperor? You will have no place there."

"Hareku offered me a title and lands when my task was done."

"Even if he holds to that, you will have no position," Hlaryon said urgently. "No power. He will not take you back into his bed, and you will find no welcome offered to a spy and an assassin, no matter whose gold paid for your deeds."

Arris fought back his anger, and tried to speak respectfully. "Forgive me, Hlaryon, but you are wrong. There may be some resentment, but I can make my own place."

"Your place is here!" said the astrologer in a trembling voice. "How can you defy the Goddess? Your creator? You were made for a glorious destiny, boy. If you turn away from it, what will you become? A petty noble in the Sapphire Palace? An aging catamite whose beauty will be gone in ten years, the object of contempt and scorn?"

"That is enough," Arris said sharply. "I will choose my own life, Hlaryon. And any life I choose will be better than the death of blood and fire."

"You would think differently after a night in Rehoman's arms," said Hlaryon. "Terai, you must convince him. He must be Yearking. The prophecies must be fulfilled."

Terai shook his head. "I'm not much help to you, Grandfather. I refused the Candidacy myself, remember?"

"That proved well for our people, and was undoubtedly your destiny," the old man said. "Arris is meant to be the Consort of the Millennium. He has no other destiny."

"Surely the Goddess would not want an unwilling Consort," Arris said.

"She accepted your friend the Prince. And she will accept his sacrifice, though it is unwilling," Hlaryon said.

"No one will force you to be Yearking," Terai said quickly, seeing Arris's sudden fear. "If I had feared that, I would never have allowed you to come to Gama. I would have brought Saresha alone."

"But you think I should do it, don't you?"

"I think you would discover that you would live more fully in one year with her than most men live in sixty," Terai said. "But it is your choice."

"It should not be," Hlaryon said. His nearly sightless eyes were fixed disconcertingly on Arris's. "He does not consider what is best for himself, or what is best for his people. The Lady feels the same. She does not wish to face the Goddess's wrath when she wakes to find a different Consort than she dreamed."

Arris turned away to Terai. "It was a mistake for me to come here. I think I had better go, before someone drags me to the altar and puts the knife in my hand." It was too bad. He had been looking forward to a bath, several meals, and a rest in Gama before he started for Deiran.

Terai's narrowed gaze measured Hlaryon's closed, stubborn expression. He nodded. "I think that would be best. I'll see to it the guards let you through." He rose and opened the door of their room.

Six armed soldiers stood outside the door, filling the narrow stairwell. Arris looked up to meet the malicious smile of Clynetra, the warrior-trained sister of the girl he had killed. "You are to remain in your room, my lord," she said softly, "until the Council arrives to prepare you for your Candidacy."

"Terai," Arris breathed.

His companion stepped forward, frowning. "Officer, what do you mean? Surely a mistake has been made. Arris is not a Candidate."

"There is no other," she said evenly, turning to Arris again. "I had hoped to challenge you to combat for my sister's honor. But there is no need. No death I could give you would be surer than this."

Arris began to sweat in the cool hallway. "I refuse Candidacy," he said desperately. "Four witnesses are required for a formal declaration. There are eight here. I . . . I, Arris, Tauena's son, refuse the offer of Candidacy for the position of Yearking, in all humility and sorrow. I am not worthy." He folded his arms. "Let me pass." Terai nodded at him in approval.

Clynetra grinned. "Hinita, take word of the Candidate's acceptance to the Lady, and tell her the Councilwomen may come when they are ready."

"Terai," Arris said, trying to stay in control of his fear, "Was this part of your plan to gain the Lady's favor? Was . . . was Saresha only a tool to use to get me here today?"

"No. I swear I knew nothing of this," Terai said. "This is insane, Clynetra. You may be able to keep Arris here, but you can't possibly force him to go through with the Ritual."

"We'll see."

"If you really didn't intend this, old friend," Arris said tightly, "then get me out of it."

"Together," Terai said. "Now."

Both crouched and sprang. Arris leaped to the side of Clynetra's sword and aimed a kick to disarm her. Suddenly he found himself thrown hard on the ground with his leg twisted up behind him and a sword at his throat. There was a groan from Terai.

"The welcome cups you two drained so quickly," Clynetra said, "were drugged, of course. Not enough for you to notice, but sufficient to dull those trained reflexes you boast. You'll both have a slight headache tomorrow. Don't try to escape again." She kicked Arris to his feet and shoved him back into the room. Terai stumbled after him. They landed on the floor, off balance, and watched the door slam behind them. A heavy bolt was drawn across.

Terai hung his head between his knees. "Fool," he cursed softly. "To spend all your life weaving intrigue and deception, then not recognizing it when it hits you over the head." He glanced sidelong at Arris. "If I had known what they planned, I would have made certain you never got within a hundred miles of Gama."

Arris got slowly to his feet and went to the window to view the unscalable surface once more. "It isn't your fault. They took your plan one step further. One or two unwilling Yearkings don't matter. Rehoman used to demand hundreds of victims every year."

"I am the Goddess's man," Terai said. "But I am also your friend. Perhaps even more so. Arris, believe me in this. I didn't want this to happen."

The younger man nodded. "I believe you, Terai. And . . . thank you." He leaned out over the windowsill. Perhaps he should just throw himself over. It would be quicker. But he would not. "You were right when you said they can't force me to go through with the Ritual. I'm not like Saresha. I know what is supposed to happen. I simply won't kill Sasha on the altar, and I certainly won't sleep with the Lady afterward. So I won't be Yearking."

Terai shook his head. "They're sure of themselves. They must have that planned as well."

He felt trapped, helpless, as he had not felt since the first days of his slavery in Deiran. He remembered his terror when he had first felt the Emperor's big hands on his shoulders, turning him around, a force he could not resist. The pain, and most of all his powerlessness as he lay in gold chains. He had come to love Hareku in time, to need him, though he had never lost his fear. The Goddess would be more demanding, more capricious, than the Emperor at his worst, without the human quality of compassion that had made Arris's slavery bearable. She would consume him bit by bit, until at year's end when she consumed him utterly.

"How could I have ever thought I'd escape this?" he said half to himself, in a dull, dead voice he scarcely recognized.

"Perhaps there's still hope," Terai offered unconvincingly. "Karillos—"

"You said yourself he had no chance, with the Goddess strengthened by the sacrifice," Arris whispered. "The Brothers Ylla are a lesser order of gods. You taught me that years ago, Terai."

"But if you can delay the sacrifice until he arrives," Terai said thoughtfully, "if you can keep from killing the Prince . . ."

Arris looked at him. "Would you want that? The chance your Goddess might lose? You've been working for the Millennium all your life."

"This is not what I worked for," Terai said. "To achieve the prophecies by deception, by force . . . it is as if Cembra had lived, and gained control of the Council as he intended, and turned them all to the shadow."

The first night of Winter Festival was still and dark, a cloak of black ice. The moon had decayed and was gone, to reappear reborn on the morrow with the new King. The whispery silence of the eerie valley of the Temple, the vastness of the grassy plain, the cold high mountains surrounding it all, conspired to make Arris feel very small and very helpless. He walked stiffly with his guards, shivering in his short white robe. His freshly washed, pine-scented hair fell unbound over his back. His bare feet were bruised by the stony path.

The Temple ahead dwarfed the Lady's cottage. Both were brightly lit against the oppressive darkness. In the cottage, the lights were warm and inviting. But the gold-spired Temple shone with the cold, pale light of the underworld, cheerless and offering no comfort. The Lossiran was perched high on one of the spires. At Arris's approach, it cast its leathery body into the air and began to sweep down toward them in great spirals. The guards shifted uneasily, many of them seeing the Vulture for the first time in their lives.

Terai followed Arris at a short distance. He would have no role in the ceremony, but they wanted to keep an eye on him. No one really thought he would try to interfere, but the Lady had ordered that he be kept under guard.

The towering, massive doors of iron and gold filigree opened outward at the guard leader's ritual knock. Arris blinked and squinted at the light of the countless lamps that hung on pillars and beams. A spearpoint nudged him in the back, and he walked forward. The crowd was quieter than usual in its greeting of the Candidate. Surely some of the priests, priestesses, and students present thought it was wrong to kill one unwilling Yearking and replace him with another. Arris glanced from side to side, but if any were sympathetic, they hid their feelings well.

The guards escorted him down the endless aisle, beneath archways and domes and bank upon bank of windows. The lamplight sparkled off jewels and gold leaf. Arris had been awed and impressed by the Temple as a child. Now it seemed a monstrosity, a thing not built by human hands, meant for a Goddess's resting place and incomprehensible to a mere mortal.

He could feel the Goddess here. She was waking, fighting her way slowly, level by level, out of the seductive dreams imposed upon her by the Brothers Ylla. She needed the meat and drink of Saresha's burnt flesh and spilled blood to waken fully and regain her old power. She wanted Arris to reign by her side.

He shuddered at the seeking touch of her mind, fearing it would prompt the same overwhelming desire he had felt when she had touched him in the Citadel. But the contact was brief. He was near the end of the long aisle. Just ahead the path widened, flaring out to a broad curving space where the press of the watching crowd thinned, until only three people stood before him.

The Lady, in a robe of black silk and a crimson cloak, smiling in welcome. A black-robed priest whose back was turned to Arris. Saresha Ilkharani, bound with silken bonds as strong as steel to a tall standing stone, the Altar of Rehoman. The Prince's eyes were glassy with fear and illness. They were on a level with Arris's. Their gazes met, and Arris looked quickly away. Saresha wore a short white robe to match Arris's, and his dark golden hair was combed to his shoulders. Arris could see him even when he did not look at him. The clouded blue of the Prince's wide-set eyes stared at him from every corner of his mind. He was lost in the color.

"Who has come to disturb the sleeper's rest?" The Lady's singsong voice made Arris look up. She was beginning the Ritual. The crowd rustled eagerly.

"One who seeks," Arris's guard chorused in the proper answer.

"You can't make me do this," Arris said loudly.

"What do you seek?" The Lady smiled at him. Arris swallowed hard.

"To wake the sleeper, and offer a gift," chanted the guards.

"I won't do it," Arris said. "Do you hear me? I won't!"

"What do you offer?"

"My love and my life."

"I won't kill him!"

"And in return?"

"To enter her presence, to sing her praises, to know her love."

"Sasha," Arris said, using skills Danae had taught him so that his voice cut below the others. "I'm sorry. They can't make me kill you. But they'll just get someone else to do it."

"They said they could make you do it," Saresha whispered.

"I won't," he said.

"Freely granted, freely given," the guards chorused. Arris had missed the Lady's question.

"Be it so." The Lady moved aside.

The black-robed priest turned and presented a cushion toward Arris. Glittering on the crimson velvet was a sickle-shaped knife. Arris backed up a step. A spearpoint pricked him. He knew this knife. He had used it to sacrifice a goat to Aghlayeshkusa once. It was a blade with a blood lust of its own, a pit-dark soul of its own. It thrummed with a low, growling note like a vibrating bass string, drawing him toward it, willing him to take hold of its handle.

No! He would not. If he touched it, if he felt that thirsty spirit in his hands, he would not be able to keep from killing.

"Are you all mad?" he heard Terai shout from the forefront of the crowd. "That blade is a thing of darkness! You cannot use such a thing in a ritual of the Goddess."

"Take up the blade, worthy Candidate, and strike," the Lady said. Her voice had subtly altered. The awakening Goddess had begun to impress herself upon her priestess, like a pouring of clay wetting the inside of a mold.

"No," he whispered.

The Lady said a word that made his teeth grit together, a word of power and command. The Lossiran flew down from the ceiling. Arris smelled its fetid breath. The wing tattoos on his back burned in response to its nearness. It pressed down on him, its vastly powerful, dimly intelligent mind urging him forward. He tried to fight. But the sickle knife had its own power, and he could not battle that and the Lossiran and the Lady and the Goddess herself all at once.

His hand reached forward and gripped the knife handle. He felt the blackness of its soul welling up into him. No. He would not strike. He would put the knife back down . . .

"You are my creature," said the Lady in a seductive

voice. "You cannot change that. Do not try. Strike. I thirst,
my beloved. Give me drink. You must strike."

He stepped forward. His arm bent at the level of Saresha's
abdomen. He knew the procedure, the careful crossing cuts
that doomed the Yearking to agony until the mercy of fire
released him at last. Only begin here . . .

Saresha's blue eyes closed. The point of the knife was
against his skin, pressing through the cloth of the white robe.
Arris could feel the unbearable tension of the Prince's muscles. He did not want this! He did not want Sasha dead, he
did not want to be Yearking. He could not fight the blade's
power. He did not have the strength, he no longer had any
power of his own.

"Gods," he breathed, "help me. Anyone, please, oh,
please help me . . ."

A familiar, hated voice spoke in his ear. "I'm not a god,"
the daimon said. "But I can help you. Promise me your
soul."

The moment was short, but Arris felt centuries older when
he whispered, "Yes. I promise. I promise you my soul. Now
get me out of this."

CHAPTER

25

THE DAIMON MATERIALIZED beside him in the monstrous form
he had seen it assume once before. Cold, scaly hands closed
over his own, lunged forward and down. The sickle blade
whined in disappointment as it cut through silken fetters, first
at Saresha's feet, then at his wrists. Arris tossed the knife to
his left hand and caught the Prince as he slumped from the
altar stone. The daimon turned with them to face the crowd.

The Lady was already half-transformed. The beauty that

had always been hers was heightened to a terrifying pitch, a palpable energy that radiated through the eerily silent building. There was a crimson glow to her dark skin, and her eyes were red-rimmed. She looked at them in imperious disbelief and raised her arms in command, calling out words in a language like shivered glass.

Arris fought the urge to obey those compelling eyes. This was the purpose for which his life had been shaped. She had created him, had made him something that would fully complement her, that would meld with her to create something greater. But he would not do it. He would not. He could sense the daimon's strength beside him, a cold but welcome presence.

Saresha leaned on him, his eyes half-closed, his skin hot and damp against Arris's. "Stand up," Arris whispered to him. "You'll have to help if we're going to get out of here."

The Prince tried to straighten, and managed a wry smile. "Just tell me what to do."

"Run," Arris said, pulling him forward. Terai had stolen a sword from a guard's belt, and Clynetra had leaped to engage him; the drug might slow Terai's reflexes, but it did not affect his years of experience. The young soldier would not stand before her former teacher for long.

The chanting of the Lady brought down the Lossiran from the ceiling of the pillared hall. It swept over the crowd toward Arris and the Prince, its rotting smell seeping through the incense, its dull red eyes fixed on Arris. He could feel the wing tattoos on his back fluttering as if alive, like a patterned spell trying to force him to be obedient to the Lossiran's will. "Aghlayeshkusa!" he cried. "I'll need more than shields against this!"

The daimon hurled its monstrous winged form at the Vulture. They rolled together in the air, shrieking in horrible voices, locked in physical and mental combat. The guards started toward Arris as his unearthly defender left him. Arris half carried the Prince as they stumbled toward Terai. The grim-faced Yaighan had wounded Clynetra in the leg, and she had fallen.

"The Goddess can't wake fully until the Prince is dead!" Terai shouted. "If we can keep him safe . . ."

Arris deflected a soldier's lunge with the sickle knife he still carried. The crowd was beginning to move forward to stop them. The daimon was occupied with the Lossiran, and the Lady's voice was becoming unrecognizable as she summoned the considerable power she could still control even with the Goddess half-asleep.

Suddenly the Temple began to shake. The towering columns shivered in their fluted bases. Windows shattered and cracked, blowing inward in a rain of colored glass. The Lossiran disengaged from Aghlayeshkusa's clawed grip and fled back toward the altar stone. Terai reached Arris's side and joined him in staring at the massive closed doors of the Temple entrance.

Brilliant streams of light, yellow and fierce as the sun, gleamed through every crack, in and around the portals. The door began to groan as if hit by a ram. The Lady's voice faltered. The crowd pressed back away from the doors, paying little attention to Terai, Arris, or the Prince as they struggled through.

"Karillos," Terai panted. "Must have gotten through . . . we've got to get out of here right now, Arris, those are gods out there . . ."

"Gods?" Saresha repeated.

"We'll be caught in the middle," Arris said. "Quickly!"

The daimon flew toward them in erratic spurts, hurt and winded from its battle with the Vulture. Scratches on its scaly form dripped foul-smelling liquid. "Can't . . . stay here . . ." it said as it passed them and opened a side door with a blast of power. Arris glanced behind him, to see the massive stones of the floor around the altar tilt from their beds and rise to stand like a great henge as the Lady prepared to defend the Couch of Rehoman from the invaders. The trained priests and priestesses in the crowd were grouping together, forming a circle of power.

"I wake!" the Lady shrilled over the confusion. "I wake . . . who comes? My enemies . . ." Her voice was uncanny, her language the ancient tongue.

"Kill the Yearking!" a priest bellowed. "Give the Goddess her sacrifice. Anyone! We must have the blood of the Horned One!"

Three young students hurled themselves at Saresha. Arris thrust the Prince behind him and stood close to Terai to meet them. The youths carried only ceremonial knives, but the

Goddess urged them on; their eyes were bright with madness, their swiftness and strength impossible.

"Don't kill them," Terai said as he lunged to wound the first student in the side. "The Goddess might be able to use their deaths."

Arris nodded and fought defensively, trying to disarm his opponents. One knife fell harmlessly to the floor, its wielder clutching a cut wrist. Arris blocked the blow of the other youth with his forearm. Then his sickle knife seemed to move of its own accord, darting in and slicing deep into the student's chest. Arris felt the glee of the blade as he withdrew it, and heard the daimon's weak laughter from the portal.

The giant front entrance bowed and crashed inward, as five indistinct, blinding figures strode into the Temple. Arris recognized the stylized forms that radiated such heat and power. Myrdethreshi the Warrior led them, wearing the full armor of a champion of a thousand years before, unearthly muscles like twisted cables moving beneath his glowing skin. The stern, forbidding, shadow-thin shape of Verchaki of the Night followed him, and after him came Sygathi the Truthsayer, Ogliatu the Eldest Brother, and Kerami the Lover, a being whose beauty and compelling grace were almost a match for the Goddess's in Arris's eyes.

"Come on!" Terai shouted, pulling Arris through the side door after the staggering Prince. The daimon flew before them, looking back over its shoulder in fear and awe at the much greater spirits that had entered the Temple.

"You dare to enter here?" an imperious female voice demanded from within. A blast of light and power was her answer. Arris did not need to look back: he could feel the battle around him everywhere on the dark plain that surrounded the Temple.

"The gate," Terai gasped as they ran. "We must get back to the White City."

Arris could see the gate ahead, standing open, slain guards at either side. Karillos stood just before it, supported on either side by Falcmet and Husayn, scarcely conscious from the effort of summoning his gods. Saresha gave a glad cry, and they looked in his direction.

The daimon descended beside Arris, holding out a hand to stop him. It had resumed the form of an oversized warrior;

Arris was amused to see that it had copied Myrdethreshi's armor, though it was battered and bloodied. "I must return to my world," it said urgently, "to heal my wounds and rest. I will study how best we may overcome the bonds in which you have imprisoned your power." It grinned at him. "I knew you would be mine one day. Now that I have your soul, I need not even depend upon an invocation to visit your world whenever it pleases me. My link with you will bring me here. And every time you kill, I will feed. I thank you for the life of the young one in the Temple. May there be many more!" It vanished in an echoing chorus of laughter.

Then the Goddess had not been strengthened by his inability to control the sickle knife. Arris supposed he should be glad of that. If Rehoman won her battle, she would come after him, and he did not think she would seek him as a lover.

"Arris! Through the gate!" Terai cried to him. He saw them standing within the portals, his brothers, Karillos, the Prince, Terai. He ran to join them, as the Temple glowed behind them with the sun's light on what should have been a pitch-black night.

An army of gold-robed priests and Prince's Companions held back the frightened people in the streets of Gama. They greeted Saresha with joy and relief, but Arris saw only hostile faces turned in his direction. Terai shifted uneasily at his side, still holding the sword he had taken from a guard in the Temple.

"Take them," Karillos whispered, leaning on Falcmet's sturdy, armored form.

Arris took a defensive stance with his sickle knife, but Husayn stood before him with a hand held out. "Give up peacefully, and return with us to the Citadel to stand trial. Or we'll kill you here."

"There are too many of them," Terai said quietly, "especially since your friendly daimon has abandoned us."

Arris stood uncertainly, feeling the blade in his hand urging him on to kill. But he did not want his brother's soul to go to the daimon. After a moment he dropped the knife, not trusting himself to place it in Husayn's outstretched hand without striking. Terai handed over his sword, and soldiers pinioned their arms behind them and shoved them toward two unoccupied horses.

"Wait," the Prince said weakly. "What . . . what will happen to them?"

"They are undoubtedly guilty of your uncles' murders, my Prince," Falcmet said in a bitter tone. "And they kidnapped you for the purpose of having you killed. One of them is a Deirani spy."

"How much did Danae tell you?" Arris asked, twisting around in his captor's punishing grip. His eyes met Falcmet's, and read the contempt and anguish there.

"She told us everything," his older brother said.

"Then you know who I am."

"Yes. And if the Consulate does not condemn you to death, I'll kill you myself. You dishonor our father's name."

"I avenged him!" Arris said in disbelief.

"Areyta was a man of honor, of principle," Husayn said quietly. "Do you think his spirit will rest easier knowing one of his sons has become a traitor and a murderer?"

"As well as an abomination in the sight of the gods, one who seduces others to commit blasphemous acts," Karillos said in weary satisfaction. "Young Danae's confession was quite thorough."

"Confession?" Terai repeated. "You don't mean to charge her with any wrongdoing, do you?"

"She knew of the presence of a Deirani spy and intriguer in the Citadel court," Karillos said. "But she did finally realize where her loyalty should be. The Regent Nievan's widow Oella has spoken on her behalf. She is repentant. We will not be harsh with her."

"Come," Falcmet said impatiently. "We must leave this place. Get them on the horses. My Prince, you'll ride with me. You aren't well enough to keep up with the pace we must take."

Arris watched Saresha closely as the Prince was helped to mount. There was no longer any evidence of the presence of the Horned One within him. No doubt the Consort had left him, gone to assist his mistress however he could in her battle with the Brothers Ylla at the Temple. He might be of some help. But the true power of the Horned One lay in his death and rebirth each winter, his incarnation in human form and his sacrifice. The cycle had been interrupted. Arris wondered what would happen now.

He and Terai were bound into their saddles. Arris submitted quietly, numb and light-headed with weariness and the drugged wine he had drunk that morning. He scarcely felt the cold on his bare legs and arms, or the abrasive rub of the leather against his unprotected skin as his legs were tied to the horse's sides. His wrists were bound on a short lead to the pommel. The captives' horses would be led, no simple trick at a gallop.

He had no intention of going to the Citadel to face trial for his acts. He suspected the new Regent might be Karillos, for his loyalty and quick action to follow the Prince. If that was so, Arris would undoubtedly be condemned to death. But this was not a good time to think of escape. First he needed to get as far away from Gama as possible.

The morning came, clouded and chill, finding them riding at a much slower pace through a rock-shaded valley some distance east of Gama. There had been no pursuit. The Kwaitl nomads had watched them go without apparent concern; the priests and priestesses had been occupied with the battle in the Temple.

Terai seemed no wearier than he had been the day before when they rode into Gama to the acclaim of the people. Arris envied him his stoic endurance. It helped that he was wearing his traveling clothes still. Arris thought that another night like the past one and he would be as sick as the Prince. He was bruised and sore and hungry, and when he allowed himself to think of everything that he had done in the past few weeks, he thought that perhaps he deserved whatever torturous death Karillos meant to grant. Danae and his brothers were right. He was a traitor and a murderer. Even his rescue of Saresha had been more for his own sake than for the Prince's.

The stones of the hillside shifted under his horse's hooves, and he slid painfully in the saddle. He drew in a sharp breath as he felt blisters tear that had formed only hours before. Terai glanced at him in sympathy, but did not speak. He wondered what Terai was thinking. His teacher had spent his entire life working toward the Millennium, and when it had come he had helped to prevent its realization. Arris was still not certain why, but he was grateful. If Terai had been one of those trying to force him to be Yearking, he did not think he would have found the courage to resist. Terai had given him hope.

"Look!" a priest hissed. The cavalcade pulled to a ragged halt as a pillar of whirling sunlight descended to hover over Karillos. The light coalesced to reveal the familiar figure of Sygathi the Truthsayer, far more weary-looking than he appeared in Temple paintings.

The priests dismounted in a rustle of gold robes and a creaking of saddles, and prostrated themselves on the ground. The Companions reacted a little more slowly, but they too dismounted and knelt, leaving only the half-conscious Prince, Arris, and Terai still on their horses.

"Most Holy One," Karillos said, rising a little to his hands and knees. "Again you honor me with your presence. I am not worthy."

"Nonsense, Karillos. You are one of our most dedicated and talented servants." Sygathi spread out his arms in benediction. "Your noble efforts on behalf of our chosen ruler for the Khalifate are most appreciated."

"Thank you, Most Holy," Karillos said. "Were . . . were you victorious?"

"The ancient powers are very strong," Sygathi said matter-of-factly. "But the Bloody One was not possessed of her full strength. We have managed to confine her to her Temple, awake but unable to go out into this world as she wishes. Still, she remains a threat."

"Is there anything your priests can do to nullify this obscene spirit?" Karillos asked fiercely. "If there is, I will do it. Be assured of that."

"One task," Sygathi said slowly. "One task only. Kill Rehoman's intended Consort. Kill him now. If he ever returns to her Temple and offers her a consecrated sacrifice, she will have enough power for freedom. For freedom . . . and revenge. This must not be."

Priests and Companions turned to look at Arris, who stared at the manifestation of the god above Karillos. "I'm the one who made it possible for you to defeat her!" he said. "Do you think I'd return there and try to free her?"

"You are her creature," said the god soberly. "Of course you will. As you are my servant, Karillos, kill him now." The pillar of light brightened and flashed.

Saresha straightened in his saddle, and spoke in a soft voice that could be heard throughout the column. "Must it be done?"

The god nodded. "I would do it myself, but he is Rehoman's creature. I have no power over him."

Karillos was already rising and walking back toward Arris. Saresha held up his hand and said in a voice of command he never learned from Nievan or Maenad, "Stop. I . . . I am the injured one here. He killed my uncles, and kidnapped me. I will do it myself."

Arris stared incredulously at the Prince. The blue eyes were stern and unyielding. "Sasha?" he whispered.

"It is my right," said the Prince remotely, turning to the god for confirmation.

Sygathi nodded approvingly. "Indeed, most favored Prince."

"Show that you can at least die with honor, Arris," Saresha said, drawing a long knife from the saddle scabbard. "Ride forward to me now. You, Leis, release his horse. Come forward with him, Terai. I want you to see this."

Karillos was smiling now. Arris felt sick. The priests and Companions were watching him avidly. Only Falcmet and Husayn had turned away. Perhaps they did not hate him so much after all. His hands trembled in their bonds.

"Well?" Saresha said softly.

Arris nodded and urged his horse forward with his knees. It picked a way through the still-prostrate priests and kneeling Companions. Terai guided his mount easily beside him. He could not believe this was happening. He should have killed the Prince when he had the chance. He would have lived at least a year longer.

He sat back to stop his horse when he reached the Prince. Terai stopped beside him on his left. Saresha walked his horse forward, leaned over, and gathered the reins of Arris's bridle from where they dangled. He laid the hand that held the reins on top of Arris's bound wrists, balancing his knife in his other hand.

Arris looked straight ahead, his jaw clenched. Die with honor? If that was all he had left, that is what he would do. The pillar of twisting flame that hid the god Sygathi was fading, as if the god's weariness was taking him back to his own lofty plane. Arris supposed Sygathi would not have to be there to know that he had died.

Then Saresha whispered, scarcely voicing the words, so that none but Arris would hear or even notice that he spoke. "Look down. Don't change your expression. I'm going to cut the ropes and hand you the reins. You take it from there."

Arris controlled himself well enough that his eyes only widened a fraction. Relief coursed through him, and renewed fear. It would take the priests and Companions only moments to remount and come after him. He would have to free Terai as well. "Why?" he breathed.

"No matter what you've done you're still the closest friend I've ever had. You saved me when you could have just run last night." Saresha raised his knife. "Go."

"Tell Danae that I'll get her family out of Deiran," Arris whispered as the knife flashed downward. It sliced the lead that connected his wrists to the pommel, then came up to cut the bonds on his hands. Arris felt a hot bite of pain as a piece of skin came off with the rope. He grinned widely at Saresha, grabbed the knife and the proffered reins, and whirled to slice Terai's bonds.

"Stop them!" Karillos shouted. "Stop them, anyone!"

Priests scampered to their feet, Companions sprang for their horses. Arris squeezed his legs together hard and was gratified to feel his well-trained horse gather beneath him to spring. Falcmet leaped in front of him to grasp at the horse's bridle, but Arris urged the animal forward and his brother was knocked aside.

"Straight up!" Terai shouted. "There's a path I know along the ridge!"

Arris whipped his horse with his rein ends and fought to keep his balance through his tired, dizzy state. Terai pulled ahead of him and rocks scattered down on their pursuers below.

"We'll make it, lad," Terai said over his shoulder. "We have to. We'll have no other chance."

They would make it. Arris was certain of it. He could not receive a gift like that the Prince had given him and fail. He was free. Free of the Goddess's plans for him, free of the burden of prophecy. He would make a life for himself in Deiran somehow. And one day he would return to face Karillos on his own ground, with his mental powers freed and augmented by the daimon's help. He would show the Khalifate gods that he was not one they could lightly order killed. He would show them all.

He looked down when they topped the ridge. Several Companions were almost upon him. Far below he could see Saresha Ilkharani's golden-curled head uplifted, watching him. So beautiful. So far out of his reach. He turned away resolutely and raced his surefooted horse across the high ridge of the Dark Hills. The bitter wind chilled his skin and brought tears to his eyes, and he laughed. He had never felt more alive.

THE ENCHANTMENTS OF FLESH AND SPIRIT
The First Book of Wraeththu

Storm Constantine

From the tired carcase of Mankind a new entity bursts forth, fully armed.

The Wraeththu were a mutation: quasi-human, strikingly beautiful, telepathic and enmeshed in strange and exotic rituals. Spurning the degenerate society that spawned them, they challenged Mankind's waning supremacy to the limits, and fought for a future that promised justice and equality *their* justice, *their* equality.

Pellaz — naive, adolescent — refused to believe the Wraeththu existed. Until exotic, striking-looking Cal 'called' him. Under Cal's spell Pellaz abandoned home and family, and set off on a bizarre odyssey, both physical and spiritual, into the very heart of the Wraeththu mystery. And it soon became very clear that a special destiny awaited Pellaz.

Futura Publications
An Orbit Book
Fantasy
0 7088 8256 0

All Futura Books are available at your bookshop or newsagent, or can be ordered from the following address:
Futura Books, Cash Sales Department,
P.O. Box 11, Falmouth, Cornwall TR10 9EN.

Please send cheque or postal order (no currency), and allow 60p for postage and packing for the first book plus 25p for the second book and 15p for each additional book ordered up to a maximum charge of £1.90 in U.K.

B.F.P.O. customers please allow 60p for the first book, 25p for the second book plus 15p per copy for the next 7 books, thereafter 9p per book.

Overseas customers including Eire please allow £1.25 for postage and packing for the first book, 75p for the second book and 28p for each subsequent title ordered.

interzone

SCIENCE FICTION AND FANTASY

Quarterly   £1.50

- *Interzone* is the only British magazine specializing in SF and new fantastic writing. We have published:

BRIAN ALDISS	M. JOHN HARRISON
J.G. BALLARD	GARRY KILWORTH
BARRINGTON BAYLEY	MICHAEL MOORCOCK
MICHAEL BISHOP	KEITH ROBERTS
ANGELA CARTER	GEOFF RYMAN
RICHARD COWPER	JOSEPHINE SAXTON
JOHN CROWLEY	JOHN SLADEK
PHILIP K. DICK	BRUCE STERLING
THOMAS M. DISCH	IAN WATSON
MARY GENTLE	CHERRY WILDER
WILLIAM GIBSON	GENE WOLFE

- *Interzone* has also published many excellent new writers; graphics by **JIM BURNS, ROGER DEAN, IAN MILLER** and others; book reviews, news, etc.

- *Interzone* is available from specialist SF shops, or by subscription. For four issues, send £6 (outside UK, £7) to: **124 Osborne Road, Brighton BN1 6LU, UK.** Single copies: £1.75 inc p&p.

- American subscribers may send $10 ($13 if you want delivery by air mail) to our British address, above. All cheques should be made payable to *Interzone*.

- "No other magazine in Britain is publishing science fiction at all, let alone fiction of this quality." *Times Literary Supplement*

- -

To: **interzone** 124 Osborne Road, Brighton, BN1 6LU, UK.

Please send me four issues of *Interzone,* beginning with the current issue. I enclose a cheque/p.o. for £6 (outside UK, £7; US subscribers, $10 or $13 air), made payable to *Interzone*.

Name _____

Address _____

_____